Shelter

BEST SELLING AUTHOR
ashley john

Ashley John

To find out more about the author of this book, sign up to his **mailing list** for exclusive content and to be the first to find out about new releases, visit his official website:

ashleyjohn.co.uk/newsletter

Also by Ashley John

Shelter

Ashley John

For Keri, Lisa, Ceri, Amy, Tee and Sam.
Thanks for having hawk eyes that make me look better.

Chapter 1

Staring out into the garden of the Havenmoore Rehab Center, Elias James slid the silver ring back through the right corner of his lip. Piercing through the already healing skin, he felt a shudder of satisfaction when it eased through. He ran his tongue along the metal, a chill of satisfaction shuddering around his slim frame.

His fourth stint in rehab had come with stricter conditions. This time it was court appointed, so he couldn't just walk through the doors. Getting caught in the backroom of a Chinese takeout place clinging onto the last thread of life, with enough cocaine in the pocket of his skinny jeans to make him look like a dealer, had almost gotten his ass thrown in jail. He was the mayor's son, so she was never going to let that happen.

Prison would have been a welcome break from sitting

around with a bunch of wackos for nine weeks, talking about his feelings and pretending he was a reformed man. As he stuffed the last of his clothes into his denim backpack, he was already thinking about where he could get his first post-rehab fix.

"Elias, your sister is here," Sandy leaned against the doorframe with her hands in the pockets of her white nurses uniform, "you ready?"

"Like you wouldn't believe."

Sandy was one of the few nurses in the place who actually seemed like a normal person. Most of the other nurses seemed to check out the second they put on that uniform but Sandy seemed to shine through it. She was giving him a smile that Elias had seen three times previously. It said '*I really hope this is the last time I see you in here*'. Elias wanted to smile back and believe it but he couldn't. He wasn't going to promise Sandy something with a fake smile, even if it would make her feel better.

Tossing the bag over his shoulder, he ruffled his short and thick black hair in the mirror, the newly replaced rings and studs cluttering his ears glittered in the late morning sun. His face looked thin, his cheekbones strong under his eyes.

Ellie was sitting in the waiting room, distracted by her cellphone. Ellie was his over-achieving twin sister and even though they shared a face, she actually had a brain capable of retaining knowledge beneath her black angular bob.

"Hey, Sis," Elias cleared his throat.

All of a sudden, he felt unexplainably nervous. He thought back to the last time he had seen her. Handcuffed to a hospital bed and coming down from the worst high of his life, she was nothing more than a blurry blob crying angrily at the bottom of his bed. For nine weeks he hadn't been allowed any visitors but he wasn't sure if she would have come if she were allowed. He knew she cared but her eyes told him that she was at the end of the road with helping him out. She was a doctor, so she understood addiction better than most but she had never been able to fix her own brother.

Elias' battered sneakers on the tiles made her look up from her cell, a frown already tightening her strong features. Hazel eyes danced over Elias' scruffy clothes, piercings and unclipped facial hair, with the same look of displeasure he had grown to expect.

"Elias," she pulled him into a quick hug and kissed him fleetingly on the cheek, "good to see you."

Ellie's eyes told a different story. He knew all too well what she really wanted to say. She would want him to promise that he was clean and that he was going to stay that way. Just like Sandy, he couldn't give her that fake promise. At twenty-six, Elias knew that the second chance boat had sailed by him many times and he had missed the last pick-up more years ago than he could remember.

"How was it?"

"Oh, you know, the usual. Lots of sitting around in circles talking about why our childhoods have fucked us up. Nothing new. Have I missed much?"

She pursed her lips, almost angrily. Despite being twins they were polar opposites in most ways. Ellie had always been the brains and Elias had been the trouble. Being stuck in her shadow meant that his mother barely noticed he was there. His father had predicted what was coming and he got a ticket out when he died in a car accident four months before the twins were born.

With a mother who didn't care and a father who he wasn't allowed to ask questions about, he failed most of his classes and left high school without a diploma, instead choosing a lonely and empty life of drugs and homelessness. Ellie, on the other hand, was on track for Tufts University of Medicine to become the brightest of shining stars.

"Mom apologizes for not coming," Ellie forced a smile.

They both knew she hadn't. Elias' relationship with her was almost nonexistent. If she couldn't throw money or her status at a problem, she wasn't interested in trying to fix it. Ellie was closer to her but he doubted they knew each other beyond their mind numbing chats about work, money and success.

"Don't tell me, she's busy?" he filled out the discharge papers.

"She's stuck in a meeting with the chief of police at the

station all day."

Elias knew she was probably hiding out in her office so she didn't have to face her problem child. *Why break the habit of a lifetime?*

"It figures," Elias gritted his jaw.

Had he really expected her to show up? It was her meddling that got him locked up in rehab again. *Anything to keep me a secret from the mindless residents of Havenmoore.*

"You know what she's like," Ellie's eyes were glued to her phone, "she's a busy woman. So am I. I'm needed back at the doctor's office in an hour so can we make it quick? I'm using my lunch hour early to pick you up."

Without any goodbyes, Elias and Ellie headed straight for her car. She didn't even try to hide how much of an inconvenience he was anymore. He didn't care. He would tell her to drop him at the bus station so he could get the cheapest ticket out of Havenmoore and hopefully out of the state.

"What's next for you?" Ellie asked, "Are you going to stay clean?"

"I'll get out of town and see where I land."

"And find the nearest dealer?" her knuckles squeezed the steering wheel, "I don't think so, Elias. You know you have to stay in Havenmoore as part of your plea deal. You can't just leave the state. Maine is your home."

He knew that but he had been hoping Ellie hadn't remembered. If he travelled far enough south they'd eventually give up looking for him. A homeless drug addict wasn't going to be at the top of the most wanted list.

"Fuck the plea. Just drop me at the station and I'll be out of your way in time for you to grab lunch."

They drove through Havenmoore in silence and it didn't take him long to realize she wasn't taking him to the bus station next to the mall on the edge of town.

"Mom's got you an apartment over the bakery on Stanley Street," Ellie sighed, "I didn't want to tell you because I knew you'd freak out. If you leave, you're only going to make things worse for yourself."

"An apartment?" he laughed, "You've got to be kidding me."

"She wants to help."

"All that woman wants is to keep her reputation intact."

This was typical of his mother. He had been sleeping rough for the past years, catching nights on sofas whenever he could. His mom had never once tried to help him out, unless she was getting something out of it. Her son going to prison would lead to somebody hearing about it but she could keep another stint in rehab under control.

"This is her way of helping," Ellie said, "she didn't have to put a roof over your head. You should use this as your chance to start fresh, Elias. Nobody wants to see you falling into that black hole again."

That black hole was all he had known for nearly a decade. Cocaine was his family, his lover and his best friend when he wanted it to be. Even on a sober and clear mind, it was all he could think about.

Ellie pulled up outside of the tiny bakery on the corner of Stanley Street, the smell of fresh bread thick in the air. Peering up at the small red brick building, he saw an even smaller window.

"It's a six month lease," Ellie joined him in looking up, "the rent's paid until the end of the lease. Gives you enough time to get on your feet."

Enough time to figure out how to get out of Havenmoore.

Ellie dropped the keys into his lap along with a basic cellphone. Without saying a word, she twisted back in her seat with a glance at the delicate diamond-encrusted watch on her slender wrist.

"You're not coming up?" he asked.

Had Elias expected that they'd go upstairs and chat with a cup of coffee? Even the thought of the normality made him ache for what he had never known. They may not have had that tight of a relationship but they had a bond neither of them acknowledged and he knew she felt it too. It was as though they'd always known what the other was thinking, even if they didn't want to listen.

Elias had given up on that bond ever physically returning. They were both two different people on different paths as they headed towards their thirties. Even if he tried to hide the slight disappointment, she would know what he was thinking.

"Ten minutes and then I really need to get back."

They headed towards a hidden green door in the dark alley beside the bakery. The smell of the bread was masked by the smell of the dumpsters. Elias was more used to the dumpsters.

Jiggling the single key in the rusty lock, the door finally opened onto a plainly decorated staircase that led to the apartment directly above the bakery. The apartment was small but clean in decoration. Simple furniture filled the space, some of it looking like it had come from one of Havenmoore's nicer thrift stores. It had all of the basics for what any normal person would need when they are starting up on their own for the first time. For Elias, it was a reminder that his mom may have put a roof over his head but she hadn't taken the time to decorate it. It screamed that it had been blindly picked by one of her many assistants because even if she didn't care what happened to Elias, her lavish tastes wouldn't have allowed her to even go to the cheap section of IKEA.

"It's nice," Ellie nodded as she looked around, "cozy."

"Yeah," Elias shrugged, not really caring what it looked like, "not compared to your place."

Ellie now had the huge, six-bedroom house on the outskirts of town. They had grown up there with their mother, not that the mayor was ever there. He remembered a constantly revolving cast of nannies and cooks, none of them sticking around to work for such a needlessly strict, yet distant employer.

"I work hard to pay my bills," there was a dig in her voice, "maybe if you worked a job, you could upgrade. You're always looking for a free ride."

Aspirations had never been something Elias had been interested in. With no high school diploma, who would employ him? All of his convictions and stints in rehab would show up as red flags on his record. Elias would struggle to get a job scrubbing toilets in a fast food joint.

"Would you hire me?"

Ellie didn't answer. She headed over to the kitchen, opening up the fridge. It was filled with fresh fruit and vegetables. Elias already knew they'd probably go straight in the trash, untouched. Cooking was another thing he had never learned.

"All of this stuff is new," she ran her fingers across the sparkling stainless steel washing machine, "must have cost her a couple of thousand dollars."

"A small price to pay to keep me under her nose so that I don't ruin her perfect life. The town square is filled with apartments smaller than this one but they'd be too close to her office. Here, I'm far away enough that she doesn't have to deal with me on a daily basis."

Ellie sighed and pinched between her brows. One quick glance at her watch told Elias that they weren't going to sip coffee. The thought was almost amusing.

"I need to go," she said, "Mrs. Doris is coming in at four. Just *stay* out of trouble, please?"

Elias collapsed on the couch, his tongue flicking against the lip ring, "I can't promise that."

"Promise me you'll try," her hand lightly brushed across the top of his head, "if not for you and if not for me, for your nephew. Kobi talks about you all the time and for some reason he adores you. He looks up to you and one day he'll be old enough to know that his uncle is an addict and a criminal and it'll break his heart."

Just the mention of Kobi made a fist tighten around his stomach. Kobi was the only person in his family that he still had a meaningful connection with, even if he was only six-years-old. He looked at Elias with innocent eyes, not caring about his constant mistakes.

"Kobi's better off without a deadbeat like me in his life."

"He is," Ellie agreed, "but I'm tired of making excuses every time he asks why his Uncle Elias hasn't sent him a birthday card again, or why he's never at his football games."

Elias hated himself for being that uncle and he hated that

Ellie was throwing it in his face the second he was out of rehab, when all he could think about was his first score.

"I'll try," he found himself saying, "but don't hold your breath."

Ellie's hand ran across his head again, more firmly this time, "Don't worry, brother, I never do."

He listened as her pointy heels clicked quickly down his new staircase. Staring around his new apartment, he pulled the new cellphone from his tight jeans pocket and retrieved his old sim card. He had smuggled it into rehab deep in a pair of socks but he had never gotten his hands on a cellphone. He scrolled straight for '*Rigsy*', his finger hovering over the green call button.

With a frustrated grunt, he tossed the phone onto the low, glass coffee table. Pushing his face into his hands, he cried out through his fingers, feeling the pull of the only two things he had ever truly loved.

Cocaine and his nephew.

***

"Help me with this one?" Caden Walker's dad, Buster Walker, cried as he attempted to pull a huge box out of the back of the pickup, "Is there a body in here?"

"My books," Caden shook the sweat from his spikey, pale hair and rushed in to help catch the other side before his dad dropped his collection of rare and vintage books, "although don't joke about the dead body."

Smiling sympathetically with his eyes, his dad heaved as he propped the box on his knees, struggling to keep his grip. They had been cleaning out Caden's half of the New York apartment for most of the day and both of them were exhausted. Caden was extra exhausted because Finn, his ex, had decided to show up, pretending he didn't know what day it was.

"That's the last of them," his dad dusted off his hands before slapping Caden on the back of his broad shoulders, "I'll leave you to get settled in."

When his dad closed the door, the reality of the situation

dropped on Caden like a Mack truck. Every inch of his old teenage bedroom was filled with boxes and bags, stuffed with years of accumulated junk. They had redecorated his old room into a tasteful guest bedroom soon after he had moved out. The furniture may have changed and the wallpaper may be different but he felt like he was slipping backwards into being a teenager. As a twenty-year-old heading to the big city to start an exciting new life, he thought he would have everything he had ever wanted by the time he was thirty. At twenty-nine, he was back in his parents' house, wondering where everything had gone wrong.

If he had known back then that he would spend eight years struggling as a journalist, writing tidbit stories and advertorials for tiny publications, only to one day come home and find his boyfriend of five years in bed with his so called best friend, he might have stayed in Havenmoore. *I can't believe I proposed to that jerk.*

Having no idea how he was going to condense his entire apartment down into one bedroom, he decided to leave that war for another time. He headed to the kitchen where his mom was making grits.

It was the smell of home. His mom, Claire, had been born and raised in Austin, Texas so the scent of the South had filled their home growing up. It was a comforting smell but it also made Caden's palms sweat. *This is just temporary.* He had been repeating that mantra ever since his parents had suggested that he move back in with them so he could get back on his feet to save a deposit for a new place, not that he knew where that new place would be. New York had always been his dream but it felt tainted and soiled. Havenmoore had always been his nightmare growing up. Caden had always felt trapped and confined in such a small, tight-knit town where everybody knew everybody's business. He had grown to love the anonymity of living in New York. There, you are just another person with a coffee in your hand, rushing around the over-populated streets trying to make your dreams come alive.

"I've made your favorite," his mom had the same sympathetic smile that his father had kept plastered across his face all day, "to help you settle in."

She spooned the white, lumpy grits into three bowls followed by a thin slice of yellow butter. He only ever had grits when he was at his parents' place but he had a feeling it was going to lose its quirky novelty.

Wiping the sweat from his brows, Caden tugged at the blue sweater clinging to his lightly haired chest as he sat down at the huge oak table in the kitchen. His mom pushed the bowl in front of him with a smile as she handed him a spoon. It was the taste of his childhood. Finn had always hated the smell of grits when he had tried to make it in New York, so it had been added to the list of things they couldn't do. Caden wondered why he had put up with that ass for so long. *It doesn't make it any easier to fall out of love with him though.*

"Smile," his mother beamed, her flame red hair shining in the afternoon light as it forced its way through her bright yellow kitchen drapes, "things'll get easier, I promise."

She rested her slightly wrinkled hand on his. His dad nodded in agreement. *Bless them.* He knew they were trying their hardest to make the transition as easy as possible but he knew nothing would make it run smoothly. Not even grits could fix that.

"I'll be fine," he forced a smile, "I always am."

"That's the spirit," she squeezed his hand, oblivious to how empty his bold statement had sounded.

Caden wanted so badly to hate Finn. He had found him bent over their bed with his best friend, Adam, right behind him. Just thinking about that sight made his blood boil but it wasn't enough to ignore the five years they'd had together. They weren't five perfect years but he knew nobody's relationship was perfect. He thought they were doing okay. He wouldn't have proposed to Finn if he didn't think they had a future together. *And then he had to cheat on me.*

One week ago, he had been living a good life. Work was a struggle but he was finally trying to write the novel he had been struggling through for most of his twenties.

"Have you thought about work?" his dad asked.

His mom shot him a look that read '*not now, Buster*'. Caden didn't expect to live under his parents' roof for free but he knew the couple of thousand dollars in the bank wouldn't last forever. The problem was, Havenmoore was a tiny town, so there wasn't much room for new people to squeeze into its economy.

"I haven't thought about it," Caden shrugged, scratching the back of his slightly tinged red hair.

The hair on his head ran down to the trimmed beard framing his mouth and it was the perfect combination of both of his parents. Even though his dad was greying, he had light brown hair in his youth but Caden had inherited a cast of red from his mother. She had always said Caden had '*strawberry brown*' hair, which he knew made no sense but he loved it all the same.

"You don't have to worry about that yet, honey," she squeezed his hand again, "you just focus on settling in."

His dad looked like he was going to say something again but Caden was sure that his mom had just sharply kicked him in the shin under the table.

"I'm not here for a free ride," he said, "I'll pay my way."

A sweet and thankful smile fluttered across his mother's lips. She would never ask him for money but he knew they didn't have enough to support an adult son again. They were both heading towards retirement and they'd wound down on the amount of hours they worked a week so they could start to enjoy life more. None of them had expected what had happened.

"I wonder if Bruce has anything at the bar?" Caden asked.

Working behind a bar was Caden's idea of hell but he supposed he could put up with it if it meant working beside his big brother. Bruce was thirty-four and he had the perfect life in Caden's eyes. He had a wife, a daughter and his own business. Caden wasn't so sure about the kids but he wanted everything his brother had.

"Things are tight at the bar," his dad said, "give him a call though. Something might come up soon."

"It's okay," Caden shook his head, "I don't want to make him feel awkward. He won't be able to say no to me if I put him on the spot."

They sat in silence, finishing up their late afternoon snack. He could tell they were both trying to think of topics to talk about that didn't involve the move, work or Finn, but it was difficult. That's what their relationship had boiled down to in the weekly phone calls and his trips home, three times a year.

"I think I'm going to use this time to finish writing my book," Caden offered.

"You are?" his mom's face lit up, "That's something. Isn't that great Buster?"

"Oh, yeah," Buster coughed and nodded, looking up from the morning paper he had started to flick through, "what you sent us was great. Be good to finally read how things turn out."

Caden had foolishly sent them half of his unfinished manuscript and his mom hadn't let it go since. Life got in the way of the ending but now he had all of the time in the world to get things done.

"Hey, I've just had an idea!" his mom snapped her fingers, "We're recruiting at the charity. Jerry's retired and we're looking for someone to fill his spot. You've still got your certificates, haven't you?"

"Somewhere," Caden nodded.

His mom was the director of a local charity, Helping Hands Outreach Program. It worked with people suffering with addiction problems, helping them get back on their feet. Before he had headed to New York, he had worked a couple of months at the charity. His mom had offered him a job, hoping he would stick around and not move seven hours away. It hadn't been enough to keep him in Maine. He had enjoyed it until Frank died. When he lost Frank, he knew he wasn't built for that life like his mother.

Sitting in his parents' kitchen, with all of his worldly possessions in boxes upstairs, wasn't the life he had wanted for himself either.

"I'm not sure," he mused, "after Frank -,"

"That wasn't your fault," she jumped in, "Frank had been an addict for forty years. I shouldn't have given him to you as your first. Sometimes they don't want saving and there's nothing you can do."

Just hearing his name made Caden squirm uncomfortably in his chair. He still thought about Frank and whenever he did, he was consumed with guilt. He thought he could help the heroin addict in his late sixties, he thought he could save him from himself. His body gave out before Caden could do anything. Logically, he knew it wasn't his fault but it didn't stop him from blaming himself.

He almost turned down the offer immediately but he stopped to think about it. He didn't totally hate the idea, even though he had been hoping to get a job that involved writing of some kind. He had thought about inquiring at the local paper but he knew that would be a long shot. The Havenmoore Herald was a tiny publication and he wasn't sure that his pathetic journalist experience in New York would get him through the door.

"It's only part-time," she offered, "which will give you loads of free time to work on your novel. It'll be a good stepping stone to getting your own apartment and if you're sticking around you can get something four times bigger for the same price you'd pay in New York."

He hadn't even told them that he had already thought about abandoning his plans to return to New York. It was a huge place but he knew he would somehow bump into Finn or Adam everywhere he went. They'd all been part of the same friend group, leaving most of his favorite places off limits.

"I guess. It would keep me busy."

"Exactly!" she grinned.

Caden looked to his dad but he didn't look so sure. He had never really shared his mom's enthusiasm for helping the people at the bottom of society's ladder. Buster was a fisher and a hard grafter. He had worked on a fishing boat since he was a teenager. Sometimes Caden wondered how him and his mom had stayed together for so long. They were coming up to their fortieth year of marriage so they clearly had the secret to success that Caden had yet to discover.

"You can start this week," she dropped in.

Choking on the water he had just sipped, he looked to her

with burning cheeks, "So soon?"

"There's no time like the present," she collected the plates and started to wash them in the sink.

He had been hoping for at least a couple of weeks to sink himself into his novel but he guessed that working could provide a more rewarding distraction, plus, he would need the money soon.

"Okay," Caden nodded, "I'm in."

"I'll get things moving. You'll have to take part in a refresher class but your old training should still stand," she bit her lip with excitement as she glanced over her shoulder, "and if you fix things with Finn, it's not like there'll be a problem leaving."

Choking on the water again, his cheeks burned even darker.

"That won't happen," Caden said sternly.

He stared at the back of his mom's red hair and he knew exactly what she was thinking. She thought they were going to work things out and he was going to move back to New York. He wanted to believe his stern reply but a little part of him hoped that too.

There must be more to life than this.

Chapter 2

Elias jumped out of the shower after the water turned cold again. It had been doing it since he had moved into the new apartment but it wasn't like he could complain to the landlord because he had no idea who that was. He had considered that it could be the baker downstairs but they'd bumped into each other when they were both tossing trash into the dumpster and he had seemed surprised to see Elias.

He turned off the water and left the warmth of the stall, tucking a towel around his thin waist as the cold tiles greeted him under foot. Wiping the steamy mirror, he stared at his cloudy reflection. His lip and ear rings shimmered brightly under the strip lighting. Dark smudges under his eyes signaled how little sleep he had been getting in the week since he had been in the apartment.

Toweling off his body, he quickly ran the damp towel over

his short black hair before tucking it back around his waist. He had worked his way through the few clothes he had but he hadn't even attempted to figure out how to use the washing machine.

Heading out of the bathroom, he kicked a beer can out of his path. It rattled along the wooden floor, hitting a stack of pizza boxes. His first welfare check hadn't been enough to score so he had spent the cash on as much beer and fast food as he could.

The rehab center would look at his drinking as an official relapse but for Elias, alcohol had never been his vice. He had only ever used it as a tool to suppress the hunger for stronger substances. If drinking six cans of beer a night meant that the itching for cocaine wasn't as strong, then that's what he needed to do.

Elias didn't even know why he was trying so hard. He had finally called Rigsy and arranged to see him on his first night but cancelled ten minutes before he was due to arrive. It wasn't because he didn't have the money; he had always been able to offer other things to Rigsy in exchange for a couple of lines. It was because Ellie's words were circling loudly in his mind. For the first time in his life, he was starting to feel guilty for his lifestyle and he hated that feeling.

Opening the fridge, he cracked open his first can of the day and landed on the couch, the towel still loosely around his waist. Flicking on the TV, he scanned the guide, settling on a trashy reality TV show. He had never had the luxury of watching much TV because he had never really had a stable roof over his head. It wasn't like he craved it. He had never seen the appeal of spending hours in front of the box watching trash but since he had nothing better to do, it was all he seemed to do. Elias was the first to admit that he had always had an addictive personality. When he was a kid, he took a liking to Reese's Peanut Butter Cups and that's all he would eat. With his mom always at work, the nannies and cooks were always happy to supply them because it kept him quiet. Now, he had replaced the cravings for drugs with watching trashy shows on MTV. It didn't feel like a fair tradeoff.

His cell vibrated, signaling an incoming call. When he saw '*Rigsy*' on the caller ID, he almost swiped the red reject button. Staring back at the TV with a huff, he slid the green call icon and pressed the phone up to his ear.

"What's up?"

"Hey, dude. I got some *premium* shit in last night. Wanted you to be the first to try it."

Elias gulped, the direct offer throwing him.

"Erm," he stumbled, "not a good time."

"Have you found another guy? Another dealer?" anger rose in Rigsy's voice, "If you're worried about the cash, don't sweat it. You know we've always had our little *arrangement*."

Blowjobs in exchange for a line always seemed like an easy deal for Elias. He was already gay, even if he wasn't out, so it didn't make much of a difference for him. Rigsy claimed to be straight but he enjoyed having a guy suck his cock far too much to convince Elias otherwise.

"It's not that," Elias swallowed the fear, "I just – I -,"

"You're trying to go clean?" Rigsy laughed, "*You?* You've been doing this stuff longer than I have."

Why did Rigsy find it so hard that he was trying to go clean? Cocaine was the first thought on his mind when he woke up and the last thought on his mind when he went to bed. It would be so easy to give into the desire, the hunger for it, but he didn't. He wanted so badly to tell Rigsy to come straight over with a bag of the stuff. His tongue was even running across his lips as he imagined the high it would give him.

"I don't know what I'm trying to do," Elias mumbled defensively, "I'm fresh out of rehab."

He heard a long sigh of exhaustion leave Rigsy. For a dealer, court appointed rehab was his worst enemy because every so often it would actually work.

"I get it, you're trying to be a good boy for a couple of days. When you're ready for me, I'll be waiting."

With that, Rigsy hung up and Elias tossed his phone back onto the table. He muted the TV and started drumming his fingers on the sofa. He thought back to the accidental overdose before rehab. That should have been enough to scare anybody off going back to drugs but it had never been that simple for Elias. If it was simple, he would have been able to tell Rigsy to leave him alone for good. Somehow, keeping the option there felt like a good thing.

He heard a key twist in the lock downstairs, quickly followed by heels clicking on the wooden steps. He didn't need to turn around to know who it was.

"I didn't know you had a key," he laughed, "but of course you do. Why wouldn't you?"

Standing up and making sure that the towel was still tightly around his waist, he turned to see his mother standing in the door. The great mayor of Havenmoore, Judy James, was finally gracing him with her presence. *I've only been out of rehab for five days.*

"Look at you," she rolled her heavily lined and mascaraed eyes, "have you stopped wearing clothes now as well?"

Her sharp black bob was slightly wavy for a change but it didn't soften her severe look. Her wide, dark eyes were framed with perfectly shaped, angular brows. A subtle berry stain covered her plump lips, which Elias didn't doubt had had a little help from a surgeon's needle.

"It's nice to see you too, Mom," Elias folded his arms protectively across his chest.

Whenever he was in her presence, the hairs on the backs of his arms would stand rigidly in the air. It was like being in a room with a rattlesnake, not knowing when it was going to attack to deliver the lethal blow.

"It didn't take you long to trash the place," she peered around the apartment as if it was the first time she had seen it.

Her stilettos sharply tapped on the floor as she walked in slowly, her knee-length pencil skirt constricting her movement. She was wearing a white blouse with a long black jacket over the top. Dumping her designer leather bag on the couch, she shrugged off her coat.

Elias dug through the laundry basket and pulled the least smelling t-shirt over his slim body, followed by a pair of green and blue striped underwear. He wasn't going to bother trying to find his jeans. She wasn't that important.

"I like the messy look," he shrugged, "makes me feel at home."

"Well, it is what you're used to," everything she said sounded like an insult, "aren't you going to offer me a drink?"

"Beer?" he opened the fridge, pulling on the seal and sipping at the amber liquid, "Or do you want something stronger?"

Hovering by the couch, she pursed her lips, her angular brows creasing up her forehead, "Didn't take you long to relapse. Even for you, that's a record."

She looked around, clearly trying to find left over lines and powder covered credit cards. He was almost disappointed that he couldn't fulfill her expectations. If she had her way, she would keep forcing him into rehab so she didn't have to worry about him interfering with her life.

"I haven't touched anything," he collapsed back onto the couch, pushing her bag and jacket onto the floor, "but you probably don't believe that."

She planted her hands on her hips as he sipped the beer. The TV flickered silently in the background and it didn't suddenly seem like such a bad distraction.

"This isn't a social visit," she sniffed as she glanced at her watch, "I have a meeting at -,"

"When don't you have a meeting?" he mumbled, almost to himself.

Coughing, she glared at him before continuing with her prepared speech, "I have a meeting in ten minutes. I just came by to tell you that we've arranged your follow up aftercare."

"Aftercare?" he laughed, "We?"

"The rehab center and I," she nodded, "and yes, aftercare."

"I'll pass," he laughed, "I don't need aftercare. I don't need anything you're offering."

"You're happy to sit on the couch I bought you," she almost sounded smug.

They both knew she hadn't supplied Elias with somewhere

to live because it was a natural motherly instinct. It was more like a points scoring system. Twenty years as the unopposed mayor meant that her publicity budget had been slimmed down. A lease on a tiny apartment wouldn't have even skimmed the top of the cash she had sitting in the bank.

"And besides, it's not optional," she stood up straight, "it's part of the deal. You have two months of follow-up care to make sure you're not using again. If they can prove you're using, you'll be sent straight back to rehab, or prison, depending on which judge you get."

"So that'll be whichever judge you can bribe to keep me out of prison?"

Her lips pursed even harder and her black eyes turned to slits. She looked like she could pounce into a vicious verbal attack at any moment but years in the public eye had given her the restraint of a saint.

"It's already arranged. A local charity has agreed to taking you on."

"Forget it!" Elias laughed, standing up, "I'll skip town. I don't care about follow up. Send me to prison. What have I got to live for?"

Elias wished he hadn't been so quick to turn Rigsy's offer down. This was just reminding him why he had never really cared about getting clean before. Why was he trying now?

"It's the Helping Hands Outreach Program," she continued, "your first drop-in will be at four, so you should probably clean up."

Elias didn't know if she was talking about him or the apartment but the way she wrinkled her nose and darted from his dirty t-shirt to the stacks of pizza boxes and beer cans, he was sure she meant both.

"Whatever," he sighed in defeat, "close the door on the way out."

Bending down gracefully, she picked up her jacket and bag. She took time to carefully fold the jacket to gently place it over the arm holding the bag. Turning on her heels, she headed for the door. For a second, she paused at the door and turned to

Elias, her eyes not quite meeting his. For a moment he thought she was going to say something but she left in silence.

Upturning the coffee table and sending his beer can hurtling across the room, he let out a cry and rubbed his face.

I can't do this. Why am I trying to do this?

***

"It's good to have you back in town," Caden's brother, Bruce, clinked their beer necks together, "here's to you finally getting rid of that leech."

Caden smiled, grateful for his brother's support. Bruce didn't need to try too hard to send the digs firing in Finn's direction. He had never kept it a secret that he had never liked him. Finn always said it was because Bruce was sexually repressed and he must want him but Caden knew his brother well enough to know that Bruce just didn't like Finn. Bruce would never have said anything to Caden when they were together but the '*leech*' was gone so Bruce didn't mind saying what he really thought.

"I'll drink to that," Caden jammed the bottle in his mouth, "how are things with you, bro?"

The conversation had been geared towards Caden's failing life so it was a nice change to push the conversation towards Bruce. Scratching the thick, ginger beard that ran up to his equally thick, flame red hair, Bruce stuck his chin out and his eyebrows rose with a sigh.

"Can't complain," he said, slapping the bar he was standing behind, "business is going as good as you can expect for Havenmoore. The Lobster Festival is here next week so that'll be good for us."

"It's that time of year already?" Caden set his beer on the bar, "I can't remember the last time I was in town for the festival."

Bruce squinted, as if he was trying to remember the last time.

"Ah, wasn't it 2007?" Bruce snapped his fingers, "Yeah, it

was. It was the year I met Lucy. You'd come back to town for a couple of weeks for dad's birthday."

Caden remembered it. He had been twenty-one and living in New York for a year. He had come back for two weeks because the first boyfriend he had out there, Jack, dumped him over email and he had been devastated. They'd only been dating for a couple of months but he remembered how hard he had tried to hide it from everyone because he felt like a fool. Caden had never been good at keeping secrets and he had dramatically let everything slip out after a few beers with Bruce. Bruce was five years older so he was always there to lend his little brother a shoulder.

If Caden remembered correctly, his advice back then had been '*screw that jerk. You deserve better*'. As a twenty-one-year-old, he would believed him. He thought there would be somebody great out there for him. He thought he had met that person in Finn. *Ha, look how that turned out.*

"I remember," Caden nodded, "how's the family?"

"Becca starts elementary school next week," Bruce bit his lip, "she's growing up so quick."

Caden was about to ask more about his niece but his eyes wandered to the giant TV behind the bar when the sound of a cheering crowd signaled the first touchdown for the Havenmoore Rangers. Caden had never been interested in football but he remembered his dad saying that the game was starting at four.

"Shit," he gulped the last of the beer, "there's somewhere I need to be. Oh, fuck. Mom's gonna kill me. I've got my first Helping Hands meeting with this guy."

Shrugging himself into the jacket, he ripped open his canvas bag and quickly looped his new ID badge around his neck.

"You'll have to stop by the house. The girls would love to see you," Bruce waved, "and if mom gives you any trouble, blame me."

"Will do."

Marching across the square, Caden pulled the thick file out of his bag, flicking to the address of the guy he had been assigned that morning. Underneath '*Elias James*' was an address and Caden let out a sigh of relief when he recognized it as the apartment over the bakery. Straightening up the collar on his shirt, he quickly walked around the corner, the smell of fresh bread hitting him in the face. It made his stomach grumble, reminding him that he hadn't eaten since the eggs that morning.

Craning his neck to look up at the small window, he tried to ignore the nerves circling in the pit of his stomach. In those couple of months he had spent working with his mom, he always got nervous when meeting somebody for the first time. It was a lottery and there was no way to know who he was going to meet on the other side of the door. Sometimes, they'd be friendly and accepting of the help that he was there to offer, but more often they wanted nothing more than to be left alone.

Ducking into the narrow alley next to the bakery he saw a green door in the shadows. It didn't have a number on the door but he knocked anyway. Wiping his hands on the backs of his jeans, he cracked his neck and pushed a smile up his stubble-covered cheeks. He had skimmed over Elias' file that morning but he had been so nervous slipping back into a job he hadn't done for eight years, he hadn't soaked up much of the information.

Clenching his eyes, he tried to muster the information on the file he had already stashed away in the bag hanging over his shoulder.

The door swung open and Caden's eyes opened wide. The jumbled words on the file in his memory disappeared when he saw the man in front of him. He didn't know what he had been expecting but he hadn't expected a man in a pair of very tight green and blue striped briefs standing in front of him. Caden's eyes landed on his package, which was jutting out under a creased grey band t-shirt. He had a slight build, differing from Caden's strong and wide frame. He had picked that up from his dad's side, which apparently all Walker men inherited, making them look like they worked out without having to try. He looked a couple of inches shorter than Caden's own six feet two inches but he wasn't short by any stretch of the imagination. With his darkly haired lean thighs crossed, his narrow hips poked out as he clung to the edge of the door, waiting for Caden to introduce who he was.

A quick reminder of why he was there sent his eyes running up to the man's face. He had black hair, a slim face and a lip ring, which his tongue was playing with. Caden was used to working with older people who fit the stereotype of '*addict*'. Elias looked younger than Caden and he was ignoring how good looking he was.

"What?" Elias snapped, "What do you want?"

Caden blinked heavily and shook his head, ridding himself of the stage fright. He was frantically trying to remember what he had picked up on the couple of days he had spent shadowing his mother but it was useless.

"Hi," Caden jutted his hand out, "I'm from Helping Hands Outreach."

Elias rolled his eyes, ignoring the hand. Stepping to the side, he kicked the door out, his toned thigh holding it in place.

"C'mon then," he jerked his head upstairs, "let's get this over with."

Nodding with an awkward smile, Caden jumped in and stopped the door from shutting when Elias started to run up the stairs, taking them two at a time. Caden tried to ignore the bounce of his cheeks in the underwear but he couldn't. *Pull it together Caden, you're here to do a job.*

Closing the door behind him, he followed Elias into the tiny apartment above the bakery. It wasn't what he had been expecting at all. It was clean and nicely decorated, if not a little simple. From what he remembered, nice housing had never been a luxury to the people at the bottom of the social ladder.

"What did you say your name was?" Elias grabbed the ID card around his neck and twisted it, "*Caden Walker.*"

Elias dropped the ID badge and jumped over the back of the sofa. He sat in the corner of the couch, his arms over the back and his thighs spread.

"Let's make this quick," Elias already sounded frustrated.

Caden took this as his invitation to get things rolling. He sat on the couch next to Elias, who seemed oblivious that everything was pretty much on show. Gulping, Caden was almost surprised how affected he was by a man in a pair of underwear. He had barely looked at another guy in five years and now he was sitting next to a semi-naked one. *Pull it together, man.*

"How've you been?" Caden pulled the file out of his bag, resting it on his knee.

"Peachy," Elias grinned sarcastically, "is that everything?"

The shallow circles under Elias' eyes told a different story. This had been the part Caden was expecting and it was always the part that made the job harder, or so he was told. The more they resisted, the harder he would have to try to get them to cooperate. Sometimes, they wouldn't cooperate and there was no way to help them but his mom had always taught him that you didn't give up on people until they gave up on you. The fact Elias even answered the door was a step in the right direction.

"Are you settling in okay?"

"You can see it's clean," he tossed his hands out, "don't I look settled in to you?"

Elias scratched the side of his face as his tongue angrily toyed with the lip ring. Similar rings cluttered his ears, leading down to a tiny plug in a stretched out part of his ear lobe.

"I'm not here to judge you," Caden delivered the line they're all taught to say when things turned sour, "I'm just here to help you help yourself."

"Cut the shrink crap," Elias laughed, "you're here because my mom wants somebody to keep an eye on me and she's too busy."

"Your mom?" Caden saw this as his way in.

"Our lord and savior," he rolled his eyes, "the mayor. That's why you're here, isn't it? Because she can't keep her nose out?"

Caden flicked open the file on his knee, hovering over Elias' surname. James. *Judy James is his mother? Judy James has a son?* Judy had been the mayor of Havenmoore for as long as Caden could remember. She was a permanent fixture in the town hall and a regular at public events. People trusted her and they liked her so she ran unopposed for most elections. The small town mentality meant that any change was usually discouraged.

"Look, Elias," Caden closed the file, "I'm here because the court said you needed follow up, but that isn't all this has to be. You can really benefit from -,"

"Don't tell me. I can become a functioning member of society? Get a nice little job somewhere? Maybe get married and have some sweet little kids and live a normal life?"

"Exactly."

"Sure," Elias tossed his head back, "aliens will land and we'll have a woman in the White House before that happens."

Elias jumped up and headed over to the kitchen. Caden watched as he poured himself a glass of water with shaky hands. It wasn't rare for people fresh out of rehab to start using again but Elias didn't seem high.

"Do you want to talk about your time in rehab?"

"Nope," he gulped the water.

"What about your mother?"

"Double nope."

"Anything?"

"No," Elias tossed the rest of the water into the sink, "if that's everything, you can go now."

Caden wasn't going to give up that easily. An average session could range anywhere from ten minutes to two hours, all depending on what the person needed. A quick glance at his watch told him he had been there for six minutes.

Elias headed into the bathroom, leaving the door open. When Caden heard the sound of peeing, he re-opened the file and scanned over Elias' file. Words like *cocaine*, *repeat user* and *serial offender* caught his eye in a flash. Snapping the file shut, he stood up and dumped it on the couch, heading over to the kitchen. Pizza boxes and empty beer cans were piled up next to an overflowing trashcan. T-shirts, jeans, underwear and socks were stacked high in front of the washing machine and dirty cups and plates were dangerously balancing by the sink.

Shrugging off his denim jacket, he rolled up the sleeves of his stiff white shirt and started to fill the sink.

"What are you doing?" Elias reappeared, tugging at his

manhood through his underwear.

"Washing up," Caden shrugged.

"Whatever," Elias sighed, heading back over to the couch.

As Caden squirted a healthy dose of dish soap into the water, Elias flicked on the TV, turning it up over the sound of the running water. Reclining on the couch, his eyes fixed on the screen as a group of reality wives argued about wine.

It wasn't Caden's job to be a cleaner but he knew that if he showed he was willing to help, no matter how he was helping, Elias might open up. Turning off the faucet and dunking the dishes in hot soapy water, he glanced over to Elias who was acting as though Caden wasn't even there.

"I never knew the mayor had a son," Caden said as he scrubbed a plate.

"That's what she wants you to think," he mumbled, "I bet you knew she had a daughter though."

Caden cast his mind back. Now that Elias mentioned it, he was sure he had seen something on the front page of the Havenmoore Herald about a daughter graduating.

"Is she a doctor?"

"Bingo," Elias rolled his eyes, "everybody knows about Ellie."

Elias shared the same black hair and dark eyes as his mother but he didn't seem to share any of her people skills. Rinsing off the soapsuds, he stacked the dishes on the strainer. Drying his hands on a towel looped over the front of the oven, he moved onto filling the washing machine with the dirty clothes. They smelled strongly of an unwashed man.

"Detergent?" Caden looked over the counter.

Elias shrugged as he turned up the volume on the TV, "How should I know?"

Sighing, Caden started to look through the cupboards until he found a bottle of detergent and a bottle of softener. Dumping them into the washing machine, he set the cycle after figuring out how the machine worked. It looked unused.

"Do you want me to show you how to use this?" Caden called over.

Elias shook his head, not looking away from the TV as he scratched his balls. Caden looked around the kitchen for more things to do. When he found some bags in some of the drawers, he started to stuff the pizza boxes into the bag along with the mountain of beer cans. *He couldn't have drank through all of these in less than a week?*

"Did you drink all of this?"

"The magic fairy helped," Elias rolled his eyes, "what's it to you?"

Elias jumped up from the sofa and marched over to the kitchen. Snatching the bag from Caden, he dumped it on the floor and pulled a beer out of the fridge.

"If there's anything you want to talk about, I'm a listening ear," Caden watched as Elias sipped the beer, "that's what I'm here for."

Elias arched a dark brow, almost amused at how hard Caden was trying. Leaning in slightly, his dark eyes pierced into Caden's, making his lips part. Elias' eyes darted down to his parted lips with a smirk.

"I can smell beer on your breath," Elias whispered, "get off your high horse."

Caden backed away, bringing his hand up to his mouth. How could he have been stupid enough to let his brother convince him to have a *'quick beer'* when he was just trying to pass through to see how the bar was going.

"I'll be honest with you, Elias. I had a beer in my brother's bar before I came here, but I'm not the one with an addiction problem."

"I'm not addicted to beer," he laughed as he drank from the can, "I just like it."

Caden opened the bag to look at all of the cans. Stomping on the pedal of the trashcan, he could see loads more inside. He had gone through enough beer in less than a week to sink a navy ship.

"Change is hard," Caden crouched on the sofa next to Elias, "I get that. I want to help you."

"What do you know about change?" Elias snapped angrily,

"Look at you. I bet you have a perfect life."

Caden had to stop himself from laughing. His life felt far from perfect; it felt like a mess.

"I was living in New York," he relaxed into the couch, "with my partner. I thought I had the perfect life but I caught them in bed with my best friend and now I'm back in Havenmoore. Trust me, I know change."

Elias peered at him out of the corner of his eye before staring back at the TV. Letting out an exhausted sigh, he picked up the remote control and switched off the box.

"You ever tried cocaine?" Elias crossed his arms across his chest, his legs wide open so that his package was resting on the sofa cushion.

"No."

"Then you have no idea what I'm going through. I'm not suffering with addiction. Cocaine isn't as addictive as people make out. Most people can take it or leave it. It's the feeling it gives you that's addictive. Do you know how it makes you feel?"

"No."

"It's like a warm hug from somebody who loves you. It makes you feel on top of the world. It makes this shit world feel bearable. You don't know anything so don't pretend you do. You're here because you need to be so let's not make this any harder than it has to be."

Turning back to the TV, Elias gritted his teeth as he breathed heavily through his nose. His eyes stared intensely at the beer can on the coffee table but he looked like he was looking right through it.

"Have you used since you left the rehab center?"

"Do I look like I have?" Elias laughed, "Do you think I'd be sitting here if I had? People think rehab is the solution but it isn't. Rehab is easy. You have people around you all day treating you like a kid who can't look after themselves. You're so frustrated that you can't take a shit without somebody looking over your shoulder that you barely notice the withdrawals. It's when you get home and you're left alone that it starts. I can't sleep, I can't think about anything else and that can of beer right there is the only thing keeping me level enough not to call my dealer."

Caden didn't know what to say. Elias was right; Caden wasn't equipped to deal with his situation. You could have all the training in the world, he was only working for a local charity who didn't have the resources to do anything other than offer support and a guiding hand. Caden wanted to be that guiding hand for Elias. The first rule was to help without letting your guard down but it was so hard to have a guard with somebody younger than him. *Any of us could have ended up like him.*

"I'm not going to pretend to know what it's like. The only thing I've ever really been addicted to was Jolly Rancher's in junior high and I only stopped eating those because my dentist scared me to death with pictures of cavities."

"Jesus, man," Elias laughed, "Jolly Rancher's?"

"I'm not trying to say I know what you're going through but I know that you've been clean for ten weeks and that's a start. You might not have had a choice in rehab but you've had a choice this week. It shows that you're strong."

Elias uncrossed his arms and dropped his hands in his lap, making Caden's eyes dart down there with them. He rested his hands on his junk and started picking at the skin next to the nail on his thumb.

"I'm not strong," he shook his head, "I don't even know why I'm not using right now. I have nothing to live for."

"Everybody has something to live for," Caden reached out and dropped his hand on Elias' shoulder.

He didn't know why he did that but when Elias turned to look at it, Caden ripped it away, folding his own arms.

"If you're done," Elias mumbled, "you can go."

The sadness in his eyes made Caden's stomach knot. Elias' arms crossed over his body, clinging to his slender bicep protectively. Any moment, he would shrink back into the furniture. Caden knew he hadn't even scratched the surface with figuring Elias out. There must have been something stopping him from relapsing, Caden just needed to figure out what it was.

"You sure?"

Elias nodded without saying anything. Caden could see his Adam's apple bob up and down as if he was trying to swallow back tears. He didn't want to leave but he knew that they would need to take baby steps if there was any chance of them building a relationship so that Caden could attempt to help him.

Pushing himself off the couch, he stepped over Elias' legs, his foot brushing against his hairy shins. Picking up his jacket from the counter, he shrugged into it. On the counter next to the phone was a blank pad and a pen. Caden knew he was breaking the rules but he quickly scribbled down his cell number.

"Anytime you need anything, I'm on the end of the phone," he tore the paper off and held it up, "day or night."

"I'm fine," Elias switched the TV on.

As Elias stared blankly at the TV, pretending that Caden wasn't even there, Caden gently slid the piece of paper under a fridge magnet of a lobster. Picking up his bag, he headed for the door, pausing to stare back at Elias. He thought about saying goodbye or offering something else but he was sure that it would fall on deaf ears.

Heading back out into the late afternoon sun, he vowed that he was going to help Elias, no matter what it took. *I'm not going to lose another one.*

Chapter 3

Elias pushed through the people waiting in line at the reception desk of Ellie's doctor's office. Cold sweat dripped from his hair and down his face. People cried out as he made his way to the front of the line, not caring about who he had to push out of the way.

"Is she in?"

Ronda, the receptionist, knew Elias. She pursed her lips and darkened her glare as she looked Elias up and down with obvious disgust.

"She's with a patient," she craned her neck to look at the vocal line behind him, "you'll have to wait in line like the rest of these people."

"Yeah! Get to the back, Jackass," a heavy hand grabbed his shoulder, yanking him back.

Elias turned to see a man who must be topping six foot, towering over him with a scowl. Elias didn't care if he was going to lose, he clenched his fists, ready to pounce on the man. The intense cravings and withdrawals mixed with the adrenaline and he was about to blow.

"Elias?" Caden's face appeared from the blur of the line, "Is everything okay?"

"No, it's not," the man answered for him, "this dude thought he could push through the line."

"I'm sure it was a mistake," Caden apologized for Elias with a smile, pulling him to one side, "what are you doing here?"

"Why do you care?" Elias yanked his arm free as Caden attempted to continue to pull him to the side, "I need to get in there."

"Are you sick?" Caden's eyes danced over Elias, looking for a sign of what was going on, "You look like you're running up a fever."

Caden's hand headed towards Elias' forehead but he batted it away. Quickly wiping away the sweat, his eyelids fluttered as he ran his fingers through his short hair. He could only think about one thing and it was driving him insane.

"Come outside for some fresh air."

"I don't want air!" Elias cried, catching the attention of Ronda who fired him a warning glance, "I need to see my sister."

Caden somehow managed to navigate Elias towards the seats lining the wall of the doctor's office. Under a poster about the effects of alcohol on the body, Elias doubled over in the chair, leaning his arms on his knees as he panted for breath. Knowing that it was all in his mind didn't make things any easier. All he wanted was something to take the edge off because alcohol wasn't doing that anymore.

Focusing on his breathing, he slowly felt his throat open up, not even realizing at first that Caden was gently rubbing his back. It felt foreign and comforting; Elias wasn't sure if he liked it. He wanted to launch at Caden, to tell him to leave him alone but the adrenaline had completely vanished.

"What happened?" Caden asked softly, his hand still rhythmically rubbing between his shoulder blades, "What's triggered this?"

"Nothing's triggered anything," he snapped, "I just need to see Ellie. I just need something to calm me down. I can't do this."

Caden's hand worked its way firmly up and down Elias' spine, the more he rubbed, the more surface area he covered. Sitting up straight, the hand disappeared and Elias stared up towards the light, not wanting to admit that Caden had managed to calm him down.

"You could have called me for some help," Caden leaned his head against the poster, joining Elias is staring at the light, "I would have come."

Elias couldn't deny that he had spent the couple of days since Caden's visit staring at the number on the refrigerator. More than once, he had found the phone in his hand but he didn't know why. Caden was just some support worker who he could already sense was trying too hard. *He's wasting his time on me, I'm beyond help.*

"You can't help me," his head rolled along the wall, "I'm just prolonging the inevitable. I'll give in eventually."

"Or," Caden sucked the air sharply through his teeth, "you keep pushing through and eventually you'll see the light."

"Fuck, man. Not everything has a silver lining," Elias clenched his eyes tight, trying to block out the rising chatter of the busy reception area.

"You're right. It doesn't. Some things are broken and can't be fixed but I don't think that's you."

"How do you know that?" Elias opened his eyes and tilted his face to stare at Caden.

Caden did the same, his pale green eyes glittering under the harsh strip lighting. A network of fine lines surrounded his eyes as his cheeks peaked into a soft smile. It made Elias' stomach flutter in a way he didn't recognize. Dismissing it as hunger, he clenched his jaw as he waited for Caden to respond.

"I don't," Caden shrugged softly, his pale lashes fluttering, "it's just a feeling."

Elias looked down to the paper clutched in Caden's hand, instantly recognizing it as a prescription form waiting for a doctor's signature. It was folded but from the letters he could see, it looked like a prescription for Methadone.

"What you doing here, anyway?" Elias asked.

Caden caught Elias' eyes on the paper and he quickly tucked it into his pocket, straightening up.

"I'm dropping something off for one of my mom's patients," he explained, "confidential."

"Heroin addict?"

Some of the older addicts at rehab had been withdrawing from heroin and they'd been allowed Methadone while their bodies were coping with the sudden loss of the drugs. They were the only people in the place allowed any kind of drug to make things easier.

"I can't say," Caden's smile said it all, "but they're in a tough place. They have it worse than you."

"Is that possible?" Elias laughed, rubbing his sweaty palms together.

The door to his sister's office creaked open and an old lady clutching a handkerchief to her nose shuffled out. Before Ronda could call for the next patient, Elias bolted, leaving Caden behind.

"What can I-," Ellie's voice trailed off when she saw her brother, a frown instantly forming, "I'm working."

She dropped her pen on the table and leaned back in her chair in front of the window looking out onto Havenmoore's floral square. Perfectly manicured fingernails clutched the edges of her expensive chair.

"Nice to see you too," Elias quickly sat in the chair, "this won't take long. I just need something."

"No," swaying her short, dark hair, she leaned forward with a dry smirk on her face, "get out of here. I have real patients to see."

"Please," he pleaded, "hear me out."

"There's nothing you can say to convince me to help get you high. I've done that before and I almost lost my license because of it, Elias. This is your mess. You clean it up."

She had only ever helped him out before because Elias

would usually blackmail her with something. It was usually something emotional to make her crack. He always hated himself for doing that but he never felt like he had any choice. He just needed something to keep his mind off the drug he really craved.

"I'm trying, I really am," he scratched his scruffy hair with both hands as his tongue flicked against his lip ring, "honestly, I didn't touch anything."

"You smell like a brewery," she wrinkled her nose.

"It's just beer. Nothing else, I swear."

Ellie's doctor eyes wandered over him, quickly examining him. His eyes may have been bloodshot from the lack of sleep but they weren't extremely dilated.

"You promise me you've not touched anything?"

"I promise," he held his pinky finger out, "pinky swear."

It was something they used to do as kids and neither of them dared to bring out the *'pinky swear'* unless they were being truthful. Ellie stared at the pinky but she didn't reach out to join in.

"I believe you," she gritted her sharp jaw tightly, "but why?"

"Why?"

"Why haven't you cracked? It's been a week, so why are you still clean?"

"Thanks for the vote of confidence," Elias tried to laugh it off.

"You've been to rehab before and you've come out making bold claims about trying to stay clean. This time, you haven't touched anything. Why?"

Elias didn't want to tell her why. He didn't want to admit that hearing that his nephew looked up to him had shaken him and got under his skin. He didn't want to be a role model to a kid. *I can't even look after myself.*

"Kobi needs an uncle," he wiped the sweat from his brow, "and I'm trying for him. I don't know why, but I'm really trying not to crack."

"You've never cared before. Does this have anything to do with the fact you nearly died this time?"

"Don't."

"No, I will," Ellie leaned across the table, "I was the first one they called. You'd taken so much coke you were about to meet your maker. You almost died, Elias. I almost lost you."

"I know!" he cried, hands slamming on the table, "Damn, do you think I don't know all of this?"

"No," she shrugged and laughed, "because you keep doing this to us! You always go back to your default settings, hurting everybody around you. You're selfish Elias, and you always have been."

"I know I'm selfish!" he said, "But I've been the only person to ever have my back, so what do you expect?"

"Don't start with that shit," she laughed, "we had the same childhood and I turned out fine."

It was Elias' turn to laugh. *Does she really believe that?* Looking her dead in the eyes, he knew she didn't believe it when she couldn't sustain the gaze.

"The difference was, you had the brains and I might as well have been invisible."

"You have a brain," she rolled her eyes, "you just never knew how to use it."

Leaning back in the chair, Elias rubbed his face, exhausted from the sudden therapy session. He knew it was a long shot coming to see his sister. In vain, Elias hoped Ellie would have helped him out even if part of him secretly hoped she wouldn't. When he heard a plastic bottle rattle on the desk, he moved his hands and opened his eyes.

"What are those?" he stared at the orange plastic.

"Anti-depressants," she pushed the bottle across the desk, "Cymbalta, from my personal stash."

Elias reached out and snatched up the bottle before his sister could change her mind. It wasn't what he had been expecting but it was something.

"Why do you need anti-depressants?" he asked.

"Well, my brother is in and out of rehab, my husband doesn't talk to me and my mother doesn't know how to hug me," she shrugged, "they're a last resort. Take them before you go to bed and they'll help you sleep. You'll wake up feeling a little calmer. It can take a few days but you'll settle out eventually and you've got enough for a couple of weeks."

Smiling, he nodded his thanks, knowing he didn't need to say it. Arching her eyebrows to the door, Ellie let him know that he had over stayed his welcome. He opened the door and the guy from the line huffed heavily as he pushed past him.

"Everything done?" Caden was still sitting in the chair he had left him in.

Patting the pill bottle in his pocket, Elias nodded, ready to get back to his apartment and away from the crowds of people. He wasn't used to having to deal with so much on a clear mind and he was starting to wonder how everybody else lived with the madness of the world without a little help.

"Hey, Elias," Caden called after him as he headed for the door.

"What?"

A warm, soft smile twinkled across Caden's rugged features, "See you in an hour for your next home visit."

"Right," Elias mumbled heading outside, "bye."

Shielding his eyes from the bright afternoon sun, Elias tried to get the image of Caden's smiling face out of his mind, but he couldn't. It had been so kind and friendly, as if he was actually looking forward to the visit. *Don't be dumb, Elias, he's being paid to be your babysitter.*

When he reached the bakery on the corner, his fingers wrapping around the orange plastic of the pill bottle, he wondered if there was more to Caden than he thought.

***

"Sweetie, is that you?" Caden heard his mom call from the kitchen, "I'm making chicken, you want some?"

"Sure," he called back as he shrugged off his jacket, "I have time for chicken."

He headed into the small family kitchen where Bruce was sitting reading the morning paper.

"What are you doing here, anyway?" Caden slapped Bruce

warmly on the shoulder, "Shouldn't you be at the bar?"

"Sharon's holding it down," Bruce closed the paper, "thought I'd come and see mom."

Their mom turned around, fingers covered in slimy breadcrumbs as she coated the chicken, "He's just hungry, that's what he really means."

Caden had to admit, he was looking forward to his mom's chicken as he sat at the table. Caden had never been able to find a chicken takeout in New York who could make it like his mom.

"I've just dropped off George's prescription for you," Caden said, "should be ready later today."

"I'll head to the doctor's office later," she nodded as she slowly started to lower each wing into the boiling oil, "how's Doctor James?"

He knew she meant Ellie but he didn't know why she was asking, "She's fine."

Caden almost stopped there but he took it as an opportunity to find out more about Elias before their next meeting. His mom hadn't told him much but he got the idea she knew more than she was letting him know.

"Did you know the mayor had a son?" he asked.

"She does?" Bruce wrinkled his forehead as he sipped a glass of orange juice, "I thought she just had that yuppie daughter?"

"Yuppie?"

"Head so far up her own butthole that she's coming out the other side. She's come into the bar a couple of times with her husband and she always acts like she's better than everyone."

"That's no way to talk about our town's best doctor, Bruce, is it?" their mom winked over her shoulder, seeming to agree with him, "And yes, I knew she had a son. Not many do though."

Caden poured himself a glass of orange juice, just like he would have done when they had been around that very table as kids. Bruce would always snatch up the bottle first, because in his words, he was the oldest and he deserved it more.

"Why's she kept him so quiet?" Caden asked.

She carried on cooking, straining the chicken out of the oil before laying it on a sheet of paper towels. Caden knew she was avoiding his question. Whenever she didn't want to answer something she would always pretend like she didn't hear while she thought of how she could steer the conversation in another direction.

"Chicken!" she dumped the huge plate in the middle of the table, "Be careful, it's still hot."

Just like when they were kids, Bruce dived in and burned his fingers as Caden sat back and let it cool. He stared at his mom but she was diving in too, even though she was usually the last to grab any chicken. She was either really hungry or uncomfortable with what Caden had asked.

Deciding it would be better to wait until they were alone, he waited for Bruce to eat his chicken. As predicted, he kissed their mom goodbye, patted Caden on the back with a promise to hang out soon and headed straight back to his bar. They all knew he never trusted anybody to look after his baby for too long.

His mom glanced awkwardly to him before busying herself with clearing away the dishes.

"Mom, Elias. What do you know?"

"Does it matter?"

"If I want to help him it does."

Carefully placing the dishes into the sink, she washed her grease covered fingers and turned around, folding her arms awkwardly across her green blouse covered chest. Caden knew what he was doing. His mom cared too much about the people her charity helped so she wouldn't ignore Caden's plea.

"This was the reason I wanted you to take Elias," she sighed, "I know too much about him and his family."

"What do you know?"

Pulling up a chair, she leaned her arms on the table and started picking at her nails. A quick glance to the chicken shaped clock over the stove let Caden know he only had twenty minutes if he wanted to get to Elias' five minutes early.

"When you were a baby, I used to volunteer at the hospital. They usually put me in the maternity ward because I'm kind to folks. Most of the time, I'd try and reassure the ladies because I knew what they'd been through. You couldn't have been out of diapers at this time. One night, in the early hours, the mayor came in wearing a huge black coat. Well, she wasn't the mayor back then but she worked at the town hall. She was still really important even back then. I was more shocked than anyone to see that she was heavily pregnant. I'd seen her a couple of months before at the Lobster Festival and I hadn't suspected anything. I was in her room when she was delivering and out came twins. One boy and one girl."

"Elias and Ellie?"

"That's them," she nodded, "but the thing is, she kept it so quiet. The next week she came into the hospital to open the new children's ward with the mayor of the time, Steven Carlwright. Lovely man he was. Died of a heart attack a couple years later and Judy jumped straight in there. She was wearing another huge coat. I expected her to say something about her new babies but she never mentioned them. There was nothing in the paper about them and nobody was talking about her growing family. Like I said, even back then she was important. Folks knew her. I thought it odd but eventually, Ellie started appearing at functions with her in these adorable little dresses. It wasn't until later that I started to notice Elias was never around."

She left it there but he could sense there was more to the story. Leaning in closer, he nodded, urging her to carry on.

"I wouldn't have thought anything of it until I saw him again a couple years later. He couldn't have been any older than ten. You know how I go into the school once a semester to give a talk to the kids about substance abuse? Well, I spotted him straight away in the crowd, sitting next to Ellie. They're the mirror image of each other and the essence of their mother. I stuck around for a couple of hours, going from class to class. When I came to their class I was struck by how different they were. Ellie was so well behaved and quiet but Elias was like a boy possessed. He ran around the class and you could tell his teacher was exhausted with him. I guessed that he was just a troubled boy but later on when I was up at the rehab center I saw him. He looked different. Skinny, pale. He didn't look like his sister anymore, nor his mother. Ellie and Judy had turned into clones of each other. Same haircuts and everything, although I'm not sure whose idea that was. I wanted to say something to him but he didn't know me. I was just a stranger who knew something the rest of the town didn't know. I was walking by his room once and I saw him crying. People were always crying in that place. Usually they'd be howling out for drugs but Elias was sobbing so quietly, he was almost choking. His tears told a thousand tales that his mouth would never speak. It was then I came to my conclusions about his mother."

"What conclusions?"

"She's not a maternal type, like me. Some people just aren't built for kids. I think she saw something of herself in her daughter. Something she could mold and shape. Her son on the other hand, I don't think it was as easy for him to follow her. Some boys are like that but most grow out of it with love and patience. I was lucky having you and Bruce. You were my perfect little boys. Judy James pushes out this image as our loving mayor but I think it's a different story behind closed doors. She's pushed her son so far away from her spotlight because she's ashamed of what he's become and I think Elias feels that. You don't turn to drugs for no reason. Most of the time, they're just trying to hide something painful."

Caden's mind was racing. So many things were starting to make sense and the more he figured out, the more his heart broke for Elias. There was a wall built so high around him and he tried to push everybody away but he was starting to understand why.

"Why didn't you tell me any of this?" he asked.

"Because sometimes you can go in knowing too much. I was hoping he'd open up to you and tell you this himself. I didn't feel comfortable working with him because I'd want to mother him and that's not what he needs right now."

Caden stood up and grabbed his jacket, more than ready for his next meeting with Elias. Pulling the zipper halfway, he stopped and turned back to his mother.

"He was in rehab for cocaine addiction?"

She nodded.

"Alcohol, other pills, where does he stand?"

"Why? Has he been using? If he has, you need to report -,"

"No," he jumped in, not wanting her to jump to conclusions about Elias, "I'm just wondering. Just in case."

She narrowed her eyes, clearly not believing her son. Caden had always been a terrible liar. She had always said it was because he had a kind and honest soul.

"Everything needs filing and reporting," she said, "this is serious. This is his fourth time in that place and from what I've heard he didn't go in there willingly. Whatever it is, write it down, for his sake. Don't let your guard down, Caden. Remember, you're there to do a job. You're there to help him and sometimes you have to do things you don't want to do, especially if you like the person."

"I know," he nodded with an awkward smile, "is there any of that chicken left?"

"You still hungry?" her maternal eyes twinkled at the thought of being able to feed her son, "I'll get it wrapped up for you so you can eat it on the way."

Caden watched as she wrapped the cooling fried chicken in foil before placing it gently in a plastic box. Grabbing his bag with Elias' paperwork, he slid it in gently, kissed his mom on the cheek and headed across town, more determined than ever to help the man he was learning more and more about.

Chapter 4

Looking around his apartment, Elias wondered if he had time to quickly tidy up before Caden showed up. He didn't know why he was suddenly bothered about it because he wasn't last time. There was something about the way Caden had been rubbing his back and showing that he cared that had awoken something in Elias.

Calm down, he's probably straight.

Scooping up a pile of laundry, he tossed it into the machine, not bothering to turn it on. When he was about to tackle the beer cans cluttering the place, there was a firm knock on the door. Stomach knotting, Elias quickly fixed his black hair in the reflection of the stainless steel fridge. Caden's scribbled down phone number caught his eye. For a second, he thought about taking it down but he didn't want Caden to know he had even noticed it.

"You're early," Elias opened the door.

"Thought I'd make up for last time," a shaky smile filled Caden's lips as he clung onto the strap of his canvas bag, "can I come in?"

"Yeah, right," Elias stepped out of the way, "I didn't have much time to clean up."

Wishing that he had taken one of his sister's '*calming*' pills, he headed upstairs, leaving Caden to follow. When they were both in the apartment, they stood behind the couch, awkwardly smiling at each other. *Why are you being so weird?*

"Coffee?" Elias asked.

"You're offering me coffee?" Caden laughed, "I guess that's progress on last week."

Elias headed for the kettle and boiled the water, not bothering to wait for Caden's response. Deciding that he was going to ditch the beer, at least for Caden's visit, he grabbed two never before used mugs from the cupboard and scooped four large heaps of the dark stuff into his mug. He scooped two into Caden's because he looked like the kind of guy who wouldn't like his coffee strong.

"I brought you some chicken," Elias heard the sound of foil and the rich smell of fried chicken filled his apartment, causing a rumbling in his stomach, "I didn't know if you'd be hungry but my mom makes the best chicken in Havenmoore and I thought it would be selfish to keep it all to myself."

"Thanks. You shouldn't have," Elias mumbled, dropping the sugar into the mug.

"It's no problem," Caden pulled the milk from the fridge and handed it to him, "I guessed it'd make a nice change from all of the pizza."

Elias finished up the coffee with shaking hands, desperately wanting to grab a cold beer from the fridge. He handed the cup to Caden, who instantly slurped the dark liquid.

"Geeze," he winced, "that's a bit strong."

"Oh, that's mine," Elias swapped the cups.

Caden took a sip of the less strong coffee with a wince but he didn't say anything. Elias had hardly had much practice at making coffee. It's not like he had lived in his own apartment to invite people around to before, not that Caden had been invited. *He's here for the court.* Elias knew Caden was practically there to spy on him.

They sat on the couch and Caden brought the box of chicken with him. He set it on the trash covered coffee table in front of them, leaving Elias to eye it up hungrily. When his stomach growled loudly, announcing that he hadn't eaten anything, Caden reached out and offered the box to him.

"Dig in," he smiled, "I've already had mine back home."

Elias plucked out a leg and wedged the coffee between his knees. The chicken melted against his lips, the mixture of the breadcrumbs and grease making his stomach happy. Caden was right, it was the best chicken he had ever tasted, even if it was going cold.

"Good, right?" Caden laughed, "I missed that in New York."

Elias nodded, his mouth full of chicken. He wanted to know more about Caden. Elias had been in and out of Havenmoore his whole life, sleeping rough and couch hopping in between rehab stints. Looking at Caden's face, he was sure that he had never seen him around town before.

"Why would you come back here after living in New York?" he licked his fingers and picked up another wing, "What does Havenmoore have that New York doesn't?"

Caden smiled softly and stared down into the coffee. Elias instantly picked up on the sadness in that smile, wondering if he should push it further. He didn't want to open up a can of worms he wasn't prepared to deal with, especially since that was supposed to be Caden's job.

"I didn't have much choice. I thought I'd be in New York for the rest of my life but I found myself in a position where I felt like I needed to come home for a while."

Elias instantly guessed that he was talking about a break up. He imagined a professional businesswoman left behind in the big city broken hearted. Elias had always wanted to visit New York but he had never managed to get out of Maine.

"So you're not sticking around here?"

"I'm undecided," he said, "I thought I'd come back and clear my head so I could finally start work on my novel."

"Novel? You're a writer?" Elias was slightly impressed.

"Kind of. I've mainly been writing advertorials and tiny articles for magazines that nobody reads. I've hardly been living the New York dream out there. It's a tough place to survive."

For Elias, Havenmoore was a tough place to survive. Just the thought that his mother was around the corner was enough to put him on edge, especially knowing that she had her own key.

"What's this book about?" Elias asked.

"You really want to know?" Caden laughed, leaning forward and pushing his coffee cup onto the coffee table, "It's pretty dumb, really."

"I scored the lowest SAT score my school ever got. Don't talk to me about dumb," he said, "go on, writer, what's it about?"

Caden took a deep breath and stared up at the ceiling as if he couldn't believe he was about to tell Elias. Surprisingly, Elias found himself wanting to know, if only to understand Caden a little better.

"Okay, so I had this idea for this story set in a medieval village. Have you seen Game Of Thrones?"

"Do I look like I've watched much TV in the last decade?" Elias arched a brow, "The mayor didn't like to pay out for the rooms with the TVs in rehab."

Elias meant it as a joke but Caden's expression dropped and the sadness returned. This time, it looked like the sadness was directed at Elias. He didn't look like he pitied him. It was more complicated than that. It made Elias feel comfortable, which in turn made him feel uncomfortable because he wasn't used to it.

"Well, my idea," Caden continued, "was about this tiny village where people trained dragons for war. The concept I had was the boys of the village are given an egg when they become teenagers and they have to look after this egg until it hatches and that's when they become men. I had this idea of a boy, about fifteen, waiting for his egg to hatch and feeling left out because his was the last one out of his peers. It all sounds so silly out loud."

"It doesn't," Elias immediately jumped in, "I still feel like I'm waiting for my egg to hatch."

Caden stared deep into his eyes, the corners pricking up as he smiled, "Me too."

Elias put the syrupy leftovers of his coffee on the table along with the chicken. When he sat back, his arm reached across the back of the couch. It was dangerously close to Caden's elbow, which was propping up his head as he stared at Elias. He wanted to pull it away but he knew that would look even weirder, so he kept it there, his body stiff as a board.

"Have you started writing it?"

"Kind of," Caden shrugged, "I've been writing on and off for the past five years but the time has never felt right. I was hoping coming back to Havenmoore would give me more time but I started working for Helping Hands and I've been busier than ever. It's keeping my mind off -,"

Caden suddenly stopped mid-sentence and sat forward, staring at the blank TV awkwardly. Elias pulled his arm back and sat cross-legged on the sofa. He fiddled with the rings in his ear as he wondered what Caden was about to say.

"Your break up?" Elias offered.

"Was it that obvious?" Caden ran his hands across his light scruff, "Damn, man. I shouldn't be talking about this with you. I'm here to help you."

"This is helping," Elias said, "I hate talking about my problems. People only ever want to talk about addiction. This is the most normal I've felt since getting out."

Caden half smiled, glancing to Elias out of the corner of his eye. It warmed Elias to know that other people in the world had problems, even if they were different. He had grown up in a world where weakness and differences were actively discouraged.

"I haven't really spoken about it," Caden said softly, "my parents don't really understand and all of my friends are his friends so it's not like I can vent to them either."

"His friends?"

"Yeah, my ex, Finn. I moved to New York and -,"

"Wait," Elias cut him off, "you're gay?"

Caden smiled awkwardly and shifted back into the corner of the sofa. Elias felt his entire body turning rigid as he stared at Caden, waiting for the answer.

"I am," he nodded, "is that a problem, because if it is -,"

"No, it's not a problem," he interrupted again, "I just – I just didn't know."

"Do you want me to wear a badge?" Caden laughed awkwardly, "We're normal people too."

Elias could tell that Caden was joking but it didn't stop Elias' heart pounding in his chest. *Just tell him you are too.* The words were there, waiting to come out. He hadn't actually spoken them to anyone before. They'd never been important, but sitting there with Caden feeling almost normal made him want to share that part of him with the world. *It'll only make things even more awkward.*

"Can I tell you something?" the words tumbled out of Elias' mouth.

"That's what I'm here for," Caden turned back towards him, a friendly smile on his face.

Elias wanted to say the words, to finally confide in somebody. Would it be a relief? He had always had so many troubles in his life, this had been one that he had pushed to the back of his mind, only confronting when he needed to use it to his advantage to get what he wanted from people; usually curious and horny dealers.

"I – I -," sweat poured down his forehead, forcing his shaky hands to wipe it away.

For once, he didn't know if they were shaking from the need to use drugs or because he was actually feeling nervous.

"What is it?"

Elias could tell that Caden was urging him to speak. Did he suspect something too? Could Caden sense that Elias was gay too? Did it matter? *Why does it matter?* Elias didn't think it did but he felt something else.

"I'm -," he mumbled, "I mean – can we get this place cleaned up?"

Caden almost looked relieved but Elias felt like kicking himself.

"Sure," he blinked slowly, "c'mon, many hands make light work. That's what my mom says."

"Right," Elias quickly jumped up, heading straight to the bathroom to stare at himself in the mirror.

Elias wanted to know who the man was staring back in the reflection, but he didn't. Elias had always been so busy distracting himself, he had never taken a minute to get to know the guy inside.

***

As they cleaned the apartment, Caden couldn't stop looking over at Elias, who was silently collecting beer cans. He could feel there was something wrong but it was obvious that Elias wasn't ready to talk about it. Caden knew he was supposed to wait for Elias to open up to him but he wanted to stick his middle finger up to the training. He wanted to help Elias, even more so since listening to his mom. He wanted to let Elias know that he had somebody who cared, but he didn't want to overstep that line. *It's bad enough that he knows you're gay, you've just gone and made things totally weird with this guy.*

"Elias, all of this drinking," Caden broke the silence, "do you think you really need it?"

Shrugging, Elias tied up the trash bag and dumped it next to the front door. Caden could tell Elias had spent the last hour glancing at the fridge, wanting to grab a can of beer. Replacing one addiction with another just gave Elias a brand new problem to deal with.

"I need something," he bit into his lip hard, "the days go so slowly. I need something to take my mind off everything."

Caden knew trying to convince Elias about the health effects wouldn't make a difference. He probably had people shouting those facts at him all of his life. They'd be completely meaningless, just the pleas of somebody put in a position to 'help'.

"Do you not have any friends you could hang out with? What about your sister?"

Elias jumped up onto the kitchen counter, a soft smirk on his lips, "When you're into drugs, your friends are your dealers. Take them out of the equation and you find yourself without anybody to call."

Caden caught Elias' eyes dart over to the fridge, but this time, his eyes landed on the piece of paper that Caden had left behind. Had Elias wanted to call Caden but felt too weird about it? Feeling his heart swell, he wanted to be that friend that Elias clearly craved. Deciding to make up his own rules, Caden threw caution to the wind, knowing that traditional methods weren't going to work with Elias.

"Do you like lobster?"

"Lobster?" Elias' tone was dismissive.

"The annual Maine Lobster Festival is in Havenmoore this weekend. If you're free, we could go?"

"Together?" Elias squinted.

"It might be fun."

Feeling his pulse increase, Caden pushed those thoughts to the back of his head. He wasn't going to deny that he thought Elias was cute and that he wanted to be there for him but he knew that wasn't his place. If he could be a friend to Elias and help get him through his court order clean and sober, that would fulfill him more than anything else.

"Lobster," Elias pondered, "I can't say I've ever tried it."

"What?" Caden's head shot back, "You live in Maine and Havenmoore's docks are the biggest for miles around."

"It was never a priority," Elias shrugged.

"I won't take no for an answer now," he crossed his arms and rocked back on his heels, "you're coming if you like it or not. How does Saturday sound?"

"It sounds like I don't have much choice," Elias laughed.

There was a carelessness and honesty in his laugh that warmed Caden. If Elias was replacing cocaine with alcohol, Caden was going to try his damn hardest to replace alcohol with friendship. He knew it wouldn't be easy but he felt like he owed it to Elias. Not because he was an addict who'd been on death's door, but because he knew the truth about the way Elias had been treated by his family, even if he hadn't told Elias that.

"That's final," Caden clapped his hands together, "it'll be fun."

"If you say so," Elias jumped down from the counter, "you'll have to show me how to use that damn machine so I can wash a shirt."

"I thought you didn't want to learn?"

"Yeah, well, I guess I've changed my mind."

Hardly containing the grin spreading across his face, Caden showed Elias how to use the washing machine and watched proudly as he loaded and started it. They spent the rest of the afternoon finishing the cleaning and taking the bags down to the dumpster in the alley.

When Caden felt their session had naturally come to an end, he felt like he wanted to stick around and somehow spend more time with Elias. *You can't suffocate him. He needs his own space.*

"I think that's enough for today," Caden reached for his jacket and bag, "I'll let you get back to your shows."

"Oh," Elias mumbled, "sure."

Was that disappointment or had Elias wanted to get rid of Caden all day? He couldn't decide. Looking around at how clean the apartment was, Caden felt proud that he had made a difference, even if it was only a small one. He thought about the paperwork he would have to fill in and how he would have to report that he had found evidence of Elias' drinking.

Finding his conscious battling with his morals, Caden swallowed and headed for the door, reminding himself he was there to work and help Elias. Would getting Elias into more trouble help him? Judging by his record that would only make things worse.

"Elias," Caden turned, his hand on the doorknob, "I shouldn't be telling you this but I have to report if I find you using any other substances, including alcohol."

"Right," Elias laughed, rolling his eyes, "course you do."

"Listen. I won't report anything if you make me a promise."

Leaning against the couch, Elias' eyes turned to slits as he waited for Caden to deliver his bargain.

"Just promise me that from now until Saturday you'll try and stay sober. If you do, I'll draw a line under your drinking until now and I won't file it."

Laughing coldly, Elias dropped his head as he scratched the back of his hair. Caden could feel the tension radiating from Elias' body and he wasn't altogether sure that he wasn't about to punch him in the face.

"Okay," Elias' head shot up, "I promise I'll try."

"Oh. You mean that?"

"I promise I'll try," he repeated.

"You still have my number. If you need me, anytime of the day or night, just call me and I'll be there."

Elias nodded, his eyes still dark, narrow slits. That was good enough for Caden. Through the angry and tight expression on Elias' face, he was sure he could feel something thankful trying to break through. Knowing that his work there was done, he headed down the stairs alone and out into the alley. The smell of baked goods tickled his nostrils but the feeling inside was much more satisfying. Walking home in the late afternoon sun, he started to look forward to their next meeting on Saturday, hoping that he would see a clean and sober Elias for the first time.

Chapter 5

Elias had spent the morning staring at his four walls, tossing a ball in the air as he scratched himself at timed intervals. When he noticed those scratching intervals lining up perfectly with the frequent commercial breaks during the trashy reality TV shows, Elias had found his mind hooked on, he knew he had to get out of the house.

Only having a couple of numbers in his phone, he didn't have much choice to get his butt out of the house. Some of those numbers would lead him into trouble so he opted for calling his sister. Caden's digits were still attached to the fridge under a lobster magnet but Elias still didn't feel right calling him, despite Caden's assurance that he was there. It had only been a couple of days since he had seen him and there were only a couple of days until they were meeting at the Lobster Festival. Not wanting to seem too interested in the man who could potentially get him thrown back in rehab, he decided it was better to keep some distance. They may have shared a sexual preference but that's as deep as Elias was willing to let the connection run.

"I can't remember the last time you just wanted to meet for coffee," Ellie sipped her latte, "actually, I don't think we have ever just met for coffee. Those pills must be working."

The pills she had given him had taken the edge off but they weren't numbing his mind completely. Now that he was forcing alcohol out of his life too, he was suddenly so aware of everything around him. Everything was louder and more vibrant than Elias ever remembered and it was driving him crazy. Every couple of seconds the sound of the steam shooting into the milk jug behind the counter made him jump.

"I needed to get out of that apartment," he slurped the thick, black coffee, "I can't watch any more TV. I don't know how normal people do it."

"Normal people have jobs," she said, "something you've dragged me away from."

"I thought you were on a break?"

"I am," she nodded, "you're lucky it's quiet today. Breaks are a luxury the residents of Havenmoore aren't too happy to let me have these days. We need some more doctors at the office but all I keep hearing about is budget cuts. I'm going to bring it up to the state senator if he shows up to The Medical Ball in a couple of weeks. And then there's that damn Obama Care. Don't even get me started on that."

When Elias started to laugh, Ellie put her coffee cup on the table and pursed her lips, shaking her jet black hair from her face.

"What's so funny?" she demanded.

"Nothing," he laughed, shaking his head, "it's just weird us sitting here chatting about trivial things. It's refreshing."

Ellie let a smile flutter across her pursed lips for a second before reaching for her cup again. No matter what he had put her through, neither of them could ever destroy that bond they'd shared since birth. It was something only twins knew about and it couldn't be explained. They didn't even need to like each other that much. They were like two peas in a pod, even if one of those peas was slightly misshapen and an off shade of green.

"Have you seen mom?" Ellie dropped the question in so casually, he had to admire her approach, even if Judy James was a subject he would rather avoid.

"She dropped by for about five minutes last week," he shrugged, "can you believe she has a key for my apartment?"

"Well, she did pay for it -,"

Elias shot his sister a *'don't go there'* warning glance and she held her hands up in defeat, backing out of the conversation. Elias had never seen the point in talking about their mother. There was no resolution to be reached and there was no solution to the problem of their relationship. *What relationship?* The window of opportunity for fixing that mess had closed sometime around Elias being in fifth grade.

"How's Kobi?" Elias headed towards the conversation Ellie didn't want to talk about.

Just the mention of her son's name sent Ellie's lips pursed impossibly tight. Elias knew there was no way she was going to let him see him and he wasn't about to ask her to.

"He's fine," she nodded, "he asks about you a lot."

Elias was suddenly regretting sending the conversation in that direction. The knife of regret and guilt twisted in his stomach again. The only reason he hadn't reached straight for his cellphone and called a dealer the second he got out of rehab was because of what Ellie had said about his nephew. That's how it had started but it snowballed into something else; something Elias didn't understand. It was as if there was a faint light, flickering in the distance, drawing him towards something he wasn't sure he wanted. The darkness was still all around, ready to claim him again at any moment. For some reason, he was pulling himself through the darkness like a madman wading through taffy.

"What do you tell him?" he swallowed the lump rising in his throat.

"The same thing I've always told him. I tell him you're sick but we hope you're going to get better soon."

The knife sunk deeper. As usual, Ellie was right. He was

sick. He had been sick for so many years.

"I want to see him," Elias blurted out.

"Impossible," shaking her head, she blinked heavily, "not until you prove you're clean."

"I'm trying," he leaned across the table, "I really am."

Ellie finished the last of her coffee and glanced eagerly at her watch. They both knew she had nowhere to be but the hectic lifestyle as one of the town's only doctors always gave her a backdoor to wiggle out of when the time called for it.

"For once, I believe you," she sighed as she pushed her arms into her long, black overcoat, "but it's not good enough. Prove you're clean, then we'll figure something out."

Ellie hovered over him and Elias could tell she was trying to figure out what the appropriate farewell was. Whenever she had dragged him out of the gutter or thrown him out of her house, they'd skipped the polite goodbyes.

"See you around," Ellie quickly leaned in, her lips lightly touching the top of his hair, "I love you."

"You too," he mumbled as she darted out of the quiet coffee shop.

Elias sat alone for a moment, looking around at the few people that were also drinking coffee. A couple caught his attention. Not because there was anything extraordinary about them; it was quite the opposite. The man was laughing at something the woman was saying, their eyes locked as their fingers ran up and down each other's arms. It looked like love. *Not that I'd know what that kind of love looked like.*

Deciding he was better off at his apartment, he finished the last of his strong coffee and headed for the door. When he saw his mother on the other side of that door, a frown on her face and a cellphone pressed into her ear, he couldn't help but think what a cruel twist of fate it was. *Why does she have to be here?*

The mayor's gaze caught his and the frown deepened. Pulling on the door, he stepped to the side, letting her inside. He couldn't imagine what she was doing in a coffee shop on a Thursday afternoon but he didn't want to stick around to find out. Hoping that she was too deep in her phone conversation, he stepped around her, itching for the freedom of the outdoors.

"Just a second," she called after him, irritation in her voice, "*Brian, I'll call you back.*"

Tossing her cellphone into the designer bag slung over her cocked arm, she crossed her stiletto topped feet, the tight pencil skirt barely moving an inch. The look on her face said '*well, aren't you going to talk to your mother?*', but Elias knew he had nothing to say to her that hadn't already been said.

"What are you doing here?" he asked, stepping back into the coffee shop and closing the door when a group of teenagers tried to push past him, "Isn't it beneath the mayor to grab her own coffee?"

"My assistant has food poisoning," her dark, well-groomed eyebrows hovered low over her heavily lined, wide hazel eyes, "Why are you here? You're not looking to score, are you?"

"In a coffee shop?" he had to laugh, "I just had coffee with Ellie."

"Ellie?" it was her turn to laugh.

"Yes, Ellie. My twin sister. You remember her? Same stick up her ass as you? Similar haircut and the same taste in clothes that makes grown men quiver in their boots."

His mother's gaze darkened as they hovered awkwardly by the door. He wanted so badly to leave, if only to escape the awkwardness. Elias knew his mother as well as he knew a stranger walking by him on the street. The mother he had grown up with was always on the local news or on the front page of the newspaper. That version of his mother always had a smile on her face. Elias had always wished that version would be the one to come home at the end of the day.

"You're not destroying that new apartment, are you?" the judgment was loud and clear in her voice.

"It's clean. Me and Caden spent hours cleaning the other -," Elias stopped mid-sentence, unsure of why.

"Caden?" she said, "Is that one of your friends?"

By '*friends*', Elias knew she meant '*drug dealing scumbags who keep making my life so difficult*'.

"He's the support worker from Helping Hands Outreach."

"Oh."

His mother frowned again and he was sure it was because of how casually he was talking about Caden. She wasn't happy unless they were rubbing against each other like two pieces of sandpaper. The fact he didn't totally hate his support worker seemed to ruffle her perfectly groomed feathers.

"Is he helping?" her red nail circled around Elias' face.

She wants to know if I'm getting help? Ha, that's new.

"If you mean, have I been using, I haven't."

"Why?" she cocked her head back.

Part of Elias was shocked that she would ask that question but another part of Elias totally expected it. Unsure of how to answer because he didn't know himself, he took this as his signal to leave the awkward conversation.

When another wave of people opened the door and attempted to squeeze around them, he backed away with them, "I'd like to say it was nice chatting, but it never is."

Back out in the open space, he wanted to feel his lungs open, but they didn't. The effect his mother had on him was like being bit by a venomous snake. Just breathing in her air made every craving for every dangerous substance he had ever taken rise to the surface.

Before he headed back to his apartment, he stole a glance through the coffee shop window. He wasn't sure if he was expecting to see his mom staring back at him, but she wasn't. Somehow, she was already at the front of the growing line, with her cellphone sandwiched between her ear and shoulder as she struggled to pull cash out of her wallet.

Taking his time to walk across town, Elias headed down to the docks. The boats were all out at sea. It made him think about the Lobster Festival and how much he was looking forward to seeing Caden again. The excitement was foreign. He had only ever looked forward to seeing somebody when they were handing over a little bag filled with white powder. Walking slowly along the edge of the sidewalk, teetering toward the beach below, he wished he had taken the chance to tell Caden about his sexuality when the opportunity had been there. *You're only making things more awkward for yourself.*

After a quick reminder that he was a twenty-six-year-old man, he kicked an empty soda can down to the dirty colored tiny strip of sand below before turning in the direction of the bakery.

Peering through the bakery window, he looked at the display behind the counter. His stomach, which was only filled with coffee, rumbled loudly. Elias was far from being able to look after himself. Regular mealtimes and feeding himself was something he had never been good at. In rehab, you get your three meals served to you at the right time but most of the time, you're too out of it to even care. When you're begging on the streets for change, food is always on the bottom of the list of priorities. The rehab had worked out his welfare checks before he left but he was yet to head to a grocery store and most of the fruit and vegetables his mom had paid her assistant to fill his refrigerator with had turned rotten.

Reaching into his pocket for some change to grab a bagel, the sight of a silver car in the reflection caught his eye. For a second, he thought nothing of it, until he saw the twinkle of a gold tooth leaning out of the driver's window. *Was that there when I walked here? No, it couldn't have been. I would have seen it.*

Elias almost didn't want to turn around but the face that the gold tooth belonged to was staring directly at the back of his head. He didn't need to look in the reflection to know that; he could feel it.

Elias dropped the change back into his pocket and headed across the road, "How did you find me?"

Rigsy beamed sinisterly, his arm hanging out of the car. His dark complexion was soft and smooth, giving no indication of how much stuff he snorted.

"I wasn't looking for you," Rigsy smirked, "I was just – in the area. I saw you and couldn't resist following to see your new pad. Nice. Looks a little small. Cozy, right?"

"Get out of here, Rigsy," Elias crossed his arms across his chest, "I don't want what you're selling."

"Who said I was selling?" Rigsy's laugh was so charismatic, soothing almost, "Maybe you're not the only one who's turned over a new leaf."

From the designer watch glittering on his wrist Elias couldn't quite believe that. Elias and Rigsy went way back. Never quite becoming friends, but always there to give each other what they needed. Now that Elias didn't want what Rigsy was offering, he wasn't sure where they stood with each other.

"I have somewhere I need to be," Elias pointed over his shoulder.

"Get in," Rigsy's voice darkened.

Elias didn't want to but he knew Rigsy well enough to know that the charming smile plastered across his lips was a façade. Scratch the surface and you find out how dangerous he really was. After a deep breath, Elias was in the passenger seat, staring dead ahead at the road as they drove slowly around Havenmoore.

An eerie silence filled the car until they found themselves in a dark alley, crammed between the town hall and the library. Being that close to his mother's place of work made Elias even more on edge than usual.

"Have you missed me?" Rigsy smirked.

"I can't say I have."

Reaching out, Rigsy cracked open the glove box. When Elias saw the piles of tiny white bags, his mouth watered and his skin itched for it. He tried to look away but he was transfixed. Rigsy fished out a bag, his hand rubbing against Elias' thigh on the way back. The bag slapped on the inside of his legs and he almost jumped out of his seat.

"What about this? Have you missed this?" he dangled the bag in front of Elias' face.

Gulping hard, Elias shook his head, a cold sweat erupting. He wanted to reach up to wipe it away but he found his hand frozen by his side, unable to move and unable to look away.

"I – I -,"

"There's no need to make this any harder for yourself," Rigsy whispered darkly, "we both know this is just a blip. I know you enough to know how much you want this."

Elias blinked but he couldn't open his eyes again. In the

darkness he saw Kobi's face, his scruffy black hair hanging loosely over his eyes so that he was looking under it. *Not just looking under it, looking up to me.* Behind Kobi, he saw Ellie, the familiar disappointment on her face. To his surprise, he saw Caden too. The man who didn't know him but seemed to care so much about helping. His stomach churned. *I'm not this strong.*

"I have no money," Elias choked on the words, hoping the excuse would diffuse the situation.

A dark and coarse chuckle escaped Rigsy's throat, followed by the metal crunch of a zipper, "When have I ever asked you for money?"

Elias swallowed hard, his eyes slowly opening. Rigsy's cock was already swollen as it jutted out through his jeans. Elias has seen it a million times because he had always done what he needed to do to get what he wanted. Sometimes he enjoyed doing it and sometimes it was a chore he would rather have finished. As Elias stared at it, watching it throb and twitch, he felt terror unlike anything.

"I can't."

"You know you want it," he gripped his huge cock at the base, "you know you want both of them."

Dropping the bag next to his cock, he left it there as temptation. In ten minutes, he could have the bag and he could be locked in his bathroom, ready to escape everything. But what happens after that? What about tomorrow?

"What would your girlfriend say?" Elias attempted to laugh.

"Nobody gives head like you, boy," Rigsy's huge tongue ran across his lips, "that's why I've kept you around."

Elias found himself leaning in towards it, like an old habit rising comfortably to the surface. Face to face with it, his tongue ran shakily across his lips, resting on the lip ring. It would be so easy. Darting down to the bag, he felt the most uncomfortable stab of pain deep inside. Suddenly, he had a conscience.

"I can't do this," his hand was already on the door handle, "leave me alone, Rigsy."

Before he could be tempted further, Elias jumped out of the car and sprinted into the dark depths of the alley. Hiding behind a dumpster, he waited until he heard the roar of Rigsy's engine before he dared leave. He walked out to the other side of town before doubling back to his apartment, changing direction every couple of minutes. It took him nearly an hour to get back to the bakery but when he slipped into the peace and quiet of his empty apartment, he had never felt so happy to be home.

Without hesitation he grabbed his cellphone and headed straight for the piece of paper attached to the front of the fridge.

***

"Where's Uncle Finn?" Becca traced her finger along the edge of Caden's light beard.

"Oh, erm, he's -,"

"He's in New York," Lucy, Caden's sister-in-law jumped up, scooping Becca from Caden's lap, "stop asking Uncle Caden so many questions."

Caden mouthed his thanks to her as she planted her in front of the TV, where she was quickly engrossed in the brightly colored cartoon on the screen. Caden didn't know how to start explaining something so serious to a five-year-old. She had spent the last twenty minutes talking about what her first couple of days in the first grade were like, pausing to ask awkward questions.

"She's too nosey for her age," Lucy laughed, "she takes after your mother. You want another coffee?"

"Sure," Caden held out the empty cup.

Lucy grabbed the cup and disappeared into the kitchen, leaving Caden sitting with Becca in their cozy den. Expensive furniture was covered in toys and books, giving it a messy family home feeling Caden knew he would never have for himself. He had been stupid enough to start talking about kids with Finn and they'd both seemed excited about the idea. *Maybe I was blind to it.* Staring at the back of Becca's flame red hair, he started to doubt that he would ever be that guy.

"Are you going to talk about him?" Lucy sat down next to him, handing him another coffee, "You've been here for an hour and you haven't mentioned him."

"I was hoping you wouldn't notice," he slurped the hot coffee.

He had only dropped by to spend time with somebody who wasn't his parents. He loved them but he was already growing tired of how much they fussed over him. He knew Bruce would be at the bar but he always got along with Lucy like she was his sister.

"What happened Caden?" she leaned in and sighed, "I thought you two were the real thing."

"So did I," Caden forced a smile, "turns out I was wrong. I caught him, y'know -,"

Caden nodded his head towards Becca, not wanting to say '*I caught him fucking my best friend over our bed in the middle of the afternoon*' in front of delicate, listening ears.

"That snake," she muttered angrily, "the pig!"

"Yep."

"I thought he was so nice!"

"He was."

"Nice guys don't cheat on people like you. Any guy would be lucky to have you. You're a saint, Caden. You're the nicest guy I know! If you weren't a giant homosexual, I'd be convinced I'd picked the wrong brother."

She smirked with a wink and Caden couldn't help but laugh. Lucy had a way with words that always managed to cheer him up. In New York, gay couples broke up every two minutes but Caden had been convinced that wasn't going to be them. He thought he had the last decent guy in New York. Finn had always been nice, if not sometimes a little neurotic. Caden had always looked past his outbursts but he couldn't look past the cheating. Finn swore it only happened once but there was something about how casual it had been that he was convinced it was more of a regular thing.

"Maybe I wasn't enough for him," Caden nursed his coffee, "Adam always had these amazing stories about the s-e-x he had with guys. Maybe that's why Finn wanted him so bad."

"If you love somebody, *all* sex is the best sex," she

whispered, obviously less concerned about Becca's ears picking things up, "I've been with your brother for nearly eight years and he still has the ability to make me -,"

"Let's not go there," he tapped her knee, "I don't think I can stomach hearing about my big brother in that way."

Lucy winked again as she tucked her bright blonde hair behind her ear. Caden couldn't explain what it felt like, not even to her. *She wouldn't understand. She has the perfect life here. I thought I had the perfect life.*

"I'm thirty this year and I have no idea where I'm going," he muttered, "I thought I had it all figured out."

"You're still a baby," she said, "there's time to figure it out again. You might meet a nice hunk in Havenmoore who'll sweep you off your feet."

Caden didn't think that was likely. He knew better than anyone how deserted Havenmoore was. It had been one of the reasons he had always dreamt of moving to The Big Apple. Growing up, he had always felt like he was the odd one out in town so the second he came out to his parents, he headed out into the world on his big gay adventure. *Maybe I settled down too quickly.*

"I don't think Havenmoore is the place for -,"

He was cut off by the vibrating of his cellphone. Fishing it out of his pocket, he stared down at the unknown caller ID uneasily. He never usually answered unknown IDs, just because they normally ended up being smarmy salesmen trying to sell him stocks, insurance and broadband. He stared at the screen, letting it ring out. He would have been happy to let the call end but something inside compelled him to answer it.

"Hello?" he said awkwardly.

"Yeah, *hi.* It's me," Caden instantly recognized *'me'* as Elias.

A smile instantly pricked up his lips, followed by nervousness. Caden knew he wasn't ringing for a social call about the weather.

"Everything okay, Elias?"

"Yeah, everything's fine," Caden could tell it wasn't, "I think. I don't know. Can I see you?"

Caden paused, excitement bubbling inside. He glanced to Lucy, who was busy watching the cartoon with Becca.

"Are you busy? I knew I shouldn't have -,"

"No, now is fine," Caden jumped in, "I'll text you my address."

"Okay. See ya," Elias hung up, an awkwardness in his voice.

Caden knew it wasn't in Elias' nature to reach out for help so he was nervous for what had happened but he couldn't ignore how pleased he was that he was getting to see Elias earlier than he thought.

"Who was that?" Lucy asked.

"Just some guy."

"Oh," her face lit up, "some guy, eh?"

"Not like that," he laughed it off, "I'm working with him for my mom's charity."

Lucy narrowed her eyes, a smirk growing across her pretty face. Caden could tell that she didn't believe him and he wasn't sure he believed it himself. He felt a pull towards Elias and he was finding it so hard to ignore. He wanted to say it was just the need to help but it felt like something more. *You're only setting yourself up for trouble.*

"I need to go," he jumped up, "thanks for the coffee."

"Make good choices," she called after him.

Caden headed across town with haste in his steps and a reluctant smile on his face.

Elias arrived at the address Caden had given him. Standing outside of the cute, wooden family home in the heart of town, he looked up to see signs of movement inside. *Do I call again or knock?*

When he caught Caden half walking, half jogging toward him, he knew that he had ripped Caden away from something. In the time since jumping out of Rigsy's car, he had tried to calm down as much as he could. Watching Caden hurry closer, he felt like a fool for even calling him. *I don't need his help.*

"Phew, I'm out of shape," Caden wiped sweat from his cheeks and rearranged his light hair, "I need to start hitting the gym."

"You were busy?" Elias bit his lip, "It's okay, I can go -,"

"No, no! I was only with my sister-in-law and I was about to leave anyway. She was trying to open the ex-file. Your call saved me from having to rip off that Band-Aid so I should be thanking you."

Caden unclipped the gate and headed towards the small house. It was painted white with a small American flag hanging from the porch. Vibrant flowers filled planters under the windows. It wasn't lavish like the home Elias had grown up in but it had a feeling of home that Elias never had.

"Mom and dad are working," Elias followed Caden into the house, "So we've got the place to ourselves."

"Cool," Elias looked around at the modestly decorated house.

On the surface, it looked exactly like the type of place he had imagined Caden would call home. He was sweet and so was the house. Caden grabbed two cans of orange soda from the kitchen and to Elias' surprise he headed upstairs. Elias followed him to his bedroom, which looked like a nice hotel room filled with boxes and bags.

"Ignore everything," Caden held the door open for Elias, "I'm still trying to decide what to do with this stuff. If I unpack, everything becomes real."

Elias squeezed into the bedroom. A window over the double bed overlooked the small back yard, a chain-link fence separating it from the neighbors. Cracking open the soda, Elias perched on the edge of the bed. Caden copied, sitting on the other side.

"I thought it'd be easier if we came up here. If my mom comes home, it'll be difficult to explain."

"Because I'm an addict?"

"Because I'm your support worker. We're meant to keep a professional distance, for safety reasons."

"What makes me so special?" Elias crossed his legs on the bed, facing Caden who was leaning against the headboard, the can of soda balancing on his jeans.

"I trust you," he shrugged, "so, what's up?"

Elias didn't know where to start. Even though he hadn't, he felt like he had done something wrong. He called Caden because he felt like he had nobody else to turn to. Did he even have to tell him what had happened? Scratching the dark scruff around his mouth, he let out a deep sigh and started at the beginning.

"Wait, this guy was trying to give you free drugs?" Caden scrunched up his face, "Why?"

Elias almost mentioned their '*arrangement*', but he stopped himself, "We go back."

"But you didn't take anything?"

"I jumped out of his car and came straight here."

Nodding, Caden carefully sipped the soda as he thought. Elias felt like he was still so weak, even if he had turned down the one thing he craved. It didn't make him feel any better because deep down, he was lusting after the drugs, even if he had walked away. A tiny part of him was cursing his stupidity and that was the most vocal part. It was so difficult to ignore the reasoning when the Elias he had known for so long was still very much there and wanting so badly to score.

"You did good," Caden broke the silence, "It couldn't have been easy."

"It wasn't," he scooted up the bed to lie against the headboard next to Caden, "I wanted to do it so badly."

"What stopped you?"

Elias wasn't about to mention that Caden had been one of the reasons. He was tired of promising people things because for an unknown reason his promises suddenly had the ability to make him feel guilty. In rehab, they had talked about becoming the person you know you are but all Elias knew was the addict. Seeing his mom before he saw Rigsy should have tipped him over the edge, but it hadn't.

"Lots of things," he mumbled, "I feel guilty for being selfish. I can't get rid of this feeling. I want to go back to normal."

"You mean, you want to start using again?"

"No, I want to stop feeling guilty."

"So you can start using?"

"Maybe," he grunted in frustration, "maybe not! I just feel so aware."

"That's good. You're aware of what you've done to the

people you care about. That's progress."

"I don't have people, not really. Not like other people do. I don't have a family like you. I don't have parents who will let me move in when things go wrong, I don't have a sister-in-law I can talk to. I just have a twin who would be happier if I left her alone and a nephew I've already screwed up. Don't try to shrink me," Elias turned his head, "I'm un-shrinkable."

"I wouldn't dare," Caden winked back, "I just think you're over thinking your intentions. You've had temptation around every corner."

"And I've nearly given in so many times!"

"But you haven't," he said, "that's what's important."

Elias knew Caden was right but it didn't make him feel any better. He knew how close he had been to sucking Rigsy's cock, just to score a line. Why did that make him feel so ashamed when he had done it countless times?

"I've never thought about the future before. I never thought I'd get to twenty-six alive. I thought I'd run out of luck by now. That sounds insane, I know, but I never put value on my life. I didn't want to be here. I didn't think I had anything to be here for but now I feel like maybe I do. Maybe there is a chance for something."

His mind flashed back to what had sent him to rehab again. He had been alone in a back room of a Chinese takeout place, snorting line after line. Even now, he couldn't remember how he had gotten there. All he could remember was how desperately he had been chasing that high, cutting more lines than he knew he should have. Nothing was making anything easier, so he carried on. The next thing he remembered was waking up in the hospital with Ellie by his side. That's when the mayor got involved. The police wanted to lock him up for how much drugs were found on him. She told him that they were trying to pin him down as a dealer but dealing had never interested Elias. He always wanted to take the drugs alone. Some people took drugs socially; Elias isolated himself and did it in solitude.

"I almost died two months ago. I almost died and I didn't even care."

"Do you care now?"

"I haven't thought about it," he said, "it's too heavy."

"You didn't die though. You got help and you're still here."

"Not intentionally," he gulped down the soda.

"Did you want to die?" the question sounded heavy and Elias didn't want to answer it.

With the ten-dollar bill jammed up his nostril, the thought had crossed his mind. He knew he was taking too much but he wasn't thinking logically. Was that because he had wanted everything to just stop or because he was just too dumb to realize what he was doing?

"I don't know."

"Maybe it was a cry for help?"

"I don't want help," Elias snapped instinctively, "I don't know why I called you. I should go."

Elias edged towards the end of the bed but Caden's hand on his shoulder stopped him. He squeezed firmly, freezing Elias. It gave him the same tingles it had in the doctor's office waiting room. Shuffling backwards, he banged his head on the headboard and stared up at the fan on the ceiling.

"I want to help you, Elias," Caden whispered, "I really do."

"It helps that you're being paid."

"That's not the point. We're similar ages. I feel for you."

"Feel sorry for me, more like. It's a pity mission. You don't have to waste your breath trying to explain it. I get it. People feel sorry for me because I'm such a loser."

"You're not a loser," Caden said, "you're just lost."

"How do I find myself?"

"Time."

Elias turned his head to stare at Caden and Caden did the same. He caught the glint of his piercings reflected in Caden's pale green eyes. He smiled softly and it was genuine, not the pathetic smile people usually gave him when they were trying to help.

"Before I left for New York, I did this job for a couple of months," Caden said softly, "I only worked with one guy. Frank, was his name. I thought I could help him but I couldn't. He died and I couldn't handle it so I left. It wasn't what I really wanted to do but I felt like I owed something to him to help him, even though he was beyond help. He was in his sixties and he had been living on the streets for years. You, Elias, you can be helped. I see it in your eyes and I see how you're trying even if you don't want to admit you're trying. I'm going to help you."

"Do I not have a choice?"

"Nope," Caden smiled, "you just need time to adjust. I know you've got things on your mind, but it'll get easier. The further you get away from rehab and what you've been through, the easier it will get."

Elias was touched. He didn't know how to help himself so how was somebody else going to do it for him? Looking around the room, the boxes caught his eyes. Caden needed help too, but in a completely different way.

"It looks like we're both burying our heads in the sand," Elias nodded towards Caden's stuff, "you should unpack and forget that jerk."

"It's not that easy," staring down at the soda can in his hands, he smiled so sadly that it almost broke Elias' heart, "I wish it was."

"Looks like we're both in the same boat," Elias nudged Caden with his shoulder, "we both just need time."

"Now who's trying to shrink who?" Caden rolled his head towards Elias, "You're not a bad guy, Elias. You're really not."

"You're not either," Elias stared down at Caden's lips, "you deserve somebody."

"So do you," Caden said, "have you never dated?"

Elias suddenly looked forward uncomfortably. Cramming the soda can up to his mouth, he thought this could be his chance to come clean about his sexuality but he couldn't say the words. If he could tell anybody, he could tell Caden, so why didn't he want to?

"I've never had time," he said, "being an addict is a full time job."

"When you're ready, I'll hook you up. My brother runs a bar so he'll know loads of girls."

Girls. Elias almost laughed but he didn't correct him.

"I don't think anybody would be interested in somebody like me."

"Why not? You're good looking and you're a nice guy."

"Why do you keep saying I'm nice? Have you ever met a nice addict?"

"That doesn't define you. You've got a new start, so take it."

Elias felt like saying the same to Caden, who was clearly staying packed because he didn't want to admit that he was back in Havenmoore. As they sat on Caden's bed in silence, Elias couldn't help but think neither of them really wanted to be in Havenmoore but for some reason, they both needed to be.

"Thank you," Elias mumbled, "for not writing me off."

"There's still life in you. Damn, you're younger than me. I'm thirty before the year's out and I'm living in my parents' guest room."

They laughed for a couple of seconds until their chests slowed down. Elias found his eyes darting down to Caden's lips again. They looked so moist and inviting. *I can't remember ever actually kissing a guy.* It was as if that urge took over him. When he found his head slowly leaning in, eyes wide and staring into Caden's, he wanted to stop but he couldn't.

To his surprise, Caden didn't pull away. He didn't lean in, he just stared at Elias, as though he was trying to understand what was happening. *Stop it, Elias!* The sound of the front door slamming made Elias pull back. Jumping off the bed, Caden headed for the door.

"Mom, is that you?" Caden called down, a shake in his voice.

"It's just me," she called up, "come down. I've picked up some lunch."

"I'll be right down."

Caden closed the door carefully, turning back to Elias. He looked like he was about to launch into an apology but Elias was the one who'd tried to kiss him. Could he try and laugh it off? He had been so close to his lips.

"I should go," Elias headed straight for the door, "I

shouldn't have bothered you."

Pushing past Caden, he ran down the staircase, taking them two at a time. He saw Caden's mom out of the corner of his eyes but he didn't hang around to explain anything. Before Caden could chase after him, Elias started to run back across town.

You're such an idiot!

***

Did he just try to kiss me? Caden shook his head as he ran his fingers over his face. *He couldn't have, could he?* Was it Caden's imagination that Elias had started leaning in slowly towards his lips? If it was, why did he run away?

"Caden, what's going on?" his mom called up.

"Give me a second," he snapped harsher thanhe had intended.

Caden wanted to head out to follow Elias but he knew he would probably be across town already. Should he go to Elias' apartment to talk about it? Would that make things even more awkward? What if Caden had imagined it?

"Was that who I think?" his mom said casually as she opened up the pizza box on the table, "I got Hawaiian, your favorite."

"Thanks, Mom," Caden picked up a slice and dropped it on the plate in front of him but he didn't start eating.

"So," she sat down next to him, "did I just see Elias running out of our house or do I need to get my head tested?"

"Yeah, he just -," Caden couldn't even finish the lie convincingly.

Picking up a slice, his mom chewed on the end, not taking her eyes away from Caden. He knew exactly what she was thinking and she was probably right. He wanted to try and diffuse the situation but his mind was racing. *Did we almost kiss?*

"You know you shouldn't give your home address to the people you work with," she said, "you're there to support them to move on with their lives."

"I know, I know," he snapped out of it, "he needed support.

He almost relapsed. I wasn't thinking."

"Did you help him?"

"I don't know," Caden mumbled.

Was he really helping Elias, or was he just making things worse? He wasn't equipped to deal with his problems, just like he wasn't equipped to deal with Frank's problems. Some courses and a couple of days shadowing his mom weren't enough. He didn't have the knowledge his mother had. She had spent her life helping people and she knew exactly what they needed. Caden on the other hand, had always been too worried about upsetting or offending people. He had always tiptoed cautiously, trying to be people's friends. *That's why Finn walked all over me.*

"It takes time," she patted his hand, "you'll get the hang of this."

"How do you know when you're over stepping the line?" he asked after finishing a slice of pizza.

"Has something happened?"

"No," it technically wasn't a lie, "I just worry that I'm too friendly with people."

"There's nothing wrong with being friendly," she shook her red hair out, "as long as you're not being taken advantage of."

"Yeah," he mused.

The problem was that he didn't feel like he was being taken advantage of at all; it was quite the opposite. Elias was vulnerable and Caden was there to help him, which made the stupid crush he was developing feel even more wrong.

"Are you going to the festival this weekend?" she asked, "Your dad's holding down a stall in the square on Saturday."

"I'll be there," he said as he slid his phone from his pocket.

Opening his call logs he hovered over the most recent number in his history. He almost called but he opted for a text. *A text is safer.*

'Hey, It's Caden. If you still want to go to the Lobster Festival on Saturday, I'll meet you outside your apartment at noon.'

Hovering over the '*send*' button, he read the message over and over, hoping it didn't have a hidden subtext. Nervously, he hit the button and dropped his cell onto the table, ready for the agonizing wait for a reply.

The phone vibrated almost instantly.

'Sure. See you on Saturday.'

Unsure of what was going on, he saved the number under *'Elias'* and slid the phone back into his pocket, knowing that he had a couple of days to figure out what to do next. *Do I bring it up or do I ignore it and hope it goes away? I'm supposed to be helping this guy, not making things more complicated.*

Chapter 7

Elias changed his shirt again and fiddled with the gel in his black hair. He tugged at the collar of the obscure rock band t-shirt, pulling it over his head when he felt it suffocating him. A quick sniff of his armpits made him spray deodorant for the fourth time. Bundling up the shirt, he tossed it across the room, sending it crashing into the wooden blinds.

"Ugh!" he cried out as he dug through the clothes on his bedroom floor.

Clothes had never been a problem for Elias. He had always dressed for convenience rather than for fashion. Most of his clothes were stolen from department stores or from the donations bin in the rehab center. Pulling a plain white t-shirt over his head, he examined his reflection in the floor-length mirror at the end of his bed. It was tight, but it hugged his body in a way that didn't make him look so skinny. After a quick scoop into the pot of bright blue gel, he brushed it through his dark hair again, adjusting it, suddenly forgetting how it normally looked.

Elias hadn't even tried to deny that he was nervous to see Caden again. It was almost noon and they were about to go to the Lobster Festival together. *I should have just cancelled.* He had been tossing and turning all night, hoping that Caden hadn't picked up on what Elias had nearly done. *Maybe he didn't notice you trying to kiss him? Ugh, who am I kidding? Of course he fucking noticed.*

Swiping the gel off the dresser in frustration, he watched as it blobbed across the wooden floor, landing messily on a pair of briefs. He wanted to calm down, hoping that Caden wasn't going to mention it. The thought that Caden was as embarrassed as he was gave him hope. The reminder set on his cellphone beeped loudly on his nightstand, sending a shiver running down his spine. He had three minutes to go until noon. Was that too late to cancel?

Heading across his apartment as he tugged on a black zip-up hoodie, he peeked through the blinds. Caden was already waiting under his window, outside of the bakery. His strawberry infused hair glittered brightly in the sun, contrasting with the beat up denim jacket he was wearing. He looked different. Was he more dressed up than normal or was Elias looking too far into a jacket?

"Hey," he couldn't look into Caden's eyes as he rounded the corner, "how's it going?"

"You look nice," Caden smiled, "I mean – new shirt?"

"It's just something I found," Elias tugged at it, wondering if he was showing off too much of the body underneath.

"Hungry?" Caden pushed his hands into his jeans.

Were they tighter than the ones he usually wore? Maybe this is how he normally dressed and he dressed a little more casual when he was working. Or maybe he had been standing in front of a mirror for an hour trying to find something to wear, like Elias had.

"Starving," Elias smiled back, looking into Caden's eyes for the first time.

There it was in Caden's eyes. *He knows you tried to kiss him.* Elias hoped Caden was going to pretend nothing happened so they could get through the day without any awkwardness.

In a strange and tense silence, they headed towards the town square, which had been completely transformed. If Elias hadn't known better, he would have thought a rock star was about to perform because everybody in Havenmoore seemed to have turned out. The steps of the town hall had been turned into a makeshift stage, where Havenmoore 106 was broadcasting live. White tents and stalls covered the square from corner to corner, the smell of fish strong and thick in the air. It seemed like a pretty big deal for the town, which made Elias wonder how he had gone his entire life avoiding it.

"Are you ready for your first lobster?" Caden clapped his hands together, rubbing them in excitement.

"Sure," lobster was the last thing on Elias' mind.

They approached the square, the buzz of the people drowning out the awkward silence between them. Wandering from stall to stall, they hovered over the different lobster themed products on offer, neither of them approaching. Glancing around the crowd, Elias wondered if the mayor was in the mix somewhere or if she had shown her face and gone back to her office to get away from the locals.

"Can I interest you in a lobster cupcake?" somebody leaned out of their stall, "Made with real lobster!"

"Elias?" Caden looked to him.

"You've got to be kidding."

With a wink and a shrug, Caden pulled out his wallet in exchange for two bright red cupcakes with decorative iced lobsters adorning the top. To his relief, they were filled with sweet red goo and the lobster theme didn't extend beyond the outside.

"You've got a little –," Caden pointed at Elias' chin.

Elias was about to reach up and wipe away the frosting but before he could, Caden's thumb dove in to scoop it up. The contact was brief but it was just as electric as it had always been. Elias watched as Caden wiped it on the empty cupcake wrapper, wondering if Caden had felt it too.

As they headed deeper into the festival, Elias wanted to bring up what had happened at Caden's house, if only to defuse the underlying tension. He hated to admit that a support worker was the only person he felt like he had in life but it was true. As much as he resented what Caden was there to do, he had grown not to hate him. He was stuck between thinking that was because Caden was gay or just that Caden was a nice guy.

"Hey, Dad," Caden waved to a balding man who was propped up behind a stall selling freshly cooked lobster chowder, "how's it going?"

"Slow," he grumbled, "when did this place become such a circus? People used to come here to eat lobster but now they come to buy the trash people are selling. I saw one woman with lobster claw earrings. *Earrings!*"

Caden's dad stretched out, wiping his hands down the front of his apron. He shared the same pearly green eyes as Caden, making the family resemblance striking. Elias felt like he was shrinking into Caden's shadow but his dad suddenly looked to him, assessing the stranger.

"Dad, this is Elias," Caden patted Elias on the shoulder, "somebody I'm working with."

"Buster," he held his hand out with a cautious smile, "pleasure to meet you."

"You too," Elias forced an awkward smile, small talk never being something he was good at.

"I didn't think you were working today?" Buster looked to Caden, raising an eyebrow.

"Oh, I'm not. Not technically. Elias has never tried lobster before so I thought I'd bring him down here."

Buster didn't just look shocked, he looked offended. Scooping two huge ladles of the hot chowder into two plastic bowls, he handed them over, refusing to take Caden's money when he offered it. Feeling put on the spot, Elias crammed the plastic spoon into his mouth.

"Well?" Buster leaned forward, "What do you think?"

"It's salty," Elias chewed the lumps, "and fishy."

"You young 'uns," he sighed, sitting back on his perch, "don't appreciate good food when it hits you in the face."

Caden nudged Elias in the ribs with his elbow, forcing Elias to take another mouthful. It wasn't to his taste at all. His palette was more used to pizza and cheeseburgers but he forced a smile.

"No, it's good," he nodded, "takes a while but it's nice."

He didn't even convince himself but Buster closed his eyes and pursed his lips together into a half appreciative smile. They left the stall and carried on walking, Elias ditching the free chowder in the first trashcan he could find.

"He's usually nicer," Caden leaned in and whispered, "he's not big on change."

"You weren't supposed to be working today?" Elias asked.

They parked on a bench in front of the town hall, where music was pumping into the crowd from the local radio station.

"I thought we could hang out," Caden shrugged, "get to know each other better."

Elias turned to look at him but Caden was squinting into the sun, avoiding his gaze.

"Like, friends?"

"Yeah, friends," Caden nodded, seeming relieved.

Elias was relieved to. It was as if the tension eased a little, even if he couldn't help feeling slightly deflated. Why had he even tried to kiss Caden? Maybe it was because he had never really kissed a guy and in that moment he wanted to try it. He wanted to push it further but he didn't know what to say.

"Isn't that your sister?" Caden pointed into the crowd.

Elias looked to where he was pointing. His sister and her husband, John, were there, with Kobi by their side. At first, he didn't want to believe it was Kobi because of how big he had grown since he last saw him.

"We can't be here," he stood up, "we need to go."

"Why, what's up?" Caden jumped up, "Let's go over and say hi."

"No, I need to leave," he pulled the hood of his jacket over his face, "Ellie doesn't want me seeing Kobi and I don't want to give her any reason to hate me anymore."

"Why?"

"Why do you think?" he laughed, "Would you let an addict near your niece?"

Caden didn't reply but his silence said it all. Elias attempted to duck into the crowd away from his sister but they'd vanished. He looked around for them, Caden hot on his heels as he tried to keep his face low. He wasn't running because he didn't want to see his nephew, he was running because he did want to see him.

"Wait," Caden pulled Elias back, "we've only been here for ten minutes."

"Ten minutes too long," he ripped his arm away, "see you around."

Elias felt the dark cloud descend over his mind, feeling every inch the loser he was. Who was he trying to kid that he could be a normal guy? Maybe that's why he had tried to kiss Caden, to feel some kind of normal?

Caden called after him, making him look over his shoulder. Ducking deeper into the crowd out of his way, Elias turned back ahead in time to see the back of a sharp black bob colliding with his face.

"Watch it!" she called out.

"Uncle Elias!" Kobi jumped up and down.

Ellie turned around, confusion on her face. Pulling his hood back, he let his sister look at him for a second, hoping she wouldn't freak out.

"What are you doing here?" she said.

"Lobster," he mumbled, "I was here with somebody."

"Oh," she turned, "John will be back any minute. If he sees you with -,"

"Don't worry," Elias avoided Kobi's excited gaze, "I was trying to get out of here so that we didn't have to do this."

"Uncle Elias, Mommy says you've been sick. Are you better yet?" Kobi tugged on his sleeve.

Elias looked down at his nephew as he peered under his thick, dark bangs. For a second, it was like looking down at a younger version of himself. The James gene was so strong, John's side barely got a look in. He looked into those innocent doe eyes, feeling guiltier than ever before. Had he ever looked at his nephew with a sober mind?

"I'm getting better, champ," Elias crouched down so that he was face to face with Kobi, "how's school?"

"It's great, we're learning about space and rockets and aliens and my teacher broke his wrist. Is that what you've done? Is that why you're sick?"

"No, kid," Elias laughed, "I'm a different kind of sick, but I don't want you to worry about that. I need to go, okay?"

Kobi's excitement lessened, breaking Elias further. It wasn't fair on him either way. Elias knew that Ellie was only doing what she thought was best and he was sure that John was dictating from behind the scenes. John had always hated Elias and he never understood why Ellie gave him so many chances. Elias didn't understand why Ellie had given him so many chances either, but she did. Deep down, he knew it was a twin thing.

"Mommy said I can't see you until you're better," he whispered, looking down to the ground, "I miss you."

"I miss you too," Elias ruffled his hair, "It won't be long."

He looked up to Ellie who was looking down at him with a mixture of anger and the same upset Elias was feeling. She was giving him a look that screamed '*don't you dare make any false promises*', so Elias decided to leave it there. He hugged Kobi, who didn't seem to want to let go of his neck.

"C'mon, Kobi," she pulled him away, "daddy will be wondering where we are."

"Okay," he sulked, "bye Uncle Elias."

"See ya around," Elias tried to smile for Kobi's benefit but the second he was gone, he couldn't maintain it.

Anger bubbled up from within but instead of being angry with everyone else like usual, he was angry with himself.

"You okay?" he wiped away a tear when he heard Caden right behind him.

"How long have you been there?" he mumbled, not turning around.

"Long enough."

They stood in silence for a couple of seconds and he felt the tickle of Caden's lobster breath on the back of his neck. They were so close and silent as the busy crowd swallowed them up.

"You don't have to try so hard to be the good guy," Caden said.

Elias turned around, confused by what he meant, "What?"

"Seeing you with him, it's clear you care for him. You don't have to fake being a good guy because you are one."

Elias only half understood what Caden was saying. Furrowing his brow, he bit into his piercing, wondering if he should still head back to his apartment alone. Looking around at the festival, he knew he didn't want to spend any more time there.

"Do you want to come back to my place for coffee?" Elias sighed, "I have nothing better to do today and it turns out I don't care that much for lobster."

"Sure," Caden smiled, "coffee sounds good, but can I make it this time?"

"What's wrong with my coffee?"

"Nothing, I just didn't sleep for three days after drinking it," Caden winked with a playful smile, "I'll get some nice cupcakes from the bakery too."

Side by side, they broke through the crowd and headed towards Elias' apartment. Watching Caden through the bakery window as he paid the guy behind the counter, he felt strangely motivated. Seeing Kobi was the assurance that he needed to know he was ready to change and he knew Caden was the person to help him through it.

***

"You've been cleaning," Caden dumped the tray of cupcakes on the coffee table as he looked around at the apartment, "I'm impressed."

There were mugs with left over coffee in the bottom of the sink but aside from that, he could tell that Elias had actually put in some effort to keep on top of things. It was a sign of progress and Caden felt a strange sense of satisfaction that he had helped him get there.

"I've got nothing else to do," Elias headed to the refrigerator, "TV has lost its appeal."

"You need to get a hobby."

Caden watched as Elias opened the refrigerator. All of the beer bottles were still there, which was a good sign. He either hadn't touched them or he had been out to buy more but from the look in Elias' eyes, he looked pretty sober.

He watched as Elias reached inside, his hand hovering over the beer. Just when Caden thought he was about to pluck two out, he reached for two soda cans, tossing one towards him.

"Hobbies are for dorks," Elias leaned across the counter while Caden hovered on the other side, "what would I do?"

"Are you artistic?"

"Do I look artistic?" he arched his dark brows, his tongue playing with the ring in his lip.

Whenever he did that, it made Caden's stomach flutter but he decided to ignore it, forcing his eyes to make contact with Elias.

"Can you sing?"

"Can you?"

"No," Caden laughed, "my hobby is writing."

"How's the book coming along?"

"It's coming," he lied, not wanting to admit that he hadn't even opened his laptop since arriving in Havenmoore.

Half of the reason was because he was terrified to pick up his book, fearing that he had forgotten how to write. He knew if he didn't try, he couldn't fail, even if it meant his manuscript lay on his hard drive, tormenting him every time he looked at the laptop's white shell. The other reason was because he was avoiding social media at all costs. He had deleted all of the social apps on his phone, wanting no connection to the life he had left behind in New York. He didn't want to know about Suzie's new haircut or Mindy's new apartment with a great view and he especially didn't want to know how quickly Finn was moving on without him. With his fingers firmly in his ears, he knew how hypocritical it was to attempt to help Elias move on with his life when he was looking toward his thirtieth birthday as the end of his life.

"What about reading? Do you like that?"

"I didn't even read my high school books," he sipped his soda, "that's probably why I never got my diploma."

"You didn't?" Caden was shocked, "Why don't you try and do that? There's a night school at Havenmoore High helping adults who never got their diploma. That'd be great for you."

Elias recoiled, disgusted at the idea. He didn't instantly dismiss it because Caden could sense the cogs turning in the back of Elias' mind.

"No thanks," he shook his head with an awkward smile, "not my thing."

"Think about it! It'll help you get a job so you can stand on your own two feet. How are you keeping this roof over your head?"

"How do you think?" Elias walked around the counter and headed towards the couch, "Mommy is paying for everything."

Caden followed him, confused as to why she would be doing that. He knew she had fixed up the apartment for him for when he got out of rehab, but everything his own mom had told him about the mayor seemed to conflict with the idea that she was helping Elias.

"Have you guys gotten closer?" Caden asked, sitting next to Elias.

"Ha! No," he rolled his eyes, "this is her way of dealing with the situation. She thinks if she has me under her thumb, she's got some control over what's happening with my life."

"Isn't that motivation enough to get your diploma? You could get a job and pay your own way. Wouldn't that be a good start?"

Elias stared dead ahead, his eyes glazing over slightly. He didn't look as disgusted this time and Caden could definitely hear the cogs turning. He knew getting Elias into a program would give him something to focus on and that's clearly what he needed.

"Maybe," he mumbled reluctantly.

"I'm not saying you have to," Caden nudged Elias with his shoulder, "think about it. I'll make some calls to see what's out there for you. There must be something you want to do with your life. Where do you see yourself in ten years?"

"I never saw myself making it this far alive, so I never got around to the whole ten year plan."

"We'll figure something out for you."

Elias flicked to look at Caden for a second, his lips pursed. He seemed reluctant to let anybody interfere with his life like that but he knew that the lure to get out of his mother's grip was something he clearly wanted.

"Thank you," Elias mumbled as he played with the pull ring on the top of the soda can, "you could be hanging out with your own friends right now."

"What friends?" Caden laughed, "They're all back in New York and I don't even know if they're my friends anymore. They were his friends first. I've never really been good at making friends. I always seem to trust the wrong people. My mom said I was always too nice for my own good and I'm starting to think she's right. I've let people take advantage of me one too many times."

"That just shows you care about people," Elias said, "that's not a negative, man. That's a good thing."

"I guess," he sighed, "but look where it got me."

"It could be worse. You could be me."

Elias winked playfully and they both laughed but deep down, Caden felt like he was in just as much of a mess as Elias. Life was happening all around him, passing him by. He was itching to do something, to start something new but the security and safety of hiding in Havenmoore was the only thing keeping him sane.

"At least I've made one friend," Caden sipped his drink.

"Who's that?"

"You," he laughed, "I meant it earlier. I know I'm your support worker but that doesn't mean I can't be your friend too. I won't be your support worker forever."

"And you still want to be friends after that?"

"I'd like that," Caden smiled.

Elias rolled his head on the couch, a soft smile on his face telling Caden that he would like it too. Caden thought back to the moment in his bedroom where he had been so sure that Elias was trying to kiss him. Caden had put it down to confusion or misplaced affection but as they looked into each other's eyes, he felt like they were looking beyond the surface. There was so much pain and sadness in those dark eyes and he could feel his own pain reflected.

"Can I tell you something?" Elias whispered, his lips barely moving, "I've never told anyone before."

He edged forward, his hot breath trembling on Caden's face.

"What is it?" Caden swallowed hard, his eyes flicking between Elias' lips and eyes.

"I – I'm – I-," he stuttered.

Caden felt his own head moving closer to Elias. He didn't know what was pulling him, but something was. It was so strong, it blurred all lines of reason and logic. Closing his eyes, he closed the gap and he felt the softest touch of Elias' lips pushing against his.

It was magnetic and electric, forbidden but right. A voice in his head was telling him to stop what he was doing but the feeling in his gut was telling him to carry on. He felt his mouth open slowly, his breath trembling against Elias' lips. A hand brushed up his thigh, squeezing his flesh tightly.

Pushing his face into Elias', he let his tongue slowly move against Elias'. Something twitched below and Elias' hand made its way deeper into the inside of his leg.

"What am I doing?" Caden whispered, almost to himself.

"It's fine," Elias whispered back.

Caden let the kiss continue for a couple of seconds but the spell broke instantly when he felt Elias' fingers start to fiddle with the buttons on the front of his tight jeans.

"No," Caden jumped up, "this is wrong. I'm sorry. I overstepped the line."

"Wait, Caden," Elias flopped against the couch, something solid snaking down the inside of his own jeans, "just -,"

"I should go," Caden couldn't look at Elias.

He grabbed his denim jacket, not bothering to put it on. Heading straight for the door, he turned back to see Elias standing, his hands behind his head and his tight white t-shirt floating above his naval, exposing the dark trail down to the elastic waistband of his underwear. Despite everything, he felt a raw attraction towards Elias and words couldn't explain it. That's why he knew he needed to go.

"Mom," he pressed his cellphone into his ear, "I think there's a problem. I've done something stupid."

Chapter 8

Elias spent the weekend tossing and turning, failing to sleep for more than a couple of hours. The kiss was weighing heavily on his mind and he had found himself propped up in the dark and staring at Caden's cell number more than once. He wanted to call, to tell him to forget anything had happened but he didn't want to forget it.

Elias didn't know what to expect from a kiss. He had obviously seen people doing it and he had obviously kissed people before but never like that. Elias had never felt such passion and heat in such a short space of time. He had wanted it to last forever. When Caden ended things and ran out, he felt like he was left hanging.

Caden was his support worker so he didn't know what he was expecting from him. He was the first person and the first man who had ever treated Elias like he was just a normal guy and he liked that. He liked feeling like just another person in the crowd and not somebody at the bottom of the pit.

After a weekend of pacing his apartment, Monday morning rolled around and he found himself cleaning up, awaiting Caden's arrival. He felt like a fool as he quickly washed through the dirty dishes, as if hoping that Caden seeing how much he was trying would make everything better. He felt like a dog jumping for a toy.

There was a knock at the door and just from the knuckles rapping on the wood he knew there was something wrong. They were lighter and softer. *Maybe he thinks I'm asleep?*

"One minute," he called down, wiping his soapy hands on an old t-shirt that had been tossed in front of the washing machine.

Pausing at the top of the stairs, he took a deep breath as he slowly closed his eyes, promising that he was going to open up to Caden. Maybe if he knew Elias was gay too it would fix things? Even if he just kept the promise of friendship, that would be enough for Elias. His eyes had been opened up to a whole new world and he wanted to explore more of it. He wanted to feel what it was like to really have somebody care about him; whether he was happy or not.

He opened the door and he saw the flame red hair but it wasn't on top of Caden's head. The hue was stronger and it belonged to a short woman in a white blouse and a pair of faded jeans.

"What?" he snapped, "What do you want?"

"Elias, isn't it?" she smiled, "I'm Claire. I'm from Helping Hands Outreach."

She tapped the badge on her chest and held out her hand with a warm smile but Elias ignored it. Poking his head over her shoulder, he shot up and down the alley to see if Caden was behind her. He was bitterly disappointed.

"Where's Caden?"

"There's been a change of plan," her smile wobbled and it widened, "I'm your new support worker."

In a stunned silence, he stepped to the side and let Claire

squeeze past him so she could head upstairs. Her perfume was sweet and sickly and it turned his stomach. Slamming the door, he took the stairs two at a time and bolted into his apartment to see Claire already making herself comfortable on his couch as she opened a file on her knee.

"Let's see," she mumbled, "where are we at with you?"

"No, this isn't right," he laughed, "there must have been a mix up. Where's my usual guy, Caden?"

She turned the files with a smile, her eyes trained on the paper but clearly not reading the words. Immediately, he knew there was something she wasn't going to tell him.

"It's quite normal for us to switch," she patted on the couch next to him, "c'mon, sit. We've got a lot of stuff to get through."

Elias did as he was told and he sat in the corner of the couch, as far away from Claire as he could. His mind was working a thousand miles a second as he tried to piece together what was going on. *Why isn't he here?*

"So, have you tried looking for a job yet?" she asked rather formally.

Immediately, he got the impression that things with Claire were going to be very different than they had with Caden. Half of the reason he had grown to like Caden was because he kept the official and formal stuff to a minimum. It felt like hanging out with a pal – *and look where that got you.*

"No," he frowned, "I don't understand. Where's Caden?"

She half smiled and softly closed the file.

"Listen," she sighed heavily, "sometimes there's a compatibility issue. It's nobody's fault."

"A '*compatibility issue*'? He quit?"

Her eyes narrowed, slightly confused, letting him know that she didn't know about their brief kiss.

"We've swapped," she said, "my son thought I could help you better. I have more experience and -,"

"Son?" he laughed, "Oh, this is brilliant."

"Has something happened?"

"No," he snapped, "let's just get this over with."

Claire started rattling through the paperwork but Elias tuned out. He felt used and tossed aside. Caden had been so full of promises to help, to get him on the right track but he had thrown him to the side like an old taco the second the heat turned up. He wasn't mad that he wasn't going to get help from Caden, he was mad that he had believed him. *I trusted him, I let my guard down to him and I never do that.*

"I need the bathroom," he jumped up and ran to the bathroom, locking the door behind him.

Staring at his reflection in the mirror, he splashed cold water on his face and watched as it dripped into the sink below. The bags under his eyes had calmed and the whites of his eyes were actually white for once. Even his skin had some color. *I can't let it just end like this.*

Frantically staring around the bathroom, he looked to the frosted window. Unlatching it, he yanked it open and stared down at the dark alley below. There was a fire escape for the bakery but it was too far to his right. He stared up at the sky, it's cloudless and bright blue vibrancy shining down on him. Hitting his hands against the frame, he cried out, his screams echoing back at him.

"Everything okay in there?"

Elias looked down at the alley again. The dumpster was directly under his window on the other side of the alley. He knew if he got the angle right, he could land on top of it. *I've seen Spiderman, how hard can this be?* Climbing up onto the window ledge, he looked down at the alley below, knowing he could have a long way to fall if he misjudged it.

With a metal bang, he landed on the lid of the dumpster in a squat, his knees crying out.

"What are you doing?" the baker appeared in the doorway, "Get out of there before I call the police."

"Call them," Elias slid off the lid and onto the ground, dusting down his clothes.

Grabbing his cellphone, he pulled up the address Caden had texted him and headed across town, not giving a second glance to his apartment.

***

Caden told his brother more than he would have liked. Bruce smoked three cigarettes in quick succession, as he listened to Caden spill his secrets. He had started talking, not knowing what he was going to say but the second he mentioned the kiss, his tongue couldn't be silenced.

"Do you like this guy?" Bruce lit another cigarette, "Or is he just a rebound? It happens, y'know."

"I wish I knew," he wondered what effect one of his brother's beloved cigarettes would have on him right now, "have I done the right thing?"

"Getting Mom to take over your job?"

Caden nodded and he could already see that Bruce thought he was a coward. *I feel like a coward.* He had toyed with all of the different scenarios in his mind of what could happen next but he could never escape that he was put in a position to help a vulnerable man and he knew he was taking advantage of him. *Is this what being with one guy for five years in New York does to a man?* Maybe it wasn't so unusual that Finn strayed. *That was with your best friend.* Was that any worse than what Caden had done?

"Did he push you off? Throw you out?"

Shaking his head, Caden wished that Elias had objected to the kiss. It would have made things easier for him. Elias' lack of reaction and total submission only served as further confusion. Something self-pitying was about to leave his lips but a firm knock on the front door derailed his thoughts. Bruce stood but Caden hurried for the door, glad of the distraction.

When he saw Elias standing in his doorway, he wished he had let his brother take this one, "Elias, what are you doing here?"

"I could ask you the same thing," his voice was filled with venom.

Sensing confrontation, Caden slipped out of the house, closing the door. Bruce would understand. Dragging Elias around the side of the house, they stood awkwardly in the shade of his mother's small greenhouse.

"You shouldn't have come here," Caden forced professionalism.

"You shouldn't have blown me off," Elias' voice rose, "sending your mom to clean up your leftovers?"

"You're not leftovers," Caden knew that Elias didn't understand why he had to do what he had done, not that he expected him to; *I don't know what I've done.*

"I thought you wanted to help me," a cold laugh left Elias' throat as he pushed himself against the wood of the house.

Caden caught Bruce's reflection in the glass of the greenhouse as he peered through the kitchen drapes. He was sensitive enough to leave them to fix their own problems.

"That's why I can't work with you. I want to help you but I can't."

"Why?" Elias demanded.

Because I want to kiss you again? Because I can't control myself? Because my life is a mess and I'm dragging you into it?

"I just can't."

Shaking his head, Elias' fingers combed through his black scruff as he stared up at the cloudless sky, "This always happens. I always get palmed off onto someone else."

"It's not like that!"

"So, what's it like?" Elias turned to face Caden, his pale skin ghostly in the shadows, "Because I'm tired of trying to figure out where I keep going wrong in this mess you people call a life. I thought you said we could be friends."

"We can, when you're better."

"You don't think I'm better?"

"That's not what I meant!"

Caden knew that Elias had been trying hard to stay clean and he felt like he had had some impact there but he knew how easy it was for addicts to slip back at the snap of a finger. There was no cure, just a constant battle.

"I'm not good for you."

"People are always telling me what's not good for me," he laughed a laugh so empty it made Caden's hairs stand on end, "it'd be nice if I could decide that for myself."

"I'm sorry," Caden mumbled, "I should *never* have let myself get so close to you. Maybe we wouldn't have -,"

Stopping to read Elias' expression, he couldn't tell what he thought of the kiss. Was Elias trying to ignore it for the sake of keeping the only friend he had ever made, or was it all he was thinking about?

"There's something I didn't tell you," Elias lowered his eyes to the ground, "we're not so different."

Puzzled, Caden turned and leaned against the greenhouse to face Elias. He caught his brother in the window, shaking his head at Caden as if to ask what was going on. Caden widened his eyes at his brother and he backed away from the window.

"What do you mean?"

"I'm like you," he sighed heavily, "I just didn't know how to tell you."

"Like me how?"

"Gay," he snapped, "I'm gay too."

Caden forced his body harder against the glass. He couldn't decide if he should be shocked or not. To look at Elias, he looked like any other guy, but he knew it wasn't that cut and dry any more.

"Okay," Caden nodded.

It was Elias' turn to look confused and Caden knew why. Elias probably thought his sexuality would magically change things but it didn't stop Caden feeling like he had abused his position. He wasn't a bad guy but he felt like one around Elias, and he hated that.

"When you kissed me, I-,"

"It doesn't change anything," Caden whispered, "you and me can't happen."

"But, I-,"

"I'm your support worker!" Caden almost shouted, "I should never have let it get to this situation. I just wanted to help you. That's all. Just to help."

Elias' dark eyes danced all over Caden's body. He braced himself for a punch, knowing that if Elias did lash out at him, he deserved it. *Do it, I won't duck.* His fists clenched by his side and

Caden readied himself, but the fist didn't meet Caden, it met the wall. There was a crack and a split, but it wasn't the wooden panels, it was Elias' knuckles. Blood spurted from the fresh cuts and Caden wanted nothing more than to swoop in and help.

"Why did you do that?"

"Because! There's so much I want to say, but I – I don't know how. I'm not good at this talking thing. I can't get the thoughts from in *here*," he tapped a finger on the side of his head, "to come out of my mouth. Not in the *right* way. Not ever."

"I'm sorry, I -,"

"When you didn't turn up this morning," Elias carried on, "I was so angry. I even cleaned up, ready for you. When I saw your mom, I felt like you'd just given up on me. It sounds so childish, this is why I never say what I think, what I feel. I just – *ugh* – I just wanted to see *you*. That's all I wanted to do this morning. I didn't want to score, I didn't want to drink, I just wanted to see you. To talk, to fix things, to -,"

Stopping himself, Elias looked up to the sky and let out a small laugh. Caden could feel that Elias was wondering why he was even trying. Caden was just another person full of false promises and he couldn't believe he had done that to somebody so fragile. *Can't you see the hurt you're already causing?*

"I wanted to see you too," Caden stepped forward, "but that's why I couldn't come. You're in a place in your life right now, and whatever this is, it can't happen."

"What place? This is the longest I've been clean since I was a kid."

It was Caden's turn to feel like he couldn't get the right words out of his mouth; the words to make Elias see that a kiss and whatever that kiss would lead to wasn't a good idea for either of them. Drugs, ex-boyfriends, rebounding and secrets weren't the foundations for a new life, for either of them. Havenmoore was supposed to have been a break away from the complications but it was only creating more. Looking deep into Elias' eyes, he felt selfish for even wanting to push him away, even if he knew it was the right thing to do.

"You'll be better without me," Caden looked to the ground,

"this is too complicated, for both of us. I'll be your friend, but I can't be any more than that."

The muscles in Elias' jaw tightened and his brows furrowed so deeply, his eyes were nothing more than shadows. He lingered, looking like there was something important and painful on the end of his tongue. Instead of speaking, he broke away, clutching his hand.

"Elias, you can come inside to get your hand -,"

A bloody middle finger over the shoulder shut Caden up. He watched as Elias ignored the gate to jump over the fence before setting off at a sprint along the road.

If this is the right thing to do, why does it feel so wrong?

Chapter 9

Lingering outside of the doctor's office, Elias hid in the shadows, pulling his hood over his head. It had been days since he had confronted Caden but he was still in his system. Lust was a stronger drug than Elias had ever experienced and the withdrawal from the thrill was the hardest cold turkey he had ever attempted.

If he understood it, it would be easier to explain away. On the surface, it was one kiss from a man he barely knew, but when he started to dig, it was a blur. A blur of bright colors, wild ideas and crazy notions he had never had before. It was akin to insanity and nothing numbed it.

He watched as Ronda headed out, pulling her purse tightly over her shoulder. She looked around before ducking into her car and driving off. The lights were still on inside so he knew his sister was still in there. He thought about waiting for her to come out but what he wanted was in there with her. Pulling the hood lower over his eyes, he slid through the door silently.

The waiting area was completely dark, aside from a light above the desk highlighting the different posters. At the end of the corridor, a bright light beamed from beneath his sister's door. He had no way of knowing that she would still be there but she had a habit of always being the last out of the building at the end of the night.

"Sorry, we're closed," she mumbled when the door opened.

When he closed the door, she looked up from her paperwork and jumped back in her chair when she saw her brother's face. The bright bulb in her lamp burned his eyes as he pulled his hood back.

"What do you want?" she looked down to her paperwork, "I'm not giving you anymore of those pills, if that's why you're here. Make an appointment with another doctor and go through the motions like everybody else."

She was already starting on the attack but he knew he could work around that. She would have to listen to him. This time was different, surely she could see that?

"Nice to see you too," he forced a smile but he didn't feel like smiling.

"Stop the niceness, Elias," she arched her brows as she scribbled away, "dilated pupils, bags under the eyes, oily hair and skin, it doesn't take a genius to work out what's happened here."

"I'm not using," he stepped forward, "I swear I'm not using."

Pinching between her eyes, she laughed softly, shaking her head with disappointment.

"Why should I -,"

"I swear on Kobi's life, I haven't touched anything. No coke, no alcohol, nothing. I want to, so bad, but I haven't."

Ellie dropped her pen and leaned back in her chair to assess her brother's face again. He yanked back the patient chair and sat on the edge of it, his fingers scrambling together frantically as his tongue probed the metal in his lip. He wasn't helping his case. He knew he looked like shit.

"You've sworn on his life before," she sighed heavily, "it's a miracle he hasn't dropped down dead a dozen times with an uncle like you."

"I swear," he said, "I promise you. I just can't sleep."

"Why?"

"Because I can't."

"Because you've been snorting coke all week and your mind won't shut up?"

Elias had done that enough times to know that's how he looked. After enough of the drug, you eventually stop getting tired and become a walking zombie, only semi present. This time was different.

"I haven't touched it since I left rehab, I -," he swallowed hard, "it's different."

"Make an appointment if you have nothing to hide," she got back to her paperwork, "I'm not losing my job for you."

If he could have, he would. He wasn't allowed any prescribed medication until he had finished his follow up and that could last for months depending on his drug tests. Even if she would never believe him, he hated putting his problems on her. It just showed how stuck he was. *I always end up here, begging for her help, pleading to the tiny part of her that can't say no.*

"I just need something to sleep," he pleaded, "I just want to sleep. I just need to sleep."

As the words left his lips, his thick and dry lids batted in a rhythmic fashion. Sitting in his sister's office made him feel like he could sleep at any moment but he knew the second those lids dropped, they'd spring right back open again with no idea how to process the swirling thoughts in his mind.

"What about those other pills I gave you? They should help you sleep."

"They don't. They just make me restless and they make my skin itch. I just want to sleep."

Elias was starting to feel like a broken record.

"What's happened to you? I thought you were past this stage. Are you still withdrawing? You can't be, not now."

I'm withdrawing from something.

"It's complicated."

"I'm not going anywhere," she shrugged, "maybe it's time you started telling me your problems instead of expecting me to just hand over the stuff."

It was the last thing he wanted to do. He felt weak. *I am weak.* Why couldn't he understand the pain in his chest or the thoughts in his own mind? *One kiss.* It meant nothing to Caden. *You're just a mistake.*

"I kissed someone."

Ellie frowned in disbelief before a smile tickled her nude painted lips, "Is that all?"

"I told you, it's complicated."

"Welcome to the real world, brother," she almost seemed relieved, "I'm not giving you anything. You need to ride this one out. Us normal people don't medicate ourselves up to the eyeballs every time we want to avoid facing our problems. Face them, because I'm all out."

"Please, I -,"

He slapped his hands on her desk, immediately regretting it when he saw the bloody mess he had turned the knuckles on his right hand into. Ellie's eyes caught it before he could pull them away.

"I punched a wall," he said before she asked, "I was angry, okay?"

"Is that going to solve it?"

"No?"

"Did it make you feel better?"

"Not really?" they still hurt.

"Who was it?"

Could he tell her? Should he tell her? Did she know that he wasn't attracted to the opposite sex? Had she always known? Ellie had always avoided talking about relationships and love with him but he had never known if that was because of the awkwardness it would present or just because she had no interest to discuss such things with her brother. Caden was the first person he had officially come out to and it was hardly the joyful and freeing experience the movies painted it to be.

"Nobody. It doesn't matter. It's not going anywhere."

She pursed her lips tightly, resembling their mother in a flash. Ellie was racking her large brain for a possible suspect but they hardly moved in the same circles.

"Ice cream helps," she shrugged, "and chocolate."

"For real?" he scooted even further to the edge of the seat, "I've barely slept in three days and you're prescribing ice cream?"

"The sugar picks you up. It's called comfort eating. That's what normal people do."

"I'm clearly not a normal person, am I?"

"Have a bath, listen to music, cry, call them, watch a sad movie, get it out of your system. You'll feel fine. You'll get over it. You're not the first person to go through this."

Feeling like he was getting nowhere with his sister, he collapsed back in the chair, closing his eyes heavily. For a second, he felt like he could actually fall asleep but the familiar feeling of falling took over him and he jolted back to reality.

"I've never liked somebody before," Elias muttered, almost to himself, "I never thought I could."

"Just tell me who it was. I won't judge."

He almost did. She had been keeping things gender neutral and her eyes were open and kind. *I can't, not like this.*

"Ice cream?" he stood up, "Will any flavor work?"

"Chocolate Brownie is my favorite," a soft smile tickled her lips.

Feeling beat, Elias headed towards the door, wondering if even talking about it had made him feel better. Maybe it was a good thing that she wouldn't give in to him so easily? *Maybe this is what I need.*

"Elias, I'm sorry," the words sounded alien leaving her mouth.

"Why?"

"For jumping to conclusions. The brother I know would have cracked under the pressure. I think I need to get to know this new one better."

Hand gripping the handle, he felt a little warmth enter his heart. Turning, he smiled and she smiled back. The twin bond was still there, under it all.

"Me too," he nodded his thanks and they didn't need to speak to know what the other was thinking.

Pulling his hood over his hair, he headed out into the chilly night. Bars and restaurants buzzed around the town square as Havenmoore's nightlife started to kick in, but all Elias could think about was putting his sister's sugar theory to the test.

***

"Are you sure everything is okay with you?" Caden's mom asked for what he was sure was the tenth time that day, "Ever since – well – you've been acting a little strange. Has Finn called? Has he said something to you?"

Caden slammed the laptop shut, his word count no different to what it had been two hours ago when he had finally dug the dreaded machine from one of his bags.

"Finn hasn't called," standing up, he pulled off his t-shirt and pulled on a crisp shirt, "I'm fine, honest."

"People who are fine don't keep saying '*I'm fine*'," she folded her arms in the doorway of his bedroom.

"Stop asking me if I'm fine then," he buttoned up the white shirt.

"How are you and Mary getting along?" she seemed to be totally unaware that Mary was part of the problem.

"We're great," he lied, "I think she's starting to trust me."

"Mary? Trusting you? Are you sure she is not just – *never mind*. I'm sure you're great at what you do. I don't know how you and this Elias kid got along, but it's like pulling teeth."

"How is he?" he asked a little too quickly.

"He's hard to read," she sent a long, red nail into her pulled back hair, "he's always on edge. It's so hard to even talk to him. One word answers, grunts. I think he just needs more time."

"Yeah, more time," he agreed, hoping that time would make things easier.

His mom left him to finish getting dressed and after a quick spritz of aftershave he was heading into town with his mom where they were meeting the rest of the family for his dad's birthday meal in a new restaurant next door to Bruce's bar. It was a little more upmarket than where they'd usually go and his dad insisted that it was completely unnecessary to make such a fuss over his sixty-third birthday, but Bruce insisted. He was trying to build up a good relationship with his new business neighbors and he had been promised a healthy discount off the price of the meal.

They pulled up outside of the restaurant, where Bruce and his dad were already chatting over a shared cigarette. The cigarette was quickly thrust back into Bruce's fingers when he noticed them jumping out of the car. If his mom noticed that he had been sharing, after quitting nearly ten years ago, she wasn't mentioning it. It was his birthday after all; he would just probably pay for it in the morning.

Before they headed inside, Bruce pulled Caden to one side and started to quiz him about Elias and if everything was okay. Caden had become an expert at smiling through the pain and he made sure to let his brother know that everything was fine and moving in the right direction.

"Welcome to *Buffitos*," a charming and handsome young man greeted them all at the door, "table for Buster? Right this way. Some of your guests are already here."

Lucy and Becca were already sitting patiently at the table. Lucy was going over the menu while Becca scribbled delicately over a coloring sheet, her tongue poking out of the side. When they all sat, Caden chose his place next to Becca very carefully. She was probably the only one on the table who wasn't going to start quizzing him about his love life or complicated situation.

"Do you like it, Uncle Caden?" Becca held up the sheet, which she was already halfway through, "It's a donkey."

"It's very pretty," he ruffled her hair as he squinted, trying to see a donkey but only seeing a cat, "you're so good. You'll have to teach me how to color."

"Okay," she nodded proudly, "but mommy says we can't color on the walls, even though there's more space there."

"Silly Mommy," Caden winked at Lucy, "I think mommy

should let you."

"And I think Uncle Caden should stop trying to make my life a living hell," she winked back.

When the entire family was in one room, there was never an awkward silence. He had been to dinners with Finn's parents and it was like pulling teeth trying to search for conversation. The difference was, his family all genuinely liked each other, so there was always something to talk about. The problem was, they all liked to know each other's business too intimately and he could sense that Bruce had told Lucy everything that had happened with Elias and she was itching to start quizzing him about the details. When Bruce promised not to tell anybody, Caden knew he would tell Lucy but that didn't bother him.

"Caden, help me at the bar?" Lucy stood up, "Can't have empty glasses on Buster's birthday."

He knew that if they called over their server, he would bring wine straight away but he wasn't going to argue. When they stood at the bar, she ordered the drinks before turning to him and waiting for him to speak.

"What?" he laughed, "Is there something on my face?"

"You know what!" she slapped him on the arm, "Why didn't you tell me about this new guy?"

Oh, God. Elias was hardly the '*new guy*'. He was '*no guy*', after what Caden had done. No matter how many times he told himself it was a pointless and dumb kiss, he couldn't ignore the strange feelings the memory conjured in his stomach.

"Really, there's nothing to tell. It was a mistake. I've drawn a line under it."

"So, he was just a rebound?"

"I guess so," that didn't feel right.

"If he wasn't, there's no point saying he was," sometimes Lucy could read him as if they were the ones who were actually siblings, "if you don't grab love by the balls, it won't grab you."

Lucy clenched her fingers tightly together in a ball grabbing motion.

"Woah, hold your horses there," Caden ran his hand over his beard scruff, "who said anything about love? It was one, ill-judged kiss with somebody I should never have kissed."

"If you say so," she rolled her eyes, accepting the bottles of wine and handing over the cash, "Finn is ancient history. If he's what's holding you back, let it go."

Finn was the last thing on his mind. Caden arrived in Havenmoore expecting Finn to be on his case about getting back together, but he hadn't heard a peep from him. He was glad of it and it only confirmed how bad they really were for each other. On paper, they should have worked, but when it came to it, distance only confirmed that Finn wasn't the settling type.

"It's bad timing. Timing is everything and -,"

"Listen to you," she put the wine bottles back on the bar, "you're trying to come up with excuses why you can't date this guy. If there's nothing concrete, I say go for it! Don't try and talk yourself out of it. Even if you just have some great sex with this guy, what's so bad about that?"

"It's not that simple," he couldn't even imagine using Elias like that, "he's troubled."

"You're scared of his past?"

"No," he meant it, "I'm scared of what I'm going to do to his future."

And there it was. The very words he had been searching for but he had been unable to say.

"The future is a book none of us have read. Stop pretending like you know what's around the corner."

"But what if I send him back to rehab? What if we kiss again and we keep kissing and then it gets more serious? What if that doesn't work out? What if I break his heart? What if I push him so far over the edge that he breaks and –,"

"Like Frank, you mean? That wasn't your fault. That was different."

She really could read his mind. *I can't lose another one.* Caden knew he wasn't cut out for this job, not in the same way his mom was.

"Just consider this for a second," Lucy picked up the wine bottles, "what if none of that happens and you just live happily ever after?"

She headed back to the table and Caden mumbled something about needing to go to the bathroom. Staring at his reflection in the bathroom mirror, he looked every inch the coward he felt. He had never been scared of the future until he found his boyfriend in bed with his best friend. He watched the future he had been so sure about, crumble before his eyes. He didn't want to crumble Elias' future. He wanted Elias to be the best version of himself but could he get there with Caden by his side, messing with his emotions?

"What do I do?" he cried at his own reflection, but it stared back blankly.

A surly looking guy appeared from a stall behind him, making Caden smile awkwardly like a fool. The guy gave him an awkward smile, before heading out without washing his hands, clearly thinking Caden was crazy. He quickly washed his hands and headed back into the restaurant. He was still in such a confused daze, he didn't notice the woman he was about to walk straight into.

"Watch it!" she cried out, a cellphone pressed into her ear.

It took him a second to realize that he was staring into the angry eyes of Judy James, Havenmoore's beloved mayor.

"I'm – I -," he mumbled, her dark gaze burning into his pale skin.

She had Elias' eyes, or rather, he had hers, but they were different. They were the same dark color, but they were devoid of the same vulnerability and softness. They were cold and shiny, like the exoskeleton of a beetle. She had the same smiling face of the woman who was on the front page of the newspaper every other day, but he suddenly felt like he knew her in a different way to everybody in the restaurant.

"You're Elias' mom," he pointed at her, unsure of why he said that.

"I'll call you back," she mumbled down the phone, not taking her dead eyes away from Caden, "who are you?"

"I work with your son. I mean – I *worked* with your son. I do some work with Helping Hands Outreach and –,"

"If you're about to ask for more funding, save your breath

because I'm not working," she cut him off with a wave of her manicured fingernails, "now if you don't mind, I was in the middle of something."

"Wait," he reached out and grabbed her arm, which he quickly let go of when she looked like lasers were about to shoot from her eyes to slice off his wrist, "Elias, he's -,"

"What? What about him?"

He swallowed hard, fear creeping up inside of him.

"How's he doing?"

"Fine," her lips pursed so tightly and he couldn't ignore how much she looked like her daughter, Ellie, "why?"

Caden glanced back to his table but the wine was flowing and so was the conversation. They wouldn't miss him for a couple of seconds. He knew he was playing with fire but he wanted to push Judy for some information. He was hoping to find a tiny glimmer in the woman that she cared for her son to ease his guilty conscience.

"How are things between you two? He mentioned that you haven't been talking much."

Her blood red lips practically vanished into her head and a tiny network of lines appeared on her upper lip, the only indication that she was old enough to have twenty-six-year-old twins.

"I don't know what you want from me, but you're not going to scare me," she leaned in, "is it money? Is that what you want?"

"Money?" he was taken aback, "I just wanted to know if you'd spoken to your son this week."

"What's it got to do with you?" she looked at him from head to toe and he was surprised he didn't burst into flames, "Who did you say you work for?"

Not wanting to get his mom into trouble, he kept his mouth shut and gulped down the rising fear as the mayor of the town gave him a look that would turn the strongest man to stone.

"It doesn't matter," Caden knew when it was best to retreat, "I must have my wires crossed."

"You must," she straightened up her suit jacket, "because if you start talking about my son to people, I can make your life hell on earth. Do you understand me? What did you say your name was?"

"Caden," he left off the last name.

"*Caden*," she gave him another once over, "my son is an embarrassment. Talk to the press, and they'll ignore you. They know on what side their bread is buttered. He stays a secret. Do you understand me?"

His mouth and throat turned to dust as he stood, unable to do anything other than nod like a simpleton. She stared at him for long, drawn out seconds before snapping out of it. With each step she took away from him, she loosened up and became the mayor everybody knew and loved. By the time she made it back to her table in her figure hugging black svelte dress, a huge, beaming smile filled her face, hiding any hint of what she was hiding in an apartment around the corner.

"We were about to send out a search party," his mom poured some wine into his empty glass, "I ordered the Carbonara for you. If you hurry, you might be able to change it."

"Carbonara's fine," he tossed back a mouthful of the wine, which garnered a raised eyebrow from Lucy, who quickly did the same to Bruce, "Mom, y'know Elias James? Is it too late to switch back?"

"Has something happened?" his mom looked around the restaurant, "Mary's not here is she? She knows she's not allowed out after dark."

"No, no, she's not here. I just had an idea of how I can help Elias. I think we can work well together."

His mom didn't question him. Making a note of it on her cellphone, she said she would get it done. Bruce and Lucy looked at each other confused but Caden hid his '*plan*' behind a wonky smile. He didn't have a plan, just a feeling. He knew he couldn't be like Judy James.

I can't abandon him. I won't.

Chapter 10

A loud knock on the door rattled Elias from his restless dreams. The second he opened his eyes, he knew he had only been asleep for an hour or two. Swinging his legs over the side of the bed, he stepped in the melted leftovers of the chocolate ice cream. It didn't help him sleep but Ellie was right about it making him feel a little better.

Picking up the nearest shirt, he sniffed it before pulling it over his head. It was a little tight, possibly shrunk in the washing machine. He couldn't entirely remember how to use it and Claire wasn't as ready to do the housework as Caden had been.

There was another loud knock on the door and he couldn't believe how eager she was to get inside. Claire was the type of woman who thought she was amazing at what she did and she might be if the whole '*softly softly*' approach works on some addicts; Elias wasn't one of them.

"Alright, I'm coming. Jesus," he cried when she knocked a

third time.

Reluctantly dragging himself down the stairs wearing nothing more than his tight briefs and a t-shirt, he flung open the door, the harsh morning sun blinding him. When his eyes adjusted, he looked up, wondering if Claire was wearing heels because she was suddenly a whole foot taller.

His stomach knotted when he squinted at Caden's face. The ice cream from the night before bucked its ugly head and the lack of sleep over the week was still playing heavily on his swollen eyelids.

"What do you want?" he spat at Caden, who was sheepishly standing with his hands clung to the strap of his canvas bag.

"I – I -," the words stumbled out of his mouth, barely above a whisper.

Elias was about to order him away, not wanting to hear what he had to say. He was about to tell him that he didn't mean any of those dumb things he had said outside of Caden's house. His fingers brushed over the thick wounds on his knuckles, a constant reminder of how much confusion he had felt.

"What? What do you want?" he demanded.

Caden's eyes brushed up and down Elias' body, lingering on the tightness of his underwear. He readjusted them, wondering if he was showing more than expected. He wasn't.

"I – just -," he stumbled again, "I can't."

Elias thought Caden was about to run away. Elias thought Caden was about to leave him again. Elias thought Caden regretted showing up outside of his apartment. Elias was wrong.

The sheepishness and awkwardness vanished and the hands that gripped the strap of the canvas bag launched out, gripping Elias around the neck. Before he knew how to process the sudden movement, moist lips pushed against his. Their noses fought for space as their mouths worked over time. He clenched his eyes, giving in to the heat. Late morning wood suddenly sprung up, making the tight underwear feel even tighter. The grip firmed and the pressure increased, sending Elias back. He stumbled up the first step, falling onto his backside. The carpet yanked his underwear down, exposing his smooth cheeks and burning them against the rough, coarse thread on the step. Caden kicked the door closed and they were covered in darkness.

He had so many questions to ask but the kiss was too good. The way Caden's tongue explored his mouth, the way the hands gripped delicately and firmly around his head, the way Caden's clothes pushed up against Elias', sending the tight t-shirt up his flat stomach, it was the strongest apology any man had ever received.

An unspoken agreement through the kiss called them upstairs. They didn't break contact, their eyes remaining shut as they opened the door to the living room. He wondered if he was still dreaming and this was a cruel trick of the mind, but he could taste the minty freshness of Caden's toothpaste, mixed in with what tasted like grits.

"I should explain," Caden panted through the kiss.

"No," Elias shook his head, their beards grating against each other, "no talking."

"Okay," he nodded.

Caden broke the kiss only to pull the bag over his head. He dumped it on the couch before pushing Elias up against the back of it. His hands travelled down to the small of his back, pulling him in firmly. It felt strong and safe. Elias' firm shaft ached painfully against the thickness of Caden's jeans. He reached out, fumbling with the clunky metal buttons. They popped open with ease, Caden's baggy underwear springing forward. He felt around, his hands brushing against the coarse hair, leading below the waistline. He danced his fingers against the elastic of the underwear, wanting to savor the feeling, but Caden groaned in a pitch higher than anything Elias had heard leave his lips before, that he had to reach for it.

Fingers closed around a solid, veined shaft. It was warm and twitching under his grasp. He begged with his kiss for Caden to do the same to him, but his hands travelled lower into his white underwear. Short, clipped fingernails dug into his cheeks, squeezing them tightly. Nobody was even touching his cock and yet he felt fit to blow.

Caden's hands left his cheeks and disappointment raced

through him. He wondered if he had gone too far, going into his pants. He opened his eyes and Caden took a step back, only to start unbuttoning the crisp, blue shirt he was wearing. He exposed his well-toned thick chest and stomach. A light dusting of hair, a similar hue to that on his head, danced across his body, inviting Elias to touch it. The shirt was tossed on the couch, leaving Elias to admire the body in front of him as he still clung to the ever-hardening shaft in his palm.

Soft lips touched his forehead. The intensity of the kiss was gone but the passion was present. Caden's fingers tugged the tight t-shirt over his head before dropping it to the floor. He reached out and brushed his growing, dark hair off his forehead. Elias bit into his lip ring, wanting to kiss him again, wanting to never do anything else but kiss him.

"This place is a mess," Caden glanced over his shoulder.

"Kiss me again," Elias closed his eyes and dove in, pulling Caden closer towards him by his cock, forcing Caden's jeans and underwear to his ankles.

Their naked torsos pressed up against each other and Caden pulled him into a tight embrace, his arms firm and strong. It felt warm, but in a way Elias had never experienced. It was a place he would happily stay forever.

"Bedroom," Caden whispered, kicking off his shoes, jeans and underwear.

Silently agreeing with his kiss, Elias started to walk backwards towards the bedroom. A pile of pizza boxes caused him to stumble but Caden's strong arms were still wrapped around him, saving him from a naked embarrassment. They both laughed through the kiss and they were still laughing when they fell onto Elias' bed. He wished he had known about Caden's visit and he wished he had known what they were about to do in the bedroom. It smelled strongly of dirty socks and unwashed man with a top note of chocolate ice cream.

Caden's tongue and lips crawled down his body, working over his chest and stomach, following the messy dark trail into the white underwear that was still containing him. Caden kissed his manhood through the fabric, teasing him for what felt like a lifetime. When he finally peeled the underwear back, his cock sprung onto his stomach and he caught a slight glimmer in Caden's green eyes. He looked nervous and unsure but Caden was the one who had done all of this before. Elias had never gone beyond giving someone a quick blowjob in a car. Elias had met up with guys discreetly to go further but they were usually on drugs and things would never perform the way they should.

The un-sureness in Caden's eyes vanished when he gripped it strongly, the dryness of his hands rubbing against Elias' warm shaft. He worked it for a couple of minutes, watching as tiny droplets appeared on the head. Elias' entire body clenched in an effort not to give in to the overwhelming urge to let go.

Caden's tongue was followed by his mouth and Elias' shaft was soon deep in his throat. He took it like a man who knew what he was doing. Elias imagined the boyfriend back in New York and how stupid he was for letting Caden go. It was like nothing he had ever felt and it made every sense in his body heighten. He could hear a customer downstairs asking how much the brioche was, he could smell the inviting fresh bread lingering up through the small gap in his window and he could feel every hair on his thighs standing on edge as Caden's body rubbed up against him.

Caden didn't question if Elias knew what he was doing, nor did he ask any questions. He kissed the top of Elias' cock before rolling over onto his back. Elias thought he would want the favor returned, but instead he slightly spread his thighs, inviting Elias to do something he had only ever dreamed of.

"Don't we need stuff? Condoms? Lube?" Elias was nervous.

"My wallet," Caden was about to get up, "I've got some –,"

Before Caden could get to the end of the bed, Elias sprinted back into the living room and pulled a thick, brown leather wallet from the back pocket of Caden's jeans. He wore 36" waist, Elias noticed, which was much bigger than his own 28". Not wanting to open his wallet, Elias ran back to the bedroom, where Caden was sitting up slightly, nervous anticipation radiating from every inch of his naked body. Elias felt like he had the figure of a teenager who was waiting for puberty to bulk them out but

Caden looked like a real man.

Caden opened the wallet and pulled out a small gold square, followed by a blue square. Elias caught a glimpse of two photographs in his wallet. One was of Caden's parents and the other of Caden and a stranger, standing underneath what looked like the Empire State Building, grinning down at the camera as it pointed into the sky. It took him a second to realize he was staring at the man who had sent Caden back to Havenmoore. He was blonde, tanned and he looked like he was packing a worked out body under that tight tank top. Before Elias could study it any further, Caden was ripping open the first wrapper and before he could ask questions, he was sliding it slowly down Elias' shaft, which fidgeted against the slimy, cold texture of the rubber.

He watched as Caden opened the second packet, which was filled with a clear liquid. That soon vanished in between Caden's legs and Elias knew that if he wanted to go back, it was too late. He stared down at Caden, unsure of why he was even here, but also not really caring at the same time. He was there and that was all he really cared about.

"I've – I -," Elias mumbled, staring down at Caden's face, "are you sure you're ready for this?"

Caden didn't say anything. He closed his eyes and dragged Elias down to kiss him. Their bodies pressed up against each other's and Elias lost himself so deeply in the kiss that he didn't notice Caden's thick thighs wrap around him; nor did he notice the hand guiding his cock into Caden.

They took it slowly at first. Elias was nervous and he didn't want to hurt Caden. He enjoyed the feeling of his solid mass entering Caden, pushing deeper and deeper, the lube aiding them each step of the way. He wanted to take it slow, to savor every second of it, but the same hunger that had taken over Caden when he opened the door, suddenly consumed him.

Elias' arms gripped around Caden's wide shoulders, his tongue forced hungrily into Caden's mouth and his hips thrust against Caden's cheeks. At first, he was unsure if this was what he should be doing right away but the high-pitched moans and whimpers escaping Caden's throat through the kiss only spurred him on.

Sweat instantly poured from his hairline to run down his body. He felt nails digging into the small of his back, edging him deeper and harder. It was unreal and unexpected. He had never done it because he never thought anything could compare to the drugs he was taking. He had been wrong; so wrong. It was better, stronger, and higher than anything he had taken. He bucked his hips, wanting the euphoria to last forever but knowing that the quicker he thrust, the sooner it would be over. He knew he should slow down, to pace himself but it was a double-edged sword. The more sensitive his cock became, the faster he wanted to go. The more Caden begged and moaned through his kisses and growls, the more ravenous the hunger inside became.

Gripping Caden's shoulders like handles, Elias pounded himself into him, feeling every inch of the man beneath him. Face twisted and cock bouncing on his stomach, Caden looked like he was enjoying every second as much as Elias.

It felt like it lasted a lifetime and a split second at the same time. If he could have chosen, it would never have ended. He would have stayed in that place forever. When he tossed his head back, the veins in his neck ripe and ready to burst, Caden's New York ex crossed his mind and he wondered how he could ever cheat on him when it felt like this. He felt his skin turn as hot as coal and then he saw a white blinding light, before it ended in a blur of fuzziness. For a split second, he was blind and deaf, no longer one with his body. His sight returned and he looked down to see Caden's hand jerking his own cock. Still inside Caden, he brushed the hand away and did the job for him, helping him reach that same place. He felt something tighten around his own cock as he watched Caden cover his chest.

Caden's eyes twitched and he wondered if it felt the same on the receiving end. Reluctantly, he pulled out and tugged the rubber off to tie it up and toss it on top of the overflowing trashcan. Exhaustion took over him and he could do nothing but collapse into Caden's side, where his body was ready to wrap around him.

It was only late morning but he felt his eyelids already

fluttering. He wanted to say something, to ask some questions but as he inhaled the mixture of man, sweat and sex, he wanted nothing more than to fall asleep in the arms of somebody he had just made love to.

***

If it wasn't for the crash of metal trays in the bakery below, Caden could have slept for a lifetime. He crawled into his clothes, looking down at Elias' naked body, glad that none of it was a dream. When he woke Elias, he looked as confused and disorientated as Caden felt. A small smile consumed Elias' face when he remembered what they had done and it let Caden know it hadn't been a mistake.

When he got ready that morning to go to Elias' apartment, having sex with him hadn't been on his mind. It hadn't even crossed his mind until he was standing in front of him and then he could think of nothing else. He had wanted to tell Elias that they had to ignore the kiss they had shared for the sake of their working relationship but that all went out of the window when he saw his face. His heart had swelled as well as the member in his jeans.

Both now clothed, they headed out of the tiny apartment, grabbed some coffee and walked slowly down to the docks. By mid-afternoon, they were sitting under the warm sun, feet dangling over the edge of a jetty as they stared out at the fishing boats scattered across the horizon. Caden could see the town's tall white lighthouse in the far distance. Sipping his coffee, he tried to spot his dad's boat but he knew he didn't always stick to Havenmoore's waters.

"I feel like I should explain myself," Caden sat his coffee in between them, "and apologize."

"Wasn't that your apology?"

"That wasn't supposed to happen."

"Do you wish it hadn't?"

Caden thought for a second but he couldn't lie. He couldn't deny that it had been the best sex of his life and that it trumped anything he had ever done with Finn, or the two guys before Finn. *I never knew I could be fucked like that.*

"No," Caden shook his head, "that was – I'd do it again in a heartbeat."

A boyish smirk played with Elias' lips as he squinted out towards the sun reflecting on the calm surface. Caden was beginning to wonder how he ever thought he could turn his back on him.

"I'm sorry for everything. I freaked and I panicked. I didn't want to ruin your chances. I thought I'd stepped over the line and I thought you'd be better off without me. I don't even know what this is."

They sipped their coffee in silence and Caden could tell Elias was trying to figure out what it was.

"It's new," Elias said, "I've never done this with anybody before."

"You've never had a boyfriend?"

Elias bowed his head, a wry smile on his lips. Caden could sense what he was about to say next.

"I never got close. That was the first time I –,"

Caden had never had sex with a virgin before and he never had Elias down as one. A tiny part of him was starting to regret what they'd done but a louder and more vocal part was wondering how he could possibly get even better with practice. The excitement made something stir, so he studied a tiny white boat in the distance and he tried to guess how many lobsters they would have caught today.

"We can't tell anybody."

"I wasn't planning to," Elias jumped right in.

"It's not that I'm ashamed, it's just that I don't want to hurt my mom. Helping Hands Outreach is her baby and something like this could ruin her reputation."

Elias smiled again as he turned to Caden, "For a second I thought it was because I'm an addict."

"You're Elias before that," Caden smiled right back, slightly hurt that he would think that, "that's all I see."

"You must be the first person to," the smile saddened and

Caden knew exactly who he was thinking about.

Caden's mind also wandered to the mayor because she had played a big part in making Caden see that he was better helping Elias than anybody, because he understood. He felt like he saw into Elias and he wasn't entirely sure why. From the first moment they'd met, it was an instinct. Caden's mom had always said he saw the best in people and it was one of the things she loved about him. After what Finn had done to him, he had wondered if he could ever do that again. He hadn't questioned Finn and his best friend spending more time with each other. An affair had never crossed his mind because he wanted so badly to believe that people didn't do that. Boyfriends didn't sleep with best friends, just like support workers didn't sleep with the people they were supposed to be helping. That brought him back to the instinct. From that very first meeting, when Elias had wanted nothing to do with Caden, he had felt a pull towards him. Perhaps this was exactly what Elias needed; perhaps this is what they both needed.

The afternoon sun licked Caden's skin as he picked at the plastic edges of the coffee cup lid. It was more than a need, it was a want and a desire. He desired Elias in a way that he had never desired another man. *Is that because it's against the rules?*

"I like you, Elias," Caden whispered, "I like you a lot."

Even that didn't feel good enough. '*Like*' seemed too tame a word to explain the ravenous fire eating away at him. There was so much more to it than that. They barely knew each other but Elias had been enough to stop Finn even crossing his mind. Caden had noticed Elias eyeing up the photograph in his wallet and he felt like a fool for even having it there. It was burning a hole in his back pocket as he sat there, but for all the wrong reasons. Elias was no more a rebound than Finn's adultery was a silly mistake. If he stopped to think about it, he had never desired Finn like that. It had just been something that happened. Ever since the beginning of their relationship, things had just happened and Caden had gone along with it. He thought that's what life was about, finding somebody in your early twenties and going through the motions. As he sat on the jetty, a man quickly approaching his thirties in a situation that some would call a mid-life crisis, he had never felt more alive.

"Y'know that thing we did earlier?" Elias said casually, "I think I want to do it again. Right now."

Caden's cock instantly sprung to attention and without wasting any time, they headed straight back to his apartment to repeat their antics, this time in the shower. After another round on the couch and another in the kitchen, Caden noticed the setting sun and he knew there was somewhere he needed to be. He dressed, for what felt like the tenth time that day and Elias walked him to the door, a sad feeling in the air.

"When will I see you again?" there was fear in Elias' voice.

"I'm not supposed to be here until the end of the week, but you have my number. Call me tonight."

Caden opened the door and was surrounded by the smell of baked goods. They kissed again, both of them dragging it out, neither wanting it to end. Caden was in a pink cloud of lust and after the best sex of his life, which had been topped by each draining orgasm, he felt like nothing could bring him down.

"The second you're free of that rehab, I'm going to shout this from the rooftops," Caden whispered through the promise, "you're too good to be my secret."

"Your secret?" Elias whispered back, "does that mean I'm yours?"

"I want you to be mine."

"I'll have to cancel my dates with Havenmoore's other eligible bachelors, but I guess I can do that," Elias winked as he pulled away, his tongue running over the metal ring in his lip.

"Sorry for the inconvenience," Caden stepped out into the darkening alley.

They said their goodbyes and the second Elias closed the door, Caden already missed him. It felt silly and immature, kind of like the high school fling that everybody should have, except for the closeted gays who are too scared to talk to the other guys they suspect are gay. It made him feel giddy and excited for the future. The consequences of what it could do to his mom were crammed up in the back of his mind, because Elias was taking up the rest.

Pulling out his wallet, he wriggled out the picture from happier times and tossed it straight into the dumpster without a second look. He walked out into the street where the baker was locking up. He shot Caden a look that said '*I know what you've been doing up there*' and he second-guessed if his cries of pleasure had been as quiet as he had thought.

When he headed into the mayor's office, Elias was still on his mind. This had been in his plan, before they jumped into bed together and he knew when the post-sex glow vanished, his mind would be back on trying to get Elias' life into a better place. He asked the surly faced receptionist if he could see the mayor but when asked if he had an appointment he was quickly denied entry to her inner sanctum.

"Can I leave a message?" his question was met with a sigh that told him his message would probably never get to Judy James, but it was worth a shot.

The receptionist tossed him a blank notepad and a heavy, expensive feeling pen. She looked like she was thinking of ending her workday so she could go home. Caden quickly scribbled down the speech he had prepared to give to the mayor. He jotted down his phone number at the bottom and signed it before sliding it back to the receptionist. Without a second glance at the note, she dropped the pad back onto her desk and gave Caden a smile that read '*please leave so I can*'.

"What's with the smile?" his mom looked up from the huge pan of surprise soup she was making, "You look like the cat who got the cream."

"Am I not allowed to smile without a reason?" he shrugged, taking a seat at the table, suddenly feeling hungry from his day of extensive cardio.

His dad glanced over the top of his newspaper and he shared the same look as the baker. Shrugging naughtily, Caden started to flick through the letters on the table. When he noticed one addressed to him, he instantly recognized the New York returnee address in the corner.

The bubble burst and he came crashing down to earth in an

instant. Not wanting to sink beneath the earth's crust and deep into his molten core, he stuffed the letter into his jeans and forced back the smile. All he had to do was think about the things he and Elias had done and it returned in an instant.

"How long till dinner, Mom? I'm starving!"

Chapter 11

They couldn't keep away from each other. From the second Caden left Elias' apartment, Elias watched the small LED clock on the stove, wondering when it was the right time to call to arrange something. They spent over an hour on the phone, chatting about nothing and everything. It was nice, so nice in fact that after they finally hung up with plans to see each other the next day, Elias wanted to call him again.

He felt obsessed and completely attached to Caden. He wondered if it was his addictive personality kicking in, or something new. He wasn't sure that people could get addicted to other people, but if it was possible, he couldn't get enough fixes of Caden.

The next day, they met up in the town square and went to a park, where they talked about everything from school to Caden's life in New York. It turned out, they went to the same schools as kids and they had most of the same teachers but they were years apart. Elias also learned that Caden seemed to be dreading his thirtieth birthday. He was acting like it was the end of his life, which Elias found hilarious.

They grabbed ice cream and sat on a bench, watching the rest of the world pass by. Their conversation died down, but the silence wasn't awkward. It was nice to sit in each other's company without forcing something to talk about. When Elias reached the bottom of his cone, ice cream running down the back of his fingers, something to talk about was walking towards them.

"Isn't that your sister?" Caden pointed Ellie out at the same time that she noticed them.

Elias looked around for Kobi, knowing that she wouldn't have come to the park alone. It took him a couple of seconds but he spotted his dark hair in a group of kids who were busy chasing birds around the grass without a care in the world.

He almost thought she would turn and head in a different direction, pretending she hadn't seen him, but she surprised him and carried on walking, even if a little reluctant.

"Hey," Elias shielded his eyes from the sun, "what's up?"

"It's my day off," she hovered, keeping her distance, "I thought I'd bring Kobi to the park. I was just coming to sit on – never mind."

"Here," Elias moved over, cramming himself up next to Caden, "don't stand because of me."

She looked suspicious and he could tell she was trying to figure out why he was in such a good mood. The last time she had seen him, he had looked like death warmed over and he was begging for sleeping pills. That had only been a couple of days ago. A lot had changed since then.

"So -," she looked out.

"So," Elias couldn't pull up a normal talking point to discuss with his twin and he could sense that she couldn't either.

Caden sat on the end, blissfully unaware as he finished off his ice cream, squinting into the sun as it lit up his hair.

"You look good," she said, "get some sleep?"

"Lots," he fidgeted slightly and he felt Caden do the same,

"yeah, I feel good."

"Good."

The silence continued for a couple of seconds and they both watched Kobi play with his friends and he was completely unaware that his mother and uncle were observing him. Elias was glad that he hadn't noticed him because if he did, he had run straight over and Ellie would probably whisk him away with another speech about him being the world's worst uncle. He couldn't blame her. He felt the cleanest he had felt in a long time but he wasn't giving his sister that impression. *Why did I have to ask her for sleeping pills? She'll never trust me now.*

"He's growing so fast."

"They do that," she nodded, "you've missed a lot."

Her words were casual, but sharp. Caden sensed it too because he gently rubbed his elbow against Elias, telling him to let it slide. He wanted to let his sister in on what had changed but he couldn't let the secret out, not after he had promised Caden he wouldn't say anything. He didn't even know what they were.

"It's his birthday soon."

"No," she shook her head, "I mean, yes, he's having a party and no, you're not invited. I can't risk it. John will never allow it."

"I wasn't -," he sighed heavily, knowing it was going to take a long time to iron out the creases of his past mistakes, "I was just saying. Can I get him something? You can give it to him."

She thought for a second, tucking her short black hair behind her diamond studded ears. A quick nod let him know that was okay. He didn't have a clue what to buy a kid turning seven, nor did he know what kind of things Kobi liked. He vaguely remembered that he liked *Hot Wheels* years ago but kids never stayed liking the same things for long. He almost asked, but that would make him look even worse in Ellie's eyes.

"You keep smiling," Ellie said without looking at him, "what's happened to you?"

"Can't I smile?" Elias laughed.

"No. It's weird. You don't usually."

Was it that obvious that he had sex yesterday? He felt like

everybody they saw could tell but it probably wasn't that visible to the naked eye. Two people, walking around a park with smiles on their face was probably a normal sight and nobody else could see the pink haze surrounding them.

"Things are looking up."

She turned to look at him, her lips still pursed. It was as though she didn't believe a single word that left his mouth. He had spent so many years lying through his teeth, he wasn't surprised she was suspicious of his every move. Even she must have noticed that he had never stayed clean this long before after leaving rehab. Elias had already broken his own record and he only had a couple of weeks until his drug test, which would spell the end of his aftercare and the beginning of his life as a free man.

"It suits you. You need a haircut," she tilted her head to look at him, "and you could take those piercings out. Somebody might want to employ you."

"I like them," Caden spoke up for the first time, following it up by a cough, "I mean, they suit him. Don't you think?"

It was Caden's turn to have Ellie's suspicious eyes on him. Elias got the piercings as an act of defiance and rebellion when he was seventeen, around the same time he started using cocaine. Back then, he thought he was the one in control. It wasn't until his early twenties that he was ready to admit it controlled him but by then, it was too late.

"I guess," she wasn't going to start arguing with somebody she barely knew, which pleased Elias, "have you started looking for a job yet?"

"Caden was talking about getting me in a GED program," he wondered if that pre-argument offer still stood, "it'll still be hard to find one but a diploma might help."

She made a throaty grunt of agreement and she almost seemed annoyed that he seemed to be on top of things. He knew she was trying to catch him out and he liked being able to be honest about things.

"My friend Jenny, she works at that big grocery store on the other side of town. I could give her your number, if you want?"

Ellie mumbled, almost silently.

"Sure," Elias nodded, "yeah, do it."

He doubted anything would come of it. They'd only need to look at his record to see that he was practically unemployable. Theft, breaking and entering, supplying and using drugs were hardly the traits you looked for when seeking out a new employee. The diploma might help outweigh them slightly, but until he put some distance between him and his last offense, he would probably have to keep living off his welfare checks.

Ellie's phone beeped and she pulled it out to check what it was. After reading a rather long text message, she sighed and crammed her cell back into her black skinny jeans, muttering curse words under her breath.

"Why is it impossible to find a babysitter in this town?" she huffed, "They always cancel. When I was a kid, we were fighting over each other to get these jobs and now girls are turning them down to go to parties with boys."

"You and John have plans?"

"We've been trying to go out for a meal for months, just the two of us. Tonight is the first night in months that we haven't both been working. He got us reservations at this really nice restaurant in Portland and - I guess I'll have to call and cancel. I'll never find somebody this late in the day. We'll just have to wait until The Medical Ball to go out."

A flicker of disappointment and exhaustion washed across her face and Elias knew his idea was bold but it was worth a shot.

"I could –,"

"No. Whatever you were about to say, don't."

"Fine!" he knew it was a long shot that Ellie would let him look after Kobi for a whole night, "It was just an idea."

"A terrible idea."

They all sat in silence again, staring at the kids playing. This was the most time he had spent with Kobi in years and Kobi didn't even know he was there. The wall he had to jump over still felt as high as ever, even though he felt like he was crawling up it. Would Ellie ever think he was ready?

"What about me?" Caden said, "I'm free tonight."

Ellie leaned forward, the frown vanishing. She was actually considering it. She looked from Caden to Kobi, wondering if it was a good idea. She knew he worked for a charity, so he was responsible and she probably hadn't figured out how close Caden and Elias were from the piercing remark.

"Are you sure? He can be a little uneasy when we're not there."

"I have a niece," was all it took to convince Ellie that it was a good idea.

She allowed her stern face a quick smile and jumped up, saying that she needed to head home to start getting ready, despite it only being two in the afternoon. She scribbled down her address on a tiny piece of paper, even though she could have just asked Elias to tell him.

"I hope you're not going to invite a girl around when the baby is asleep so you can make out," Elias nudged him as they stood up.

"I'm not that kind of babysitter," he nudged back, "I thought we could hang out but did you see her face when that girl cancelled? I thought she was going to cry."

"I don't think I've ever seen her cry," Elias tried to think back.

Even at their grandmother's funeral, Ellie had kept the same stiff upper lip as their mother. Elias had cried, sobbed even. She was one of the few family members he had actually been close to and she was the only connection he had to his father, not that she liked to talk about him either. He could tell it was too painful and he never saw her that often. It was no secret that his mom and grandmother hated each other. When she died around Elias' tenth birthday, he felt like she had left him to deal with the mayor on his own and he hated her for it. His tears at her funeral were as much grief as they were fear.

"Well, I guess we can still hang out," Elias shrugged, "just call me when they've gone."

They walked in silence until they reached the gate of the park and it wasn't until Elias looked at Caden that he sensed some slight friction.

"I don't think that's a good idea," Caden clenched his eyes, "It's just – your sister – she seemed pretty *sure* that she didn't want you to see him and kids don't keep secrets too well. If she found out, it'd come back to me and how would that look."

"Right."

It made sense, it just surprised him that Caden was taking Ellie that seriously. Ellie didn't want Elias to see Kobi because she was convinced he was going to slip up at any moment but Caden surely knew that Elias wasn't going to? They walked back to Elias' apartment in a stuffy silence, only talking when they were sitting on the couch.

"Do you trust me?"

"I trust you," he nodded, "but your sister doesn't and I can't change her mind."

"I know, I know," he sighed, "I just feel like she'll keep moving the goalposts every time I make some progress."

"It's still early days. Give her time. It's only been a couple of weeks."

Elias knew he was right, he just wished he could fast forward to the bright future people always talked about. He felt like he was waiting for a better version of Elias to take over and win people back. Would that ever happen? It suddenly struck him that he was treating life like a rehearsal. *I thought the coke would have gotten to me by now.*

"That GED program. I want to do it," he nodded, "I don't want to be '*Elias the ex-addict*'. I don't know what I want to be, but I want to be something."

The proudest smile Elias had ever seen spread across Caden's face. It was the face he had always expected from his mom whenever he aced a test in elementary school. She had never bat an eyelid because Ellie's score was always guaranteed to be better. Elias always felt like a spare and that his mom put all of her legacy eggs into Ellie's basket. Caden looked at Elias like he was the only thing in the world that mattered. He had looked at him like that ever since they'd first met. At first, he had thought it was patronizing but he liked it.

"You'll be a great something," Caden leaned his head against the back of the couch, "we'll figure it out. Something will naturally fit you."

"We'll see," Elias had never been exceptionally good at anything, except fucking up – *If fucking up was a job, I'd be the boss in no time.*

"I feel like that too. We all do. I'm doing this job to pay my mom back. I want to write, but I don't have the balls. I'm scared to fail so I don't try."

"Let's try together. I'll get my diploma and you can finish your book. Deal?"

Elias held his hand out and Caden looked down at it, scared to make such an unbreakable promise on something he clearly didn't believe in. He accepted the handshake nonetheless, even if it was a little shaky.

They spent the rest of the afternoon discussing potential jobs for Elias and potential book titles for Caden. They didn't have sex and they didn't need to. When they weren't enjoying each other's bodies, they were enjoying each other's minds and that relieved Elias. He wondered if the amazing sex had clouded things and Caden would realize what a mistake he had made, but he stuck around until he needed to get ready to leave for Ellie's. When he left, he kissed Elias so deeply on the step of his apartment, it made him wish they'd spent their afternoon doing other things, as well as talking.

"Can I see you tomorrow?" Elias asked.

"I'd already counted on it," Caden bit heavily into his still moist lips.

Elias didn't go back into his apartment until he couldn't see Caden anymore. He folded his arms and stared up at the blue sky. It wasn't until the baker appeared to toss some bags in the trash that he realized how strange he looked. The baker glared at him through slits, his face covered in flour and sweat. Already missing Caden's company, he headed up to his apartment, with no idea what he was going to do.

***

Caden's mom found it hilarious that he had agreed to babysit, making the same comparisons to teenagers that Elias had. His dad commented that it wasn't that different to his day job, which they both took offense to. His mom assumed he was doing it for the money and she told him he could cancel to free up his evening but he said he didn't mind. His mom assumed that he would spend the evening with them, watching some cop show on TV until one or all of them fell asleep from the suffocating heat of the log burning fire. Eventually, she was going to notice him spending a lot of time out.

Ellie's house was nice, so nice that he had to check the address twice to make sure he had the right place. It was in a part of town that he walked past every day after high school, marveling at the beautiful buildings, set back in their own lavish gardens, all encased in an ornate, wrought iron fence. He even had to buzz to be let through the gate. As he walked towards the front door where Ellie was already waiting for him, handbag on her arm and scarf around her elbows, he wondered how a set of twins from the same mother could have such drastically different lives.

"You're early," she smiled, "and so am I. John's at the restaurant already. Had to go straight after work. All the numbers are on the fridge and eat whatever you want. The nice wine's in the cellar, so help yourself. Kobi's bedtime is eight but he might be restless because I'm not here so if he can't sleep, warm cookies and milk usually work. If they don't, well, I guess he can stay up, but no later than nine-thirty. Got that? Nine-thirty? If it's any later he'll be Damien from The Omen in the morning and I'm doing the school run. We shouldn't be too late. Midnight at the *latest*. We're both working and - ,"

"Have a nice time!" Caden nodded, practically pushing her out of the door, her spicy and floral perfume filling the hall.

She looked at him, as though she was about to start rambling again but she quickly turned on her heels and headed for the gate, an excited and girlish spring in her step.

Caden kicked off his sneakers, feeling rather underdressed

for the house. It was big, bigger than anything a Havenmoore doctor could afford, which made him wonder what John did for a living. Pulling his canvas bag over his head, he followed the sound of cartoons as he checked his watch. He had an hour and a half to entertain Kobi before attempting to get him off to bed. He had looked after Becca plenty of times to know that it could go one of two ways. Kobi would be eager to show Caden how well behaved he was and he would happily go to bed at the asked time, maybe trying to push his luck by asking for cartoons in bed, or, he would point blank refuse, he would draw on the walls, set fire to the cat and become '*Damien from The Omen*' twelve hours earlier than scheduled.

Kobi was sitting cross-legged in front of the TV, watching a brightly colored Japanese style cartoon. It wasn't in English but it had subtitles. His head bobbed along and he seemed to be following what was going on. He looked up warily at Caden, before looking back to the gigantic TV screen that was so big it was practically a cinema-size but it still didn't fill the vast room with the impossibly high ceiling.

Perching on the edge of the sofa, Caden waited for Kobi to approach him, not wanting to force anything. By the time of the first commercial break, he was glancing over his shoulder with curiosity and by the second, he decided to wander over to stare at Caden from the sofa's arm.

"I remember you," he said, "you were with my Uncle Elias at the Lobster Festival."

Caden had almost forgotten about that. It always surprised him how freakishly good kids memories were. He wondered if it was because they had less things to worry about. Did bills, work, money and relationships cloud your memory, making you forget how great it was when you were younger?

"You did. What's this you're watching?"

"Anime," he said, rather proud, "it's my favorite. Well, my new favorite. Mommy says I change my mind too much but Daddy says I'm entitled to. It's from Japan. Sometimes the voices are in English but they never match the mouths so I don't mind reading the words on the bottom."

"How do you keep up? I keep losing track."

"It's really easy," he boasted, "I can read really fast. My teacher said so."

He was a couple of years older than his niece but he still had that childlike wonder that you always hope they don't lose when puberty hits.

"Do you like to read?"

"Sometimes. If Mommy gives me her tablet, I read books on that but she doesn't always let me because she says she's shopping."

"What about real books?"

Kobi shrugged, a slight look of confusion on his face. He wanted to make a remark about '*kids these days*', but he knew how old that would make him sound and feel.

"Daddy says they're useless," Kobi added, "he says they're dust collectors and our cleaner, Helena is allergic to dust. That's what Mommy said. She said she must be allergic to dust because she never cleans under the bed."

Caden held back the laughter as Kobi spelled out his parents' relationship, not understanding what he was actually saying.

"I love books. I love the smell."

"What do they smell like?" Kobi scrunched up his face.

Zipping open the bag that held his laptop and the current book he was reading, he plucked out the thick copy of *The Bone Clocks* by David Mitchell. Opening it in the middle, he inhaled the ink and wood pulp that always brought him comfort, even if he didn't know why. He offered it to Kobi, who gave it a quick sniff. He didn't seem as impressed.

"Smells like words," he shrugged, "are you Uncle Elias' friend?"

Just hearing Elias' name made Caden miss him. They'd only been apart for a couple of hours but he couldn't help but think that they'd be together now if he hadn't offered to babysit.

"We are friends," he nodded, deciding if Caden didn't understand the true nature of their relationship, a six-year-old wouldn't, "I like him a lot."

"I like him too," he looked sad, "but Mommy says I can't see him because he's sick and Daddy says that he's a waste of space and a drain on society."

The words fell out of his mouth without the weight John probably originally said them with. He felt sorry for Kobi because he wouldn't understand the real reason he couldn't see his uncle. He was being punished, deprived of somebody who loved him and even though it was Elias' fault, Kobi wouldn't get that until he was older. Caden hoped before that happened, everything would be fixed and they'd be able to make new, happy memories. Caden was going to make sure of that.

"When can I see him?"

"Soon."

"You promise?"

Why did I say soon?

"Hopefully," Caden's smile was weak.

"That's not the same thing," Kobi scowled, "A promise, you have to put your little finger out and then if you break that promise, your finger falls off and a carrot grows in its place. That's what Sammie Harris said and Sammie Harris is always right about these things."

"I don't doubt it."

Kobi held out his little finger but Caden couldn't promise. He was sure, so sure that Elias was on the right path now, but he couldn't speak for Ellie. From what he could figure out, her husband, John, didn't like Elias at all.

"Your show is back on," Caden nodded to the TV, hoping to be able to get some of his book written after spending all afternoon telling Elias that he could do whatever he set his mind to.

"I've seen this one before," he shrugged, jumping up on the couch next to Caden, "it's my birthday next week. I'm having a party. Are you coming?"

"I don't think I'm invited."

"I'll invite you," Kobi shrugged, leaning his head against his hand as he let out a wide yawn, "I'm allowed to bring ten friends and no more. Mommy is bringing loads of her friends even though it's my birthday. Daddy isn't coming because he's working. He's a lawyer so he'll be in the courts with the Judge and the Judy."

"You mean Jury?"

Kobi shrugged and yawned again, his eyelids flickering. It wasn't even half past seven and he was already falling asleep. Caden half hoped Kobi would stay awake to distract him from having to work on his book. *Coward.*

"I asked if I could have Uncle Elias as one of my friends but Mommy said he wasn't a friend and Daddy said if he came he'd call the police because of what happened last time but I thought it was really funny when he fell asleep in my cake. We all laughed about it at school and everybody thought he was the best uncle ever."

"You really miss him, huh?"

Kobi nodded again but he didn't speak. He sunk deep into the back of the sofa, making it look huge. It only took a couple of minutes of the colorful cartoons for his eyes to close and only another couple for his chest to softly rise and fall. Scooping him up in his arms, Caden carried him upstairs. Luckily for him, Kobi's bedroom was labeled out of the many white doors on the landing. His bedroom was filled with toy boxes but it was starkly neat and tidy for a little boy's bedroom. Placing him gently on the bed, he looked down at his flickering lids, noticing how much he really did look like his uncle. He wondered if this is what Elias would have looked like when he was a kid. He imagined Elias that age, living in a house very similar, wondering why his mom wouldn't hug him or why his sister had more brains. Closing the curtains and flicking on the night light that projected stars on the ceiling, he left Kobi to his dreams, knowing that he would wake up in the morning refreshed, probably not remembering that anybody but his parents had been there the night before.

When he was back downstairs, he watched the cartoon for a couple of minutes but the constant flashing commercials advertising crazy toys and movies he didn't want to see soon started to irritate him. He flicked through the channels, most of which were blocked. *Why didn't I ask for the parental code?* Glancing to the shiny white surface of the laptop that poked out of his bag, he flicked off the TV, knowing that he would have to face it eventually.

He was greeted by a picture of him and Finn, standing in front of the Disneyland Castle as his screensaver. It was the vacation of a lifetime and it cost them both most of their tiny savings. Looking at the happy smiling faces, he could almost forget that they spent most of the vacation arguing and they flew home a day early. After he quickly changed the wallpaper, he navigated his way into his messy folders and found the manuscript. The second it opened, he felt guilty for not working on it. The word count told him that he had gotten thirty thousand words into the book. *Pathetic.* Scrolling slowly to the bottom of the document, he started reading where he had left off, hoping it would jog his memory. *This is trash.* Paragraph by paragraph, he scrolled up, reading it out of sequence and deleting each paragraph. *Did I write this?* Wondering why he had ever tried to write a fantasy book, he closed the document and opened a new page. When his fingers started typing, he didn't know what he would write about but when he was taken to a New York apartment on a bright afternoon, he soon knew where it was going. When he got to the part where the main character, Haden, caught his boyfriend, Glynn, in bed with his best friend, Ant, he stopped writing and slammed the laptop shut, angry that his brain had recycled that memory. Nobody would want to read that. *I don't even want to read that.* The letter from Finn was still burning a hole in his back jeans pocket. He had toyed with it all night, unable to open it. He had held it up to the light, hoping he would be able to make out something but he couldn't. A small part of him wanted to hear the feeble and pathetic excuses but another part knew it would only make him angry. At first, he had had no idea why he had even written a letter but then he remembered how he had been refusing to log into any social media and how he had changed his cell number. Pulling out his phone, he scrolled through the contacts before selecting one and pressing it into his ear.

"Hi. It's me. I need to see you."

Chapter 12

Elias approached his old childhood home, the feelings of old flooding back in a heartbeat. No matter how long he spent away from it, it still had the ability to make him feel like that useless, pointless child all over again. *Will that ever go away?* He was about to knock on the door but he remembered that Caden was inside and he had just buzzed him through the gate. The gate was a new touch and he wondered if it was to keep him away from the house. He wouldn't put it past John to go to that extreme. Elias had turned up at the house enough times in the middle of the night to warrant it.

"Hi," Caden was waiting for him on the other side of the door with a kiss, "Kobi's asleep upstairs."

"I thought you didn't want me here?"

"Technically, you're not seeing Kobi. You're seeing me and I really missed you."

Elias was glad to hear that because he had spent the last couple of hours watching some trash about a gang of fame hungry sisters who all had long black hair and large butts.

Caden showed him through to the living room, not that Elias needed showing anywhere. It may have been redecorated many times since he lived there as a kid but it was still the same underneath. His mom had handed the house over to Ellie the second she found out she was pregnant and Elias was sure she was glad to be rid of the place. She spent their whole childhood avoiding it. Ellie said it was because it reminded her of their dad but he was sure it reminded her of her children. She was much more suited to the sterile, luxury apartment on the outskirts of town.

"I tried writing," Caden pushed his laptop off the sofa, making room for Elias, "but the words wouldn't flow. I wonder if I'm cut out for it."

"Didn't you write in New York? For newspapers?"

"Kobi could have done that. They gave me the information, I just filled in the blanks with a couple adjectives and connectives. Writing fiction is a whole different ballgame."

Elias kicked off his shoes and crawled up on the couch next to Caden. He hesitated for a second before he nuzzled into Caden's warm side. Instantly, he felt at home, despite being somewhere he would happily watch burn to the ground. Caden flicked on the TV and settled on an old black and white horror movie after a short search. It didn't matter what they watched, he was just glad to be in his company.

"How did your sister afford this place?" Caden wrapped his arm around Elias' shoulder, pulling him in even tighter.

"She didn't. My mom owns it. She gave it to her."

"Just like that?"

"Just like that."

It's what she does. She gave Ellie her grand house in the suburbs; she gave Elias a shoebox in town and ignored their existence the rest of the time. It was all part of her control game, always letting them know that she was really in charge of them and the town, even if she had never been able to pin Elias down.

"I didn't tell you, but I spoke with your mom earlier this week. It was my dad's birthday and I bumped into her in that new restaurant and she flipped out. I mentioned you and she flipped out even more. It was like seeing a whole different person to the woman everybody sees at public events."

"She actually let you see her without her mask on?" Elias seemed surprised, "Aren't you lucky?"

Elias wasn't surprised that the mention of his name caused her to let her guard slip. Caden was lucky to get out of there without a gag order or a threat to sue. Not much could derail her record breaking tenure as mayor of Havenmoore but the revelation of a son who was a criminal and an addict might just make that train shake enough for somebody else to sneak into the lead to snatch her crown. He always wondered who Judy James would be if she wasn't mayor.

"I feel like if we just get you all together, in one room, we could really make progress."

Elias wriggled out of Caden's grip to check if he was being serious. The middle of his brow was pinched in thought and that almost made Elias laugh.

"There's no progress to be made," he made sure he sounded final, "there's no relationship."

"Every wall can be rebuilt. You're still family."

"A wall without foundations is just a pile of bricks," Elias moved even further away, "you don't have to keep being all support workery with me. I thought we were beyond that?"

"I still want to help you. I still have a job to do."

Elias couldn't tell if he was being serious. He stood up and walked a few steps into the center of the living room as the movie soundtrack suddenly picked up, ancient screeching violins rattling through the dulled down surround sound.

"I don't need that kind of help. I have what I need. The help has been done."

"There's still more we can do," he felt Caden stand, "Helping Hands Outreach has a great -,"

"No!" Elias laughed, "Why are you slipping back into shrink mode? Jesus, Caden, this is why I didn't like you at first. That shit doesn't help me. It *irritates* me. It gets under my skin and it makes me doubt my sanity. This is the first time I've ever felt sane. The first time I've ever felt like maybe I could have some chance at getting out of this turd hole. I don't need you to tick boxes with me. They're all ticked. Job done. In a couple of weeks, we'll be out of that situation and everybody will congratulate you on an amazing job keeping me clean and then by the time they find out we're a couple, it'll be too late for anything to be against any dumb rules."

Elias' skin burned as his heart raced. His mind was so clear; it was processing so much at once. He had got so used to chemically slowed functions, he forgot what his mind could do.

"I just want to help."

He felt a hand on his shoulder but he shrugged it away so he could turn around. A genuine look of hurt dragged down the corners of Caden's eyebrows.

"You are helping," Elias looked up to the ceiling, "this is what I was trying to tell you when you quit. Just you being near me is all the help I need. You make me feel safe, you make me feel calm and you make me feel normal. It's like you're shelter from all of the things that turn me bad. When I'm with you, I'm not thinking about drugs or my past or any of that, I'm just thinking about you and me. Ever since that time I nearly kissed you in your bedroom, you're all I've been able to think about. I stopped drinking because you told me to. I turned down free coke because I promised you I wouldn't. I don't understand it because I don't think there's an explanation. Fate is a bullshit thing that hippies believe in, but if I believed in it, this would be it. You didn't even live in Havenmoore. You didn't even work in this job. We should never have even met, but we did, and something happened and that's all I need. I don't need counseling or sessions or therapy, I just want to be normal. That's all I've ever wanted."

"I make you feel normal?" Caden's cheeks burned bright, as though he felt stupid for even trying to suggest family therapy.

"Like you wouldn't believe. I've never had an anchor. You're my anchor."

"You make me feel so un-normal," he said, "but in the best way. My life in New York, with Finn, it wasn't real. I convinced myself of all of these things until I thought they were true. I thought we were untouchable and in love and it wasn't. With you, I don't have to convince myself of anything. The only thing I had to convince myself of was to stop seeing you and I couldn't even do that for long. I think I – I know I – I want to – I -,"

Elias could feel what was coming next. He could feel the weight of the words about to leave Caden's mouth. He wanted to hear them but he feared them too. He dove in, capturing Caden in a kiss so tight, they both fell back onto the sofa. The words were there, as their lips merged. Caden caught his tooth on Elias' lip ring and they both laughed through the kiss, not stopping. That's how he knew it was there. It was easy and effortless. It was the first relationship in his life that he hadn't needed to try for. His sister, his mom, his dealer, his doctors, his counselors all wanted something and expected something and when Caden wasn't trying to do his job, that's when he truly felt like nothing was being drawn from him, other than the man he was inside. That was the man Elias didn't know existed, but the man Caden had awakened.

"We shouldn't," Caden moaned as his hand travelled down to Elias' already hard shaft, "It's not right."

"He won't wake up."

Elias wasn't sure of that but his authority, as an uncle, seemed to be the permission Caden needed. He rolled onto Elias, switching their places. His fingers fumbled with the belt on Elias' jeans, freeing his cock in seconds. He stood up, yanking his own jeans and underwear down. He produced a condom and rolled it down Elias with such speed that it was snapping around the base before he registered what was about to happen.

Lying flat on the comfy couch, Elias' breath trembled, the anticipation and hunger fresh in his mind. He knew what to expect this time and he was ready for it. They'd used all of the lube the other day so Caden spat into his hand and used that instead. Mounting Elias, he pressed his lips deep against his, their noses squashing together and their facial hair becoming one. He slowly slid down Elias' shaft and the deeper he went, the harder their kisses became. This time, it was Caden who was in control. Elias laid back and let it happen how Caden wanted it to. His knees on either side of Elias' chest, Caden slowly found his rhythm as his hips swayed and twisted back and forth.

Not having control over the speed or pace was like torture for Elias. He wanted to take it to the place where Caden started to let out high pitched groans but this time, it was him doing the groaning.

The kissing stopped but the riding sped up. Caden clenched Elias' hair, gripping it in his fist. He stared down at him, his green eyes glittering around his burning skin. They were still fully clothed and only a minute ago they'd been on the brink of an argument, but as they stared deep into each other's eyes in the middle of an act so intimate, Elias could feel the words that he had stopped Caden saying and this time, he wanted to hear them.

Caden straightened his back and sped up, clutching onto the front of Elias' clothes for support. They were both trying their best to stay quiet but the quicker they fucked, the harder it became to muffle the moans. The horror movie played on in the background but the sinister music didn't take away from the whirlwind of lust and passion that had enveloped them.

"I'm so close," Elias gasped all of a sudden.

He thought Caden was going to slow down, to torture him by taking away the climax, but he didn't. He dove in, to join their faces again, his hips speeding up still. When he didn't think they could go any faster, they did, forcing Caden's grunts so close together. He shot back up and started massaging his own shaft. When he started that, he slowed down a little, but Elias was so close, he couldn't hold back even if he wanted to. Gripping one of Caden's shoulders, he started to fuck him, his buttocks bouncing off the scratchy material of the couch.

A noise louder than either of them had been expecting left Elias' mouth, making Caden use his free hand to clamp it over his lips. The orgasm didn't end and the noise escaped through Caden's fingers. The tingling eventually stopped, just in time for him to see Caden's face tighten up. Despite his own orgasm ebbing away, he knew how in the zone Caden would be; how ready and willing he would be to do anything to reach that high. Resting his chin on his chest, Elias leaned in and took the shaft into his mouth, using his hand to work the exposed flesh. Within seconds, Caden was clenching his buttocks around Elias' still solid cock to release his own load.

"That was -," Caden's voice was cut off by the slamming of a door, "shit!"

It was a quick scramble for belts and jeans as hurried heels marched across the hall. Elias knew the house well enough to know that they didn't have long. He yanked off the condom, forced his wood into his underwear and yanked the jeans over the top. Wearing a floor length black gown, Ellie stormed into the living room to see her brother holding a condom and her babysitter buckling his belt, looking as surprised to see them as they were to see her.

"What -," she gaped.

"I – I -," Caden stuttered.

"You've both got some explaining to do," she pursed her lips so hard that the red lipstick almost vanished into nothing.

***

"I thought I could trust you!" she screamed, less concerned about waking Kobi than they had been, "And here you are, fucking the one man I didn't want in my house on my antique sofa. Will you stop carrying that thing around and toss it in the trash?"

They followed her into the kitchen and Elias sprinted over to the cupboard under the sink where the trashcan was concealed. Caden was so embarrassed that he didn't know if he should start apologizing or just leave. He kept looking to Elias but he looked far too shell shocked to respond. He was her brother so he could imagine it was even weirder for him. He once walked in on Bruce and Lucy having sex one Christmas when they visited him in New York, but hadn't seen Bruce left holding the condom between his thumb and forefinger.

"I can explain," Caden offered, "we can explain. It's not what it looks like."

"So you haven't just fucked my brother on my antique

sofa?" her voice was almost dolphin-register, "Or am I missing something?"

"Technically, he wasn't fucking your brother," Elias mumbled.

"Oh, forget it! I don't want to know after all," she slapped her hands over her ears, "I told you! I told you I didn't want you near my son. And you come here and you do this! Did you have sex with him to see Kobi? Did you think it'd distract him? Is that what this was about?"

She seemed hysterical but Caden couldn't ignore the apparent lack of a husband and the mascara streaks that had been hastily wiped away from her cheeks.

"Oh, Ellie, don't be so dumb. It doesn't suit you!"

"He wasn't here all night. I called him long after Kobi fell asleep. I didn't invite him here for that. It just *happened*."

"You're his support worker, aren't you?" she shook her head and her pin straight black hair sprung out from behind her ears.

"We're kind of a thing," Elias added, "it's not what you think."

"So you're gay?" it was like she didn't know who to attack first.

"I wanted to tell you but I couldn't. Like you said, he's my support worker."

"I've always known," she shook her hands, "that's not important. You think I didn't know how to check an internet history? You were hardly discreet about it."

Caden could tell that Elias was the embarrassed one now. They stared at each other silently and they seemed to be communicating without using their voices.

"So you thought you'd use my brother for a quick fumble?" she turned on Caden, advancing towards him with an outstretched finger, "he's vulnerable and he's an addict and -,"

"- and he's standing right behind you," Elias cried, "damn, Ellie, it's *not* what you think."

"What is it? *Please.* Somebody explain what is going on under my roof. I'm so sorry for asking so many damn questions! I just *assumed* the babysitter wasn't going to turn my living room into a cruising hotspot. I bet you were on that Grinding thing, weren't you? That gay app? Is that how you got him over here? Did you know he used to live here?"

She was reflecting all of the concerns Caden had had about what he was doing with Elias. She made it sound so seedy and dirty. He felt wrong and ashamed, which is why he quit Elias in the first place. He was overwhelmed and Ellie wasn't backing down. Her finger seemed to be growing with every second and he flinched, expecting it to spike through his eye without a moment's notice.

"No," was all Caden could say.

"Give him a break, Ellie," Elias rolled his eyes, "this isn't the first time we've done this."

"How long has this been going on?" she turned back to her brother, "Is this who you kissed when you came begging me for pills? I thought you said that could never work? I thought you said it was over?"

"Look at me!" he laughed, "You said yourself how I was smiling. You said that today! Remember?"

She backed down slightly, shrinking a little. Caden shook his head and took the opportunity to finish buckling up his belt.

"My mom could lose everything over this," Caden almost choked on the words, "if this gets out while he's still under this court thing, everything will fall in."

The gravity of the situation suddenly fell on him. How could he do that to his mother?

"You can't tell anybody," Elias said, "not yet."

"Don't tell me what I can and can't do!" she cried, "In my house."

"This is no more your house than it is mine," Elias laughed, "we're twins and I was born two minutes and 30 seconds before you, so I'm the oldest. When that old witch dies, this won't be yours. This is hers and it will become ours, unless she's put it in her will."

The uncomfortable silence and small cough from Ellie spoke volumes. Elias looked like he was about to burst into a full blown attack but he just laughed silently, shaking his head as he stared at the floor.

"I bet she's left everything to you, hasn't she?"

"You can't be trusted!"

"Right," he nodded, "you used to say that when we were kids. You were always the responsible one and I was always the leftover. The *mistake*."

"That's not true."

"Isn't it?"

"Don't turn this on me! You're the one who went against the one thing I asked. Don't think I'm going to forget that so easily."

Caden couldn't handle it. Their voices were rising with each word and any moment, Kobi would appear at the top of the stairs with sleep in his eyes and no idea what was going on.

"Just stop it!" Caden cried, "You're twins. Stop fighting over every tiny detail. Ellie, I'm sorry I invited him over. I just wanted to see him. I just wanted to spend time with him. The other stuff, it just happened. It wasn't the reason, I swear. I would have asked him to go before you got home. I never wanted you to – I just – I *love* him."

"You what?"

"You love me?"

Caden swallowed and closed his eyes. When he opened them, he would be asleep in front of the horror movie with Elias asleep on his shoulder and it would have all been a bad dream. When he opened them, he had almost identical twins, both glaring at him with the same disbelief in their eyes.

"I can't help it. I know it's fast. I can't explain it. I've tried explaining it to myself but don't they say you know when you know? I was with somebody for five years and I never felt like this. I never felt so – in love. It's insane, I know but -,"

Elias pushed Ellie to the side and she stumbled into the kitchen island as she tripped over her heels. Hands gripped Caden's face, pulling him straight into Elias' lips. It was brief and heated but when he pulled away, those same lips pressed against his ear and whispered four words.

"I love you too."

That was it. He felt it. The fireworks that people always talked about were an understatement. It felt like an atomic bomb had just been detonated in his stomach. Five years of '*I love you too*' from Finn could never compare. This was the real thing, unexplainable, irrational, irregular love.

"Jesus Christ," Ellie poured herself a large glass of wine, "are you two for real? He was in rehab about three weeks ago."

Leaning against the counter, she ran her nails through her hair. It was obvious to Caden that she had more on her mind than her brother for once.

"Could you just try and be happy for me? Just once?"

"I am," she sounded offended.

"Why were you home so early?" Elias looked around the kitchen, "Where's John?"

She drank half of the wine and topped it up instantly.

"I don't know where he is," fingers tightened around the glass, "we had a fight in the middle of the restaurant."

She collapsed onto a stool at the breakfast bar, as if delayed shock was just hitting her. Her shaking hands dragged the vat of wine up to her lips but she could barely drink any through the trembling.

"He started talking about divorce and custody. It all started over something small. It happened so fast. I made a comment about his weight affecting his health when he tried to order the Steak Diane and that was it. He exploded, in front of hundreds of people. Some of my patients were in there. It was mortifying. I didn't mean to upset him. I didn't want to be that person. I didn't want to be like – it doesn't matter."

Elias walked over and wrapped his arm around his sister. Despite everything they'd been through, it was obvious they did love each other. Nothing could take that away and even if they buried it deep away beneath layers of bitterness and anger, it would always come to the surface when one of them needed the other. Caden wondered if that's why Ellie had always been the one to give into Elias when he would beg. In his file, Ellie was referred to as '*the enabler*' but Caden could imagine how difficult it was to turn down a brother when he was in a desperate place. He tried to imagine Bruce in pain, begging for money for one last fix. He knew Bruce would never get to that place but he still didn't like thinking about what it would be like to be in that position. He would want to believe that Bruce meant it was the last one. *No wonder she doesn't want to trust him ever again.*

"Can you not work it out?"

"I don't know if I have the energy," she gulped down a large mouthful of red wine, "that's why I wanted tonight. *Needed* tonight. I thought if we just put a date in the calendar and do something together, we'd get back on track. I'm being honest, things haven't been fine for months. He's been gaining weight and he's been distant. The weight isn't important. That's not the problem. It causes arguments. It's like I can't *stop* myself. We've been at each other's throats, barely talking. He spends a lot more time at the office and – and -,"

Tears started tumbling down her cheeks and Elias looked as surprised to see them as Caden. Neither of them seemed to know what to do as the stern doctor and daughter of the mayor cried in her kitchen, clutching wine like it held all of the answers.

"What is it?"

"Ronda," she choked, fighting back the sobs, "thinks she saw John with another woman leaving a hotel on her trip to Portland. I thought she was joking but when I checked where John's conference was, it was Portland. And the woman she described, she sounded just like his receptionist. Twenty-one and tits under her chin. Blonde, of course. I thought it was a one off, or mistaken identity, or maybe he was just helping her outside. I convinced myself every relationship had one of those incidents. Marriage is *hard* work and I didn't want Kobi to grow up like we did, without a dad."

"Oh, Ellie," Elias looked to Caden for some help, "John is a jerk."

"You've never liked him," she sniffled.

"Because you were always too good for him. Mom told you not to marry the first guy who proposed. Maybe she had a point?"

"Wait, you're siding with her?" Ellie wiped away the tears.

Even Caden couldn't believe his ears. Caden had never heard Elias talk about her like she was his actual mother before. Perhaps there was something there, even if it was just a glimmer. Caden thought about the note he had left with the mayor, wondering if she had read it.

They hung around, until Ellie seemed to forget what she caught them doing and she was too consumed by her own problems, which were being consumed by wine. Caden wanted to mention that it had to stay secret but he got the impression that she wouldn't start airing his dirty laundry when she barely wanted to air her own.

"We should go," Elias whispered as Ellie washed the wine glass, "do you want to stay at my place?"

"Sure," Caden nodded, "I'll help her up to bed. I think she's had a lot to drink. Can you grab my bag from the other room?"

Elias didn't question it. He seemed relieved to be dismissed from sibling duty. He probably wasn't used to it. Caden wasn't used to it. Guys were different. He was usually the one with the drama and even he wouldn't cry in front of his brother. Their relationship didn't work like that and neither of them would know what to do if they started.

Ellie didn't want help up the stairs but he did walk with her. He told her about his plan and she listened. He bent the truth and told her that the mayor had already agreed to be a part of it. When he said that, she agreed too, as though scared to miss out on something her mother was in on. When she was tucked up in bed, he headed back to Elias and they walked arm in arm through the dark to the bakery.

He'll understand. It'll help.

Chapter 13

Salty bacon and creamy eggs tickled Elias' nostrils and the smell of a freshly cooked breakfast woke him for the first time since he had moved into his apartment. Pulling on a t-shirt, he rubbed his eyes and headed into the kitchen. He was met with the sight of Caden's smooth bare cheeks as he cooked breakfast, in nothing more than a tiny, yellow apron.

He was about to make a joke but he decided to observe as he worked, unaware that he had a guest. It was the first time he had woken to Caden in his apartment. It didn't feel empty, cold or too big, like it usually did. He could almost forget that he was living under one of his mother's many roofs.

When he remembered what they'd said to each other the night before in Ellie's kitchen, he smiled. When he remembered how those words had practically driven Ellie to the brink of her sanity, he felt bad for his sister. Elias was falling in and Ellie was falling out. For once, he was the happier twin and he was going to try and enjoy it.

"Morning," Caden grinned when he turned to put the eggs back in the fridge, "how long have you been standing there?"

"Long enough," he flicked his lip ring and glanced down at his naked lower half, where his morning wood was standing to attention.

"Not around naked flames. Safety first."

"Butt cheeks are fine, right?"

"Exactly," Caden slapped his own backside and winked with a playful smile, "c'mon, let's eat. We're going to Ellie's. She called and she wants us there."

"She called?" Elias screwed up his face, wondering why they were being summoned, "What does she want?"

"Didn't say," he shrugged as he placed the plates on the other side of the counter, "but I said we'd be there at eleven."

"And what time is it now?"

"Erm," Caden bent over the counter to check the time on the stove, "just past nine."

"Good," Elias spat into his hand, the other already spreading Caden's cheeks, "we have time for two breakfasts then."

By the time they finally got to the second course, covered in sweat and lacking the apron and t-shirt, the bacon and eggs were stone cold, but they wolfed it down like hungry dogs.

"I need to head out. I promised my mom I'd do something for her," Caden pulled on jeans, sans underwear, "I'll be ten minutes. I'll shower when I get back. You can join me."

It wasn't a question, it was an order and it was an order Elias was all too happy to obey. Despite just being used and spent, the morning wood sprung right back and he knew it would still be there when Caden returned from his errand.

He collapsed onto the sofa, resisting the urge to touch himself. Caden softly kissed him on the top of his head before darting out of the door. The absence in his heart was instant and he didn't doubt that it was love he was missing.

***

Checking that Elias wasn't curtain twitching in the apartment above, he quickly jogged across the square towards the town hall. The doors were already open but he knew if he got there early enough, he might beat the receptionist to her game or at least catch her off guard.

Silently celebrating when he saw the empty desk, he slipped past it like he belonged there, despite his creased t-shirt, sticking up hair and morning breath. He paused outside of her door, the words '*Madame Mayor – Judy James*' engraved on a permanent gold plaque. He almost knocked but he knew a knock could be ignored. He tried the handle and when it wasn't locked, he walked right in.

"Emily, cancel my ten. I have one of my headaches coming on – who the *fuck* are you?"

The niceness switched off and '*one of her headaches*' seemed to vanish instantly as she jolted up alert in her chair.

"We've met before," Caden said, "I work with your son. I left you a note earlier this week. Did you get it?"

The glare in her eyes let him know she had. This time, he wasn't going to let it shake him. He was still in the haze of an intense orgasm, he had a full stomach and he had the love of a good man. One mayor was nothing.

"I think you should leave," she strained a smile and nodded to the door, "before I call for security."

She could call security but Caden hadn't seen any walking around and he guessed that security threats weren't priorities at half past ten in the morning. Closing the door, he wasn't leaving until she listened to him and agreed with what he had to say.

***

When he arrived at his sister's house, she was acting so strange that Elias wasn't entirely sure why they'd been asked to show their faces. His theory that she had wanted to talk about their sofa antics was blown straight out of the water. It wasn't mentioned and her wide-eyed expression told Elias to forget it ever happened, which was unlike Ellie. She could hold onto things for months, years if the thing called for it.

Ellie also didn't mention her husband, nor did she mention her breakdown in the kitchen. When Elias tried to steer the conversation in that direction, her eyes widened even more and he was so scared they were going to pop out of her face, he decided to take the same vow of amnesia.

"Drink?" her smile was fake, "I have soda, or orange juice if you want something a little more fresh."

"Soda is fine. Are you going to tell us why we're here, or do I have to start guessing?"

Ellie produced two cans of soda and he noticed a shake in her hand. When she passed a can to Caden, Elias noticed her eyes holding his for a little longer than what felt natural. Caden was smiling a little too much too. *What is going on here?*

"Where's Kobi?"

"School. Are you guys hungry? I could make us a snack."

"We've just had breakfast," and then some, "Ellie, stop the wholesome mother routine and tell me why we're here. In all of the years you've lived here, you've never once invited me here, so what's changed?"

"I just wanted to be nice," she twirled a piece of black hair around her index finger, "extend an olive branch. It's clear you're trying so I thought I would."

He wanted to believe her but it felt like a lie. Elias knew Ellie enough to know that she didn't extend olive branches because she was always the one to wait for those branches to be extended to her. She had always been the same way. When they were kids, Ellie's best friend, Mia, lived three doors down. They did so much together; anyone would think they were the ones who were twins. One day, Mia took one of Ellie's dolls home and lost it, which caused Ellie to blow up at her friend. It wouldn't have been that important to Ellie but it was an antique doll their grandmother had given her. She never spoke to Mia again and Elias had always known that she missed her, but she would never admit it. The months passed and the seasons changed but Ellie would never make the move to repair the friendship. She refused to apologize for shouting at Mia and Mia was too scared to go anywhere near Ellie. Eventually, Mia and her folks moved out of town and they were never seen or spoken about again but Elias saw his sister's face when that moving van drove away. Even back then, she had that stiff upper lip to conceal all of the emotions she was bottling up.

"You're up to something," he said, "tell me or I'm leaving."

Ellie looked to Caden again, this time begging him to help her. Elias felt like he was the only one not in on the joke as he stood between them, clutching an unopened can of soda. A knock at the door caused Ellie to jump on the spot, seemingly glad of the excuse to leave.

"That'll be her," she mumbled as she walked off.

"Are we expecting somebody else?" Elias turned to Caden.

Caden shrugged, clearly avoiding his eye contact. If he wasn't sure if Caden was in on things, he sure was now. Ditching his soda, he headed for the front door. It wasn't a woman, it was John, Ellie's husband. He was standing on the porch, looking like he didn't want to come in. Ellie's arms were crossed protectively over her chest and she was keeping her distance. Elias didn't like John but it was sad to see. *Is this what it all boils down to?*

"I just want some things. I'm at a motel out of town. It's easier for work that way."

"Alone?"

"Don't do this, Ellie. This doesn't have to be that hard," his words were final.

"It was a dumb fight in a restaurant. Don't turn it into something it isn't," she tried to laugh it off.

"It's not just that, is it? We've been sleeping in separate -," he looked over Ellie's shoulder to spot their audience, "what is he doing here?"

Ellie quickly turned, embarrassment on her face and tears forming in the corners of her eyes. She didn't look angry to see Elias standing there, she actually looked relieved. If he wasn't mistaken, her eyes were crying out for her brother's help. Elias stepped forward, compelled to be there for his sister, despite their problems.

"I think you should go," Elias rested his hand on Ellie's shoulder, giving it a tight squeeze, "she doesn't want you here."

"You're kidding?" he said this to Ellie, "I've been gone one night and you've let this scumbag move in?"

"He hasn't moved in," Ellie wiped away a tumbling tear, "if you want your stuff, come when I'm not in. I'll call you."

Ellie slammed, locked and bolted the door in her husband's face. He tried his key but he couldn't open the door more than a couple of inches. His begging for a change of clothes for work turned angry within seconds. Ellie listened but she seemed detached from his words, the face of a woman who'd heard it all before. Elias had always thought Ellie had the perfect life, protected by her high metal fence, leaving the real world problems on the sidewalk. As he watched her stiff upper lip melt away, he knew he had been so wrong.

"Are you okay?" Elias asked when the door finally closed again, "I can go if you want. Is this why you asked me here?"

"No, *stay*," she wiped away the tears, "it's fine. I'm fine. I've been kidding myself. He's right. Separate bedrooms are just the start of the problems. Maybe this is for the best."

She didn't sound convinced but she was putting on a brave face for her guests. Elias looked to Caden for help, knowing that he was the one with the breaking up experience. He was still hovering at the end of the hallway, looking awkward and out of place.

They sat in the living room, all of them avoiding the couch Caden and Elias had spoiled. Ellie and Elias sat next to each other and Caden perched on the arm, checking his watch every couple of seconds.

"Hang on," Elias suddenly remembered, "you weren't expecting John, you were expecting a woman. You said, *'that'll be her'*. Who were you expecting?"

He looked from Caden to Ellie and they both looked to each other, neither of them talking.

"I thought it was Mom," Ellie gave it up, "we were supposed to have a family counseling session here. We thought it would be better if we didn't tell you because you wouldn't have come."

Elias jumped up and walked around the coffee table so he could see both of them. He instantly knew they were both in on the plan and from the way Caden was staring at the ground, he was the ringleader. *He promised me he wouldn't do this.*

"Caden?" he demanded, "Anything to share?"

"Elias, I thought it would be better if I didn't tell you. I thought if I got you all in one room at the same time with me, we could talk about things and get somewhere."

Attempting to calm his anger with a technique they'd tried to teach him in rehab, he counted back from ten, only making it to seven.

"I told you I *didn't* want this! Don't you think we've tried this before? Don't you think promises have been made in these sessions? They've always been broken."

"You've broken them," Ellie sounded angry now, "you always ran back to the drugs."

If it were only that simple, he would be able to accept it. Promises of support and care from his mother and sister hadn't lasted more than a couple of days, sometimes a couple of hours. They'd always end up in the same strained place, where none of them knew how to interact or communicate as a family. Elias had given up on that ever happening long ago. Why was Caden trying to drag it all back up now?

"You promised me," Elias looked to Caden, "is it that easy for you to break these promises?"

"I'm trying to help. I still have a job to do. This was part of the timeframe. You have your first drug test in two weeks and I knew it had to be before then or I'd get in trouble with the center for not going through everything."

"Fake the paperwork! You didn't actually have to organize something. I could have told you she wouldn't show."

"She promised me this morning that she would be here. I actually believed her. Maybe she's running late?"

He saw her this morning? Elias almost laughed, feeling like a fool for not questioning where Caden was really going when he ran out, still licking bacon grease off his fingers.

"You'll get nowhere with that woman," said Elias, "stop trying!"

"I thought I could help you all get somewhere better. You can't all keep going on like this."

"Why?" he cried, "Huh? This is my family, not yours. Just because you have the perfect family, it doesn't mean we do. It's broken."

Ellie started shaking her head, a dry and silent laugh moving her lips, "Have you ever wondered why? You're impossible to trust. Are you surprised she wants to wash her hands of you? I'm not."

"This all started before that and *you* know it. Stop editing our childhood, Ellie. It wasn't all sunshine and roses like you remember it was."

"C'mon, it wasn't that bad!" she didn't sound as convinced this time around, "I mean, she wasn't around much but it was fine. Her husband died when she was pregnant. How was she supposed to cope? You wouldn't *listen* to anybody. You always thought you knew best. You were wild and nobody knew what to do with you."

"I was a kid! What was I supposed to do?"

"I didn't go off the rails."

"That's because your wheels were firmly glued to the rails. You were the straight A student. You had it all. See what happens when we try to talk about this stuff? We always end up in the same place. Elias is always wrong and everybody else is just putting up with him."

"That's not true," Ellie sighed, "I wanted you to get clean. It wasn't *easy* for any of us. The first time you came out of rehab, I thought it was the fix. I thought I'd get you back but it didn't last long. I even had hope the second time. The fourth time, I just wanted to drop you off in that apartment and never see you again. I couldn't deal with you anymore, Elias. I don't think you realize how difficult it was to live with a brother who you couldn't talk to. You've been clean for weeks now but I'm so terrified that you'll fall off the wagon any moment. It's happened before and – it's *so* hard. *So fucking hard.* You've been so selfish for so long and it's blinded you. I've been here this whole time and I know our relationship isn't as great as it should be but all you had to do was stick to your promises. You could have done this years ago. Do you not think I wanted my brother? I wanted you there when I was pregnant and when I was struggling to raise Kobi. Do you have any idea how hard it was for me?"

Elias shook his head. He couldn't even remember Ellie being pregnant. His memories of that time were sketchy and vague.

"Of course you don't. You say none of us have been here for you, but the truth is, you haven't been here for us either. You can talk about broken promises but what about the things you shouldn't need to promise? I've done everything I could for you and I know I shouldn't have kept giving in to you but I didn't know what else to do. I didn't want to see you suffer but I didn't realize I was making things harder for you. All I've ever wanted is a brother who I didn't have to lay awake at night, wondering if he was still going to be alive when I woke up. When you overdosed again this year, I actually felt relieved because I knew I hadn't been losing sleep for nothing. Every time I think you can't disappoint me anymore, you do."

Elias had never heard such honesty from his sister. It felt like an outpour from years of built up anger and hurt. He knew that's how she felt but he had never stopped to think about it. She was right, he knew he was selfish but he didn't know how to be any other way.

"What do I do? What do I do to make this right?" Elias blinked back the tears, looking from Ellie to Caden for answers.

"Let's make a new promise," Caden said, "no more secrets. No more lies. No more holding it all in. Can you both do that?"

Elias wiped away the tears, not wanting to cry because he wouldn't know if he would be able to stop himself. He stared at Ellie, urging her to show that she was willing to do that. When she nodded her head, he felt a weight lift from his shoulders. He didn't care about the unspoken rules, he walked straight over to her and grabbed her in the tightest hug he had ever given anybody.

"I'm sorry," he whispered through her dark hair, "I'm so sorry."

"Me too," she whispered back.

There was no need to talk anymore because it was all there in the embrace. The promise was different this time because they both wanted it. For the first time in his life, he felt like they were both on the same side.

"This isn't right," Caden stood up, "you shouldn't be doing this alone."

He ran into the hall, leaving them alone. Elias pulled away from the hug and he followed Caden.

"Where are you going?"

"I'm going to give Madame Mayor a piece of my mind," he didn't turn around, "her time is up. She's not getting away with this anymore."

Elias knew he should have tried to stop him, but he couldn't. He forgot all about Caden arranging this behind his back because the passion poured from every part of his body. He wasn't doing it to upset Elias, he was doing it to try and make things better. When he joined Ellie in the living room and he saw the genuine smile and the shared relief, he knew that Caden had helped after all.

"I'd pay to see this," Ellie laughed through the tears.

Chapter 14

As Caden bolted up the grand stone steps to the town hall, he didn't know whom he was more angry with; Judy for breaking her promise, or himself for believing her. Ignoring the various sign-in desks, he headed straight for the mayor's reception desk, where the receptionist Caden had been stopped by was busy talking on the phone.

"Is she here? I need to see her," he demanded.

Apologizing to whomever she was talking to on the phone, she hung up, already looking like she had the ready made excuse on the end of her tongue.

"The mayor has requested that you leave," she smiled bitterly, "you can't be here."

"I'm not leaving," he laughed, "she can request all she wants, I'm not going anywhere until she talks to me."

The receptionist rolled her eyes and typed something on her computer for a couple of seconds, glancing to Caden between every word.

"What are you doing?"

"Writing down everything you say," she mumbled, "for the police report."

"What police report?"

"You're harassing the mayor of Havenmoore," she said it as though it should have been obvious, "and the police will want evidence when I hand it over."

Police report? Evidence? Caden should have been scared but he wasn't. He wasn't even surprised.

"Listen to me," he leaned across the desk, not able to hold the anger back, "if you don't let me see the mayor, I will turn this town upside down until I find her. She promised she would be somewhere very important today and she broke that promise. I need an explanation from that woman."

"The mayor is a very busy -,"

"Too busy for her children?" he slammed his hands on the desk, "You can write every last word of this down and hand it over to the police. I don't care. That woman needs to face what she's done to her own kids."

"Kids?" she stopped typing and arched an eyebrow, "I thought there was just one? The doctor?"

"Exactly," he nodded, "and that's the problem. She has twins. *Two*. Two kids. *Not one*. Where is she?"

The receptionist tried to hide her confusion behind her false lashes and heavy mascara but it was obvious she had no idea about Elias, just like the rest of the town. The mayor was public property in their eyes but they only knew the abridged version of her life. They all knew the lies and façade but they didn't know the witch who lay beneath it.

"I can't tell you," her voice shook, "she told me not to."

"Listen, Emily," he read her name badge, "I know this is just a job for you and you don't want to get in trouble but this is important. I need to see her and it needs to be right this minute."

Emily looked from Caden to the screen as she battled her conscience. They both knew she could lose her job if she told him. For a moment, he thought she would but her eyes narrowed and she started typing again.

"I will call the police," she avoided Caden's gaze.

As the anger bubbled over, he ran around the side of the desk and straight through the door to her office. To his surprise, there she was, reading the morning paper with a sandwich on a plate next to her desk. Not wanting to take any chances, he closed the door and twisted the metal lock into place.

"How did you -," she closed the paper, "leave, now."

"No, I won't leave," he walked straight over to her desk, slamming his hands on the antique oak, "you promised me you'd be there. You promised me you'd come and try."

"Something came up," was that a smirk on her red lips? "I'm a very busy woman."

"How long are you going to keep lying to yourself? How long are you going to keep ignoring the cries of your children?"

Judy leaned back in her chair, already looking exhausted by his surprise appearance in her office. Had she really thought that she could get away with this, again?

"Don't pretend you know what you're talking about," she rolled her wide eyes, "if you know what's good for you, you'll leave."

Caden felt the draw of the door. He felt the familiar fear creep up inside his chest. It would be so easy to run away and rule her out, just like Elias had but he remembered why he was there. He was there for Elias. He was there to help Elias. *She can't keep hurting him like this.* As much as Elias pretended he didn't care about her dismissal of her son, Caden knew it affected him more than he would ever admit. How could it not?

"I told you, I'm not going anywhere," he sat in the chair opposite her, "your kids were just both in tears, promising each other that they were going to work on their relationship. You should have been there. You were supposed to be there."

He thought that would shake her lip but it didn't. Not a single muscle in her ice-cold expression shifted.

"How touching," she said, "I don't see what this has to do with me."

"Because you're their mother," he leaned forward, "and you

should be ashamed of yourself."

"Ashamed?" her eyes rolled again, "I'm not the one who takes drugs."

Caden wasn't sure if she didn't understand or if she just didn't care about her kids, or, just didn't care about Elias. Was that all she saw when she looked at him? Drugs? He was so much more than that, so much better than that and if she bothered to get to know her child, she would see that too.

"You stupid woman," he shook his head, "you stupid, stupid woman."

"How dare you! I'm the mayor of this town and I could have your head for that," she cried, "now *leave* my office right this second before I call the police and have you arrested for trespassing."

"Call them," Caden pinched between his eyes, "I don't care right now. I just can't get over how *heartless* you are. You've ruined your son's life and you don't care."

"I've done nothing but help that boy. Who put that roof over his head? Me. You think you can just turn up at the last minute and start throwing accusations around. He's probably told you all of these horrible lies about me. I bet he forgot to mention how many times I've saved him from going to prison."

"You've saved yourself," Caden shook his head, "that's all you've done. You care more about your reputation than your family."

This time, her face did change. All of the muscles in her face appeared to drag down into her lips, forming the tightest scowl he had ever seen. She looked like she could spit venom at any moment.

"How dare you," her voice deepened, "how dare you speak to me like this."

"Somebody needs to make you *see* how wrong you are. Everybody is too scared of you. When was the last time you hugged one of your kids?"

For a second, it looked like she was trying to think about it and Caden almost thought she was going to produce an answer to shock him, but she didn't.

"Get out."

"What about when your son nearly died taking an overdose?"

"Three."

"What about when he came out of rehab and expected to see you there?"

"Two."

"Or when he was a kid and all he wanted was his mom to come home and spend time with him."

Judy jumped up to her feet so fast, it shocked Caden into doing the same. They stared at each other like wild animals trying to find the deadliest place on the body to attack.

"Why do you care so much?" she looked him up and down.

"Somebody has to," he decided it was better to hide his true feelings.

"What makes you think I don't care?"

"If you cared you would have showed up today."

She scowled again, the dimples in her chin shaking as her brows hovered low over her hazel eyes.

"I – I -," she stuttered before reaching out and delivering a swift and sharp slap to Caden's left cheek, "get out of my office before I drag you out with my own hands."

Gripping the stinging handprint on his cheek, Caden took a step back, staring at her with pure shock. She sat back in her chair and straightened out her blouse before resuming her place in her newspaper.

"I don't know how you sleep at night," Caden whispered, still clutching his fire-stung cheek.

"Easily."

Elias was right. She was a lost cause. Caden hadn't wanted to believe that a mother could be so cold and heartless but she was. He thought about how much Elias cared for Kobi and how much he cared for his own niece, Becca. They weren't even parents but they both seemed capable of love. The woman sitting in front of him, reading the sports pages of the paper didn't look like she was capable of loving anything or anybody.

Tail between his legs, he left the town hall. He didn't know where to go, so he let his legs carry him to Elias' apartment. When the door opened and he saw that Elias was back home, he pulled him tightly into his arms, understanding his pain better than ever before. The stinging in his cheek was only a fraction of what Elias must have felt for so long.

"I'm sorry for dragging this up," Caden whispered into his ear, "you were right. She doesn't care."

Elias didn't look surprised as he led him up to the apartment where the bed was waiting for him. They made love slower and more passionately than Caden had ever made love to a person before.

***

"You shouldn't beat yourself up so much," Elias pulled the frozen lasagne from the freezer and tossed it in the microwave, "some good came from today."

Sitting on the sofa in nothing more than his boxers, Caden smiled a little but Elias could tell it was still weighing heavily on his mind. He had never had anybody fighting so hard in his corner before and it felt strange, but in a good way. He could see how much it upset Caden that he couldn't fix everything.

"I've got my drug test and then we're free of this," Elias set the microwave and joined Caden on the sofa, "when it comes back clean, we can really start."

"She's always going to be around the corner though, isn't she? What will she be like when she finds out about us?" said Caden.

"I don't care," Elias rested his head on his shoulder, "she'll probably pretend we don't exist and keep living her life. She's not important. When you left, Ellie said that she believed me when I said I was staying clean and she said the second I get those results in my hands, I can see Kobi whenever I want. Isn't that great?"

"Hmmm."

"I couldn't have done it without you," he whispered, "you saved me from myself. I would have relapsed in a second if you weren't so tough on me."

"Yeah."

Elias sighed, wanting to shake Caden out of whatever he was in. He knew how his mother could be, but he had had twenty-six years to adjust. Caden seemed shell shocked by her and no matter what Elias said that wasn't budging.

"We could eat out tonight? We haven't even been on a real date yet. And then tomorrow, we could go to the high school and ask about the GED program."

Caden seemed to snap out of it. He rested his head on Elias and reached out to run his hand gently across the hairs on Elias' thighs.

"I'm sorry."

"Just forget her. What do you say?"

"About?"

"Eating out."

"Oh, yeah. Sure. That sounds like fun."

"It can be our first date. Well, it can be my first date too. I can't say I've ever been on one and alleys with dealers don't really count, do they?"

Caden didn't laugh at Elias' joke. There was an unshakable tension in the air and he wanted to get rid of it. It made him wish that he had tried to stop Caden from running out to find the mayor. A tiny part of him thought he might have gotten through to her but he should have known better. She's unreachable, even when she's sitting in front of you.

A hurried knock on the front door made Elias jump up. He looked to Caden, wondering if they were expecting anybody, but Caden shrugged. Grabbing his t-shirt from the corner of the kitchen counter, Elias headed downstairs.

"Is he here? My son, is he here?" it was Caden's mom.

"Claire, what's up?" Elias tried to sound casual as he pulled the baggy t-shirt down over his tight, ripped jeans.

He looked down, realizing he was wearing Caden's shirt. Crossing his arms across his chest, he hoped she hadn't been paying attention when she last saw him.

"Is my son here?" she repeated nervously, looking over his

shoulder.

"Mom?" Caden's voice came from the top of the stairs, "Wait, what are you -,"

"Oh, no," her face landed in her hands, "I swore it wasn't true. I told myself it was all in my head. Caden, how could you do this?"

Her face burned and her bottom lip trembled, as she looked straight through Elias, to her son, who was standing on the top step in nothing more than a pair of underwear. There was no explaining their way out of this one.

"Mom, I can explain."

"Oh, Caden," a sad smile took over her trembling lips, "you don't realize the trouble you've gotten yourself in."

"I think you should come in," Elias stepped to the side, scratching the back of his head, unable to look at his lover's mother.

Caden quickly dressed and made them all coffee but Claire was too shaken up to drink. She couldn't look at them. The shame and disappointment was obvious and it was making Caden keep his distance by the kitchen counter as she perched on the edge of Elias' couch.

"Is this why you asked me to switch with you?" she directed her question at Caden, almost pretending that Elias wasn't there, "How long has this been going on?"

"I tried to stop it, I *swear* I did, but – I *couldn't*. I love him, Mom. It just happened. If we don't tell anybody, we'll be in the clear in two weeks and everything will be fine."

She shook her head, her auburn curls bouncing over her clenched eyes.

"It's too late," she tucked her hair behind her ears, "I got a call from the rehab center an hour ago telling me that our contract with them has been suspended, pending investigation."

Elias knew instantly what had happened and who caused it. Caden looked horrified, frozen to the kitchen counter.

"W-What?"

"They wouldn't tell me why, but the second they mentioned your name, Caden, everything just slipped into place. I hoped it wasn't true. I prayed I was wrong and that it was something else. Something *I had* done."

"Mom, I -,"

"You *can't* have sex with the patients!" she cried, "It's against everything *I've* worked my life to build. You signed an agreement. You've stepped over the lines, Caden, and there's no going back from it. I could lose my license over this. Do you understand what you've done?"

A shaky nod was all Caden could manage and Elias felt unfair that he was getting all of the blame when he was the one who'd pushed it in the first place. He had been the one to try and kiss Caden the first time.

"This isn't all of his fault," Elias spoke up.

"Don't blame yourself," she turned and smiled to Elias, "Caden should have known better."

She had the *'you're just an addict, you wouldn't understand'* look in her eyes that he was so used to. It made him feel like he was shrinking back in the sofa, unworthy of adult and serious conversation.

"I love him," Elias stood up, "I don't care. I love him."

Joining Caden's side, he looped his fingers through Caden's, squeezing them tightly, letting him know that they were going to face it together. Caden squeezed back but he couldn't look up from staring at the carpet.

"How can you love each other?" she laughed, "It's not even been a month yet. How? What about Finn? A stack of letters came for you over the weekend, all from New York. Don't you want to read them, to work things out?"

Caden dropped Elias' hand, stuffing them in his jeans pockets. Was there something else Caden was keeping from him?

"I don't care what he has to say."

"You're engaged! You can't throw five years away like that, not for a fling like this. I don't mean to upset you, Elias, but my son is fresh from a serious relationship and -,"

"Finn cheated on me with Adam. He broke us. Whatever we had, and I don't think it was real love, it's broken. Drop it, Mom. I told you, I love Elias. I'm *not* going to explain that. I don't need to."

Exhausted, Claire flopped back into the sofa and started picking at the skin next to her red painted nails. It was like everything was crumbling before her. Had she been hoping that Caden was going to fix things with Finn? Was that ever an option?

"He's been writing to you?" Elias asked Caden.

"I've had one letter from him and I didn't open it!" Caden yanked his bag up from the coffee table and dug out a crumpled up letter, instantly ripping it in two, "I don't care what he has to say. I've moved on."

Elias watched the letter pieces flutter to the ground, wondering if Caden had actually moved on or if he just wanted to move on. It suddenly felt like there was another person crammed between them.

"Finn is a nice boy. People make mistakes."

"And Elias isn't nice?" Caden laughed, "You don't know him like I do. Nobody seems to. Elias is – Elias is amazing. He's been through *so* much and he's still standing in front of you. If I were him, I would have given up. Finn used me. Finn was scared of being on his own and so was I. That's why we made it to five years. It was fear of the unknown, not love."

"Do you think me and your father would have been together for thirty years if we gave up when it got tough?" she cried, "Relationships are hard work!"

"I was tired of the work. Everyday, there was some struggle to get through. I've not felt like that once with Elias. It's easy. It's natural. It's real. What's wrong with that?"

Claire stood up and straightened out her jacket. She walked over to her son and cupped his cheek in her hand. For a moment, Elias thought all was forgiven, but then she opened her mouth.

"You were always too quick to see the best in people."

She moved on and her hand found it's way onto Elias' shoulder, "You don't have to love the first person that shows you some attention. Just know that."

With that, she left, leaving behind what felt like a ticking time bomb. They turned to each other, begging the other to say that she was wrong first.

"She doesn't know what she's talking about," Caden laughed, "she's just angry that I've messed things up for her. It changes nothing."

"Are you sure?" Elias bit into his lip, forgetting about the lip ring, almost chipping a tooth.

Caden reached out and dragged Elias into a hug. At first, it felt like a hug to tell him everything was okay but after another couple of minutes, it felt like Caden was clinging to Elias, trying to reassure them both that it was all going to be okay. Elias' heart was racing, denying everything Claire had said. He knew he loved Caden and he could feel Caden loved him. His experience with love within his family had never been as clear as the love flowing between them.

"We'll fix this," Elias changed position and it was his turn to pull Caden in, "my mother won't get away with this. Not this time."

The microwave signaled it's end and the smell of tomato sauce and cheese filled the kitchen. He reached inside and gripped the plastic, forgetting all about gloves. He yelped and pulled it away, a fresh burn forming on the ends of his fingers. Running it under the cold water, he thought about how his mother had burned Caden and it got him thinking about how he could burn her.

There was one person who could ruin everything for her. *Me.*

Chapter 15

Over the next couple of days, Caden didn't leave Elias' side. They locked themselves up in his apartment, watching endless streams of reality TV, ordering enough takeout to feed a frat house and having enough sex to put anybody off it for life.

On the fourth day of their forced exile, Caden felt the walls starting to cave in. They grabbed clean clothes from the washing machine and headed out to Bruce's bar. Not for a drink, but for that date they'd been talking about but never had.

In the evening, Bruce had started serving food to compete with the new restaurant next door. Some of the tables had couples at them but the evening was wearing on and soon, the bar would be full of college students and the town's workforce ready to let their hair down.

"I've got a table in the back. It's quieter," Bruce winked to Caden, fully aware of what was going on.

The table wasn't much quieter than the rest of the bar but he appreciated the gesture. When they were both sitting and

Bruce was taking their drinks order, he gave Caden the '*we need to talk*' eyes. Those eyes made Caden wish he had gone to the restaurant next door, instead of going to his brother's bar to save a few bucks. Now that he was effectively unemployed and faced with the worst writer's block of his career, the little money he had in his account was going to dry up faster than a California reservoir in the middle of a drought.

"I never saw the appeal of bars," Elias looked around, "the last thing I want to do when I drink is dance."

"You'd hate New York. There's a bar for every person in that city, two even. When they say it never sleeps, it's true."

"Do you miss it? New York I mean?"

Caden thought he would but he didn't. Just thinking about the crowded streets gave him a headache. Everybody walked like they were always ten minutes late and in the middle of the day, the city was impossible to navigate. It made Havenmoore look deserted but he didn't mind that. It made him wonder if he was coming up to that time in his life that made people hate the volume of nightclub music and start talking about the good old days like they were so much better than what was currently happening.

"I'm happy here," Caden reached out, gripping Elias' hands, "with you."

Elias smiled, and for a moment, it felt like they were a normal couple without the stress of the town on their shoulders. Judy James hadn't reached out or caused any more trouble for them but he knew it was only a matter of time before she found out that they were together. She got Helping Hands Outreach shut down just because of how Caden spoke to her so it only made him wonder what she would do if she found out the truth. *No more hiding.* Elias had been bent on revenge for the first couple of days but Caden managed to convince him that they should stay low and wait for her to make another move. If she didn't, they were in the clear. Caden doubted that would happen.

"I never thought I could be happy in this town," said Elias, "I've spent years avoiding it, sofa surfing and sleeping on the streets, just so I could stay out of it. I always ended up back in

Havenmoore."

Caden excused himself, telling Elias that he was going to check where the drinks were. He knew Bruce was withholding them on purpose so that he would have to collect them, alone.

"Mom's waiting for you to call," he said as he poured a beer for a student, "she's not happy with you."

"I don't know what to say! I feel like I've ruined her life. She'll never forgive me."

Losing his mother like that was his biggest fear. The last thing he had wanted to do was ruin her career but he had been so blinded by love, he had let the ball drop, just long enough for Judy James to pick it up.

"Of course she'll forgive you," Bruce laughed, "she loves you. She adores you. She's just angry that you didn't tell her. I think she can look past her job, she's retiring in a couple of years anyway. It's the lies she doesn't like. She always said you were the honest one out of us and it's just a shock."

"A shock that I'd find a guy I really liked?"

"No, you dufus!" Bruce cried, "Shocked that you'd keep it a secret. If you'd have told her she could have prevented this happening. Could have protected you."

Caden wasn't so sure. Bruce was looking at her through rose tinted glasses because she wanted to push him and Finn back together. She hated the thought that two people who seemed perfect for each other could fall so far apart. Caden had hated that too but finding Finn fucking Adam over his favorite bedspread had been the biggest blessing in disguise. It had freed him.

"I'll fix it," Caden accepted the two glasses of cola, "I don't know how, but I'll fix it."

"Just apologize," Bruce shrugged, like it should have been obvious, "she said you told her that you loved this guy?"

Caden was sick of having to defend his heart and the look on his face must have showed that because Bruce stepped back, holding both hands up in retreat.

"I'm not judging you, bro! If you love him, go for it. I told Lucy on our second date. She thought I was crazy and I probably was, but I just knew. Seven years later and we're still here with Becca. I look at her and I feel that same feeling I felt on that second date."

"Really?" Caden was shocked to hear his brother open up so much.

"Are you dumb? You can't ignore love."

Bruce tossed the towel over his shoulder and headed across the bar to serve a group of professionals in suits and ties. He took the drinks back to the table, Bruce's words heavy on his mind. *I can't ignore love.*

"Sorry," Caden brushed away the heaviness and smiled.

"It's fine. I got a text from Ellie. She wants me to go to this medical ball thing with her this weekend. I think she was supposed to take John and I don't think she wants to go alone."

Caden thought about how sour their relationship had become. Ellie had seemed so excited to go on their date when Caden arrived to babysit but by the time she returned, that excitement had been drained. He felt sorry for her. She seemed like a nice girl, under it all. She was a little too much like her mother but she had absorbed it all in Elias' place.

"You're invited too," Elias slid the phone to him.

Caden read over the message and even though he wasn't mentioned, she said he could '*bring a plus one*', "Are you sure she means me?"

"Who else?" Elias narrowed his eyes "You don't have to come."

"No, I want to. It'll be a good chance for us to dress up."

"I don't own a suit," Elias ran his hands through his dark stubble, "I suppose I'll have to buy one."

Elias' phone beeped again and it was a message from Ellie, saying that if he needed a suit, she would take him to the late night mall that night to find something. It was spooky how in tune they were with each other. Caden found it even spookier how long they'd spent fighting, considering how close they really were.

"I have something," Caden didn't mention it was the suit he had bought for the small engagement party they had back in

New York two years ago, "I think it'll still fit."

That was Caden's way of stepping back from the shopping trip to give Ellie and Elias time to talk alone. Elias smiled in a knowing way, clearly excited that his sister was keeping up her end of the deal. It was obvious he had never expected her to involve him in her life so soon after years of being kept at arm's length.

Food turned out to be microwaved and cheap tasting but neither of them complained, knowing it was a free meal out of the house. Caden suggested that they go to the grocery store at some point so they could get some food to cook. Without even meaning to, Caden had moved in with Elias, despite it not being agreed to. If Elias had a problem with it, he wasn't mentioning it. Caden loved being so close to Elias and it was a relief to be out from under his parents' feet. It was clear they'd grown used to their own space after nearly a decade of living alone and even though they'd never tell him that, he knew they were heading toward suggesting that he find a small apartment in town.

Everything had been temporary since arriving in Havenmoore, except for Elias. He seemed to be the only thing that Caden could see in the future. He didn't even know how long the roof, supplied by Judy James, would stay over their heads. She could pull the rug out from under them at any moment and it was clear, even if they weren't talking about it, that they could feel it coming. Elias had Ellie and that huge house but Caden didn't want to jump from place to place like a nomad. It wasn't helping the feeling of unrest he was feeling toward turning thirty.

When Caden tried to offer his brother some money for the food and drinks, Bruce flat out refused to Caden's relief.

"Before you go, can I talk to you really quick?" Bruce whispered to Caden so that Elias, who was shrugging into his jacket, couldn't hear.

"Wait for me outside, I need the bathroom."

Caden headed towards the bathroom and Bruce followed. Standing in the lemon-scented hallway, Bruce looked around him before speaking.

"It was the mayor that ratted you out, wasn't it?" Bruce ordered with a tone of '*don't lie to me about this*'.

"How did you know?"

"I didn't. It was a guess, a good guess by the sounds of it. Whatever you've done to her, apologize and move on or she'll ruin your life."

A girl, possibly a student, left the ladies bathroom, wiping her damp hands on her denim skirt. She gave them both a suspicious look before squeezing through them to get back to the bar.

"What aren't you telling me?"

"There's a reason a new restaurant opened up next door. Remember when next door used to be a burger joint, ran by that guy Karl?"

Caden vaguely remembered eating there once with Bruce on one of his New York visits back to Havenmoore. When he originally left town, it had been a bookstore, so it was hard to say.

"Kind of," he shrugged, "what does that have to do with me?"

"The mayor got him shut down," Bruce gripped both of Caden's arms, "and she made Karl's life so bad that he left town. He wasn't happy about how long it was taking to have one of his permits granted. He was trying to get a liquor license so he could stay open later. Business wasn't great and he saw how great I was doing next door. I didn't mind because a little competition can drive sales up for you both and he was a nice guy. After four months of waiting, he went to the town hall and he caught the mayor in the hall. It was by accident really, he was only going in to leave a message with the permit people. It turned pretty ugly pretty quick. He said it was like she morphed into someone else and she got so angry that he'd brought that to her. When he told me, I said he'd probably caught her on a bad day.

"Then, loads of things started happening. There was a review in the paper from the food journalist, ripping his place to shreds. He hadn't even been in to eat! Karl knew him and he would have recognized him in a flash. It was really bad for business. Then, there was another article about his hygiene, suggesting he had rats. Karl was borderline OCD so I knew that was garbage. He used to come and help me clean the cellar out every couple of months. I'd pay him because he was so thorough. Then, he was shut down. Somebody claimed that they'd been sold liquor there and that was it. No investigation, it was sold and nowhere else would hire him. He couldn't even get a job in McTuckey's, so he moved out of town to work on his uncle's ranch down south until he found something. She's a dangerous woman, Caden. She owns this town. I think she owns most of the people in it. She can make your life hell with the snap of her fingers. Mom knows what she's really like. I told her all of this months back and she was the only person in town not surprised."

If Caden wasn't scared before, he was now. He knew what the mayor was capable of but he didn't know she acted that way with everybody, not just Elias. If she didn't like somebody, they weren't welcome in Havenmoore. *Why did I cross her?*

"What else can she do?" Caden tried to laugh it off but it sounded warped and fake, "She's already taken her shot."

"I don't know," Bruce stepped back, stuffing his hands in his pockets, "but I'm sure she'll find something. Karl saw none of that coming and by the time he figured it out, he was being lynched. Don't think this is over. Does she know about what you're doing with Elias?"

Caden shook his head.

"Make sure she *never* finds out," Bruce tilted his lips into a sympathetic smile, "if she hates him as much as you and mom make out, that'll be dangerous information to a woman like her."

Bruce left Caden standing in the hallway and he couldn't seem to move. Four more students pushed past him to get to the bathrooms before he remembered Elias standing outside waiting for him.

"Get lost?" Elias laughed.

"Yeah," he tried to laugh too but as he looked across at the town hall, he noticed the light in the mayor's office was still burning bright.

He knew it was a stupid idea but he couldn't shake the image that she was in there, plotting his demise.

***

Standing on the corner outside of the closed bakery, Elias pulled the collar up on his jacket, slightly nervous about seeing Ellie's white car pull around the corner. He knew he was worrying about nothing but he couldn't remember the last time they'd spent time with each other and it not revolve around his addiction.

As it started to softly rain, Ellie showed up, five minutes early but Elias had already been waiting for ten.

"You're here," she sounded surprised.

"So are you," the awkwardness he had been dreading was there.

Elias jumped into the passenger seat, slightly damp from the sudden downpour. It was already seven but Ellie knew of a mall that didn't close until ten. She offered to buy the suit for him and he knew better than to try and offer her money for it.

"Has Mom called?"

"No. Was she supposed to?"

"She said she would," Ellie mumbled as she pulled onto the freeway, "has something happened? She seemed angry with you."

"When isn't she?"

Ellie gave him the *'that's not funny'* look but he wasn't joking. Was Ellie still holding out hope for their mother to suddenly sprout a heart in that cavern? Elias wasn't.

"What did Caden say to her?"

"I don't know," Elias shrugged, "but I can guess."

"He didn't tell you?"

"I didn't want to know."

"Well she's pissed. I know that. I heard about what happened with Claire's charity losing the rehab contract. I bet she's cut up about that. I've worked with her a couple of times over the years on different projects. She's a nice woman."

There was a hint of accusation in her voice, as if blaming

Elias for her losing that job, completely ignoring that it was their own mother who had caused the storm. He imagined her calling the rehab center, mentioning her name and suggesting that they find another charity to deal with the aftercare.

"How's Kobi?"

"Fine. It's his birthday on Sunday. I have to work, but we're having a little party for him on Tuesday. You're welcome to come."

Elias turned to his sister, not sure if he heard her right. He replayed what she had said in his mind before letting himself get excited.

"Seriously?"

"I wouldn't ask if I wasn't. When's your drug test?"

His stomach sank when he remembered that it was on Tuesday. With Helping Hands Outreach being sacked so close to his drug test, the rehab center didn't bother starting him with another support worker, satisfied that most of the boxes had been ticked. It was no secret that all they cared about was that he passed the test. That way, everybody had done their job and they could pat themselves on the back.

"Tuesday," he winced, "same day."

"It's fine. It's in the morning, right? They usually are. Just come in the afternoon. We won't be starting until he finishes school. It's a surprise and showing him that you're clean and healthy will be the best surprise you can give him."

She said all of this without a smile as she focused on the road but he could tell what a big deal is was for her to make that step. He was silently grateful, not wanting to make anything anymore uncomfortable than it always was.

They pulled up outside of the mall, which was surprisingly busy for half past seven on a Friday night. Ellie wasn't one for wasting time shopping and Elias quickly found out that she usually hired a buyer so she could be in and out of the mall in an hour. There was no buyer this time, so they headed straight to the suit shop John usually bought his work suits from. Elias instantly felt out of place in the environment. He looked down at his ripped at the knees skinny jeans, obscure band t-shirt and old, beat up leather jacket, wishing that he would put a little more effort in.

"You're going to need a full tuxedo set," Ellie marched with purpose to the back of the store to where the tuxedos were kept, "what size are you?"

"Erm."

"You don't know your size?" she sounded surprised.

"Sorry, I've been a little busy and I was banned from prom, remember?"

"Vividly. I was on the committee. It was me that banned you. Go and call that shop assistant and we'll get him to measure you up, if he's quick," she glanced at her watch as if she had somewhere to be, "John's picking up some things and I don't want to leave the house empty for too long in case I come back and he's taken more than his share."

Surprised that she was still going ahead with kicking him out, he ran across the store and grabbed a teenage girl, who was busy texting under the counter. The second Elias told her what he needed, she sighed and jumped up off her chair to be led over to where Ellie was.

"Hi," Ellie shook the girls hand, "I need a tux for a ball. My brother, he doesn't know what size he is and we don't have much time, so if you could measure him up, that would be great."

The girl forced a half-smile as she produced a length of measuring tape from her pocket. She instructed that Elias take off his leather jacket and when he did, her hands jumped and danced over his body, quickly jotting down numbers as she went. When she vanished up the inside of his leg, he gave Ellie a '*is that supposed to happen?*' eyes. Ellie nodded with a smirk.

"What's the occasion?" the girl asked, faking an interest, most likely because she was on commission.

"It's The Medical Ball," Ellie answered for him.

"The Maine Medical Ball?" the girl's ears pricked up, "My dad's going to that! He's a consultant. You're a doctor?"

She squinted at Elias' band t-shirt, trying to read the bright red calligraphy. Ellie almost choked on her laughter.

"No, that's me," Ellie laughed.

"What's with the laughing?" Elias tilted his head, "I could be a doctor. Could I be a doctor?"

The girl gave Elias a look that clearly read '*don't drag me into this*', but when Elias didn't back down, she looked him from toe to head.

"You look like you're in a band," she shrugged, "doctor's don't have piercings."

"Told you," Ellie grinned proudly, "those piercings are going to stop you from ever getting hired."

"I think they're cool," the girl offered.

Elias suddenly took a warming to her but before he could thank her, she disappeared into the back to find something for him to wear.

"This is like the one my dad is wearing," a long, black suit bag was covering her face, "this one is in your size, but the pants will be a little long. We do offer a tailoring service if you need it."

She handed Elias the bag and showed him to the fitting room, which was a lot nicer than he was expecting. It wasn't the usual cramped cube with a curtain, it was a whole room, filled with mirrors and a sofa in the middle. To his surprise, Ellie followed him in and sat on the couch. It was nothing like the changing rooms he used to steal his clothes from.

"Oh, come on, you think that I've never seen you naked?" she rolled her eyes, "How many times have I found you passed out, covered in your own vomit? Who do you think gave you a bath?"

He genuinely couldn't remember that happening but he didn't know if his lapse in memory or her admitting to doing that was more embarrassing.

Elias stripped down to his underwear, glad that he was wearing a clean pair. He quickly scrambled into the pants and as predicted they were about four inches too long for him. He shrugged on the shirt, waistcoat and jacket and left the bowtie undone around his neck.

"You need to tie that."

"I think it looks cooler like this," Elias checked himself out in the mirror, "makes me look like Frank Sinatra."

"It makes you look like a hobo," Ellie jumped up and tied it for him, "just admit you didn't know how to tie one."

"I never had a reason to learn."

The girl brought in a pair of shoes for him to try on and she helped him fasten the tricky laces, turning up the pants while she was down there. They all stepped back and observed the sight in the mirror. At first, he thought he looked as uncomfortable and cramped as he felt, but looking at his reflection, he almost didn't recognize the man staring back. The last time he had worn a suit was for his grandmother's funeral but he couldn't even remember what that looked like. Staring at him in a full tuxedo was like looking through a window into a parallel universe.

"How does it feel?" Ellie circled him, checking over every detail of the suit when the girl left them alone, "It looks like a good fit."

"It is," he turned around, "makes my butt look perky."

"Caden will be happy about that," the joke sounded strange coming from her mouth, "I mean, yeah. You look good. Really good. It's almost like it's not you."

She sat down and he caught her looking at him with a sad smile.

"I can take my piercings out, if you really want me to," he turned around, "just for one night. We can tell people I'm your hot new boyfriend. Somebody will tell John and he'll die with jealousy."

"It's not that," she shook her head, "keep them in. They make you."

"Can I get that in writing?"

"It's you," she bit into her bottom lip, "it's really you, isn't it?"

"Ta-da," Elias shook his hands by his side, slightly confused.

"No, I mean, it's you. You're here and you're present. It's like you're free."

"I feel free," he shrugged, "although these are a little tight in the junk area."

He changed out of the tux and before he could look at the

price, Ellie scooped it up from him, leaving him to get changed again. Checking out his reflection in the mirror, he noticed that he didn't look as deathly skinny as the last time he had looked in a mirror. He remembered that all too well. In the rehab center, there was a long, floor length mirror right in front of the bath and you couldn't avoid it whenever you stepped out. He thought it was so people could really see themselves and he always wondered if it was one of the psychologists tricks to scare people into changing their ways. He had seen a skeleton back then. He was nothing more than a bag of bones, clinging onto life and thinking of one thing and one thing only.

Now as he looked at himself, he saw the one thing he had only ever wanted to see. A normal guy.

"You coming? We need to get your hair cut too," Ellie called in.

Smiling at himself, he allowed a moment of pride. Ellie was right. It really was him and it had never felt so good to admit that. He quickly changed and headed out to see Ellie paying for the clothes and shoes. He saw the bottom line and he nearly choked but he didn't say anything. She had offered to do this for him and he knew it meant as much to her as it did for him. He wasn't going to ruin it for her. It probably made a nice change to be buying something other than drugs for her brother.

When they left the barbers, his thick, black hair considerably shorter and neater, they stopped off for coffee and a slice of cake, where Ellie dropped a bombshell on their rather nice evening together.

"Mom's going to be there tomorrow night," Ellie said it as casually as if she was chatting about the weather, "she is every year. She always does a speech thanking the medical professionals in the town. It's always the highlight of the evening for most people. Not for me, because she always mentions me and that's when everybody stares at me to see if I stand up to the mayor. My dress has to be -,"

"You knew when you asked me?"

"She sits at a different table, don't worry," Ellie sipped her coffee, "practically on the other side of the room. You probably won't see her."

Elias knew she would make a point to bump into him to deliver some cutting remark. He suddenly remembered that Caden was going to be there too and after everything that had happened, it was an explosion waiting to happen. He could hardly un-invite Caden, nor could he tell his sister he wasn't going to go to avoid his mother. *Why should I keep having to avoid her?*

"That's fine," he swallowed his worries, "no problem."

Ellie squinted at him as she wrapped her mouth delicately around a large piece of carrot cake. She was clearly trying to sense the underlying tension but he wasn't going to let their mother ruin what had been a fun shopping trip with his sister. She seemed to ruin everything but this wasn't going to be one of them.

"What time is it?"

"Quarter to ten," Ellie checked her gold watch, "we should go."

"I need to get a gift for Kobi," Elias suddenly remembered what Caden had told him about his new obsession with Japanese cartoons, "he likes that thing doesn't he? Amie or something like that?"

"Anime," she rolled her eyes, clearly sick of hearing about it, "but you just being there is going to be enough."

Elias pulled out his wallet and he had one crinkled up twenty-dollar bill stuffed in the corner. His next welfare check wasn't coming through for another nine days but he had never been able to turn up to one of his own nephew's parties with an actual gift, sober. *I'll starve if I need to.*

"I have a lot of years to make up for. Is there a book store in this place?"

Ellie abandoned her cake and stood up, tossing her handbag over her shoulder

"C'mon then," she urged, "this place is going to close any minute. I know of a store that sells the manga comics he likes. If we run, we'll be able to blackmail our way in before the shutters start coming down."

"Manga? I thought it was Anime?"

"It's the same thing. One's comics, one's TV shows. I don't know. Kobi knows the difference."

Like children, they sprinted across the mall, practically sliding under the shutters before the storeowner tried to close them. He tried to tell them he was closing for the night but after begging that it was a matter of life or death, he let them in if they promised to make it quick. It turned out that Ellie knew a lot about Manga and Anime and what Kobi liked and especially what he didn't like. He was glad because he knew nothing when it came to the bug-eyed colorful drawings. She grabbed a stack and when the total came to thirty-six dollars, she footed the rest of the bill when she saw him digging in the bottom of his wallet for cash he knew he didn't have.

It was nice having Ellie on his side. She wanted him to succeed just as much as he did and it was a good feeling. Even knowing that he was going to be in the same room as his mother wasn't going to dampen his spirits. He would have his sister and his boyfriend there and they were all he needed.

Chapter 16

Elias walked towards Caden's parents' house, asking again if it was okay for him to be there. No matter how many times Caden assured him everything was fine, he was finding it hard to believe. He didn't doubt that Claire was a nice woman, she had seemed like a nice woman when she was acting as his stand in support worker, but he wasn't sure that enough time had passed since their relationship had caused her to lose the majority of her work.

"I called her last night and I apologized and everything is fine. She's not a bitter woman. She wouldn't be able to hold a grudge if she tried."

Entering the house for a second time was a lot different than the first. The first time, he had come with Caden, alone and confused. Elias had needed somebody to talk to because he felt close to relapsing. This time, he was wearing a tuxedo and ready to go to The Medical Ball with somebody he had fallen in love with. The second he stepped over the threshold, he could feel life buzzing through the small, yet inviting home. He instantly felt the tension that had been laid out by Claire in his apartment vanish the second his new shoes landed on the soft carpet. The smell of delicious food he didn't recognize floated from the kitchen, where most of the noise seemed to be coming from.

"I bet she's cooked," Caden laughed, "I told her there'd be food at this place. Cooking is like her natural defense mechanism. Do you think you could eat two meals tonight? It'll make her feel better and she'll love you if you finish a plate."

"Sure," Elias was grateful for being hungry, although he wasn't sure how far the well-fitting tuxedo would stretch.

They walked into the kitchen to be greeted by Claire at the stove with Buster and Bruce waiting on whatever she was cooking. The second they stepped into the kitchen, she pulled them both into hugs in turn, apologizing over and over for the way she acted in Elias' apartment. It seemed the shock of what had happened had worn off and now that she knew about the mayor's meddling, she was less angry with them because it was being directed somewhere else.

"I told my son. I told him all about that mother of yours. No offense, but she's always been this way. If only more people in this town knew about her true side, she wouldn't be so quickly reelected every year!"

"It'll take a lot to unveil the wizard behind the curtain," Caden sat next to his brother, "or in this case, the witch. Maybe somebody will drop a house on her?"

Elias felt strangely at home with Caden's family. Perhaps it was the common dislike of his mother or witnessing something he only thought existed on television, but he felt like he could easily fit in somewhere like it. Was this why Caden was so eager to try and reunite Elias' family, so he could experience this?

When invited, Elias sat across from Caden and next to Buster. Buster was quiet, busying himself with what looked like tax paperwork. Bruce on the other hand was talking all about the bar, telling a story about a fight that kicked off the night before between rival college football teams. The story ended with Bruce pulling the two ringleaders apart with his own hands and throwing them out on the sidewalk. How much of it was true, Elias wasn't sure, but they all laughed the same. He reminded Elias a lot of Caden, just a little older and with a more boyish sense of humor. It was obvious that the two brothers cared for each other, in an under the radar way, similar to how he and Ellie were becoming.

Claire ladled generous helpings of a mystery stew into each of their bowls and Elias didn't want to ask what it was, not wanting to come across as the fussy guest. It was delicious and he soon figured out that the big chunks of dark meat were beef. It practically melted on his tongue, making him want to know how meat could do that.

"This is really good," he didn't need to fake it.

"It's one of my specials," she smiled proudly, "I just throw it all in the slow cooker and hope for the best."

"It's delicious, Mom," Caden scooped it into his mouth, "you need to start writing these recipes down as you do them so you can give them to me."

"You know that's not how I work. I like to make it up as I go along. Where's the fun in following a recipe? Did you know Caden is a good cook, Elias?"

Elias didn't but he didn't want to admit how little he actually knew about the man he was claiming to love. There hadn't been an opportunity for them to cook because they'd been surviving on takeout for most of the week.

"I get by," Caden blushed, "I can make a few recipes."

The conversation quickly turned to work and after his parents spent a good ten minutes reminding Caden that he needed to finally finish writing his book, it quickly moved to Claire and Helping Hands Outreach. It turned out, things weren't as bleak as they'd all thought. Working with Havenmoore's rehab center was only one contract and Claire had spent the last couple of days contacting other centers and hospitals in towns nearby. This eased Elias' conscience and he could sense that it did the same to Caden's.

"Until I find something, I'll just volunteer here and there," a carefree smile filled her lips, "I have enough money saved up to fall back on. If you'd put away ten percent every month, like I told you, you'd be able to get your own apartment, Caden."

Elias hadn't ignored that Caden was practically living with him, but he hadn't brought it up either. He didn't want Caden to think he didn't want him around, because he did. The truth was, he dreaded the day that he would wake up and Caden wasn't next to him, sleeping softly in his bed, hugging the covers with his legs in the way he did.

"You don't get an extra ten percent when you're living in New York. Everything is so expensive out there. And I barely made a penny with Helping Hands Outreach. It's hardly the best paying job in the world."

Claire started rattling off different jobs she had heard were available in town but Elias could tell none of them were of interest to Caden. Even if he acted like he was no good at it, his heart was in writing. He may have only been writing fluff pieces that nobody read in New York, but at least he was writing.

"Did you get references from your jobs in New York?" Buster spoke up.

"I never thought it was important."

"Oh, I feel like I've failed as a parent. No references and no savings and you're nearly thirty."

"Thanks for the reminder," Caden half smiled, half grimaced.

Bruce, who was on the other side of thirty seemed to find this funny and even though Elias was still a couple of years away from the milestone, he understood his cold feet about leaving his twenties with nothing to show for it, mainly because he had absolutely nothing to show for his own life up until this point.

"Speaking of New York," Claire snapped her fingers, dropping her spoon in the empty bowl, "I have those letters somewhere."

"Mom, you really don't -," Caden was cut off by a dismissive wave of her hand and she returned from the living room with a stack of ten or so letters.

Whatever this Finn had to say, he really wanted Caden to hear it.

"Jesus, dude," Bruce laughed, "is Hogwarts trying to contact you? What does that loser want?"

"You should at least open one," his mom pushed the pile toward Caden, but he pushed them straight back, "just to see what he wants to say."

"He doesn't get to say anything," Caden finished his stew and leaned back in his chair, "that's the beauty of moving away, changing your phone number and avoiding social media. Silence."

"Caden," his mom said in a tone as though she was about to tell him off, "you can't bury your head in the sand."

"I'm not!" he laughed, "New York was me burying my head in the sand. This is me living in the open. Sure, I have no job, no money and no hope but I have something more important than that."

For a moment, Elias wasn't sure what he was about to say but when the fingers reached across the table to intertwine with his, his heart almost stopped. It was times like this that put into perspective the doubt his head might be feeling towards his heart. Those little unexpected blips, when he wasn't sure if he was still breathing were what he found himself living for. Every unexpected kiss, delicate touch, soft breath on the neck, they all electrified his whole body, while making his heart and stomach flip in unison.

"Toss them out, Mom," Caden ignored the letters to look deep into Elias' eyes, "I have everything I need. Finn's last words can stay buried. I have no urge to help him clear his conscience anytime soon."

It wasn't his mom who tossed them into the trashcan by the refrigerator, but his dad, Buster. As if they were nothing more than old potato skins, he opened the lid and dropped them in without a word. When he returned to his paperwork at the end of the table, he fired a quick wink of support at his son.

Claire quickly cleared the table and Bruce had to leave to get home to his family. Buster vanished into the living room, quickly followed by Claire when she finished washing the dishes.

"What time do we have to be at this thing?" Caden checked

his watch.

"I said we'd be at Ellie's by six."

"So, that gives us an hour and forty-five minutes to get me dressed, undressed and then dressed again. What do you say?"

Caden had a naughty glint in his eye that Elias couldn't ignore. The moment Caden even hinted at something that involved being naked, Elias was already imagining all of the things they could do.

"I'll meet you up there, I need a glass of water," Elias let go of Caden's hands, "but I think you should use that thirty second head start to get nice and naked for me on that nice, big bed of yours."

Caden leaned across the table and kissed Elias softly on the lips, making him feel guilty for what he was about to do. When Caden ran off through the living room towards the stairs like an excited kid, Elias had to pluck the top letter from the trash and stuff it into the inside pocket of his tux. He knew nothing about Finn and he wasn't sure he wanted to but a ravenous curiosity had taken over him and he needed to know what the cheating ex had to say for himself, even if Caden didn't.

Patting the lapel down to make sure the letter wasn't showing, he headed through the living room, politely smiling to Claire and Buster as he headed upstairs to take advantage of their son's nakedness.

***

When they were both re-dressed in their suits, they quickly fixed their hair and attempted to brush out the creases before jumping in a cab to head over to Ellie's house. When they arrived, Ellie was already waiting for them in the hallway, wearing an elegant black dress that draped over one shoulder before hitting the floor. Her black hair was slicked back over her ears, letting her minimal makeup speak for itself.

"You look beautiful," Elias kissed her on the cheek.

"I should for what that stylist charges for an hour," she kissed him back, "c'mon, I think I just heard the car pull up."

It turned out that Ellie wasn't driving them to the function and when Elias mentioned that he thought she would, she found that hilarious. A stretched, black limo picked them up. It felt a little excessive for just the three of them, but Caden had a feeling she had it booked for when John was supposed to be her date. He wasn't going to complain. Sipping champagne in the back of a limo on their way to a party wasn't the worst way to spend a Saturday night.

"Kobi's with John. He's staying at his mother's. I bet she's so pleased. She never liked me."

"Is this really the end?"

"I think so," Ellie checked her reflection in the reflective metal of the ice filled champagne bucket, "I was always too scared to end it because I thought I'd miss him but it just feels like a weight being lifted off my shoulders."

"I know what you mean," Caden could relate and Ellie smiled sweetly at him through the metal as she fiddled with her hair.

The drive was short but Caden knew it was less about the drive and more about the grand entrance. They pulled up outside of the Nova Theatre in the heart of Havenmoore. It usually played old movies during the day and newer blockbusters in the evening, but tonight, it was the setting for The Medical Ball. The grand red brick building was decorated with Romanesque white columns, which were lit up pink for tonight's celebrations.

A valet opened the door for them and they let Ellie get out first, so she could have her moment of looking stunning on the red carpet.

"There's something I didn't tell you," Elias whispered, "I wasn't sure how to. My mom's gonna be here tonight."

Elias followed up that bombshell with a quick kiss on the cheek before joining Ellie on the short red carpet up to the entrance. Jumping out of the car, Caden slammed the door and hung back as Ellie and Elias walked up to the building arm in arm. *Is it too late to leave without them noticing?* The limo drove away, leaving nothing but a cloud of gray dust from the exhaust.

When they were inside the building, they walked by the box

office and the crowd of people directed them through the building to the giant conference room that sat adjacent to the old theatre. The whole way, he stayed two steps behind Elias, unsure of if he should try and drag him away from his sister to question him. Looking around at the faces in the crowd, he smiled, knowing that any minute he would see the one woman in Havenmoore that he didn't want to see.

"Thanks for the warning," Caden mumbled to Elias when they were sitting at their table in the grand hall.

It was ornately decorated, everything either red or gold. A stage sat at the far side of the room and luckily, their table was right in the back. According to Ellie, if you didn't work at the hospital, you were always put in the back as though an afterthought. Other doctors with affiliated offices in extended parts of the state filled their table but it didn't look like they'd come for the conversation.

"I knew you wouldn't want to come if I told you. Anyway, I only found out last night too."

"You're right I wouldn't have come! That woman has it in for me."

"She has it in for everyone," Elias rolled his eyes, "and I wanted you to come. Look around. When will we ever get to do something like this? It's like we're on the Titanic or something."

Caden looked around, knowing that Elias' heart was in the right place. Sitting under the twinkling glass chandeliers at a table with more knives and forks than he knew what to do with made a nice change from sitting in front of the couch eating takeout, even if he did love doing that with Elias. Finn had never approved of takeout. It was one of the *'you'll get fat if you eat that'* foods that were practically banished from their apartment.

The night zoomed by and when Caden finally relaxed, they started to have fun. The rest of the guests at the table opened up after a couple glasses of wine each and they all started sharing medical stories. Caden and Elias didn't have much to add to the conversation but they joined in where they could. Ellie even seemed to be relaxing and having a good time. If her sudden divorce was on her mind, she wasn't letting it affect her. She was effortlessly charming and witty when the time called for it. It reminded Caden of how easily the mayor could slip between two personalities when it was called of her. Elias seemed to be the only one in that family who was one person all of the time and he respected him for that.

Every so often, Caden would glance around the hall to see if he could spot her but she was nowhere to be seen. Elias noticed and rested his hand on his knee, as though telling him to relax. They drank, Elias having soda, and ate delicious food late into the night, until it came to the thing they'd all come for. One by one, awards were handed out, some of them serious and some of them humorous. Ellie picked up the award for the best local doctor and she delivered a short and humble speech before floating back to her chair.

When the awards wrapped up, Caden thought the night was about to end but there was one more person who wanted to speak on the stage. He turned back to the table, his mind a little blurry as he tried to remember exactly how many times his wine glass had been refilled without him noticing.

"Brace yourself," Elias mumbled, nodding back to the stage.

The crowd erupted into the loudest applause of the night and Caden knew there was only one woman who would demand such admiration and attention. He turned back to see the great Judy James, slowly making her way across the stage in the most ridiculously designed dress he had seen all night. It looked like a wedding dress, fitted at the waist and branching out in a huge circle around her, but made entirely of black silk. Tiny black diamonds started around her knee, draping down the floor length and puffy material, making her glitter darkly with every swaying step. Everybody else was seeing the adored mayor of Havenmoore but Caden was seeing somebody as dark as the jewels attached to her fabric.

The smile on her face was similar to the smile Ellie had been sporting all night. She looked humbled by the applause and grateful to even have been asked to speak. Caden saw right through it. All he had to do was look into her eyes to know the real woman that everybody else either didn't know or ignored for the sake of her local celebrity factor.

"Thank you, thank you," she grinned, her perfect white teeth visible from across the room, "really, you're all too kind."

The applause died down and Caden quickly noticed that he and Elias were the only ones who hadn't put their hands together. Judy looked out into the crowd, no doubt looking for her teleprompter. He was sure that her eyes landed on him, if only for a split second but Caden was sure that she would never be able to see him through the dark in the crowd. For now, he was invisible.

"Do you think we can sneak out before she's done?" Caden whispered over his shoulder to Elias, not taking his eyes off her in case she transformed into a huge dragon, or something equally as terrifying as her other face.

"You're not going anywhere," it was Ellie who spoke, "after her speech, that's when the party really starts. They clear out the tables and a DJ comes out."

Caden didn't care about dancing to a DJ and he knew Elias didn't either but he also knew that Elias wouldn't want to leave his sister's side all night because she had invited him. Caden understood that. It was too soon in their fragile and new sibling relationship to start ditching each other in the middle of parties.

"I'll keep it short because I know you all want to get on with your evening," the crowd roared and Caden could feel the excitement for what was to come next, "I just wanted to thank you all, personally. I wanted to say thank you to every single one of you who works day and night to keep the people of my town safe. Without you all, Havenmoore wouldn't be the great town that it is."

"Oh, please," Elias scoffed, which was met by a hurried '*shhh!*' from the other guests at the table next to them.

"As most of you know, my very own daughter, Ellie, is one of the best doctor's our town has and I couldn't be more proud to not only be the mayor, but to be her mother."

A spotlight suddenly landed on them, blinding Caden. Ellie seemed to be expecting it, because she squinted into the light, reflecting her mother's grin as she clapped her hands with the rest of the crowd. It was so fake that it almost sickened Caden.

"As long as you're here, protecting our town, I'll make sure I'm in office, protecting you."

The crowd roared even louder and Caden was sure this time that she made direct eye contact with him as she delivered that final line. It felt like a warning, telling him that she wasn't going anywhere and he would be a fool to push her.

Swallowing the growing lump in his throat, he found himself clapping along with the chorus as sweat trickled down the sides of his burning face.

***

When his mom finished her speech, the transformation was almost immediate. Everybody stood and the real mingling began as the waiters vanished with the tables and chairs. The lights dropped, being replaced by glitter balls and strobe lights as the music cranked up. Everybody looked ready to party but Elias felt ready to get out of there.

"This really isn't my thing," he muttered out of the corner of his mouth to Ellie.

"One hour," she smiled as she waved at somebody across the room, "there's a couple people I need to talk to."

Ellie thrust herself deep into the crowd, laughing and joking with people she seemed to know, leaving Caden and Elias to awkwardly stand where their table and seats had been only a couple of minutes ago.

The music was making him feel sick and he hadn't even touched the wine that had been topped up over and over until it was almost spilling over the edge. He only had a couple of days to go until his drug test and he didn't want a stitch of anything to show up in his system.

Just when he thought he couldn't feel anymore uncomfortable, he caught a glimpse of a pompous black gown floating through the crowd in his direction. He turned, hoping she was heading toward Ellie but she had her back to them. Turning to Caden, he mouthed a desperate '*help*' but Caden looked just as terrified of her.

"Elias," she nodded, the fake smile still plastered across her face.

"Mayor," Elias sucked the air through his teeth, "nice dress."

Her smile tightened as she looked down at her dress, unable to tell if it was a genuine compliment or a backhanded insult.

"What are you doing here?" she directed this question at both of them.

"I was invited," Elias stood up straight, "we both were."

"By your sister, I assume?"

"Yep," Elias backed away, "if you'll excuse me, I need to -,"

Before Elias could back away, thick and sharp claws tightened around his scrawny bicep, digging straight through the expensive suit jacket.

"Don't walk away from me," she snarled through her red-lipped smile, "I don't know why you're here but you need to leave. If you're trying to mess things up for me, I suggest you -,"

"For once, it's not about you," Elias laughed, shrugging his arm away, "I came for Ellie. You probably haven't heard but her and John are splitting up."

Her face didn't falter but he could tell by the flickering in her eyes that she didn't know and she was trying to work out why Ellie hadn't told her. For once, her all seeing eye had failed her.

"Since when have you and Ellie been so close?" she arched a fine brow.

"Caden helped us see the error of our ways," he said sarcastically.

"Caden?" his mother smirked, pleased with herself, "You mean you're still seeing this man after he was so unceremoniously fired?"

Feeling like he had just landed Caden even further in it, he edged closer to his lover so that their shoulders were touching. He wanted to wrap his fingers through Caden's, but he resisted, not sure if that was the best decision.

"Give it up," said Elias, "leave him alone. He's done nothing wrong."

"On the contrary," her dark eyes shifted over Caden's entire body, "I was informed that you were no longer working with my son."

The words *my son* sounded strained and foreign coming from her lips. The dislike was so strong, it was easy to forget that she had given birth to him.

"He's not here as my support worker. He's here with me."

"With you?"

"Yes, with me," Elias straightened up, "I need to find my sister because I'm not in the mood to party. Not anymore."

Elias turned, grabbing Caden's hand in the process. He didn't care what she knew now. He loved Caden and he didn't care who knew it. When you've stooped as low as she had, trying to cast Caden out of her bubble, there wasn't much wriggle room to go any lower. Elias told Ellie that they were leaving and before she could argue, he dragged Caden towards the doors. He darted up the few steps that led up to the corridor, which led to the exit and to freedom.

"Wait up," Ellie called after him, "what's happened?"

Without stopping, Elias told her that nothing had happened, he was being preemptive before his mother could strike again. When Ellie told him that he was overacting over nothing, he stopped, Caden still by his side, silent, probably from the fear of what else could be done to him. *Maybe I shouldn't have come after all.*

"I just want to take these clothes off and go to sleep," Elias tugged at the tux, suddenly feeling like it was suffocating him, "tonight's been great. Thanks for the invite."

"Elias, I -," Ellie sighed, giving up halfway, "see you later."

Grateful for the permission to get out of there, Elias pulled Caden towards the door but when he heard his name bellowing down the corridor, they both stopped in their tracks, turning to see the mayor gliding effortlessly down the corridor. Her dress was floating behind her and she had a look of contained fury in her eyes that could make a weaker man melt if he didn't know her like Elias did. He was sure he felt Caden melting in his palm.

"Don't you dare leave," she extended a finger, freezing him

to the spot, "you've got some explaining to do."

"I don't need to explain anything to you," he tossed his hands out, letting go of Caden's, "you're nothing."

"I'm your mother," she growled, looking around her as the people passing up and down the corridor stopped to see what was going on between the mayor and two strange men.

"No, you're not," he laughed, "you just *happened* to have twins. I was your curse, your punishment."

Her lips became a thin slit, her entire jaw tightening, ready to unleash whatever poison she had been storing up.

"If you're my punishment, I want to know what I did to deserve a child *like* you."

"Anybody would be lucky to have a son like Elias," Caden spoke up, "you're just blinded by your own self importance."

"You," she laughed in Caden's face, "why are you even here? What do you want with my son? *Money?* Is that what you want?"

Elias felt Caden falter on the spot but he wasn't going to let her talk to him like that. Caden had been more of a family to Elias over the last weeks than she had ever in his whole life. Caden had given him more love and made him feel more wanted than she had ever. The void he had always been looking to fill was suddenly filled and there was no way he was going to deny that.

"We're together," Elias looped his fingers through Caden's shaking digits, "we're in love."

Judy James looked ready to spit her poison straight in his face as a wretched smirk twisted across her blood stained lips. In disbelief, she darted between them, trying to figure out if it was a sick joke.

"Are you trying to ruin me?" she leaned in, "Why are you always trying to destroy me?"

"You really think this is about you?"

"Who else is it about? The drugs, the crime and now this. You just want to *embarrass* me. You want me to *react*. You've *always* been the same way."

"Maybe if I had a mother who cared for me, I wouldn't have

needed a reaction," Elias tightened his grip on Caden's hand, "this isn't about you. This is about me, for once."

"It's always been about you," her voice deepened, "and your childish little problems. Grow up and join the real world. Without my support, you would be dead."

She was probably right, but alive, at least she could attempt to manipulate and shape his life to keep him in her shadow.

"Support? You throw me in rehab every chance you get and then you push me to the side, hoping your money will fix the problem."

"I'm a busy -,"

"Yeah, a busy woman. I know. You should get that tattooed on your forehead like a catchphrase. It's all I've heard from you since I was a fetus. '*I'm a busy woman. Too busy to be your mother. Too busy to really help you. Too busy to love you. Too busy to give a fuck*'. I'm over it. I don't *need* you and I never have. I thought that maybe, just maybe, you'd see that you're the problem and you always have been but that would mean pulling your botoxed head out of your own ass and that was never going to happen, was it mayor?"

By now, the crowd had thickened but they were all so deep in the moment, they weren't noticing the dramatic gasps and questions as the drama unfolded.

"You'll regret that," she spat.

"Do your worst," falling back on his heels, he tossed his hands out, "you can't possibly bury me any further, can you? Do your absolute worst, Madame Mayor. I don't care anymore. Take the apartment. Cut off my welfare checks. Throw me in rehab and lock away the key. I'm *done* with your games. You win."

"This isn't a game."

"It's always been a game," Elias lowered his voice, heartbreak filling his cracking voice, "you're a terrible mother and you always will be."

Elias couldn't stick around to see the aftermath of the bomb he had just thrown. The second he felt tears starting to sting his eyes, he had to run as far away from her as he could. He ran out into the street, across the road and into the park opposite the Nova Theatre. The air was thick and stuffy and it wasn't helping the tightening in his chest. Collapsing on a bench, he felt angry with himself for the tears he couldn't stop falling down his cheeks. He wasn't crying because he was upset, he was crying because he was frustrated. Twenty-six years of built up frustration poured through his tear ducts and he couldn't stop them.

"Elias," Caden ran towards him, "Elias, are you okay?"

"No," he cried out, "I'm not okay. I'm angry. I just want to - "

Screaming out, his fist collided with the wooden bench but all it did was hurt the knuckles that were still hurting from punching the side of Caden's house. He hated himself for getting so wound up over her.

"I'm so proud of you," Caden's hand slid over his shoulders, pulling him in to his warm body, "you should have seen her face. She looked genuinely shocked. I've never seen it like that before."

"I don't care."

"I'm sorry."

"Why are *you* sorry?"

"Because I was the one who was trying to push you two together. I was wrong. I was so wrong. There's no saving that woman. She's as deep into her own hole as she can be."

He knew Caden was trying to make him feel better but it was only making him feel worse. Shrugging away Caden's hug, he stood up, staring up at the dark, cloudy sky. He searched for the moon, even some stars, but it was completely blank.

"I just don't understand her," he wiped away the slowing tears, "and I don't understand why she always gets to me. I wish I was as strong as Ellie, but I'm not. Every time she'd do something like this, I'd have drugs to fall back on. Now what do I have? I just want to make it all stop."

"You have me."

Caden stood and immediately drew Elias into a kiss. The noise, the anger, the frustration and the tears stopped. He felt like an idiot for letting the hatred blind how important Caden was to him.

"I know," Elias leaned his forehead against Caden's, "I'm sorry."

"Don't apologize. There are some cabs lined up outside the theatre. How does crawling into a bed with a movie sound?"

It sounded like the only place Elias wanted to be.

Chapter 17

A knock on the door woke Caden from his deep sleep. Rolling over, he peered into the dark, unsure if it was day or night. Elias was by his side, stirring from what looked like a lighter, more restless sleep.

"What time is it?" Caden's voice croaked.

"Half past ten," Elias squinted at his cell display, "I'll get it."

Elias pulled the first clothes he could find over his naked body, leaving Caden to roll back over into his pillow. His eyelids fluttered and he noticed how easy and quick it would be for him to fall back asleep. He flirted with the idea for a moment but he decided to pull himself out of bed, not wanting to waste the day wallowing.

Caden ran his hands over his scruff, noting that he needed a shave. His light hair was a little longer on top than usual but he hadn't had much time to fit in a haircut. After a quick spray of deodorant, he climbed into his jeans and a baggy white t-shirt. He rescued his phone from the wreckage of the clothes that had been torn off the night before and was instantly alarmed by the amount of missed calls from his mom, twelve in total, all from the last hour.

"I think I need to head home. Something's up," Caden stretched out, scratching his chest through his t-shirt as he wandered out of the bedroom, the sleep disappearing from his mind.

Elias was clutching a newspaper to his chest in the middle of the living room, his eyes wide and surprised to see Caden.

"Sure," Elias nodded.

"Since when do you get the paper?"

"I don't," he answered a little too quickly, "it must be a mistake. The mailman dropped it off with my mail."

"He hand delivered it?"

"My mailbox is full."

"Right."

Caden stared at the back of the newspaper, the sports pages of no interest to him. Elias was acting weird and it was as though he couldn't wait to get rid of Caden. Maybe the time had come that Caden had overstayed his welcome?

"I'll throw this out," Elias hurried past him, tossing it in the trashcan.

He didn't just stop there, he pulled out the half empty bag and tied it up. He clutched the trash bag in his fist like a prized possession. Elias usually waited until the trash was overflowing before he changed it.

"What's up?" Caden folded his arms, "You're acting all spacey."

"I'm fine, just tired!" Elias grabbed the kettle, "Coffee?"

"I should go and see what she wants. I put my cell on silent before the ball last night and I forgot to turn it back on. Is this about last night and your mom?"

"Yes!" Elias nodded, "That's exactly what it is. It's still on my mind. You should go if you're mom is looking for you."

Elias practically pushed Caden out of the door so fast he barely had time to grab some socks and shoes. Putting it down to delayed insanity from the shock of finally confronting his mother, Caden kissed Elias on the cheek before heading home. Now that they were nearing the end of September, the air was clear and still but there was an early morning ice in the air, making Caden wish he had grabbed a jacket before leaving. He looked down at his t-shirt, his nipples cutting through the fabric, right next to what looked like a coffee stain. He looked every inch of the unemployed loser that he felt these days.

When he got to his parents', there was no ambulance or cop car outside, so he calmed down a little. The closer he got to the house, the more he had convinced himself that something fatal had happened but seeing how calm the house looked from the outside he knew his mom was probably just eager to tell him something. Maybe she heard about what happened at the doctor's ball last night? Part of Caden hoped so because that meant the town would be talking about the mayor and maybe they'd start to doubt her picture perfect veneer.

"It's only me," he called as he opened the door, "Mom? Dad?"

"Caden!" his mom appeared in the kitchen door, a manic smile on her face, "I've been calling you."

"Sorry, my cell was on silent. What's up? It's not Granny, is it?" he suddenly remembered his granny in Portland and his heart stopped.

"Granny is fine. She'll outlive us all."

There was an uncomfortable quality to the way her smile beamed at him while her entire body blocked his view into the kitchen. Was somebody there? He tried to look around her but she reacted by bending like a character from The Matrix. Using her hands behind her back, she closed the kitchen door and hurried across the living room.

"Believe me when I say I tried to get him to leave."

"Who? What's happened?"

She looked over her shoulder to the kitchen door, a look of guilt taking over her face.

"He said he wasn't going until he spoke to you. He was really persuasive."

It didn't take long for Caden to piece things together. When he figured out who was sitting at his mom's kitchen table, he wanted to turn and go back to the safety of Elias' apartment, no matter how strange he was acting.

"You're kidding me?"

"Just let him say his piece and then he'll go."

Caden didn't want to hear Finn's piece. He didn't want to help him move on and he didn't want Finn to think he could worm his way back into his life by jumping on the interstate.

"Please, just talk to him," she grabbed him when he tried to turn and leave, "just five minutes."

Failing to see why his mother was even so invested in it, he still decided that he was going to give Finn five minutes of his time and no more. It would hopefully put an end to the endless stream of letters and that would be worth it. *It'll be like ripping off a Band-Aid.*

Not in the mood for confrontation, Caden pushed a smile forward. It faltered when he saw his ex-boyfriend, or rather, ex-fiancé, sitting at his mother's kitchen table, hugging a cup of coffee.

"Cadey," Finn stood, his extraordinarily long eyelashes batting like a camel trying to keep away the on coming sand storm, "it's really you."

"Who else would it be?" Caden sighed, closing the door behind him, "What do you want?"

Sitting back down, Finn sipped the coffee, avoiding Caden's harsh gaze. He looked good, great in fact, but Caden was looking at him through different eyes. Instead of feeling utterly heartbroken at the betrayal, he was wondering how he could have ever loved somebody so vapid and empty. A muscle-hugging shirt showed that he hadn't been too affected to miss his daily, sometimes twice daily, trips to the gym. His cropped, almost white hair was brushed away from his tanned face, letting all of his perfectly symmetrical beauty shine. It didn't give Caden the warm feeling it used to, it just left him feeling a little empty.

"I want us to talk."

"You drove seven hours to talk? You must have left New York last night?"

"I had to," he was directing his words at the coffee cup, "you've been unreachable. All of your profiles are down, you've changed your number and you're ignoring my letters. You're a hard man to reach."

Did Finn not understand that was intentionally directed towards him?

"I needed some space. I didn't want to talk to anybody."

"We all miss you," Finn shrugged, "I miss you."

Sitting at the table, making sure that he was on the opposite side and out of touching distance of Finn, he leaned back in the chair, wondering how quickly he could get out of there.

"We?"

"Your friends. Everybody. It's not the same without you."

"How's Adam? He was my friend."

"Please, Caden," Finn looked up to him, his bright crystal eyes doing all of the work, "I thought if I gave you enough time, enough space, you'd move on from that."

What about Caden's body language didn't say that he had moved on? He had spent years by Finn's side, feeling grateful for his love. Now, he was sitting as far away from him as possible. He was even leaning back in his chair, recoiling his head, because he was still too close.

"I've moved on. You and Adam are welcome to each other."

"It wasn't like that. It was one mistake. One time."

Caden laughed. They both knew it was more than once. Nobody would admit it was anything more than a dumb mistake but dumb mistakes don't suddenly happen ten minutes after the fiancé left for work. If he hadn't gone back for the laptop he had forgotten, he probably would never have caught them. Or, he would have caught them but in six months, or a year. It didn't make any difference to him. It was a blessing in disguise.

"We're over, Finn. I've met someone."

"Who?" Finn laughed, "You're going to throw away all those years for a guy you've known for a month?"

"I'm not the one who threw it away, I'm just the one making sure it doesn't get jammed in the garbage shoot."

Taking in a deep breath, he vowed that he wasn't going to let Finn make him feel guilty. He focused on Elias' face in his mind, instantly thinking clearer.

"Who is he?"

"That doesn't matter."

After a long pause, Finn finished his coffee.

"Is it love?"

"Why does it matter to you?" Caden stood, "Even if I hadn't met a guy, you wouldn't be able to wriggle your way back into my life, Finn. You broke whatever we had and if we're honest with each other, it wasn't as great as we thought."

"But I still love you," Finn's words didn't make Caden's insides twist, they just made him exhale with frustration, "I want us to try again. Come back with me. We can start again. I'll cut Adam out and we can just -,"

"Stop, Finn," Caden didn't want to hear anymore, "desperation doesn't suit you. Look at you, you're gorgeous and you could have any guy you want. You only want me because it didn't end on your terms. That isn't love, that's a fear of being alone. Goodbye, Finn."

Feeling like he had given him more than the five minutes he deserved, Caden gave him one last smile before leaving him alone in the kitchen.

"Caden?" his mom rose from her chair, stuffing the morning's paper under her arm, "I – I – how did it go?"

"You were right. I did need to talk to him. I feel so much better."

"Oh, good," she seemed surprised, "where's Finn?"

"Still in the kitchen," he shrugged, "I'm going back to Elias' apartment. Let me just grab some more fresh clothes."

"Didn't you work things out?"

"There's nothing to work out," Caden said as he ran up the staircase to the guest bedroom, "but I feel so much better knowing that I've made the right decision."

He stuffed as many clothes as he could into a duffle bag, knowing that he wanted to spend as much time with Elias as possible without having to come back here. Not because he didn't want to see his parents, because he did, he just needed space from his mother's questioning for a while.

"Have you seen the morning paper?" she asked, still clutching it under her arm, her bottom lip quivering.

"What? No. If Finn doesn't leave, call the police or something. Tell them he's trespassing. He's got this fear of authority. I don't know. I'll call you."

"Caden, wait -,"

Sighing, he opened the front door and tossed the duffle bag over his shoulder, "Mom, me and Finn are over. Just accept that."

The morning sun was still frosty but it had never felt so warm on his skin. As he headed back across town, leaving Finn behind, he felt truly ready to start the new life set out in front of him, no matter how unknown and scary it was. It had taken seeing Finn again to know that he wasn't scared of turning thirty after all, he was just scared that he had wasted the whole of his twenties living a life that didn't suit him.

With a renewed bounce in his step, he stopped off in the bakery to pick up some bagels and coffee. The baker, who he had learned was called Billy from the frequent visits downstairs gave Caden the strangest look. He wasn't the friendliest man but this morning, he looked more disgusted than normal. Caden shrugged it off, wondering how loud they'd been in bed last night.

"Two cream cheese and bacon bagels," he pulled his wallet from his back pocket, "and two coffees."

Billy poured the coffee into two cardboard cups, not taking his judgmental eyes away from Caden. Feeling uncomfortable under his gaze, he decided to occupy himself counting the donuts in the glass display box next to the counter. When he reached the thirteenth donut, his eyes wandered over the morning's Havenmoore Herald. He would have ignored it because the sight of a local newspaper only reminded him that he wasn't pursuing his writing passion but he couldn't ignore it when his face was plastered across the front page.

Dropping his wallet to the ground, he picked up the paper,

lifting it up with disbelieving hands. Elias had tried to hide it from him and so had his mother. As he read over the headline, he felt something bitter tasting speed up his throat at lightning speed.

***

Elias didn't know how long he was planning on keeping the front page of the newspaper from Caden but when he heard the front door slam and heavy footsteps run up to his apartment, he knew that the cat was well and truly out of the bag.

Clutching a copy of the newspaper in his fist, Caden burst into the living room, a look of panic and confusion on his face.

"How can she do this?" he shook the newspaper, "I'll never work in this town again."

Looking over his own copy, which he had fished from the trash the second Caden left, he let the headline sink in. '*Support Worker Sex Scandal*' shone proudly next to a blurry video surveillance shot of Caden. Just from the town hall reception backdrop of the image, it wasn't difficult to see where the finger pointed.

The mayor had been clever in not giving too much away. The story covered the whole of the front page and most of the third page but it was mainly fluff, fleshing out the few facts they had. All they knew was a support worker, working for a local charity took advantage of an addict under his care. Elias' name wasn't mentioned, but why would it be? That would work against the mayor, not for her. On the surface, this looked like a direct attack on Elias but he knew better. There was nothing else she could do to Elias, so she had to hit him where it really hurt and that was the man he loved.

"There's no going back from this," Caden's hands were fisted tightly in his disheveled hair as he paced the apartment, "the whole town will be talking about this."

There was nothing Elias could say to make things better.

"This is my fault."

"This is her fault," Caden shook his head, "but if you hadn't said anything at the ball, this wouldn't have happened."

The last thing Elias had been expecting was Caden to agree.

"I thought you were proud of me for standing up to her?"

"I was," he cried, "I am, but, we should have known she'd do something. You should have known she would kick back when she had the chance."

"I should have known?"

"She's your mother!"

"Barely. You probably know as much about that woman as I do."

The tension was rising between them and even though neither of them really wanted to turn on each other, it was too easy. Elias' reputation or public image was nonexistent. He had spent years in the gutters of Havenmoore, unseen and ignored. Caden, on the other hand, had everything to lose. He came back to Havenmoore for a fresh start and so far his fresh start had bitten him at every turn.

"How can she get away with this?" Caden picked up the paper again.

"Stop reading it," Elias attempted to pull the paper out of Caden's hands, but he was clutching tightly, "you're only going to make it worse."

"Worse? How can it be worse than this? This article makes me sound like a dangerous sex criminal for falling in love with you. You're not the one being referred to as an *'unstable and dark character with troubling motives'.*"

"So we'll be unstable and dark together," Elias stood up, "we'll get through this. Dogs will be using this as their bathroom tomorrow and people will already be forgetting about it."

Elias wasn't sure. He knew how small Havenmoore was and a scandal like this would give them gossip room for as long as they wanted to drag it out. People would likely add to and embellish the story until Caden became a Hollywood style villain in the eyes of the people walking the streets. Judy James was a clever woman, Elias had to hand that to her.

"You've never had to live with anything like this!"

"I've been through my own shit storms, Caden."

"You chose your path," he pointed in Elias' face, "you kept using drugs and pushing people away. I never asked for this. I never asked for my life to be ruined."

He almost couldn't believe what he was hearing. The words leaving Caden's mouth sounded like they were somebody else's. He wished they were. They weren't. His lips were moving and the sounds were coming out in his voice, hurting Elias in the one place that Caden had always avoided.

"Maybe you shouldn't have gotten so close to me then."

"Maybe!" Caden cried, his face burning, "What am I going to do?"

Elias walked over to his living room door, not wanting to believe what he was hearing, "I think you should leave."

Caden looked up from the paper, shocked as Elias opened the door. Elias couldn't believe that he was holding the door open and waiting for Caden to go. He didn't want him to. He never wanted him to leave. He needed Caden by his side, even if he was being hurtful. Words hurt but it wasn't Caden's words that had caused the problem, it was his own. As he stood holding the door, he hoped Caden would refuse to leave so they could fix things.

"Is that what you really want?" Caden blinked heavily.

Elias nodded before he had time to think about if it was what he really wanted. What he really wanted was Caden's arms around him but he felt like he had gone too far to the edge.

"After all of the times I've been there for you -," Caden stopped talking and dropped his head heavily.

Before Elias could make everything right, Caden was already hurrying down the steps to the street with a copy of the newspaper in his hands. Elias waited by the door, hoping Caden would run back up those steps at any moment so they could embrace and promise never to fight again. He didn't. Seconds turned into minutes and minutes turned into a lifetime. He was left alone with nothing more than his thoughts. They were screaming at him, calling him a fool for pushing away the one good thing he had in his life.

Times like this were usually the ones that would push Elias

over the edge. If he had a line of cocaine in front of him, he would find it difficult to turn it down. He needed the voices in his mind to stop. Every sentence replayed on a constant loop, each loop growing louder and louder.

Picking up his copy of the newspaper, he grabbed his jacket and headed straight for the town hall. The receptionist told Elias that the mayor was working from home but she looked like she instantly regretted telling him that information. With only a couple of bucks in his wallet, he ditched taking a cab and headed towards the apartment building where his mom lived.

Elias had only been once before, but it was the only building of its kind in Havenmoore. It was as close to a gated community that you could get in a small town like Havenmoore. As luxurious as luxury apartments came, it stood four stories high, all glass and steel. The reception area was manned by a security guard behind a desk, who spent his days watching screens and Elias knew there was no way he could just march in.

Looking up and down the quiet street, he spotted flowers tied to the roadside. He hated himself for doing it but he plucked out the freshest bunch, trying to ignore the cards of sympathy for the accident that must have taken place there recently. The name card in the bouquet he had stolen was still there, written out to a woman named Brenda. He left the card in the flowers, promising to Brenda that he would put them straight back when he was done. It wasn't like he was going to give his mom flowers.

"Flower delivery for Judy James," Elias deepened his voice, hiding his face with the flowers as much as he could.

He wouldn't put it past his mother to have his picture behind the security desk on a list of '*Do not let inside*'.

"There's no delivery in the book," the security guard sighed, scratching the side of his head, "just leave them here and I'll get someone to send them up."

"I don't mind doing it. I think they're from her boyfriend."

"She has a boyfriend?" the young guy laughed, "I didn't think old frosty panties had it in her. Go on."

There was an electronic buzz and the door to the elevator clicked open. Not wanting to hang around, Elias headed straight for the elevator at what he thought was an acceptable speed. He couldn't believe how easy that had been.

He pressed the button for the top floor, placing the flowers gently in the corner of the elevator for him to come back to when he was leaving. Rescuing the newspaper that he had stuffed down the back of his jeans, he straightened it out and looked at Caden's blurry and pixelated face. He wondered where he was and what he was thinking. Was he regretting everything that he had said, like Elias was, or was he feeling lucky for an exit off the crazy train? Elias couldn't blame him if Caden decided to never speak to him again. *I hope I know him better than that.*

The elevator doors slid open slowly, revealing the top floor corridor. It had a silence that only money could buy. Underfoot, carpet thicker than sponge cake cushioned his sneakers and wallpaper that looked like it had been spun from pure silk lined the surrounding walls. It was the kind of delicate elegance his mother had always adored. To Elias it was bland and pointlessly extravagant. He had never understood why people liked to throw their money at such nonsensical things.

He firmly knocked on his mother's door. She probably had cameras in the hall that he couldn't see so she could decide if she wanted to open up. If she didn't want to open the door to him, he would kick it down.

"Who is it?" a croaky voice called from within.

Swallowing hard, Elias straightened up his spine and stepped into the view of the peephole he knew she would be peering through.

"Who do you think?"

Agonizing seconds ticked by and he was sure the security guard was about to drag him out on her request. To his surprise, he heard the chain being removed and the door slowly opened.

He didn't know whom he had expected to see but a woman he didn't know stood in front of him. It was his mother, but he had no memory of ever seeing her like this. A thick, white robe was wrapped around her body; her hair hadn't seen a brush and her face didn't have a stitch of makeup on it. Without the dark eyeliner, her eyes looked smaller and more human. She wasn't wearing her usual ferocious red lipstick but a similar color surrounded her nose as she sniffed deeply, a tissue clamped in her hand.

"What do you what?" she sounded nasally, "How did you get up here?"

Elias held the front page of the newspaper in front of her face. He was sure she would fake shock or surprise but her slightly swollen eyelids didn't flutter.

"Are you a delivery boy now?" she scoffed, "Just when I thought it couldn't get any worse."

"Don't play games," Elias pushed by her and marched into her apartment without an invitation.

She had redecorated from what he could remember but he was sure that she redecorated twice annually anyway. It was simple and stylish, everything white, glass and chrome. She had a perfect view over the town and in the distance, he could see the back of the town hall. He could imagine her sitting in front of the window with a glass of red wine clutched in her long stem wine glass, staring over her empire with a twisted and shrill cackle.

"Please, do come in," she slammed the door, "I'm sick."

"Karma?"

"Flu."

It was messier than he expected, which made him think that she had cancelled the maid for the day. There was no evidence of her working from home, like the receptionist had said. A mug of half-finished soup sat on the coffee table, surrounded by tissues and pill bottles.

Clutching her robe together, she stared at Elias through her puffy eyes and he couldn't decide what that look in her eyes was. Had she been expecting him, or was she shocked that he would dare turn up at her apartment without calling ahead.

"Why would you do this?"

"Do what?" she pulled her robe tighter.

"This," he jabbed Caden's photograph, "ruin somebody's life."

Her red eyes flicked to the picture for a second but they

didn't hold. Shrugging, her brows tilted innocently and she headed into her open planned kitchen to fill the kettle. She sliced a lemon wedge in half and added it with honey to a glass mug. She didn't offer to make her son a drink.

"I don't know what you're talking about," she mumbled as she poured in the boiling water, "I haven't had a chance to read the morning paper. Anything interesting in there?"

There was a hint of amusement in her voice. She knew that Elias wasn't stupid and her denial was all part of the game. *Why does she love games so fucking much?*

"You know what's in here," he slammed the paper on the coffee table, knocking over the soup bowl with a clatter, "you got your minions at the news desk to print this phony article about Caden. I didn't think even you would stoop this low."

"Phony?" her dry laugh was followed by a cough, "Tell me that article isn't true."

"So you have read it?"

"I can guess," she turned with the boiling water cupped in her hands.

She took a deep sip, seemingly unaffected by the rising steam hitting her in the face. It just reminded him that she was empty and made of iron. Where her heart should be, a lonely slab of crumbling coal swung from a piece of fraying string.

"You've ruined a life."

"He did it to himself. I didn't force him to have sex with a rehab patient under his care."

"This isn't about him, is it? This is about me. You did this to get to me."

Placing the mug on the kitchen counter, she walked over to the couch where she sat down slowly and crossed her legs. Even though she was clearly trying to cling onto her power, she looked vulnerable and frail. She looked human. Elias had never seen her as a real person before but the mask had slipped away and he was seeing the woman. He still didn't like what he saw.

"Why would I want to do that?" she arched a brow.

"Because you hate that I'm moving on with my life? You hate that I'm finally clean and you hate that I've found somebody

I actually love, but you wouldn't know what that's like, would you? You've always been alone and bitter."

Her lips pursed and her gaze darkened, as though attempting to send him crashing through the glass to fall to the ground below.

"Your father was a weak man. Just like you. I was better off without him."

Elias couldn't believe how coldly and bitterly she was talking about his dead father, her dead husband. All Elias knew of him was the one picture his grandmother had shown him as a kid. He tried to think back to that picture but it was a blur.

"I know I'm weak," Elias shrugged, "do you know that you're evil?"

"You've never respected me."

"It's a two way street."

"You need to earn my respect. I'm your mother. It should be given."

"Just like love should be given to a child, you mean? What about Ellie? How did she gain your respect? By being a submissive angel with a perfect GPA and a matching haircut?"

Judy rolled her eyes and let out a deep sigh. She had never had any interest in listening to her son. She was blind to her own faults. *At least I faced mine.*

"I should respect you?" she stood up slowly and floated over to him, her robe getting caught up in an invisible wind, "My son, the drug addict, and now this. You're suddenly gay and hooking up with your support worker. Why do you have it in for me? It's one scandal after another with you."

She was in his face, so close that he could smell the lemon on her hot breath. He wanted to back away but he didn't have the power.

"I've always been this way but you were hardly a person I could talk to about it."

"I'm your mother, not your friend."

"And never shall the two meet? You don't even like me, do you?"

"I don't like what you keep doing to me."

"What do I keep doing to you?" he laughed, "All I've ever tried to do is get as far away from you as possible but you won't let that happen. You throw me in rehab every chance you get. You do stuff like this to somebody I love. You don't even like that me and Ellie are friends. Why? What have I ever done to you?"

"You could ruin everything," she hissed, "you're trouble and you have been since the day you were born."

"This is all because I was a problem baby? Did I have horns, or maybe a six-six-six burned into my forehead? Tell me? What have I done that's so bad?"

"Everything!" she cried, "Your behavior, your grades, your attitude, the drugs and now this! You're the thing people crave to talk about. If any of this ever got out, I'd be out of office in seconds. People would look to me like you're my fault, like I didn't raise you right. They'd question me. They'd look at you and they'd pity you but you know what you're doing. Why can't you just be normal?"

"Be more like you, you mean?" Elias finally found the strength to take a step back, "I'd rather end it all now. I've had my problems but I can sleep at night knowing that I'm not a bad person. You are rotten to the core and you can't even see it."

Picking up the newspaper, he headed for the door before he truly blew up. He didn't know what she could do if he hit another nerve but she would find something. *I never predicted this.*

"You should be more grateful," she spat after him.

"Why? What have you ever done for me?"

"Who paid for those rehab centers? They aren't free. That apartment you are using for God knows what. I gave you all of that."

Elias paused at the door, clutching the newspaper close to his chest. Staring down at her plush cream carpet, he felt an overwhelming outpour of emotion. It wasn't a feeling of being grateful; it was a feeling that she would never understand, no matter how many times he told her.

"I never asked for any of that," he whispered so quietly he wasn't sure her hawk ears would pick it up, "I just wanted a mom who loved me."

He dropped the paper in the hall and retrieved the flowers from the elevator. He hurried through reception so fast that the guard couldn't question why he was taking the flowers with him. After placing Brenda's flowers back where he found them, he turned and looked up to her apartment.

He hadn't expected to see her, but there she was, staring down at him. As clear as day, he could see her eyes staring at him. No, they weren't staring at him, they were staring through him. He wasn't even sure that she was looking at him after all. From that distance, he couldn't tell and it could have been a trick of the light, but she looked like she might be crying.

She wouldn't.

Chapter 18

"Pee into this cup," Charlene muttered, "and sign this."

Charlene and Elias knew each other well, not that he would call them friends. He wasn't sure Charlene was the type of woman who made friends easily. Her bedside manner was something to be desired and she treated her patients with enough tough love to straighten out the most crooked addict. It was there in her voice, that she expected him to fail the drug test. This time, it was different because the court was involved. If he failed this test, he would have to go before a judge to explain himself and it would likely end with him in prison. Elias accepted the cup gladly, wanting it to be over as quickly as possible. He knew he was clean and now he could finally prove it to the rest of the world.

"Anything to declare?" she stared down at him from across the desk.

"Nope," he smiled, scribbling his signature on the sheet of paper in front of him, "what's today's date?"

"The twenty-second."

Of course it's the twenty-second. With everything going on, he had almost forgotten that it was Kobi's birthday. As he headed for the bathroom cubicle, he scanned the faces in the waiting room. Caden wasn't there and Elias had expected him to be. Despite their big fight, this was an important day for Elias and they'd been looking forward to it together.

He filled the cup and was immediately shown into an examination room by one of the doctor's. He was new and seemed a little less jaded compared to Charlene, who had been at the rehab center as long as Elias had been showing his face in the corridors.

"Everything is looking good," the doctor unstrapped the heart rate monitor from Elias' arm, "your blood pleasure is a little high but that's to be expected."

After cramming a tiny light up Elias' nose, he concluded that there was no sign of recent drug use, although signs that the septum was slightly damaged, which again, was to be expected. The urine sample was picked up, along with a cutting of Elias' hair. He had never actually made it to this point in the program so he didn't know what to expect. The nine weeks locked up was the easy part, it was the aftercare he had always fluffed. *I wouldn't be here without Caden, he should be here.*

"The results? Will they come in the mail?"

"Oh, no. It'll only take a couple of hours."

"That quick?"

"That quick. It's all changed," the doctor smiled, "so, how are you feeling?"

Elias lied and told him that everything was fine. He wished it were, because it had been. The newspaper had pushed a great wedge between him and Caden. They should have stuck together and faced the mayor as a team, so what had happened? Conversation with the doctor quickly turned to sports and Elias faked his way through a perky chat about baseball, nodding and smiling at the right points.

"How long's this going to be?" he asked Charlene again, tapping his fingers on the reception desk.

"Is there somewhere better you need to be?"

Elias checked the clock over the desk. It had been hours since his samples had been taken away and it was edging ever closer to three, which was when Kobi's party started. He would make it in time, but there was somewhere else he wanted to be before that.

The door opened and he jumped, turning around to see who it was. It wasn't Caden and it was another stamp on his chest. *Why did I tell him to leave? Why did I push him away when he needed me?*

"Did you hear about that guy in the paper?" Charlene whispered to one of her co-workers, "Everybody's talking 'bout it. Sissy said he worked with a guy from our place. They didn't name it in the paper but we're the only center close. It's crazy, isn't it? You never know who lives on your doorstep."

Oh, God. What have I done?

"Mr. James? Elias James?" another new face in another white coat appeared through a door, clutching paper in her hands, "Will you come with me please?"

She waited for Elias to walk over before she headed back through the door. They walked quickly down a long corridor, deep into a part of the rehab center he had never been to before. Or had he? Withdrawals were the worst. Coming off a drug you're hooked on takes time, a lot of time. The days blur together and you don't know your head from your ass for weeks because the drug is all you can think about. Those nine weeks had felt more like five minutes and even though he had faked his way through the last couple of weeks, pretending he was fine and fixed, he wasn't. He came out ready to find a fix, so what changed? *You suddenly developed a conscience.*

"In here," the female doctor smiled, opening a door to a consultation room, "take a seat Mr. James."

"It's just Elias," his hands were deep in his pockets, picking at the fabric, "is this going to take long? It's my nephew's birthday party in an hour."

"How old is he?" she took a seat opposite him.

It wasn't like a usual consultation room. Her desk was pushed up against the wall, so their chairs were facing each other without the barrier of a computer. She crossed one leg over the other and latched her fingers over her knee. Elias didn't think he would be going anywhere soon.

"Seven," he said, "do you have the results?"

"I do," a smile tickled the corners of her glossy lips, "it's good news. There are no traces of any illegal substances in your blood. You passed with flying colors."

"Great. So can I go?"

"Not so fast," she laughed softly, "there are some things I'd like to talk to you about."

She was friendly, but in a different way to the male doctor he had seen earlier. A quick glance of her name badge told him that her name was Monica. Her hair was flame red and her face was pinched. He put her somewhere in her forties but she looked good for her age.

"This is your fourth time at this center and the first time you've been ordered by the court to attend," she started, "it's also the first time you've turned up to give samples and it's the first time on record of the treatment being successful."

"Awesome," it already felt like old news, "why does this feel like I'm in trouble?"

"You're not," her laugh was soft, "but it's my job to give you advice for what happens next. I read your file, in the event that you passed or failed, so I'm familiar with your case. What changed?"

"What do you mean?"

"Well," she plucked a file from a drawer in her desk and flicked through the pages, landing on a pink page, "the first time you were here, you completed the program but you were back here again a year later but you only stayed for four days. The third time, you got two weeks to the end and then you vanished and the fourth time, well, you had no choice after your overdose and arrest."

There was a choice, but the mayor had made sure this looked like the only choice. He wondered how he would have fared doing a couple of months in prison for drug possession. Maybe it would have been easier than what had happened?

"I guess I just woke up," he sat back in the chair, sensing that he wasn't going anywhere fast, "I left wanting to score but my sister, she made me realize something."

"Ellie," she nodded, "I know her. Were you at The Medical Ball last week?"

Monica narrowed her eyes, a knowing smile on her lips as she recognized Elias.

"Yeah."

"It doesn't take a genius to figure it out," she tilted her head, "everything in the paper. We only have three male patients in aftercare and you're the only one young and attractive enough."

"Whatever you've read, it's only half of the truth. Caden isn't a bad guy like my mom wants you to believe."

"The mayor?" she furrowed her brow.

"Nevermind."

"Your sister. How did she help you?"

Ellie hadn't set out to help him. She hadn't even realized what she had said. She had been so angry, she had wanted to hurt him but it opened his eyes for the first time.

"My nephew, Kobi, he looks up to me. It's probably because he doesn't know me, but she made me see that if I didn't at least try, I'd never know if I was a good enough uncle for him, which is why I really need to get to his party."

"You will," her smile was sweet, but she wasn't going to hurry things along, "and Caden? Your support worker? Is he still in the picture?"

"He was," he knew he probably shouldn't be admitting any of this to her, but what more damage could he do, "but I don't know anymore. He was supposed to -,"

Elias suddenly realized that this was the last place Caden would show his face. *Maybe he's waiting for me to get out so we can meet up and talk?*

"I'm not judging," she raised her hands gently, "no criminal charges have been pressed and nothing has been confirmed. That article was nothing more than gossip but I suspect he's laying low for a while."

"Maybe. We had a fight. You want to know the reason I

stayed sober? It was him."

Monica's hazel eyes softened slightly, the romance warming her cheeks. She nodded for Elias to open up, to continue but he wasn't sure he wanted to.

"He was a distraction. Caden was something to focus on and I – I guess I fell in love."

"The world's most powerful drug."

"You could say that," he nodded, "but I think I messed it up. That stuff they said about him in the newspaper, it was my fault. I said the wrong things to the wrong people and this was my punishment. He'll never speak to me again after this."

"I've been divorced twice but I'm still an old romantic at heart. People will talk no matter what you do. You may as well be happy with a guy you love."

Monica's words made sense but it was idealistic. He could already feel the glow of what they'd had wearing off. Not because he felt any different about Caden, but because he was scared that they were kidding themselves. They were fragile and they didn't know each other as well as they were acting like. He didn't know what Caden's favorite color was, nor did he know his favorite TV show. Could you really love somebody you've practically just met? His heart said so, but he had nothing to compare it to.

"I'm going to recommend that you meet with a counselor," she started typing on her computer, "I think it will really help you."

"Can we skip that?"

"You may have climbed down from the tree, Mr. James," she sent something to print, "but you're not out of the woods yet. There's still a long way to go. You've done brilliantly getting to this stage but you have a long road ahead of you."

"I'm not going to relapse, if that's what you're saying," he was almost offended, "the reason I've never stayed clean is because I've never been off the stuff long enough to actually think about it."

Monica gave him a soft smile, the kind a mother might give to her child when she wanted to believe them, not that he had seen that smile from his mother, but that's how he imagined it would look if she had. He could tell Monica had seen hundreds of people like him, all swearing to stay clean. He wondered how many came back, frail and shaking because their bodies were screaming out for a substance it should never have had? Rehab wasn't the cure, Elias knew that. Rehab got him clean, Caden kept him clean. If he didn't have Caden in his life, could he stay clean? *I don't even want to think about that.*

"Can I go now?" he stood up, not wanting to give her room to chat more, "I really do need to be somewhere."

"Sure," she handed over a piece of paper, "hand this in at the desk and they'll schedule for you to come back to see the Counselor."

He wanted to refuse to take it but he knew that he could get out of there quicker if he just accepted the paper. He checked the time on his cell and he had fifteen minutes before the start of Kobi's party to find Caden. Was it enough time to apologize for being such a jerk? Maybe Caden was worrying about it as much as he was? They hadn't called or texted but maybe they were waiting for the other to do it first? Too many maybes and not enough answers for Elias' liking.

"Congratulations, Mr. James," she handed over his results, "you should be proud of yourself."

"Sure," he nodded, feeling less proud and more anxious.

As soon as he handed the paper into the receptionist, he bolted out of the center with his results in his back pocket. He hoped he would be able to say that he never had to see it again but he was scheduled to return in three weeks.

First, he headed to his apartment. Caden wasn't there, despite having a key. He checked every room twice for a sign that somebody had been there but nothing had changed since he had spent a lonely night there. There was no note on the refrigerator and no message on the voicemail. Swallowing his fear of finding out what was in store for him, he headed for the door. His silenced cell phone started vibrating in his pocket and for a moment, he thought it was a sign from above, letting him know that Caden was looking for him too.

It wasn't.

It was Ellie.

Reluctantly, he answered the call.

"Hey," he closed his eyes, hovering on the top step of the staircase, "what's up?"

"What isn't up?" she snapped, a mixture of children's screams and laughter surrounding her, "The cake woman dropped off the cake and let's just say she's going to be getting an angry and very public message on her profile when this party is over. I asked her to make a cake of one of Kobi's favorite anime characters. Haraso, or something like that. I'm looking at it right now and it looks like somebody melted a Lego figure's face and then stuck it on a little girl's head. I need you to run to the store and get something, anything that I can stick candles in without giving these kids nightmares. Cindy's brought her kids half an hour early so I can't go myself."

When she paused for breath, Elias inhaled with her, forcing a smile on his face, not wanting to let her know that he didn't want to do it. He couldn't say no on Kobi's birthday.

"Sure thing," he nodded, his eyes still clenched, "chocolate or vanilla?"

"It's your call. Are you okay for cash?"

"I got it."

"I'll pay you when you get here," she mumbled, "listen Elias, I gotta go. *Charlie put that down*! You're a lifesaver."

She hung up and hurried off to rescue whatever Charlie was holding. Elias grabbed the manga comic books from under his bed, which Caden had helped him wrap neatly in a comic book style wrapping paper. Everything he wanted to say to Caden, he couldn't say over the phone, but he would have to try. Ellie had taken away those precious fifteen minutes, which had quickly turned into five by the time he was at the grocery store.

With the biggest cake he could find in the shape of a caterpillar, he tossed the dollar bills at the check out girl before jumping in a taxi to Ellie's. When they were on the road, he pressed his cellphone into his ear, each ring making his heart quiver.

"Pick up, pick up!"

"Huh?" the driver asked through the mirror.

"Sorry, not you. I'm on the phone."

Caden didn't pick up. It went to his voicemail after the fourteenth ring. What he had to say definitely couldn't be said over a message so he tried again. He counted the rings again and on the fourteenth, he was back to the generic recording asking him to leave his message after the beep. He hovered over the picture of Caden that he had taken for the profile picture. His smile was beaming, so carefree and easy. Would he ever show Elias that smile again? He was about to try calling again, unbothered by how desperate it looked but the car stopped and he was outside of Ellie's house.

"Keep the change," he told the driver as he grabbed the cake box.

The outside of her huge white house had been decorated in colorful balloons that screamed '*I hired a party planner so my kid's birthday party is better than your kid's birthday party*'. At the same time Elias arrived, three other cars pulled up. Parents, followed by their kids clutching gift bags hurried towards the gated entrance, which for one day, had been swung open and garishly decorated with a neon green and blue banner letting everybody know that it was '*Kobi's Seventh Birthday Party*', just in case people didn't already know.

Elias hurried inside, heading straight for the kitchen. A plastic solo cup was already clutched in Ellie's fist but he guessed it was filled with a little more than orange juice.

"Thank God," she cried when she saw her brother, "let's see it."

He suddenly had a thought that she wasn't going to be as easy going about the random design he had chosen but she seemed happy that the cake wasn't as horrifically themed. The offending cake was already deep in the trash so nobody could ever see her mistake.

"How much do I owe you?" she reached for her purse on the edge of the kitchen counter.

"On me," he knew he didn't have much money in his own

wallet but he was grateful just to be there.

Ellie appreciated the gesture but she still slipped a twenty-dollar bill into his jacket pocket, despite the cake only costing him fourteen.

"Where's Caden?" she glanced over his shoulder, "Is he not here?"

"I don't think he's coming."

"Why? Is he busy?"

The blank expression in her eyes revealed that she was in the minority of people who hadn't seen yesterday's paper. When he mentioned it, she looked even more confused. Between work and the party planning, she didn't have time to read the paper. After a quick search on her cell phone, she scanned over the article, her hand rising to her mouth.

"Poor Caden," she sighed, "how did this -,"

Ellie stopped herself, apparently putting two and two together in time to figure out who it was.

"And now we're in a fight, I think," Elias clung to the wrapped gift for support, "when he found out, I said some things, we both did. We got carried away but I haven't seen him since yesterday."

"Call him?"

"I have. Twice. No answer."

"Maybe he is busy after all?"

"Yeah," he forced a smile, trying not to show how worried he was.

When Ellie vanished to play her role as hostess to the rapidly thickening crowd of parents, all eyeing up the wine bottles on the opposite side of the kitchen, Elias checked his cellphone in vain. *No new messages. No new calls.* The empty notification screen stung but he wasn't going to give up. He called Caden again to be greeted with the voicemail after fourteen rings. Just when he was about to try again, a small figure ran in from the garden, grass stains on his knees and a blue party hat on his head, reminding Elias of why he was there.

"Uncle Elias!" Kobi screamed at the top of his lungs, running and jumping into Elias' arms.

He was heavy, so much heavier than the last time he had picked him up. It was a reminder of how much of his only nephew's life he had missed.

"You came!" he exclaimed, so much joy in his airy voice, "You really came!"

"I wouldn't have missed it!" he dropped Kobi back to the ground and examined him over with sober eyes, "Look how big you've grown! You'll be as tall as me soon."

"Maybe even taller," he grinned, "is that for me?"

Kobi was eyeing up the brightly wrapped gift on the counter. The official pile of gifts was neatly stacked on a large round table in the hall, most likely waiting for all his friends to arrive so Kobi could open them in front of everyone. Elias could only remember one party from his childhood and he was sure, looking back, that the nanny at the time, Jenny, had arranged it instead of his mother. Despite that, his mother tried to control the day and insisted that he open his presents in front of all of the guests, which he hated. The mayor got him a stack of encyclopedias. Elias had only been nine.

"Can I rip it open?" Kobi clutched the gift, looking around for his mom.

"Only if you keep it a secret," Elias ruffled the thick black hair poking out from the party hat.

"I'm good at keeping secrets," he puffed out his chest, "daddy's living in a hotel but I have to tell people he's away on business."

He didn't seem affected by the divorce yet but Elias guessed that was because he didn't understand the seriousness of it. The novelty would probably blind him because he would get two birthdays, two Thanksgiving dinners and two Christmases, but one day it would hit him. Maybe he would be lucky and suppress it until later on in life where it might all pour out in a therapy session if his own future relationship turned sour.

"Manga!" he clutched them to his chest, "How did you know?"

"Good guess," all of the credit went to Caden, which was another slap to the face, "are they the right ones?"

"They're awesome. Does this mean you're all better now? Mommy was saying that you weren't sick anymore."

Elias was touched that Ellie had laid the groundwork for him. The drug test was folded messily in his back pocket but Ellie hadn't asked to see it yet. He guessed she was too distracted with everything else going on, for once in her life, her brother wasn't her biggest problem.

"I'm all better," Elias crouched down so he could be face to face with Kobi, "and you're going to be seeing a lot more of me now. I promise you that."

Kobi flung his tiny arms around Elias' neck, giving him a tight, choking hug. The outpouring of love he had felt from an innocent child like Kobi was just as strong, if not stronger than what he had felt from Caden. *Different, but powerful.*

With his first opened gift, he ran into the garden to show his friends. Elias felt proud when the boys all gathered around him gasping with jealousy. *Have I just become the cool uncle?*

The clown arrived and the party finally settled down for a while. Standing at the back of the crowd, Elias watched as the other parents looked on as their kids laughed. They all had soft smiles on their face as they watched the children with such unquestioned adoration. Elias had never seen that smile from his own mother.

"You've checked that phone every ten seconds since you got here," Ellie nodded when they were both in the kitchen, slicing up the caterpillar cake, "you can go if you want."

"No, I'll stay. I want to."

"You've made his day, Elias. You don't have to stick around. Last year when you came to his party uninvited, you couldn't wait to leave after passing out in his cake but that was for a different reason. You actually have a real life issue to deal with."

She was giving him permission to leave but he was scared to go in search of Caden. What would he find? A man waiting with his arms open or a man who never wanted to see him ever again? He wished he had an idea of how these things worked. Caden had been in a serious relationship; was he playing by a set of post-fight rules that Elias didn't know?

"What if he doesn't want to know me? I've ruined his life."

"How?" she laughed, licking chocolate frosting off her thumb, "You two are clearly made for each other."

"You think?"

"I know it. You seem to help each other from what I can see. That's what a relationship is all about. Becoming a unit and fighting the world. That's what John and I never had. I got pregnant so fast and then we married and things just became about work and getting through the week."

She seemed saddened by the ending of her marriage but she didn't seem shocked anymore. It had settled in and she seemed to have accepted that it was for the best. Elias found that sad because even though he didn't like John, it was the end of something they'd sworn to stick to. Caden had sworn to stick by him - *so why did I ask him to leave?*

"What if this has broken what we had? I don't even know his favorite color," it sounded pathetic out loud.

"So?" she laughed, "That stuff comes with time. Love is like a jigsaw. You have the box, you just need to put all of the pieces together."

"What if those pieces don't fit?"

"You'll never know if you don't try," she cut the last slice and dolloped it onto a paper plate before handing it to Elias, "you've wasted enough of your life chasing something that didn't matter. Start chasing something that matters."

"What if it just doesn't work?"

"Too many what ifs," she shook her head, her sharp black bob springing out from behind her ears, looking longer than it usually did, "if it doesn't work out, you've had a good month together, haven't you?"

"Yeah," he shrugged, "but I need more than a month. It was too fast. I want more months. So many more months."

"Then I'm kicking you out of the party," she grabbed his shoulders and steered him toward the door, "get out of here and go find your bliss."

"What's gotten into you?"

"I'm happy," she squeezed his shoulders firmly, "for the first time in a long time I have nothing to worry about. Well, my impending divorce and crumbling family unit, but John isn't going to drag this out any longer than it needs to be. A clean break, that's what he said."

She opened the door and Elias fell out onto her doorstep, the cake still clutched in his hand. He looked at his sister and she did look happy.

"Your hair looks different," he noticed that it was past her jaw for the first time since they were thirteen.

"I'm growing it out," she plucked the cake out of his hand and stuffed it into her mouth, "call me."

Licking frosting off her fingers, she closed the door, allowing Elias to leave the party in a dignified and sober way. It felt good. Feeling invigorated, he stepped through the open gate, ready to fight for what he wanted.

***

Waking up, face down in a couch he didn't recognize, Caden looked up, a crick forming in his neck. Sitting up, he rubbed his shoulders as his mind came forward. *Why am I asleep in my brother's living room?*

The quickly forming headache reminded him of the bottle of wine he drank with Lucy, pouring out his heart to her until the early hours. Patting down his pockets, he couldn't feel his cell phone. After a quick turn out of the couch, he still couldn't find it.

"Morning, or should I say afternoon?" Lucy appeared in the door, "It's just past four."

"Four pm?" Caden jumped up, "Why didn't you wake me?"

"We were up till five and you must have needed it. Coffee?"

Following his sister-in-law into the kitchen, he had the strangest feeling that he was supposed to be somewhere but he couldn't even start to think about it until he had at least one coffee flowing through his blood.

"Why aren't you working?"

"It's Tuesday," she said, "I don't work Tuesdays."

"Tuesday," he mused, wondering why Tuesday meant something to him.

"Have you thought about what you're going to do next?"

Sipping the hot coffee, he was about to say it was too early in the morning to talk about that but he remembered that he had slept away most of the day.

"I'm just going to lie low and plan my next move," the newspaper was probably still circulating the town, shocking and intriguing the residents of Havenmoore.

"I meant about Elias."

Caden sighed and leaned against his hand as he stared out of Lucy's kitchen window and into her garden. The sky was slightly grey, reflecting how he felt. If he had known what was happening with Elias, he wouldn't have had to turn to wine.

"He told me to leave."

"People say things they don't mean. I'll fix you a sandwich, you must be starving."

Lucy didn't wait for a response and like a typical mother, got to work making him a peanut butter and jelly sandwich. Caden's stomach gurgled as he watched her make it.

"Have you seen my cell?" he looked around the kitchen for it.

"Nope," Lucy passed him the sandwich, "when did you last have it?"

"I don't remember," he remembered hovering over Elias' number, wanting to call but not having the courage to actually do it, "Tuesday! Shit! Today was Elias' drug test at the rehab. Oh, damn. I said I'd be there."

"Pre-fight or post-fight?"

"Pre, but I promised. I need to go. I need to find him and talk. This is dumb. The newspaper, that's not his fault, it's his mom's. He was in the line of fire when I needed to explode and he got hit when he shouldn't have. I need to go. I can't sit around here all day talking about fixing this. I need to go and fix it."

"At least eat your sandwich?" she pushed the plate closer

toward him.

Caden thought about it for a second but he knew he had already wasted so much time sleeping off his hangover. Pushing the plate back to Lucy with an apologetic kiss on the cheek, he grabbed his denim jacket, pulling it over his creased white t-shirt.

Wasting no time, he headed straight for Elias' apartment. His knuckles crashed down on the door. There was no answer but that didn't stop him from knocking. What if Elias had been sleeping the day away too?

"Elias?" he pushed his mouth up to the door, "Are you in there? It's Caden. I'm – we *need* to talk."

Clenching up his fists, he hit the wood hard, pressing his ear firmly against the green peeling paint. There was no answer. When he turned, Billy the baker was leaning against the dumpster with a cigarette hanging from his lip, all of the words from the newspaper article written all over his face.

He was about to offer an explanation to the greasy, little man but he tore away, the need to find Elias growing in his chest every second. Walking around the corner into the small town square, he stared at the town hall but he knew the mayor wouldn't know where Elias was anymore than he did. Turning on the spot, he scanned the faces in the crowd, looking for somebody or something familiar.

Caden found that familiar face, but it wasn't Elias. He watched as Finn opened the door to one of Havenmoore's tiny guesthouses. In the summer, the town attracted a small tourist crowd but in September, they were usually empty, waiting for the hot weather to roll around again. Almost not believing his eyes, he bolted across the square, heading straight into the guesthouse.

The noise of the square disappeared to be replaced with the soft hum of violins, crackling from an old radio behind the counter where an elderly woman was sitting on a stool, a book wedged in her hands.

"Where did that guy go?" he asked the woman, who finished her page before looking up.

"I don't want any trouble," her voice was husky and aged, "unless you're looking for a room."

"I need to speak to the guy who just came in here. Finn's his name. Is he staying here?"

The woman didn't look like she was going to tell him but before she could tell him that, Finn appeared at the foot of the stairs, summoned by Caden's voice. He had a soft, nearly smug smile on his face as he stood with his hands casually hanging from the pockets of his too-tight jeans.

"Looking for a room?" he smirked, "I've got a twin if you want to share?"

"You'll have to pay for that," the old woman coughed, "I'm not running some kind of hotel. You pay per person in these parts."

"I'm not looking for a room," Caden snapped, "I want to know what you're doing here."

Finn narrowed his eyes on Caden and Caden could tell that he was trying to think up a story to excuse his presence. Caden was sure that Finn would have ran straight back to New York with his tail between his legs the second Caden told him that he wasn't interested in the heartwarming reunion Finn had planned.

"There's a small coffee shop next door if you want to talk," Finn stepped down from the step, taking a small stride towards Caden before bouncing back on his heels with a carefreeness that Caden envied, "or we could do this here?"

The woman snorted without looking up from her book, which she was back to reading even though it was obvious her ears were pricked to listen to every single word. The thought of having coffee with Finn didn't sound fun but neither did starting an argument in the reception of a guesthouse with an eighty-nine year old audience member.

"Fine."

Caden told Finn that he didn't actually want to drink coffee because he didn't plan on sticking around for long but Finn came back with a drink for each of them. Caden was even angrier that he got him his favorite, a Salted Caramel Latte. A latte wasn't going to be a big enough Band-Aid. They sat at one of the tables on the sidewalk outside the coffee shop. The sun was already starting to set and there was a chill in the air but Finn didn't seem affected as he smiled, looking around the square as though nothing strange was going on.

"Why are you still here? You always hated coming here with me. What was it you called this place? The waiting room to hell?"

"It's quiet here," Finn sipped his coffee, "maybe I've changed. People can change."

"Oh, I know people can change. I've changed since I got back here but you're not getting away with pretending you have. Why are you really here?"

Finn narrowed his eyes across the table, his firm and solid chest pushing through the tight red t-shirt he was wearing. As the sun lowered in the sky, it cast a golden glow on Finn's pale hair.

"There's been a water leak at the apartment," he said with a tightening in his jaw, "I found out when I was about to drive back, so I thought I'd stick around for a couple of days until it was fixed."

"Liar," Caden sighed, "you always do that jaw thing when you're lying."

Finn smirked, clearly caught out.

"Would you believe me if I told you I just wanted a couple of days here to see why you were so sure you wanted to stay for the rest of your life?"

"Nope."

"You obviously know me inside out," Finn leaned in, "because I still think it's the waiting room to hell."

Caden could see right through what Finn was trying to do. He was trying to show Caden how much they really knew each other but he felt like the version of Caden that Finn thought he knew was still in New York, where it would always stay.

"If you're here to try and convince me to come back with you, it won't work."

"Why?"

"Because I've moved on."

"With that addict?"

"Don't even pretend like you know him."

"I know that he's got a little coke habit," Finn sipped his coffee innocently, "bad habit to kick."

"And yet he's kicked it. He's clean."

"How can you be sure?"

Caden wasn't. He hadn't seen the results from the rehab and he suddenly had a dark thought that Elias was avoiding him because the results weren't what they'd expected them to be. *No, he hasn't relapsed. I'd know.*

"We're not here to talk about Elias."

"He's the problem," Finn's bright blues rolled around in his sockets, "he's what's stopping you from seeing how stupid all of this is, Cadey. If it's a mid-life crisis, we can work through it, together. We can pretend this last month didn't happen. It was a blip."

"Our relationship was a blip. A long, blind blip. Elias is the reason I've come to my senses," there was a bite in his voice, "why are you here? Don't make me ask again."

The sweetness and light vanished from Finn's face and his head lowered slightly. Peering under his perfectly groomed brows at Caden, he almost looked genuinely upset.

"I can't make rent," he exhaled deeply, "New York is expensive. When I was driving back, Adam told me that he saw the super knocking on my door talking about eviction."

"Adam?" Caden laughed, "Still hooking up with him? Why come back here? Why not go to New York and stay with one of your friends until you worked something out?"

Finn's silence said it all. He had a look that cried *'a man has needs'* written all over his face.

"Because I'm two months behind with the rent," he whispered, leaning across the table with the cardboard coffee cup clenched tightly in his hands, "do you have any idea how difficult is was to keep up that lifestyle when you were practically earning nothing? When you left me, it became even harder and I couldn't keep up."

"I've only been gone for a month."

"The bills have been piling up for months."

"So? What does this have to do with me?"

"Because you didn't complain when I was buying all of that expensive stuff for the apartment. You helped me get into this situation."

Caden had grown used to the life that Finn supplied but now that he was out of it, it felt like all of the lavish things he liked to do were just distractions so Caden didn't notice that he was fucking Adam and probably other men behind his back.

"I still don't get why you're staying here."

"Because," he sighed, "I wanted to convince you to come back with me. We could work things out and we'd move past this."

"You mean my tiny rent contribution will keep your head above water? I'm sorry that I didn't earn as much as you but it's not my fault that you have expensive taste."

"It's not just about money, Cadey," Finn let go of his coffee cup and darted his hands across the table, grabbing Caden's, "I really do miss you."

Looking down at the hands, he could almost believe him.

Chapter 19

Elias didn't know how long he had been standing on the corner watching Caden and Finn talk but he couldn't look away. When he saw Finn's hands grab Caden's, he waited for Caden to pull them away, but he didn't.

He instantly felt sick and dizzy as the pieces of the puzzle started to slot into place. *This is why he didn't call you. This is what he's been doing.* He felt his heart clench tightly in his chest as his legs suddenly reanimated. Running around the corner to his apartment, he paused before opening the door, leaning against the wood as he stared up at the darkening sky.

He waited for the sickness to pass but it didn't. Just thinking about how quickly Caden could move on made him want to throw up. Billy, the baker appeared at the door, tossing a tray of burnt muffins into the dumpster. He looked Elias up and down, shook his head and headed back inside.

Elias felt pathetic. Love had blinded him and turned him into a fool. Caden had helped him get clean but had he just been a project until the ex decided to run over from the big city? Elias knew he had been a distraction, but he didn't know how much of one he had been.

When he finally found the strength to dig his apartment keys from the bottom of his pocket, he headed up into the darkness, the optimism and hope he had felt when leaving the party suddenly draining away, leaving him completely empty.

In a fit of rage, he started tossing around the clothes in his bedroom until he found the suit jacket from the ball. With shaking fumbling fingers, he felt the inner lining of the jacket rip under his touch as he searched for the letter he had fished out of Caden's trashcan. The envelope was crinkled, the artfully neat handwriting addressed to Caden mocking him. Maybe Caden finally read one of those letters and realized what he was missing out on?

Heading into the kitchen, he dug under the sink, knocking everything all over the floor. The washing detergent box split, sending white powder across the white tiles. Elias didn't care how much of a mess he was making because he found what he was looking for. A bottle of vodka was buried deep in the back. It had been one of the first things he had done when he got the apartment. A habit he had always found hard to break. Always hide something in case they think they've taken everything. He had forgotten about it, letting it mingle in with the spray bleach and fabric softener. When he really needed it, it was the first place his mind went.

With the unopened bottle in one hand and the letter clenched in the other, he crashed on the couch. First things first, he cracked open the vodka. It was odorless but he could practically taste it. Taking once quick swig, he was surprised at how strong it tasted. Had vodka always been that strong? Screwing the cap back into place, he let it fall onto the couch as he felt his mouth and throat burn.

Next, he ripped open the letter, pouring over two double-sided computer-typed pages of Finn's deepest feelings. The first half of the first page was filled with apologies, the second half with excuses, the second side with the great memories they had shared and then a whole page dedicated to begging and promising to change if Caden forgave him.

How could I ever compete with this? All of Caden's memories with me revolve around my problems.

Scrunching up the letter, he tossed it across his apartment. It didn't make him feel any better. The vodka was next to go. Letting out a deep and angry scream, he launched it at the wall. It drastically missed where he was aiming for, hitting the wall mounted TV. It cracked and tilted, creaking desperately as it hung from the wall with one remaining bracket.

He could break everything in the apartment but it wouldn't make him feel any better. He could drink every bottle of vodka he could get his hands on but it wouldn't make him feel any better. The one thing he knew could make him feel better was the one thing he had been stupid enough to lose.

Pulling the drug test from his back pocket, he let the results mock him for a second before ripping it into as many tiny pieces as his crumbling fingers could.

***

"I'm leaving. I'm not listening to this anymore," Caden stood, leaving his coffee untouched, "there's somewhere I need to be."

"You're going to him, aren't you?" the sweetness had turned to begging and the begging had turned to rage, "When are you going to grow up? You're nearly thirty and you're running around like a lovesick teenager."

"So?" Caden shrugged, "I'll take that any day over a fool who stays with somebody who cheats on them."

"Mistakes happen!" Finn stood and started following Caden across the square as he headed to the line of taxis on the corner, ready to search the entire town for Elias if he had to.

"They do. It was a mistake for you to stay here."

Trampling through the flowerbeds of the grassy common area, Caden zipped up his jacket as the night slowly crept in early, signaling the end of summer and the start of fall. Soon the town would be filled with pumpkins and for once, he would be around to see it. Nothing was going to drag him away from Havenmoore as long as Elias was there. A damning newspaper article and a desperate ex-boyfriend were not going to be the things to stand in his way.

"Caden!" Finn's shriek was so loud, Caden felt the busy town square silence suddenly as everybody turned to see what the drama was, "Stop running away from me."

"I'm not running away, I'm walking away. Stop following me."

Finn caught up with him and a hand wrapped around Caden's arm, dragging him roughly around. He looked into those crystal and cold eyes as they searched for something to say to make Caden change his mind.

"Cadey, Cadey listen to me," Finn ran the back of his hand up and down Caden's stubbly cheek, "we can get through this. I'm sorry. I fucked up. I wasn't thinking."

Caden looked down to the hand gripping him as perfectly manicured nails tightened around his jacket, digging into his skin.

"Let go of me," Caden struggled, "you're hurting me!"

"What you're doing is hurting me," Finn lost all control of his volume as he entered hysterical territory, "why don't you want me?"

Caden stared at his soft, tanned skin. When they'd first met, Caden was convinced that Finn was out of his league. They'd met at a party, both of them with dates they didn't like. They found each other in the kitchen, searching for alcohol and they ditched the party and were soon back at Finn's apartment, in his bed. He had wanted him so much then, but that was just physically. Finn was beautiful but he was emotionally empty. Like a technically good painting missing that little extra sparkle, Finn was missing the extra that Elias had in abundance. It was nothing to do with want, it was all about need.

"We're over," Caden cried back, "I'm not telling you again."

With his free hand, he grabbed Finn's wrist and yanked him off with so much force that Finn stumbled backwards, falling into the flowers, squashing them even more. A crowd had lined the edges of the square, all gasping dramatically as they watched the scene unfold in silence.

"Get up," Caden crouched to help Finn up, "just go back to New York."

"Get off me!" his loudest screech yet, "Just leave me alone."

Caden knew Finn better than he would like to admit. Finn would happily put himself in a situation to be made fun of, that's what made him the life of every party. One thing he didn't like was when somebody else put him in that situation. He was a man who hated losing control and embarrassment was his Achilles' heel. Scrambling to his feet, he wiped the dirt off the back of his skinny jeans and headed straight for the guesthouse with his head down. Caden knew that he wouldn't see Finn again. This was his version of a retreat and if Caden was right, Finn would be packing his bag and jumping into his car the second he was back in his room.

The crowd all watched to see what Caden's next move was going to be. When he remembered the front page of the newspaper he had adorned, he could see the recognition in the eyes of most of the people staring at him. They were probably waiting for the next scandal to emerge so they could watch his downfall. *Let them wonder, I have somewhere I need to be.*

Turning back to the cabs, somebody caught his eye. Not because he recognized them, not at first, but because they were hurrying along the sidewalk with a phone pressed into their ear. They were so engrossed in their call, they hadn't noticed the public show that was happening right under their nose. When the crowd reanimated, Caden noticed who the person was. Judy James. Anger bubbled up inside him as he watched the woman who had ruined his life walk by without a care in the world. He would have let her vanish out of sight but she did something unusual that caught his eye. Instead of running up the steps of the town hall, she stopped outside to drop her cellphone into her bag.

Walking forward slowly, Caden mounted the sidewalk and stood next to one of the taxis.

"Where to?" a voice in an accent he didn't recognize mumbled through the window, "Hey, you, do you want a taxi or not?"

Caden looked down to the man for a second before looking back up to watch the mayor. She was pretending to look in her purse but her eyes were darting around the square from underneath her angular haircut. She was looking to see if she was being watched.

"Dude?" the driver asked, "Get in or get off my patch."

"Sorry," Caden stepped back without making eye contact.

The mayor had him transfixed because she looked like she was up to something. After a couple of seconds of watching her, it became obvious that she wasn't just looking to see if she was being watched, she was waiting for somebody. Creeping along the sidewalk with his head down, he got as close to her as he dared. Leaning against a lamppost as it flickered into life, he watched her out of the corner of his eye.

A figure, all dressed in black appeared in front of her. Caden thought it was a false alarm at first because he walked right by her and into the darkening alley next to the town hall. When she followed him in seconds later, still glancing around to make sure she was still invisible, he knew he had to follow. It could be anything or nothing but it didn't feel like nothing. It felt like she was up to something she shouldn't be and Caden was desperate to get something he could use on the mayor. It wasn't for revenge but for insurance in case she furthered her attack on him.

"That's not the price we agreed," she hissed as Caden hovered at the mouth of the alley, leaning against the cold brickwork.

"I'm not here to negotiate," a dark, gravely voice snapped, "you want a job done and you know I'm the only one who can do it. Unless you want to do it yourself, Madame Mayor?"

"You know I can't," she was attempting to whisper but her deep voice bounced and echoed between the two buildings, letting Caden hear the desperation in her voice, "I just need him out of the way. He's a threat. Here. Take it. You'll get the rest when you've done your part."

There was a long pause. Caden guessed the stranger was counting whatever cash she had just handed over.

"Take this too. It's a key to his apartment," she said.

It didn't take Caden long to figure out whose apartment she was talking about and if he was in any doubt, the man's next words confirmed it.

"Elias isn't going to come easily. He ran away from me last time."

"Just do what you have to do, Rigsy. I need him silenced."

"Whatever you say, *Mom*," he laughed sarcastically.

"I'm doing what is best for my child. It's only a matter of time before he relapses. The sooner he's back in rehab, the sooner he can actually get better."

"Sure," the voice laughed, "whatever helps you sleep at night."

Firm and heavy footsteps headed along the uneven stone alley, forcing Caden back into the shadow of the town hall, hoping he would go unseen. He hoped it looked like he was waiting for somebody and not spying because whoever this man was, he didn't sound friendly. The hooded figure zoomed by him but he managed to see a flash of dark skin. The mayor emerged over a minute later and she too was too wrapped up in her own thoughts, because she walked right by Caden without a flicker of recognition.

"*Rigsy?*" Caden whispered, sure the name meant something to him.

Chapter 20

Leaning over the railing, looking out into the dark water, Elias scattered the tiny pieces of his drug test, unsure of why he had clung onto it for so long. Late night fishing boats dotted the horizon, the beam from the lighthouse illuminating them as they bobbed up and down on the waves. Elias wondered what it would be like to live out alone at sea where nobody could hurt him; *and where I couldn't hurt anybody.*

A six-pack of beers sat next to his foot but he hadn't opened one. After smashing his emergency stash of vodka, he felt like he needed to replace it and for once he didn't go for the strongest thing in the shop. He still couldn't bring himself to drink it. Alcohol had never been his addiction but it worked at calming his mind. That's all he wanted it for. *I want to forget seeing Caden holding somebody else's hand.*

The day should have turned out very differently. Elias had gained his official sober status, he had gained back his nephew and sister's trust but he felt like he had lost so much too. It wasn't until the tears tumbled off his chin that he even realized he was silently crying.

Reaching down, he picked up one of the beers. He dangled it over the edge of the railing, staring at the shiny label under the moonlight. It didn't excite him, it left him feeling empty but he still used the jagged metal that he was leaning against to pop off the metal cap. With a soft plop it sunk into the water below, disappearing into the darkness.

The beer was warm and bitter, not at all like he remembered. It reminded him of old socks and after a couple more mouthfuls, he sent the bottle crashing into the water to rejoin its cap.

"You're supposed to drink that," a familiar voice made him jump back from the railing, "or are you craving something stronger?"

Why Rigsy was walking towards him wearing all black, he didn't know and he wasn't sure he cared that much.

"I'm not in the mood for you," Elias' voice was croakier than expected.

Ignoring him, Rigsy approached and leaned against the railing next to Elias. After kicking open the bag, Rigsy grabbed one of the beers without asking and quickly popped off the cap with his bare hands.

"I was passing and I saw you," Rigsy offered the information before Elias had time to ask, "planning to jump over the edge?"

"What's it to you?"

"Can't a man ask a question around here?" Rigsy darted his brows playfully, the mouth of the bottle resting against his tongue.

"Just get out of here, Rigsy. I'm not playing your games."

They stared at sea together, a cold blanket wrapping around Elias' shoulders as the night turned colder. He would have grabbed his jacket but he hadn't been thinking. The port hadn't been his first destination but it's where he found himself when he stopped walking. It felt like he was standing on the edge of

Havenmoore and it still didn't feel far enough away from the heart of the town.

"I thought you'd had it all figured out now that you're clean. Trouble in paradise?" Rigsy asked, "Or has that new man of yours realized you're crazy?"

"How did you know about him?"

"I know everything," he winked playfully, "I have eyes all over this town."

"You sound like somebody else I know," he mumbled bitterly to himself.

"Want to talk about it?" Rigsy tossed the empty beer bottle as far out to sea as he could before stuffing his hands in his pockets and turning to face Elias properly.

"We were never friends," Elias laughed, "don't pretend like we were. Why are you here?"

"I told you, I was passing and I saw you."

Elias looked out to where the wooden jetty rejoined the sidewalk and he knew it was possible that Rigsy could have seen him. The majority of the port was pretty well lit, which he guessed were for the surveillance cameras watching the boats and the large, metal containers.

"If you're not trying to jump, why are you here?" Rigsy asked.

"I don't know," Elias mumbled, "I should go home."

"Wait," Rigsy reached out and grabbed Elias' arm, "I lied, I was looking for you. Shareen, my girl, she kicked me out. Somebody told her about some of the stuff I've done. I came to find you to see if you'd told her but it wasn't you."

"How do you know it wasn't me?"

"Because I know you," Rigsy smiled, biting his plump and dark lip with his almost too white teeth, "and you can't lie, kid, not to me. We go way back."

"For all the wrong reasons," Elias pulled away from Rigsy's soft grip, "I need to go."

"Let me drive you," Rigsy offered, "my car is close. It's late and this town isn't as safe as people pretend."

Elias should have known not to get into Rigsy's car but he

was a familiar face and for once, he didn't want to be on his own. When they pulled up outside of his apartment and Rigsy asked if he could come up for a beer, Elias nodded and led the way, unsure of what was happening. With shaking fingers, he found his keys deep inside of his pocket and instantly dropped them on the ground. With a deep laugh, Rigsy bent down and picked them up for him. He leaned into Elias' side, opening the door for him. The bitter beer was hot on his breath, tickling his neck in the cold night.

The door opened and he hurried inside, letting Rigsy follow him. When he was in his apartment, he half hoped that he would find Caden there but it was as empty and dark as he had left it.

"What happened in here?" Rigsy pulled back his hood to reveal that his dark Afro hair had been cut right back to his scalp.

"I took out my anger on the TV," Elias turned on the table lamp sitting next to the couch, "we won't be able to watch anything, so if you want to go, you can."

"I didn't come to watch TV," Rigsy whispered, closing the door behind him.

Elias felt trapped in his own apartment. It wasn't the sip of vodka or the two sips of beer that had invited Rigsy into his apartment, it was his own stupidity. One of the counselors at the rehab center had once said that Elias was his own saboteur and he was finally starting to see why. From the plastic bag, he grabbed one of the beers and handed it to Rigsy, opting for a can of soda from the fridge for himself.

"Soda?" Rigsy laughed, "Who are you and what have you done with the Elias I know? Have a beer."

"I'm fine," he cracked open the soda, "I'm not drinking."

"Why buy beer?"

"Because I'm weak and I'm selfish."

"It's not selfish to want to forget," Rigsy sat on the couch, putting his feet on the glass coffee table.

Elias wasn't sure he agreed. He had spent the best part of a decade trying to forget the emptiness within. *I could have used that time to do so much with my life.* He sat next to Rigsy, leaving enough of a gap between them. The way Rigsy kept looking at him with soft doe eyes made something stir within. It was only a fragment of the way Caden had made him feel but Caden had his New York boy. *Maybe I should be selfish?*

When Rigsy asked what had happened with his boyfriend, Elias reached for a bottle of beer and cracked off the cap, ready to let everything flow.

***

Caden arrived at Ellie's, expected to be greeted by the locked gate but it was open with slowly deflating balloons hanging from a birthday banner.

"Caden?" Ellie was in the kitchen with a glass of wine firmly in her grip, "If you're here for the party, you're a little late. John's just picked up Kobi."

"I'm not," Caden was practically panting from running across town, "it's Elias, I think something is going to happen and I can't find him. Have you seen him?"

Ellie told him that Elias had been to the party but had left early to find him. An elevator dragged his heart down to the deepest pits of his stomach, forcing him to grab onto the edge of the counter. His imagination was playing tricks on him, torturing him with reasons why he had never found him.

"It's the mayor," Caden's voice was shaking, "I think I saw her talking to a drug dealer. I think she's trying to set Elias up for something, I just don't know what."

Ellie didn't ask any more questions. She grabbed her keys from her purse and headed straight for the door. Caden didn't ask how many glasses of the nearly empty bottle of wine she had drank, but he knew she was their best chance of finding Elias before Rigsy did.

***

"It was my own fault," Elias tried to take another sip but he had already finished the bottle without realizing it, "I drove him back to his ex. I told him to go, I just never thought he would. I thought he'd try and fight. I thought if I gave him some space, some time, he'd want to talk to me. I don't know why. I'm nothing special. Mr. New York is practically a model. I hope they're happy together."

"No you don't," Rigsy reached his hand over the back of the sofa, the soft glow of the bulb licking his dark skin warmly, "you want them both to be miserable."

"No, I want him to be happy," Elias' eyes glazed over as he imagined what Caden and Finn were doing right at that second, "even if it's not with me."

"You mean that?"

"Yeah," it hurt to say it, "I love him enough to know that I'm no good for him."

"Love?" Rigsy laughed, "Overrated."

"Don't you love your girlfriend? Your baby?"

Rigsy's eyes narrowed on him and Elias was sure that a nerve had been hit, "What's love got to do with it?"

"Tina Turner?"

Rigsy chuckled softly, his fingers reaching closer to Elias across the sofa, "You're funny. That's what I always liked about you. You have lip."

"Lip?"

"Attitude," Rigsy sipped his beer, the liquid wetting his lips, "you were never afraid of me. That's why I liked you."

The more Rigsy told Elias that he had always liked him, the more he was starting to believe it. Would it be so bad if they ended up in bed together? *Of course it would.* He knew it would be like crawling into bed with the devil and selling his soul. For what? A cheap thrill? *It won't make you stop thinking about him. It won't fix your breaking heart. You'll have to face it sooner or later.*

"You kept me around because I was good for business," he said, "I sent people your way when they needed a fix."

"That wasn't just it," Rigsy shook his head softly, "we had some good times, didn't we?"

"Did we?" Elias couldn't remember any.

"Remember that club I took you to in the city?"

Elias vaguely remembered something but he didn't

remember having much fun. He remembered doing four lines in a dirty bathroom and then finding himself on his knees in front of Rigsy as a thank you.

"Drugs. That's all we have in common."

"That's not all," Rigsy gripped his thick bulge in his jeans, "there were other things."

"It always came back to drugs."

"We're not doing drugs right now," Rigsy's fingers finally connecting with the side of Elias' face, freezing him.

At first, they softly touched his cheek but they didn't move. They were cold to the touch and they confused Elias. When they started to move in small circles, brushing against his dark stubble, he felt dizzy.

"I need to use the bathroom," Elias stood up, "that beer has gone right through me."

Locking himself in the bathroom, he leaned against the door. On the floor, Caden's clothes were mixed in with his own. *What am I doing?* Rigsy may have been the one to stroke his face but Elias had let him in to his apartment. In Rigsy's eyes, that was probably an invitation into his pants. Letting go of the door, he walked slowly over to the mirror, taking in his own reflection. A normal guy with dark hair and piercings stared back at him. There were signs of sleep deprivation under his hazel eyes, but he looked normal. Isn't that what he had always wanted? He didn't feel very normal. He felt broken. Closing his eyes, he could see Caden holding Finn's hand again, making him grip the edge of the sink. How could he move on so fast? *Did he really love me?*

Leaning over the sink, he felt the beer about to repeat on him. On reflection, he didn't even know why he drank the beer. He thought it would be easier to talk about Caden and he thought that would make it easier to move on. It hadn't done either. All it did was make him feel guilty for attempting to alter his mind with external things. *I thought I was over this dumb game.*

Caden's aftershave caught his eye next to the sink. Just seeing it, he could almost smell that clean and fresh scent that he loved so much. He reached out for it, seeming to enjoy the torture. Fingers trembling, he pulled off the cap and inhaled deeply. A pink mist descended over his closed lids. It was as if Caden was right in front of him.

Ditching the aftershave, he left the bathroom, ready to tell Rigsy to leave. He didn't care where the night was going he just knew it wasn't going anywhere with Rigsy. He was new to relationships so he could set his own new and fresh rules, not based in his selfish need to hurt himself and everyone around him.

"You need to go, Rigsy," Elias said the second he left the bathroom.

Rigsy snorted the fresh lines of cocaine on Elias' glass coffee table. Pulling on his nostril, he blinked heavily before shaking his head.

"Oh, this shit is fresh," he laughed, holding out the rolled up twenty dollar bill to Elias, "here, try it."

"What? No," Elias took a small step backward into his kitchen, "I'm not touching it."

"Why? You have nobody to please. You said yourself that guy is out of your life," Rigsy laughed darkly, "c'mon, live a little."

Elias watched Rigsy snort another line, quicker than the first. He knew the feeling all too well. At first, you'd feel nothing aside from a slight tickle in your nostril. Then, slowly but surely, the white line would start to alter your mood, making you happy. It would make you do things you didn't want to do. It would make you say things to people you wouldn't normally. It would turn you into a person you wanted to be, a better person, a nicer person. Despite all that, he knew what it really turned people into. When that greatness wore off, it would turn you into the worst kind of person. It would make you desperate and angry. You'd do anything you needed to do to get to that temporary place. The old Elias would have reached for the line in a heartbeat, wanting to hurry to that place so he could forget the real place he was in. Standing as he was now, Elias knew that wasn't an option, no matter how weak he felt.

"It's not about Caden. It's about me. I think you should

leave."

Rigsy stood, suddenly seeming to grow wider and taller in Elias' living room. He knew that two lines weren't enough to get Rigsy to that happy place. A seasoned professional like Rigsy needed more.

"No charge," he tilted his head, his heavy brow casting dark shadows across his face, "take it."

The room shrunk around Elias. He looked to the door, wondering if he could get there before Rigsy. *Why did I let him in?*

"I told you," he faked strength, "I'm off coke. I'm off ruining my life. I have other people to think about now."

"Like the ex who left you the second things got tough?" he laughed bitterly.

"Like my nephew, my sister," he said, "myself."

"Adorable," Rigsy mocked, "are you lying to yourself or me?"

"I'm not lying," he believed his own words, "I've been clean long enough to know that I'm better than that stuff."

"Two months and you're practically a saint."

"I'm no saint."

"So why are you acting like one?"

"I've told you. I'm staying clean."

"We both know you'll crack. Maybe not now, but one day. Something will happen and it will be too much for you to deal with and you'll turn to your old friend and you'll be chasing white lines faster than you can get on your knees to pay for it."

Elias almost believed him. It was something he had done so many times, so what was different this time?

"You're wrong."

"You know I'm not wrong."

"Leave."

There was a loud knock at the door and they both looked together. He knew who he wanted to be on the other side of that door but he knew it wouldn't be him.

"Elias?" it was his sister, "Are you in there?"

Rigsy lifted his finger to his lips, motioning for Elias to be quiet. Just as he was about to scream out, he looked at the coffee table. It wouldn't take Ellie long to jump to conclusions.

"Elias, if you're in there, this is important," she banged harder on the door, "please, answer the door."

Elias didn't care if Ellie believed him, nor did he care what assumptions she was going to jump to. The look in Rigsy's eyes was enough to scare him. Taking his chance, he darted for the door. His hand closed around the handle, but he wasn't fast enough. Rigsy must have sensed what he was about to do, because thick fingers closed around his mouth, pulling him tightly into his firm chest.

"She doesn't need to know we're here, does she?" Rigsy growled in his ear, the coke kicking in, "Let's just stay like this. She'll go away."

"Elias?" this time it wasn't Ellie.

"Caden!" Elias attempted to scream but Rigsy's fingers turned it into inaudible nonsense, "Caden!"

"What did I just say?" the hand tightened, "I have a job to do and you're not fucking this up."

Rigsy dragged Elias towards the coffee table, where two fresh lines were waiting for him. He thrashed and kicked but nothing he did seemed to affect Rigsy. He was a dealer and a dangerous one at that. He could handle skinny men in their late-twenties in his sleep. It was a lost fight from the second he let Rigsy into his apartment.

"Please," his cries were muffled as the tears appeared on his cheeks.

***

"I know he's in there," Caden pressed his ear against the door, "the light's on. Look, you can see it around the edges of the door."

"Maybe he went out?"

"It wasn't on when I came before."

"Maybe he came back?" Ellie looked up and down the alley, "And left again?"

She didn't look convinced and with each passing second, she

seemed to be taking Caden's story less and less seriously. The wine was clearly setting in and she was talking herself out of believing that her own mother would pay somebody off to set up her brother.

"This doesn't feel right," Caden's fingers ran through his strawberry blonde hair, grabbing fistfuls of it, "I don't know where else he could be."

"Caden, when you get to know my brother, you'll learn that he's not predictable. As far as we know, he's skipped town or – I don't know – maybe he's -,"

"I know what you're going to say," he silenced her with his hand, "don't. He's changed."

"I'm just saying," she shrugged, wrapping her arms across her body as a wind picked up around them, "I'll check the window out front. I might see movement. He could be in the shower?"

"He always showers with the door open," he mumbled, almost to himself, "Elias?"

His cries were met with silence. Desperation ran through him, making him regret every decision made over the last couple of days. *I should never have walked out. I should have fought for him. I shouldn't have left it this long.*

"I think I saw a shadow," Ellie called out from the front of the bakery, "I can't tell."

Caden was about to join her at the front of the bakery but the sound of smashing glass froze him to the spot. The wind was growing stronger, playing tricks on his ears. He wasn't sure if it had come from the apartment or from the other side of the alley.

"Did you hear that?" Ellie appeared at the mouth of the alley, "Sounded like glass smashing."

"I can't do this," Caden took a step back from the door, leaning against the dumpster, "he's in there, I know it."

Using his shoulder as a battering ram, he launched his body at the door. It creaked under his weight, but it didn't budge.

"What are you doing?" Ellie shrieked.

"It looks easy in the movies!"

His ego wounded, he rubbed his shoulder pathetically. He

was about to try again but he heard more smashing. It sounded denser than glass. He thought about the table lamp next to the couch.

"Move," Ellie pushed Caden to the side, "the weakest part of a door is next to the lock. Everybody knows that."

"They do?"

He guessed the wine was to blame for her sudden braveness but he wasn't complaining. The door swung open on impact with her foot.

"See," she stood back proudly.

"I loosened it up for you."

Feeling like he had already wasted more than enough time, he took the stairs two at a time, hoping that the sounds hadn't come from the apartment. *Please be okay, Elias, please.*

"Elias!" the deep scream from his throat was barely vocalized when he saw the man dressed in black from the alley, on top of Elias as he rolled around on the floor in the mess of broken furniture.

There was no doubt in Caden's mind of what he needed to do. No decision-making or split second regrets. The man he loved was in danger and he would go down trying to save him. Grabbing fistfuls of Rigsy's loose jacket, he dragged him off Elias. He had the element of surprise on his side and by the looks of it, a drug dealer under the influence of his own merchandise.

Clenching his fist, he struck Rigsy in the middle of his face. He tumbled back, landing flat out on the remains of the broken glass coffee table. His fist ached but the true pain was blinded.

"I'll call the police," Ellie was already digging in her purse.

"Don't," Elias stood up, "there's drugs. I'll be -,"

Before he could finish his sentence, silent and painful sobs tightened his face as he fell into Caden's body. There was no question if this was the right thing to do. Caden was through with the questions and talking.

"I love you," he whispered into Elias' dark hair, "I love you so much."

Chapter 21

Three coffees, one long explanation and a drug flushing down the toilet later, the police finally arrived. Rigsy had already fled, bolting for the door the second he woke up from Caden's surprising punch. It turned out that was the first time he had punched somebody, which flattered Elias.

"Wait, so you're telling me somebody broke into your place, trashed it and took nothing?" the police officer closed his book, a look on his face that he was close to clocking off for the night, "Are you sure they didn't take anything?"

"I'm sure," Elias nodded, Caden's arm still firmly around him as they sat on the couch, "I have nothing to take."

"The TV?" the police officer nodded at the now broken 42" screen, "They broke it instead of taking it?"

"Have you ever tried to rip a TV off a wall?" Ellie's tone of authority made the police officer back off, "My brother's told you everything he knows. It was probably kids, drunk kids looking for a cheap thrill. You should be out there looking for them instead of questioning my brother."

The police officer ended up apologizing before leaving.

"I can't believe she'd do this," Elias exhaled deeply when they were all finally alone, not wanting to believe what Caden had seen.

"She said she'd pay him the second half when he finished. She didn't say what it was but finding him here made it all clear. I didn't want to believe it either," Caden pulled him in close, "but we know what she's capable of."

"Our own mother," Ellie shook her head heavily, "I just -,"

"I know," he clenched his sister's hand, "welcome to the shitty end of the stick."

Ellie busied herself with cleaning up the glass and when the vacuum was stored away in the cleaning cupboard Elias didn't know he had, she left them alone, promising to send someone in the morning to fix the door that now wouldn't lock. Caden jammed a side table up against the door and the bottom step of the staircase so it wasn't opening anytime soon.

When silence finally fell on the apartment, Elias leaned into Caden's shoulder, smelling the aftershave first hand. It felt so good to be back in his arms.

"I'm sorry," Caden whispered gently.

"Why?"

"For leaving."

"I told you to."

"I knew you didn't mean it," lips pressed against the top of his head, "do you forgive me?"

"There's nothing to forgive. I'm the one who should be sorry. I drove you right back into his arms."

"Whose arms?"

"New York boy's. I saw you, holding hands in the square."

Caden pulled away, a look of confusion on his face.

"You saw that?"

"It's fine. I don't blame you."

"No, Elias. We weren't *holding* hands! He came to town a couple of days ago, the morning I was on the front page of the paper. I would have told you, but we got into a fight and I thought he had left. I saw him this afternoon when I was looking for you. He's staying in the guesthouse and I wanted to know why. He *grabbed* my hands but I pulled away. Me and him, we are as over as over can be."

Elias pulled away from the hug, moving to the end of the couch. Dropping his face into his hands, it all sounded too good to be true. He believed every word Caden said but he couldn't believe that he had reacted in the way he did.

"I did all of this for nothing," Elias mumbled into his hands, "I thought you were leaving. I thought you were going back with him."

"Why would I do that?"

"Because I'm no good for you," Elias stood up, "I read one of those letters he wrote you. I stole it from your mom's trash. It sounded like it was perfect. You have so many memories and all I've done for you is ruin your life. That newspaper is as much my fault as my mom's because I dragged you into my mess."

He walked through where the coffee table would have been and leaned against the fireplace where the TV used to be. When he felt Caden's hands carefully tightening around his shoulders, it was the most comforting thing he had ever felt.

"You didn't drag me. I fell," Caden whispered, "I fell for you so hard."

Elias turned around, his eyes closed. Inhaling deeply, he felt Caden's body heat right in front of his. It was a feeling he thought he would never be lucky enough to feel again. He wanted to cry, but not out of frustration or anger, out of happiness. It was too good to be real, making him clench his eyes even harder.

When he opened them, Caden's lips were against his, forcing him to close his eyes again. His knees buckled under the kiss but Caden was there to catch him.

"I hate thinking about his hands on you," Caden pressed his forehead hard against Elias', "you should have a shower."

Elias nodded, wanting nothing more than to crawl into bed with Caden by his side, "Okay."

"I'm joining you," Caden kissed him again, "I'm not letting you out of my sight ever again."

All of the confusion and crossed wires melted away. His mother became a problem to deal with another day because he only had one thing on his mind now. Looping his fingers around Caden's, he pulled him toward the bathroom without breaking the kiss. They both fell into the door and Caden fumbled with the handle behind Elias' back. Their clothes were off in seconds, leaving their bodies pressed up against each other, neither of them wanting to break the contact so they could step into the shower.

It was Elias who broke first, feeling the cold air kiss his backside. Ripping open the shower doors, he fell inside, dragging Caden in with him. Caden twisted the water tap and ice cold water shot out between them. The water quickly turned warm and then hot, filling the tiny bathroom with thick, blinding steam.

"Turn around," the passion heavy in Caden's moan.

Elias turned, aware that this was something new. He should have been scared, he should have been nervous, but he wasn't. He wanted to feel Caden as close as possible. *I need him.* Caden twisted Elias' neck, kissing the side of his mouth sloppily as the hand pulled his cheeks apart. He broke the kiss to spit into his hand before letting a finger slowly explore Elias.

He writhed and moaned from the new feeling and he surprised himself by not hating it. The louder he moaned, the harder Caden kissed him and the deeper the finger went. Elias was soon flat against the wet tiles, his arms searching the smooth surface for something to grip to as the finger was soon replaced with something thicker.

A couple of minutes of un-comfortableness were greeted with what felt like a lifetime of pleasure. Elias was glad of Caden's arms gripping his body in a vice like hug because the feeling was blinding. The water cascaded between their bodies as Caden pushed himself deeper and deeper into Elias.

The intimacy was unrivaled. Elias had never felt more connected with another person, which only made the ending even harder to accept. When he was finished, Caden twisted Elias back around to send him to that same ecstatic place. He was quickly reminded of that high that he could happily spend his life chasing.

They finished the shower by taking turns washing each other and then drying each other before falling on top of Elias' bed, with the weight of the day pushing them into the cold sheets. Elias was exhausted and not just from the sex. He wanted to believe that it was all over because he had Caden by his side but it wasn't.

"What are we going to do about her?" Elias mumbled into the dark, not even sure if Caden was still awake.

Caden rolled over and pulled Elias' body into his, kissing him softly on the back of the head as he cradled him in his arms, "I have an idea, we need to start communicating in a language your mother understands."

"What language?"

"Secrets," Caden whispered.

Elias could only spend a couple of seconds thinking about what Caden was talking about before sleep dragged him away heavily.

***

The sun was starting to rise when Caden found himself halfway between sleep and consciousness. An early morning wind, signalling an oncoming storm fluttered the curtains through the open window. The room was cold so Caden rolled over to pull Elias in closer. He rolled into emptiness.

Blinking open his tired eyes, he found out what had stirred him from his sleep in the first place. He sat up in bed, watching as Elias frantically stuffed clothes into a tiny backpack.

"What are you doing?" Caden rubbed his eyes, "What time is it?"

"Packing," he looked like he didn't have time to talk, "and I don't know. I woke up and I couldn't get back to sleep and I just wondered why we were still here. After everything that has happened, why are we still sitting in this apartment, waiting for her to do something else to us? It'll only be a matter of time before she gets bored of my happy ever after. She hates seeing people win over her. She failed last night but that doesn't mean she'll fail every time."

Caden shook away the remains of sleep as he checked the time.

"It's half past five in the morning. Come back to bed," Caden patted the empty space next to him, "we'll talk about it in the morning."

"The morning will be too late," Elias emptied what was left in his underwear drawer onto the bed before digging for the best pairs to pack, "after what she did to you and then the whole thing with Rigsy, she'll have something else planned. I was thinking the reason she got him to come here was to get drugs in my system. If she was doing that, she's planning something else."

"What else can she do?"

"I don't know," he scratched his hair frantically, his naked body lighting up as the hazy, gray sky outside started to lift, "random drug test? Police raid? She'll think of something. It will never end."

"It'll come back clean every time."

"I didn't even tell you did I?" Elias suddenly stopped, "I passed my drug test yesterday morning."

"I know. I didn't even doubt it."

Elias let himself smile for a second before grabbing more clothes to pack. Caden got out of bed and pulled the clothes and the bag out of Elias' grip.

"Where would we even go?"

"I don't know," he rested his hands on his head to look out of the window, "New York? You know it there?"

Caden admired the muscles in Elias' shoulders. They were pulling up the muscles in the small of his back, making his cheeks stand out.

"New York is expensive. We don't have any money."

"So?" Elias looked frantically around the room, "We'll make some. We'll figure it out."

"Elias," Caden grabbed his hands, "just calm down for a second. I told you last night, I have a plan."

"Plans don't work with her. She always has something up her sleeve."

Elias reluctantly let Caden pull him back into bed. Crawling under the sheets, Caden wrapped his entire body around Elias who curled up into a ball. It was a perfect fit and within seconds, Elias was fast asleep. For Caden, it wasn't going to be that easy. Watching the sun rise on a new day in Havenmoore, he let the plan roll around in his mind over and over.

As though Elias had predicted it, they were both awoken when the sun had fully risen with a knock on the door. Caden didn't even remember falling asleep but now he felt more tired than he had at five in the morning. Checking the time again, it was now past ten and the room had warmed up slightly.

"I'll get it," Caden rolled out of bed, leaving Elias to fall back asleep as he dressed.

Pulling out the table that was jamming the door closed, he propped it against the wall and let the door swing open. Squinting at the police officer in front of him, he tugged on the tight t-shirt, realizing that he had grabbed one of Elias' shirts in the hurry to get to the door.

"Is Elias James in?" the police officer, who looked like he was in his mid to late thirties, close shaven and good looking, spoke with a familiar tone in his voice as though he knew Caden wasn't the man he was looking for.

"Is this about the break in last night?"

"No," the officer frowned, "is he here?"

"He's in bed. It was a rough night last night."

"Can I come in?"

"Can I ask why?"

The officer smirked at Caden playing his hand. His eyes darted up and down Caden's attire. Tight bright yellow underwear and a t-shirt riding up his stomach was hardly threatening.

"We received an anonymous call that he was in breach of his suspended sentence terms."

"Anonymous?" Caden laughed, "You mean the mayor?"

"I didn't take the call," the officer had a '*I'm just doing my job*' look on his face.

"What are these terms?"

"I can't discuss them with you."

Caden reluctantly stepped aside to let the officer inside. He was Officer Burton, who he quickly learned was a familiar face to Elias. They weren't friends but they seemed friendly with each other. Caden guessed this was thanks to Elias' frequent arrests.

"We received an anonymous call," he repeated again, "that you bought and used an illegal substance. You'll know this is breach of your suspended sentence terms and could result in you being called in for arrest. I don't have a search warrant but it'll make things easier if you come down to the station for a voluntary drug test."

"I had one sip of vodka and a bottle of beer last night," Elias said as he buttoned a pair of skinny jeans around his waist, "but I've been clean for over two months now."

Officer Burton looked skeptical, just like most people did when Elias told them he had changed. Caden wondered how long he would have to wear the '*addict*' label before people gave him the fresh start he clearly craved.

"He did a drug test yesterday," Caden remembered what Elias had told him in the early hours, "can't you just use that?"

"Can I see it?"

"I don't have it," Elias stuffed his hands into his pockets, "I ripped it up. Can't you just call the rehab place?"

Officer Burton pulled out a pad, checking over the details he had been given before knocking on Elias' door.

"The call was made early this morning, so we'll need a fresh sample."

"Is that all it takes for you to drag him in? An early morning tip off?"

"It's a voluntary visit," the officer assured Caden, "but if he doesn't come, we might have to put a warrant out for his arrest to take a sample. This is a serious case and Elias is facing prison time if he's found to be using again. When he was last arrested, he had enough drugs on him to make him a suspected dealer and the judge takes dealing really seriously."

Elias shook his head at Caden as though telling him not to worry and that it was going to be fine. Caden wasn't so sure. He felt the authority of what the officer was saying, he just hoped that Elias was telling the truth about not using any of the coke that Rigsy had tried to force on him.

"Let me grab my jacket," Caden said as Elias headed for the door.

"Stay here," Elias said.

"No chance," Caden ran into the bedroom and quickly dressed in his own clothes, pulling on dirty underwear, two odd socks and ramming his feet into two different pairs of shoes, "I'm not letting you go to the station on your own."

"It's just a formality," Burton said, "honestly, if you're as clean as you say, you'll be in and out in no time."

As it turned out, it wasn't '*in no time*'. When they got to the station, they spent nearly two hours sitting in reception with the other criminals who needed processing. When Elias was finally called, Caden had to stay behind, staring at a poster about an upcoming unregistered gun amnesty that was being held in the state. When Elias didn't return for another hour, he found the number for the doctor's office and asked to speak with the doctor.

"Hello?" a hurried voice said.

"Ellie? It's Caden. I'm at the station with your brother."

"The station? What? Why?"

He told her all about the anonymous tip that had been called into the precinct and she was still reluctant to want to believe that it was their mother. Even though she was reluctant, Caden got her to admit that it didn't look good.

"But why would she do this after she's paid for him to go to rehab so many times? She's even paying rent on his apartment. He would be homeless without her. I don't get why she'd try to get him in trouble."

"As a lesson? To get him out of the way? Why does anybody do anything? Because she wants something. She ruined my life with the snap of her fingers because I said something she didn't want to hear. She's been on the warpath since she found out about us. Think about it, if she gets Elias into prison, or at least back into forced rehab, he's out of the way again."

"But why? I still don't understand why she'd want to do that."

"Because he's a problem and he needs fixing."

There was a long silence and Caden would have thought the line had gone dead but he could hear Ellie softly typing in the background.

"What are you going to do?" she asked.

"I have an idea," Caden said, "I wasn't sure it would work but she's just handed me the biggest weapon to bring her down."

"What weapon?"

"Elias."

"Elias? How is he a weapon? I gotta go Caden, there's a patient at the door. *Hello Mr. Rodgers, I'll be with you in just a - no this isn't about your prescription, please, just take a seat –* Caden, I'll call you back."

She hung up and at that moment, Elias reappeared, unaccompanied.

"It'll take 24 hours," Elias shrugged casually, "they told me not to leave town. They think I'm going to fail."

Caden stood, pulling Elias into a hug, garnering strange looks from the middle aged desk clerk who was sporting an eighties perm. She raised both her brows and looked down at her desk.

"C'mon, let's go to the town hall," Caden said as they walked out into the late-afternoon haze, "I'll tell you what we're going to do on the way back."

"Can it wait one more day?" Elias zipped his leather jacket up to under his chin, "I want her to think she's won. I want to rub that clean result in her face."

Chapter 22

The sun rose early the next day and Elias rose with it, restless and ready. He spent a couple of minutes watching Caden, hoping that he would never see a day where he wasn't the first thing he saw in a morning. Mouth slightly ajar and eyelids flickering from his dreams, he looked the picture of perfection and it made Elias feel an emotion he had rarely felt before; he felt lucky.

The noise of the shower woke Caden and he was quickly joined for an early morning example of why he felt so lucky. When they were both out of the shower and clothed, Elias couldn't hold off anymore. He packed his clothes and gathered what little belongings he had and they headed to the precinct. Everything he owned fit into one bag no bigger than that a high schooler would take to school but it didn't matter to him. Possessions were temporary and he was searching for something a little more permanent recently.

"They're not ready," the clerk slurped her coffee without even needing to look up to see that it was him, "take a seat and

I'll call your name."

Tapping his foot on the slightly dirty tiles, he chewed down on his nails waiting for the results to come back. He knew they'd be clean but it didn't stop him wondering.

"You'll be fine," Caden gently stopped his leg tapping with his hand, "are you sure you want to do this?"

Elias nodded, unable to speak. They'd spent the night going over everything, rehearsing what he was going to say, over and over. It felt like he was preparing for a test and the precision of his words would determine if he would pass or fail.

After a couple of hours nervously waiting and passing back and forth, the clerk finally called him over with one finger and an irritated purse to her lips.

"Sign this," she dumped a clipboard in front of him with a pen already attached, "must have been another crank call."

"Get them a lot for addicts, do you?" Caden seemed angry.

The clerk didn't reply. Snatching the clipboard from him, she told them they were free to leave but Elias wasn't going away empty handed.

"Framing it?" she sighed when he asked for a copy of the results.

She seemed reluctant to get out of her seat and she let them know it with the heavy grunt that left her lips when she eased herself out of the chair. It let out a creaky plastic sigh of relief, leaving her to disappear, getting another of the officers to cover for her.

When she returned with a small white slip of paper, he snatched it out of her hand and practically ran out of the door, jumping into one of the taxis parked in a neat row in the corner.

"Clarince Road, please," Elias snapped the safety belt across his chest.

"Not the town hall?" Caden asked.

"We need to see Ellie first. This plan affects her too."

Caden didn't object, instead pulling a ten dollar bill from his wallet to pay the driver. Havenmoore usually had quiet roads but today, every possible car was pulling out in front of them and crawling at a snail's pace. When Elias' knee started tapping again,

Caden gave it a reaffirming squeeze and reminded him that the mayor wasn't expecting them so she wasn't going to be waiting.

Once at Ellie's, he relayed every detail of the plan over to her, asking her if she would play her part.

"Are you sure you want to do this?" she asked softly.

"She set me up, Ellie," he showed her the results, "she hoped I'd fail this."

Ellie read over the paper a couple of times, soaking in the medical lingo that Elias hadn't been able to get his head around. All he saw was the big red '*Negative*' stamp next to every tested substance.

"Maybe you're right," she mused.

"You know I am."

When Ellie agreed to her part of the deal, they quickly walked across town towards the town hall. Caden suggested calling for another taxi but Elias felt sick from the anticipation. He hoped the walk in the late September breeze would calm his stomach but it didn't. When they were standing at the foot of the town hall, he took a second to compose his thoughts.

The rehearsed speech had vanished.

"Do you remember everything you want to say?"

"Yes," he lied, "let's just get this over with and then we can move on with the rest of our lives."

Side by side, they jogged up the half a dozen stone steps to the large dark oak doors. Acting like they belonged, they walked past the various security guards and they were soon standing in front of the receptionist's desk.

It wasn't the same girl Elias had seen before. Probably fired.

"Hi, um, one second," the young boy, who couldn't have been any older than nineteen, mumbled as he squinted at the screen, his tongue poking out in frustration, "oh, shoot. Erm – hi. How can I help?"

"We need to see the mayor," Elias straightened up, faking authority, "is she in today?"

"Do you have an appointment," he scratched the back of his head, "oh, where did it go. Sorry, it's only my second day. I keep losing the damn thing."

Elias noticed the appointment book poking out on the corner, buried under scattered pieces of discarded paper. Sensing an opportunity to do this a different way, he reached out and grabbed it.

"Is this what you're looking for?" he handed it over with the biggest smile he could muster.

"Ugh, thank you," he accepted it with an even bigger smile that spread across his smooth, unmarked skin, "I have a feeling she'd kill me if I lost something."

There was already a jaded tone of bitterness in his voice, as though he had already seen the real side of the mayor she fought so hard to hide.

"We have an appointment at one," Elias glanced at Caden who was furrowing his brow in confusion, "under the name Charles."

"Charles, Charles – hmm, I don't see it," he was sweating heavily from his thick, dark hairline, "I – just give me a second."

The receptionist reached out for the phone but before he could call the mayor and foil their plan, Caden jumped in, quicker thinking on his feet than Elias.

"Y'know, I bet it was that old girl. What was her name? Stacy? Claire?"

"Emily," the new guy said.

"No wonder she was fired," he leaned across the desk, winking at Elias out of the corner of his eye, "useless thing she was. Always losing things, forgetting to write appointments in the book. I'm surprised she lasted as long as she did. I'm sure you're a much better receptionist – I didn't get your name."

"Jo," his voice was shaking, making Elias wonder if he was even younger than he had suspected, "short for José Luis. My parents are Mexican but they moved here in the eighties. You don't think – you don't think she'll *fire* me do you? I promised my mom I'd get a job to help out around the house. My dad, he died and, *oh, God*, she's going to fire me, isn't she?"

The words poured out of his tiny mouth at lightning speed, the sweat trickling quickly down the sides of his face. It hadn't taken much to fluster him and Elias felt guilty because what they were about to do could result in Jo getting fired. He almost took a step back, admitting that he had gotten the day wrong and he would call back to make another appointment. *This can't wait and he'll be better off not working for her. She'll break him.*

"It's really important," Elias leaned in and joined Caden, doubling the pressure, "we'll just go right through and we won't mention anything about the book."

"She's not in," he stared desperately into Elias' eyes, "If she comes back and you're here, what will she do?"

Caden and Elias looked to each other and Elias could see the same look of doubtful sympathy in his eyes.

"I'm sure it'll be fine," Caden smiled.

"I should call her."

"No!" Elias called out, "She hates being called on the cell when she's out."

"She does?"

"Emily did that all the time," Caden added.

"Shit."

"Yeah," Elias nodded, "if you know where she is, we can swing by and talk to her. She'll really want to see us today."

Elias thought there'd be a couple of minutes of soul searching and deliberation but Jo blurted out her whereabouts instantly. When they knew she was cutting the ribbon at a new park near Havenmoore Elementary, Elias thanked him and Caden told him that there were always jobs going in McTuckey's if he wanted to get out before he was pushed. Jo nodded gratefully and Elias wondered if he was already considering the job that had made him crack under the pressure in a couple short minutes.

"Poor kid," Elias mumbled, "that's what she does to people."

"He kept checking you out," Caden laughed.

"He did not!"

"He so did. Don't worry, it's only because you're the cutest guy in this town."

That little compliment was the pick me up Elias needed to find his inner strength as they walked towards the elementary school. When they reached the gates and he could see a small group gathered on a patch of grass with a new climbing frame, he felt ready.

Before they walked over, he clung to the metal bars, looking in at the school as though he was looking in at a prison. Elementary school had been the happiest part of his childhood and even that gave him an uneasy feeling. Even then, as a small child, he had been able to sense that his mom was different to other kids in his class. He wasn't allowed to call her mommy and he didn't have any stories to share about her. She was there in the morning before school and she was there at the end of the night. Their first nanny, Leticia, had been a caring woman in her late thirties and for the first years of his life, he looked at her like she was his mother. The mayor sacked her when she suspected that she was stealing from her but looking back, Elias was sure it was because she didn't like how loving and caring she was towards her children. A string of less caring, stricter or lazier nannies followed, constantly changing faces every couple of months when the mayor would come up with a reason to get rid of them.

"Did you come here too?" Elias asked Caden.

"Yeah. Me and Bruce both did. We would have been here at the same time."

Elias didn't remember him. They were a couple of years apart and he could barely remember the names and faces from the people in his class. He wondered if that was down to the drugs or down to wanting to forget everything that had happened during his childhood. Staring at the building reminded him of all of the disappointments he had felt when him and Ellie would be the only kids in their class not to have their parents at their recitals and plays. His report card went ignored while Ellie's was poured over in obsessive detail. Even back then, she had been the one with potential.

"Was it a good school?"

"I loved it here," a fond smile filled Caden's lips as though he was remembering a really good time, "it was awesome when Bruce was there too."

Elias wondered what it was like to have somebody to share it with. Ellie had her group of friends she was the leader of and Elias was the outcast who nobody wanted to eat their lunch with because he was the disruptive one.

As they left the gates and headed towards the new park that he was sure used to be the teachers' parking lot, he tried to shake away those bitter and deeply buried feelings but they rose to the surface with each step. It was fueling him and a new script was being written in his head, re-writing the one Caden had helped him come up with.

They lingered at the back of the crowd for a couple of minutes, watching the mayor socialize and network in the growing crowd of people. She was so deep in her conversations, the carefree smiles and laughter were almost believable. *Maybe she's laughing because she thinks I'm locked up and out of her way.*

"Look at her," Elias whispered to Caden, "she's convincing, isn't she?"

"That's what makes her so scary."

Elias ducked his head every time she looked in his direction but she didn't seem to see him. He was probably the last person she expected to see. After a couple more minutes, she walked to the front of the crowd and a hush fell as they waited for their leader to address them. Standing in front of the red-ribbon blocked gate in a long, shocking red trench coat, nipped in tightly at the waist she smiled through her red lips, thinking of what to say about a new children's park next to the elementary school. Elias knew she was about to create a stunning piece of fiction.

"Thank you all for coming out today," her voice travelled through the small crowd without the aid of a microphone, "I'm so honored that the school asked me to open this wonderful new play area for the sweet children of our town."

Elias couldn't suppress the laugh. Some of the people around him looked, one woman even putting her finger on her lips to silence him. He covered it up as a cough and he was left alone.

"Being a mother," the words tumbled effortlessly out of her mouth, "I understand how important it is to have a safe and caring environment for a child. It gives me great pleasure to announce this park open!"

She was handed a giant pair of scissors by a waiting man and when the photographer was in position, ready to capture to moment, she snipped on the ribbon slowly. Her smile didn't flicker as the bulb flashed over and over in her face and she didn't look away from the camera's lens.

"She'd make a *great* president, don't you think?" one woman with an eager looking little girl clutched to her hand whispered to another.

"Oh, I know. She's so nice and so fashionable. I'd *die* to know where she got that coat. Imagine being friends with her."

"I bet she doesn't have time for friends!" the woman replied, "She's *always* so busy. Such a giver."

"Too busy for her own kids," Elias couldn't help himself and when the gate was finally opened, they walked forward, making sure to give Elias a suspicious once over.

He waited for the crowd to thin, knowing she would naturally see him if he stayed where he was. Lingering by a shiny new trashcan, he watched as she chatted with some of the mothers as they walked into the gated park. The sparkle was still there but he could tell that she was trying to leave. When the last woman gushed over the mayor, the smile vanished and the eyebrows dropped. She muttered something to her assistant and he laughed darkly, causing her to roll her eyes and let out a huge sigh. Now that the mask had been dropped, he could tell that she was still sick from the last time he had seen her. It was hidden well under her professional and flawless makeup. She didn't look nearly old enough to have twenty-six-year-old twins.

Checking her cell phone, she headed down the new path, her sharp heels clicking and the tails of her coat hurrying behind her. She walked right by Elias and Caden, her eyes planted firmly on the screen. Feeling the opportunity slipping away, Elias followed, slinging the backpack over one shoulder.

"'Scuse me, mayor, I just wondered if you'd kiss my baby. I'd be *ever* so grateful," Elias did his best impression of one of those adoring, babbling women.

She turned around, the coat flying with her. The second her eyes landed on her son, Elias could see the shock alive in those dark pupils.

"What are you doing here?" her voice deepened and lowered, "Tony, wait in the car."

The assistant nodded and hurried over to a waiting black car on the edge of the sidewalk.

"I just thought I'd come and support my mother," he artfully arched one brow, "did you think I'd be somewhere else?"

The pinch in her jaw gave it all away. She could try and hide behind that face of steel but Elias could see right through it.

"I'm busy. I have somewhere I need to be," she snapped as she turned around.

"I know what you did," he blurted, "I think you'll want to hear what I have to say."

The mayor didn't stop walking at first but she suddenly ground to a halt, as though curious to find out how and why her plan had failed. Turning slowly, she jerked her head over to the school. Knowing that she wanted to be somewhere with no witnesses, he followed, motioning for Caden to stay behind. He hadn't planned on doing it alone but it felt like the right thing to do. Not for her, but for himself.

She walked across the schoolyard, the click of her heels echoing louder than Elias thought possible. Each step was like the crack of thunder, signaling a brewing storm.

They walked through the reception unseen and headed for the school hall. It was empty, with all of the kids in class. As though setting the scene for their showdown, the mayor walked across the dark polished floor, not stopping until she was standing in front of the high stage, dead in the center. Behind her, a full band of instruments lay unused, waiting for band practice to begin. Elias had tried learning to play the guitar in third grade. He doubted she even knew that.

"What do you want?" she said, no volume control on her voice.

Stopping a safe distance away from her, he racked his brain for where to start first, deciding to start with what he remembered of the speech he had rehearsed.

"I know you paid Rigsy to set me up."

"I have no idea what you're talking about," the words were instant, not even bothering to ask who Rigsy was.

"You paid a drug dealer to get me to take drugs so that you could call the police and have me arrested," feeling braver, he took a stride forward, "and you were seen. You weren't as careful as you thought."

Considering her options, she stared darkly at him, her shoulders pushing back, "That's quite a story you've cooked up."

"It's true."

"Prove it."

She was enjoying the game of cat and mouse. It was as though she lived to win the games she played. Losing wasn't an option for her and she would win any way she had to.

"Caden saw you paying a man in the alley next to the town hall, four days ago."

"He must be mistaken," she shrugged, "I was on a business trip four days ago."

"Yours is the one face in this town nobody would mistake. He saw you paying a drug dealer to set me up so you could get me out of the way. What were you trying to do? Get me into prison? Or rehab again? Or were you just trying to show me that you were the big bad wolf and you could blow my house down if you wanted to."

Her cheeks burned darker and more vibrantly with every word. She looked as though she was about to storm out, not wanting to hear her own plan reflected back at her by the son she never thought intelligent enough to see through her.

"If that was true, why aren't you in prison?" she sounded like she really wanted to know.

"Because I'm clean," he pulled the paper out of his pocket and unfolded it, "he didn't succeed. Do you realize how dangerous he is? He attacked me and tried to force me when I said I didn't want to. I told him I was done with that stuff but he told me he had a job to do, a job that you paid him to do. If Caden didn't kick my door in, I don't know what would have happened."

Her expression faltered, her dark lashes flickering before widening and narrowing on him. Rose red lips parted but they didn't speak. He stepped closer and held out the drug test. She looked down at it and he was unsure what she was going to do with it but she reached out and snatched it forcefully. To his surprise, she scanned over it, her face remaining still.

"Two months," she tossed it on the floor, "a new record."

Elias turned around, clenching his hair in frustration. He wanted to scream out so loud that the walls caved in.

"Do you enjoy this?" he cried, turning to face her again, "Do you live to make me feel worthless?"

"I'm too busy for that."

"Is that why you paid him to get rid of me, so I wouldn't be a threat to your busy life? Was I getting too involved, too noisy? You act like you're so disgusted in how I've been living but you liked that I was too high to cause you any problems. Now that I have my mind back, I see what you're doing and I'm taking notice. All of those strings you're pulling, people are starting to see. Ellie is seeing what I've always seen."

"Your sister is buying this story?" she laughed, "It's a fantasy. Drugs can cause paranoia."

"Read that online?" his voice grew, "Because you didn't come to a single one of the family sessions when I was in rehab. You didn't visit me once."

"I'm -,"

"Busy. I know. Change the record, Mom."

Hearing '*Mom*' from his lips made her recoil her head slightly, her face tightening even more.

"What do you want from me?"

"Nothing," Elias whispered, "absolutely nothing. I didn't come here to listen to your excuses, I came here to tell you something."

She tried to step back slowly but she bumped into the stage. Elias reacted by copying her movement while making sure there was enough distance between them.

"What kind of mother does something like that to her own

flesh and blood?" he couldn't help himself, "I'd gotten so used to you but this was a new low. Can you believe I thought there was a tiny glimmer of hope that you'd one day change? Can you believe I thought you'd be there when I got out of rehab?"

"I – I -,"

"Save your breath. Did you know Rigsy had a thing for guys? He could have done more than feed me drugs but that wouldn't have bothered you, would it? You wouldn't care if he snapped my neck and left me dead on that apartment floor."

"That's not true," her voice returned to her.

It shocked him that she would even react to something like that. Her way was usually to make a cutting comment to gain the upper hand.

"Where did you even find him? You must have known I knew him. Go on, admit it."

Her eyes darted between Elias', her lips parting and closing as her mind wrestled with the right words.

"I don't know what you're talking about."

"He could have killed me!" he shouted.

"He wouldn't have, I -," she stopped herself.

It was as good a confession as Elias needed and he could see the shock in her eyes that she had let that much slip.

"I thought you didn't know him?"

"He was only supposed to make you take drugs!" she cried, "I found him through your court case. You mentioned him. I didn't -,"

"We're not talking about candy here! Rigsy isn't somebody you cross. He's a dealer. You should have been trying to set him up, not me. He's a danger to the people in this town. Those people out there that you pretend to care for, he sells them stuff worse than what I used to take and he ruins their lives, but you don't care about that. All you care about is power and that's why you wanted me gone because all you see me as is a threat. A scandal that you can't sweep under the rug."

Her head shook slightly, her pin straight jet black hair moving with her. Her hand darted up, sweeping it back into place.

"Is this how you think a mom should be?" his voice cracked, "You see me actually trying to change and you try to send me straight back to the place I've been festering in for years. Do you think that is normal?"

"There's nothing normal about our family."

"Finally! Something we agree on. You're right. Growing up as the mayor's kid was a curse. It ruined my life. You ruined my life. If this is how you show your motherly love, you can keep it."

Elias' entire body was shaking. He couldn't remember any of the original plan because all he could see were his mother's eyes, staring deep into his. She looked scared and angry. Ready to explode at any moment and ready to drag him down when it happened.

"What would I know about motherly love?" her voice was small, "I didn't have a mother, or a father. At least you had one."

"Did I though? Where were you? Did you ever come to this room to see me on that stage?"

When he pointed to it, she turned around to look at it before darting back to the intense stare.

"That stuff isn't important. I had nobody there for me and I turned out fine," she almost looked like she believed that.

"Don't you get it?" he laughed softly, "That's the most important thing in the world."

Her brow furrowed in thought, as she absorbed what he was saying. Was she actually listening to what he was saying? *I won't hold my breath.*

"I put a roof over your head. I paid for everything, on my own. Your dad had to go and die before you were even born, leaving me to do it on my own. Do you think I had any idea what I was doing?"

Elias never heard her talk about his father. All he knew about his father was what his grandmother had told him in the few years she was in their lives.

"You didn't try."

"How would you know?" it was her time to laugh, "I wasn't always the mayor. I wasn't always where I am now. You were four when I came into office. Those first years, I tried so hard on my own, but I couldn't do it. I needed something to bury myself in. Is that so bad?"

"You sacrificed your kids for your job?"

"How do you think I paid for that nice, big house? How do you think I'm paying for that apartment you're living in, rent free? *Hmm*? By putting my job first."

She really was blind. He had always wondered if she understood where she had gone wrong or if she was just ignorant, so convinced that she had always done the right thing.

"We would have rather been homeless with no money if it meant we had a mom who loved us."

"I -," she choked, "this has always been you. Ellie is fine."

"Ellie learned to hide it."

She looked shocked and that surprised Elias.

"You had everything."

"We didn't have you!" he couldn't hold it back and his voice echoed around the entire hall, "The whole town had you. You were *their* property. If I wanted to see my mom, I'd turn on the local news or look at the paper. I'd wait for you to come home and I'd wait to see that smile that everybody else saw. You never did. You treated us like possessions you could pass around to keep out of the way of your job. Do you know what that does to a kid?"

Her shocked expression only deepened. Leaning fully into the stage, she frantically looked around the hall as though looking for an escape from her son's truths.

"Don't try and blame your behavior on me. I didn't force you to take drugs. That was all you. You were bad from the first day. You wouldn't stop crying. Ellie, she was a good child. You, you tortured me. You wouldn't let me sleep and it never got better."

"Is that why Ellie got the better deal? Because she was a quiet baby?"

"She tried. She was *good* in school. You, I had the principal on the phone twice a week! You can't blame that on *me*."

"Who else?" Elias hissed with frustration, "I wanted your attention. I wanted something from you. You were blank, even when I was in trouble."

"So you took drugs for attention?" she snorted, "You're living in a fantasy land."

Taking a step back, he looked down at the ground, focusing on the red and white tiles and noticing the tiny grains of dirt in the grout.

"No," he shook his head, "I took drugs to forget you."

"What?" she laughed even louder as if it was the funniest thing she had ever heard.

"I took them to block out the pain," he started looking at the ground but quickly faced her, wanting her to feel every word, "to forget that you never hugged me, or that you never told me you loved me. I took them because I didn't want to be a part of it anymore. It started as an escape but it made things worse. It turned me into something else and I got deeper and deeper into that hole and you were willing to send me back there to shut me up?"

"I paid for your rehab," her voice lowered again, "I wanted you to get clean."

"So why pay Rigsy?"

The school bell rang and the sound of children spilling out of the classrooms echoed around the huge hall. She looked over to the door and he could sense that she wanted them all to hurry in so she could slip outside.

"You wouldn't shut up," she looked back to him, "all you've ever done is cause me trouble."

"Maybe at first," he admitted, "but I wanted to get as far away from you as possible and you kept dragging me back. What's that old saying? Keep your friends close but your enemies closer?"

"Do you want me to admit that I'm a bad mother? Is that what you want from me?"

Her voice was frantic, almost hysterical. The hum in the hall died down as a second bell sounded out. Ringing out through his mind, the sharp sound of the bell suddenly reminded him of all of the things he had wanted to say. He hadn't wanted to confront her about her parenting or the way she treated him. He wanted to threaten her, to deliver Caden's plan.

"No," Elias stepped back, tossing his hands out, "it's too late for that. I came here to tell you to leave me alone. Both of us, me and Caden. No more threats, no more plans, no more newspaper articles. You leave us alone and if you walk by us in the street, you look the other way. I want nothing to do with you. After the things you've done, I don't care if I never see you again."

Elias didn't sound as convinced as he had wanted to do and she didn't look as placid as he had expected. He saw the same shiny look in her eyes that he thought he had seen when looking up to her apartment window.

"If you ignore me, I'll expose your deepest darkest secret. Caden said something and it made me realize all along that I had the power to cut you off all this time. It was right in front of my face, I just needed somebody to notice it. I've been playing your game all this time, lying low and floating silently along so you can keep your power trip running, but I'm done with that."

"What secret?" she muttered.

Elias took a deep breath, feeling the weight of the world on his words.

"Me," he shrugged, "I'm your secret. You've fought so hard to bury any mention of a drug addicted son because you knew what it would do to you. Information like that will ruin your winning streak in this town and people will see the real you. It'll all be over for you."

"The paper would never buy it," she shook her head, "I know the editor."

Elias laughed. He couldn't believe she was still trying to push her manipulation tactics.

"I didn't even mention the paper. I know that much. You can control them but you can't control everything. I'll post it all over the internet, I'll tell anybody who will listen, I'll even print out posters and stick them on every surface in town. I'll tell the world about Judy James' drug abusing, criminal son."

"You wouldn't."

"I will," he nodded sternly, "I don't care if people know

because I've changed. Secrets are weapons, Mom, you know that. You just need to know when to use them."

"If you hate me so much, why don't you just leave town?"

"Because you'll win," Elias didn't mention that he had been close to.

"You sound like -,"

"You?" he cut her off.

She nodded, a strange look in her eyes. He wasn't sure if he was imagining it but he thought she looked slightly proud in a twisted way.

"So do it," she said.

"I don't want to," he raised his brows, relaxing the muscles in his face, "not if I don't have to. I don't want to be like you. Drop it and leave us alone and I'll keep my mouth shut. This is me taking responsibility for my own life. I'm ending this cycle."

To his surprise, she looked like she was considering it. They stood in silence, the only sound coming from the pounding in Elias' chest. He felt strong and powerful. He wondered if this was the kick she got every time she blackmailed somebody.

"Fine," was all she said.

It was that simple. He looked deep into her empty eyes, shocked that she would agree to it. He was relieved but he didn't feel the sense of freedom that he thought. He still felt weighed down. Part of him was shocked that she would agree to let herself be cut completely out of his life. A flicker of hope that had been burning silently in the back of his mind for as long as he remembered had still been burning, after everything she had done. All it had taken was one simple *fine* to blow it out. There had been another option, clear to all of them. An option that anybody else would have taken. She was never going to apologize and she was never going to promise to change.

"I'm staying with Ellie until I get on my feet," he tossed her the apartment key, "thanks for the roof."

"You don't have -," she left it hanging mid-sentence, "fine."

He wondered how that sentence was going to end. You don't have to, you can live there? You don't have a chance getting on your feet? He wasn't going to ask, even if he was dying to know.

Without saying a word, he stood and looked at her for what felt like a lifetime. She looked stunned and exhausted but she didn't look saddened that her son didn't want to know her. *Maybe this is what she's wanted from the start?* Slinging the backpack higher up his shoulder, he clutched onto the strap, finding the power to finally look away and turn around.

"Goodbye," his words sounded final.

Elias intended those to be the last words he would say to her and he meant them. Walking away, he felt like he had told her more in those last ten minutes than he had in his whole entire life.

"Elias," she called after him.

Stopping in his tracks, he turned around. The mayor was staring dead at him, her head tilted down so that her eyes were nothing more than shadows as the afternoon sun shone down through the high windows.

"Good luck," she said as she stuffed her hands into her pockets before disappearing through another door.

Elias gave her enough time to get out of the school. He imagined that she was running back to her car, ready to lock herself in her office so she could start plotting something. It seemed like the most logical step but for some reason, he actually believed her.

The final '*good luck*' could have been interpreted as sarcastic, an ominous warning even. The blank tone was open to interpretation but the smoldering wick on the blown out candle clung onto the thought that maybe, just maybe, it was genuine; the closest thing he was going to get to an apology.

"What happened?" Caden ran toward him when he opened the school gate, "Are you okay?"

"It's done," exhausted, Elias fell into Caden's chest, closing his eyes and inhaling his scent deeply, "c'mon, let's go home."

Chapter 23

Waking up in Ellie's guest bedroom would have been strange for Elias but he woke up in the arms of Caden. They were wrapped tightly around him, just like they had been when they'd fallen asleep, making plans for their future. Caden vowed to write a book, Elias vowed to get his high school diploma and a job and then they vowed to live happily ever after in their own house one day with two dogs, whose names they had yet to agree on.

"Morning," Ellie was already up when Elias wandered downstairs at what he thought was an early hour, "sit down, I'll make you some breakfast."

"Shouldn't you be at work?"

"I'm working the late shift. I don't start until twelve."

Stretching out and yawning, Elias sat at the breakfast bar, about to protest his sister making him breakfast but realizing the last time he attempted bacon and eggs with Caden, he had almost set the pan on fire.

"Still like it extra crispy?" she smiled over her shoulder, "There's OJ in the fridge. Help yourself."

A part of Elias thought it would be weird moving in with Ellie but it felt comforting, especially since she admitted that she was glad to have someone in the house now that Kobi was split between his two parents until they came to a more permanent solution.

"Thank you," he said when she placed the plate in front of him, along with a bottle of ketchup and a small cup of coffee.

"Don't worry about it. I usually do it for Kobi."

"No, really, thank you. Thank you for letting us stay here."

With a quick shrug and a smile he knew she didn't need thanking. Gaining back his sister had made everything else worth it.

"You were right when you said this place was as much yours as mine. I was just mad at you. I'm thinking of selling this place."

"Won't John get half in the divorce?"

"It's in my name," she said, "mom signed everything over to me and she made me sign a pre-nup before the marriage. She insisted on it, in fact."

Elias shuddered slightly at her mention, disguising it as a yawn. He felt Ellie sense it because she didn't push the subject.

"If I sell, I want you to have half the money," she said it as casually as if she was commenting on the morning's news that was playing silently on a small TV mounted to the wall.

"What? Why? Are you kidding me?"

"Do I look like I'm kidding?" she arched her already filled in brows, "I want you to have something from all of this. You don't deserve to struggle until you get your diploma and that will take some time, won't it? You could use it to get your own place. You could do so much with it."

Elias let himself get excited for a second but then he realized the truth of the situation. The house might be in Ellie's name but it was his mother who had paid for it. It was the house he had grown up in as a child and he hated it because of that. Being back here on the other side of the storm felt easier but he still felt the memories lingering like ghosts. It would be tainted money and he knew it would be too easy.

"Thank you," he grabbed her hands in his, "thank you so

much, but I can't. I don't want it."

"Elias!" she laughed, "This house is worth -,"

"I don't want to know. Whatever half is, put it in a fund for Kobi's college. Let him have a good start."

"What about your start? You're not a lost cause, not anymore."

"I know," he smiled, biting his lip ring, "that's why I need to work for it. It might mean I'm moving with you if you move but it will be temporary. I appreciate the gesture and I hope you don't think I'm being ungrateful but I need to do this."

She smiled back without offense, "I understand. You need to be the one to get where you want to be."

"No more free passes."

"And no more rehab."

"I'll drink to that," Elias lifted the coffee mug before taking a long, deep sip, "nice coffee."

"Fifteen dollars a jar, it should taste nice," she winked before sliding off the stool to go and get dressed for work.

Glancing at the time on the TV, he saw that it was only past ten. He watched the news ticker scroll across the bottom of the screen, reciting the early morning news for Havenmoore. Budget cuts, a rescue dog saving a blind woman from getting hit by a car, hospital staff charity ball; nothing of real interest or importance.

When he finished the bacon and eggs that he had drowned in ketchup, he felt a pair of thick, heavy hands loop around his shoulders.

"Morning," Caden's husky morning voice whispered in his ear, "I thought you'd taken off in the night."

"You wish," Elias grabbed Caden's hand, softly kissing his fingers one by one, "you're stuck with me now."

"Forever?" a gentle kiss tickled his ear.

"In this life and the next."

Spinning around in the chair, Elias faced Caden who was shirtless and only wearing a pair of loose boxers. Running his hands down the softly muscled torso, Elias pulled him in by the cheeks to carefully brush their lips together.

"I can cope with that," Caden gently bit Elias' lip, "that's if you can cope with me?"

"I'll try," he slid to the edge of the chair, wrapping his legs around Caden's waist, instantly feeling something hard brush against his thigh.

They kissed deeply, the sugar infused ketchup passing between them. Elias almost forgot where he was as his desires took over him.

"Child present!" Ellie's shrill cry echoed around the kitchen.

Jumping back, Caden quickly slid onto one of the stools and Elias dropped his hands into his own lap to see Ellie clutching Kobi's eyes as he scratched at his sticking up bed hair.

"Mom, I've seen you and Daddy kissing," he tried to pull her fingers away, "and I've seen him kissing that new lady."

Ellie coughed loudly, letting go of her son's eyes. He blinked heavily and yawned, giving them a rub as he shook the last remnants of sleep. Elias checked the news again, completely forgetting that it was Saturday.

"Morning, Uncle Elias," he yawned, "morning Uncle Elias' boyfriend."

"Morning," they chimed in unison, smirking at each other.

Caden had turned beetroot red as he peered through his fingers, his body hunched over the counter. Ellie busied herself with making them all bacon and eggs, Elias happily taking a second helping. Ellie swore they shouldn't get used to it because she wasn't going to be doing it every morning but Elias knew that she loved being busy and she loved feeling like she was helping people out. For all her faults, she cared deeply, even if she didn't always know how to show it properly. That's why she made a brilliant doctor. She could hide her emotions when she needed to be professional headed but she still cared enough to get the job done right.

"Grandma Judy!" Kobi cried.

Elias jumped up in his seat, turning around. The hallway was empty. He turned to look down at Kobi, who had ketchup dripping down his chin. Elias followed his gaze to the TV where the mayor was standing on the front steps of the town hall silently.

At first, he wasn't shocked to see her. She was always on the news, announcing one thing or another. It wasn't until he saw the *LIVE* symbol flashing in the corner that his stomach knotted.

"Turn it up!"

Ellie grabbed the remote, turning the volume up so that his mother's voice was blasting through the kitchen, just as it had in the hall the night before.

" – so it's with a heavy heart that I stand before you to tell you that this will be my final term as mayor. I wanted you all to hear this from me first. After twenty-two years in this honored position -,"

Elias tuned out as she rambled on, unusually without her large and beaming public smile. She was delivering her lines to the unseen reporters who she no doubt called early that the morning.

"What is she doing?" Ellie wondered aloud.

"She's lost it," Caden looked to Elias who was staring at the TV but staring right through it.

"Mayor James," a microphone jutted out from the bottom of the screen amidst the chatter of reporters, "what will you do next? Do you intend on running for state senator now that Jacob Fines has stepped down?"

"No," her answer was final and blunt, "no, this is me bowing out of politics."

"Why?" another microphone and another reporter's voice, "What's inspired this sudden change? What will you do next?"

Pausing for a moment, she cleared her throat and looked down at the podium she was standing behind. For a moment, he thought she might be reading off a script that one of her assistants had prepared for her but her eyes weren't searching, they were staring blankly, just like Elias had been a moment ago.

"I'll take this time to write my memoirs and do the things I've missed out on for the last two decades," she paused and her gaze wandered from the reporter, right down the lens of the camera beaming into Ellie's kitchen.

It felt like she was looking right at Elias and it unsettled him.

"What have you missed out on, Mayor?" the first reporter cried, sensing that his chance was running out, "What is it you want to do?"

The pause was so long Elias thought she was going to ignore the question.

"I want to spend time with my family. Thank you, but I need to get back to work. There's still another six months left and I intend on using them to serve this town."

She bowed and smiled slightly before heading up the steps as the reporters cried questions at her back. She vanished inside without a second glance over her shoulder. The screen cut to the reporters in the studio who was summarizing what had just happened as the tickers all changed to the breaking news that Judy James, the long running and much loved mayor of Havenmoore was stepping down.

Elias sat in shock, staring at the ketchup stains and bacon fat on his plate. He could feel Caden and Ellie's eyes on him but he didn't have the reaction they were looking for.

He was running over what she had just said, as though his mind had recorded it live.

'I want to spend time with my family.'

At first, he wanted to dismiss it as another one of her lies but it felt like the most honest thing she had ever said.

"What just happened?" Ellie leaned against the counter, shock taking over her face, "I – I – I can't believe it."

"Elias, are you okay?" Caden's hand travelled over his back, rubbing him sympathetically, "Say something."

Elias looked up from the plate, shaking his head slightly, he looked back to the TV, which was muted again as it replayed clips of the announcement. He saw her lips silently say *'I want to spend time with my family'*, her eyelids flickering on the word *'want'*.

"She's either having a mental breakdown," Elias exhaled heavily, "or, she means it."

He shared a moment with his twin that nobody else could see or hear. With just the blink of her lashes, Elias knew that Ellie believed it. Could it be true? Was this her way of admitting that she had listened, for the first time, to how Elias really felt?

Suddenly, the simmering candle in the back of his mind reignited, flickering brighter than it ever had done. He felt sick and dizzy but the weight that had pressed down on his shoulders in that hall suddenly vanished.

"I believe her," he nodded, "is that crazy?"

He looked to Caden, desperate for him to explain things, even though Elias was the only one who'd been there in that school yesterday.

"Whatever happens next," Caden grabbed Elias' face, forcing him still so he could look into his eyes as he sat in Ellie's kitchen in a pair of boxers and nothing more, "I love you and I'll be here for you, no matter what happens."

"Me too," Ellie nodded, a small excited smile flickering across her lips.

"Me too!" Kobi cried out, throwing his arms around Elias' waist.

Sitting in the kitchen with a sober mind, the man he loved stroking his cheek with a gentle thumb, his nephew hugging him unconditionally, his sister secretly smiling at him and his mother talking to him through the TV, Elias felt like the fight was finally over and he didn't care who had won.

Epilogue
One Year Later

"Hurry, you're going to be late!" Ellie ran across Elias and Caden's tiny apartment, attempting to shoo them through the door.

"Give me a second," Elias looked in the mirror leaning against the exposed red brick wall, "are you sure I look okay?"

Caden appeared in the reflection behind him, wrapping his arms around his waist and giving him a reassuring kiss on the neck, "You look perfect."

Caden adjusted the black graduation cap on Elias' head so that a tuft of Elias' black hair jutted out of the front. Ellie was tapping her foot at the door, fiddling with the black hair that had now grown beyond her shoulders. Elias turned to kiss Caden on the lips before taking another look at the apartment they'd moved into two weeks ago. The relator had described it as a *comfortable studio with great light and close to transportation* but in reality it was a tiny apartment above an old factory, overlooking the docks. It had a tiny kitchen running along the back wall, an even smaller bathroom and a bedroom that just about fit their new bed.

Elias didn't care, because it was theirs. He had been waiting tables in Bruce's bar for most of the year, saving every last dime and cent so that he could move out of Ellie's guest bedroom. Things wouldn't have suddenly moved so quickly if Caden's book hadn't been picked up by a small publishing house. The advance meant they could put down a deposit on the only apartment they could afford and their little pot of savings let them buy enough self-assembly furniture to fill out the tiny space.

They jumped into Ellie's car and headed to Havenmoore High. Wearing a graduation cap and gown at twenty-seven felt strange, especially since he hadn't done it with his class when he was in senior year. The ceremony was a small, low-key event, organized by some of the people in his adult GED program. At first, Elias was against the idea because he just wanted to grab his diploma and get out of there but now that he was sitting in the gown, feeling strangely nervous, it felt like a right of passage that he finally needed to do.

"Do you know your book launch over in Portland?" Ellie eyed up Caden through the mirror, "Can I bring a plus one?"

"Who?" said Elias.

Ellie averted her gaze but he could tell from the creasing around her eyes that she was smiling, "Just some guy."

"Some guy?"

"Now that the divorce is finalized and I've finally moved, I thought it was time to get myself back out there."

"What guy?" Elias asked again.

"His name is Tim. He's a medical student working at the clinic. And he's -," she paused and cleared her throat, "- twenty-two."

"Course you can," Caden laughed.

She thanked him and Elias resisted the obvious 'cougar' and 'toy boy' jokes because he was happy that she was ready to date. John had dragged out the divorce for as long as possible, not giving her the 'clean break' he first promised. Months of court hearings and fighting over Kobi were finally over and with John now out of state, Kobi got to stay home with his mom most of the year, only spending certain breaks with John.

Pulling up outside of the high school, Elias breathed in deeply, clutching Caden's hand for support.

"You've got this," he whispered, kissing him on the hand, "you'll be fine."

"Do you think she'll come?" Elias asked.

"I sent her the invitation," Ellie pulled her keys out of the ignition, "and it's not like she's busy these days."

The mayor had stepped down in a blaze of glory, cementing herself in the Havenmoore history books as the mayor nobody wanted to see leave. The campaign to replace her was fierce, with more candidates than usual stepping up to take over her spot. It ended up going to Sandy Crawshaw, who also had short black hair and a designer taste for fashion. People in Havenmoore didn't seem to like change.

They walked through the high school, to the sports hall where the graduation was taking place. With only twenty-one students in his class, all of whom were older than Elias, the hall was pretty empty. Family and friends milled around, nibbling snacks and drinks from the table full of food pushed up against the back wall.

Just a quick scan of the faces told him she wasn't there. Had he really expected her to come? His interactions with her over the past year had been more strained than he had expected with them only ever being in the same room when Ellie was there. Occasionally, she would ask him a vague question and he would answer, but it was like they were strangers, neither of them able to forget what had been said over a year ago in the elementary school.

"I remember my graduation," Caden looked around the hall, "right here. I tripped on that step right there."

He pointed to the five steps up to the stage that Elias hadn't noticed and now all he could think about was not tripping.

"I was sick on mine," Ellie said, "right before I was supposed to go up, I ran off and hurled in the hall."

"Why? Didn't you have the best GPA in the class?"

"Exactly!" she said, "I knew everybody would be looking at me thinking that. It was unbearable."

Elias didn't have the best GPA in his class but he had done enough to graduate and that's all he cared about. He didn't mind waiting tables in Bruce's bar but he wanted to do more. Over the past year, Caden's mom, Claire had warmed to their relationship and he was happy to call her a good friend. She had regained her contract with Havenmoore Rehab Center and she was eager to sign Elias up because she was sure his story would inspire and help others. Elias wasn't so sure how inspiring he could be but he liked the idea of helping people get through the same situation he had been in. He wanted to be that shelter for people, just like Caden had been for him.

The principal of the school, joined by the only two teachers who taught on the program headed up to the lectern on the stage and people gravitated towards the rows of metal seats. Elias held Ellie and Caden back, sitting on the last row as though it was going to make him feel less nervous. It didn't.

Waiting for his name to be called, his foot wouldn't stop tapping on the tiles and he was sure it was echoing all around the hall but he couldn't stop it.

"Elias James," the principal read from the list.

"That's you," Caden nudged him, "go on."

Elias was frozen, unable to move. When Ellie stamped on his foot, he finally jumped up, feeling all of the eyes on him. He felt sick, just like Ellie had and he wished Caden hadn't told him that story about tripping. He walked as fast as possible but it felt like the stage was miles away, shrinking into the distance.

When he finally reached the stairs, he took them carefully and breathed a sigh of relief when he reached the top in one piece. He looked out to Caden, who winked at him with a beaming smile. Ellie had her cell in her hands and he guessed she was recording the whole thing.

"Congratulations," the principal smiled warmly, holding out his hand to shake with the diploma in the other.

The nerves got the better of Elias as he shook the diploma

and grabbed the hand, which garnered a soft hum of laughter from the watching crowd. He started to feel himself calm and when he gladly accepted the diploma, it felt heavy in his hands as though it was a flashlight, streaming ahead at a future of new possibilities.

After posing for the photographer with his diploma, he turned back to the crowd, looking for Ellie and Caden. He saw them out of the corner of his eye but he wandered beyond them to the figure standing at the back of the hall in a sand colored trench coat. When his eyes met his mother's, all of the moisture drained from his mouth.

He hung back with the rest of the class until they all had their diplomas. They posed for a class photograph in front of the stage and then they tossed their hats in the air, because according to Stacey, one of the women in his class, it wasn't a real graduation if you didn't toss your hats in the air. Elias knew they were all trying to recapture their lost youth, as though performing the rituals turned back the clock but he found that it did. He never realized what he had missed out on, until the hats came crashing back down again with the diploma clutched in his fist.

Metal scraped on the tiles and people started to mingle again, picking at the food leftovers. By the time Elias joined Ellie and Caden, they'd spotted her at the back but they were hanging back, waiting for Elias to make a move.

Walking slowly towards her, he noticed something different about the way she was dressed. Her coat was open, hanging loosely from her shoulders and under it she was wearing a simple, lilac top and fitted, blue jeans. He couldn't remember ever seeing her in jeans.

It wasn't until he was standing in front of her that he could look her in the eye. An uncomfortable looking smile was tinging her lips but he could tell she was trying her best to look natural.

The awkward seconds ticked by before she reached out and brushed a piece of white thread off his black gown.

"I'm proud of you," she said.

The words sounded unnatural coming from her lips and he

knew they felt unnatural but he didn't care. She had never even tried to say the right thing, no matter how forced it was. The gesture was all he needed to hear. He smiled back at her, and her own smile softened, her cheeks lifting and her eyes squinting.

"Thanks for coming," he said.

She nodded and turned to Ellie who was walking to them. She seemed to calm down with her there. It was going to take a long time to rebuild the bridge, but at least his mom had laid the first brick.

"Who's hungry?" Ellie said, "Let's go back to my place and I'll do my special roast."

"Sounds good to me," Caden nodded.

"Me too," Elias said.

He expected his mom to make an excuse so she could bow out of the back door without having to say anything else. If she did, he wasn't sure that he would mind. She had showed her face and she had seen him graduate and that was more interest than she had ever shown before.

"Sure," she nodded.

Even Ellie looked surprised but she tried her best to hide it. They all headed outside together, in silence. Words weren't needed to know how everybody was feeling. It felt new and scary but when Caden looped his fingers into Elias', he knew everything was going to be okay.

Shelter

Also by Ashley John

Joshua & Ezra
BOSS
STEELE

Surf Bay
Lost & Found
Full Circle
Saving Michael
Love's Medicine
Sink or Swim

George & Harvey
The Secret
The Truth
The Fight

Romance Standalones
Shelter
Cabin Nights
Unlikely Love

Shelter

About Ashley John

Ashley John lives in the North of England with his fiancé Reece, and his two cats, Jinx and Jeremy.

He's a sucker for a gripping love story. His characters are fighters, strong and complex, and they'll do anything to get the happy endings they deserve (and there is usually tears and heartache along the way). Ashley is best known for his best selling Surf Bay series.

When Ashley isn't writing, he uses his creativity to paint and draw, and when he's not being creative, he's usually taking a nap.

To find out more about Ashley John, visit his official website and blog at **ashleyjohn.co.uk**

Thank You!

I would just like to say the biggest thank you to **every single person** who has supported me, and more importantly, my work. If you picked up this paperback, thank you!

I appreciate every book sale, every comment and every email **so much**!

Without you guys, I wouldn't be doing this. You give me the strength to share myself and my life, so thank you.

Don't forget to leave a review for **Shelter** on **Goodreads** and **Amazon**!

Made in the USA
Middletown, DE
16 March 2016